THE CLAYBORNE BRIDES

Julie Garwood

The Clayborne Brides

WHEELER
PUBLISHING, INC.
ROCKLAND, MA

★ AN AMERICAN COMPANY ★

Published in Large Print by arrangement with Pocket Books
a division of Simon & Schuster Inc. in the U.S. and Canada.

Wheeler Large Print Book Series.

Set in 16 pt. Plantin.

Library of Congress Cataloging-in-Publication Data

Garwood, Julie.
    The Clayborne brides / Julie Garwood.
        p.   cm.—(Wheeler large print book series)
    Contents: One pink rose — One white rose — One red rose.
    ISBN 1-56895-515-4
    1. Love stories, American.   2. Man-woman relationships—Montana
—Fiction.   3. Brothers—Montana—Fiction.   4. Large type books.
I. Title.   II. Series.
[PS3557.A8427C57   1998]
813'.54—dc21   97-47190
                                                                      CIP

Prologue

Long ago there lived a remarkable family. They were the Claybornes, and they were held together by bonds far stronger than blood.

They met when they were boys living on the streets in New York City. Runaway slave Adam, pickpocket Douglas, gunslinger Cole, and con man Travis survived by protecting one another from the older gangs roaming the city. When they found an abandoned baby girl in their alley, they vowed to make a better life for her and headed west.

They eventually settled on a piece of land they named Rosehill, deep in the heart of Montana Territory.

The only guidance they received as they were growing up came from the letters of Adam's mother, Rose. Rose learned about her son's companions from their heartfelt letters to her, for they confided their fears, their hopes and their dreams, and in return she gave them what they had never had before, a mother's unconditional love and acceptance.

In time, each came to know her as his own Mama Rose.

After twenty long years, Rose joined them. Her sons and daughter were finally content. Her arrival was, indeed, a cause for both celebration and consternation. Her daughter was married to a fine man and expecting her first child, and her sons had grown to be honorable, strong men, each successful in his own right. But Mama Rose wasn't quite satisfied just yet. They had become too settled in their bachelor ways to suit her. Since she believed God helps those who help themselves, there was only one thing left for her to do.

She was going to meddle.

Time of Roses

It was not in the Winter
Our loving lot was cast;
It was the time of roses—
We pluck'd them as we pass'd!

—Thomas Hood (1798–1845)

Book I

ONE PINK ROSE

One

Rosehill Ranch, Montana Valley, 1880

Travis Clayborne was thinking hard about killing a man.

The youngest brother had only just returned home from the southern tip of the territory and planned to stay one night before he resumed his hunt. Thus far, his prey had managed to stay a step ahead of him. He had thought he had him good and trapped near the gorge, but then the elusive devil had vanished into thin air. Travis grudgingly admitted he would have to tip his hat to this stranger who had outwitted him. He might also have to compliment him on his survival skills. Then he'd shoot him.

He'd taken to the notion of doing in the culprit right away. The enemy's name was Daniel Ryan, and the sin he'd committed wasn't forgivable by a son's measure. Ryan had dared to take advantage of a sweet, innocent, genteel old lady with a heart of gold—Travis's own Mama Rose to be exact—and in Travis's heart and mind, killing him was almost too good for him. Now Travis was trying to convince himself that justice would be on his side.

That evening he waited until their mother had gone to bed to discuss the atrocity with his brothers. They sat side by side on the porch with their booted feet propped up on the railing, their heads tilted back, and their eyes closed.

Harrison, their brother-in-law, joined them a moment after Rose went upstairs. He thought the brothers looked content and was about to tell them so when Travis declared his intentions. Harrison sat down hard in the chair next to Douglas, stretched his long legs out, and then begged to differ with Travis. He said that the law should take care of the thief, and that this person, like every other man and woman in this fair country, was entitled to a trial. If he was proven guilty, he would be sent to prison for his punishment. He shouldn't be murdered in cold blood.

None of the Claybornes paid any attention to Harrison's pontificating. He was an attorney by trade, and it was in his nature to argue about every little thing. All of the brothers thought it was kind of sweet the way Harrison believed in justice for everyone. Their little sister's husband was a decent man, but he was from Scotland and, in their minds, naive about the laws in the wilderness. Perhaps in a perfect world the innocent would always be protected and the guilty would always be punished, but they didn't happen to live in a perfect world, now did they? They lived in Montana Territory.

Besides, what lawman in his right mind would take the time and trouble to hunt down a garden snake when there were so many deadly rattlers out there just waiting to strike?

Harrison refused to bend to the Clayborne way of looking at things. He was appalled by Travis's

4

decision to go after the culprit who had robbed their mother; he reminded Travis that he had a duty as a future attorney to behave with honor. He also suggested Travis reread Plato's *Republic*.

Travis wouldn't be deterred from what he proclaimed was a sacred mission. He leaned forward to look at Harrison when he gave his argument.

"A son's first duty is to his mother," he declared.

"Amen," Douglas muttered.

"It's clear to all of us that Mama Rose was duped," Travis continued. "He asked to see the gold case and the compass, didn't he?"

"I wish she hadn't told him about it," Adam interjected.

"But she did tell him," Douglas said. "And I'm guessing as soon as she mentioned it was gold, that's when he asked to see it."

"He knew he was going to steal it then," Cole said.

"It was clever of him to let the crowd separate them," Adam said.

"Mama Rose told us this Ryan fellow is well over six feet tall. He's bulky too," Douglas reminded them. "Bulky probably means he's got more muscle than most. Seems peculiar to all of us such a big man could be pushed around by a crowd. He meant to steal it, all right."

"For God's sake, Douglas, you cannot assume—" Harrison began.

Travis cut him off. "No one takes advantage of our mama and gets away with it. It's up to one of her sons to right this wrong. Surely you can understand how we feel, Harrison. You had a mother once, didn't you?"

"I wouldn't bet on it," Cole drawled out, just to get Harrison riled up.

His brother-in-law wasn't in the mood to take exception to the remark. "Your reasoning is twisted," he said. He waited until the derisive snorting had stopped before he announced that Travis's plan to shoot the thief was premeditated murder.

Cole laughed at Harrison, reached around Douglas to slap him on his back for saying something so amusing, and then suggested Harrison start thinking about a way to get Travis released from jail should he be arrested for doing a son's duty. He also suggested Travis simply drag the culprit back to Montana and let all the brothers shoot him.

Harrison was nearly ready to admit defeat. It was impossible to talk sense into any of the brothers. The only thing that was keeping him sane was the fact that deep in his heart he knew none of them would ever commit cold-blooded murder. They sure enjoyed talking about it though.

"How do you know the man you're after is really Daniel Ryan? He could have made up the name," he remarked. "He could also have lied about being from Texas."

"Nope," Cole said. "He told Mama Rose his name and where he was from before she started talking about the presents she was bringing to us."

"Thank God she didn't tell him about the other

gifts. He probably would have stolen my pocket watch," Douglas said.

"I'll bet he would have taken my map too," Adam interjected.

"And my leather-bound books," Travis added.

"The thief's from Texas, all right," Adam said. "He had a peculiar drawl in his speech."

"That's right," Douglas remembered. "She thought it was . . . What'd she call it, Travis?"

"Charming," he replied with a frown.

"Never did like the names Daniel or Ryan," Cole announced. "Come to think of it, I don't have much use for Texans either. Can't trust them."

Harrison rolled his eyes heavenward. "You never did like anyone or anything," he reminded him. "Do me a favor and don't say another word until I go upstairs. You're making me forget I'm a logical man."

Cole laughed. "You're the one who insisted on moving back into Rosehill with your wife. I'm part of Rosehill, Harrison, like it or not."

"Mary Rose needs to be with her mother during her confinement. I'm not about to go from town to town with Judge Burns and leave her alone in Blue Belle. And by the way, the next time you tell her she waddles like a duck, I'm going to punch you. Got that? She's a little emotional right now and doesn't need to be told she's as big as a—"

Cole wouldn't let him finish. "All right, we'll stop teasing her. She sure is getting pretty, isn't she?"

"She was always pretty," Adam said.

"Yes, but now that she's carrying my nephew, she's even prettier. Don't you dare tell her what I just admitted, or she'll never let me live it down. My sister likes to torment me whenever she can, and frankly, I can't imagine why."

He noticed the gleam that came into Harrison's eyes and knew the man was about to say something to provoke him. Since Cole wasn't in the mood to argue tonight, he decided to turn the topic back to the more pressing business at hand, catching a low-down, thieving garden snake who had slithered all the way up to Montana Territory from Texas.

"Travis, are you going to leave tomorrow?"

"Yes."

"How was it decided you would be the one to go after Daniel Ryan?" Harrison asked. "If the Texan really did steal your brother's compass, and I'm only willing to concede that the possibility exists, then shouldn't Cole be the one to go after him? The compass was meant for him."

"Cole can't go anywhere just yet," Adam explained.

"He was to lay low until old Shamus Harrington calms down," Douglas added.

"What did you do, Cole?" Harrison asked, already dreading the answer.

"He defended himself," Adam said. "One of Harrington's sons thought he was faster with his gun than Cole and forced a shoot-out."

"What happened?" Harrison asked.

"I won," Cole said with a grin.

"Obviously," Harrison snapped. "Did you kill him?"

"No, but almost," he admitted. "It was really kind of strange the way he came after me," he added. "Lester had fallen in with a gang passing through Blue Belle, and the word on the street was that they were planning to rob the bank in Hammond, Saturday next," he added.

"Does seem odd he'd come after you," Douglas agreed. "Lester's been strutting around acting like a big man in front of his new friends. Maybe he wanted to impress them."

"I heard they goaded him into the shoot-out with you," Adam said. "Dooley told me they acted like they knew who you were, Cole."

"Dooley's been hanging around his friend Ghost too long," Cole said. "You can't take anything either one of them says as fact, Adam."

"They probably heard of your reputation," Douglas suggested.

"They were just looking for trouble," Cole said. "Besides, everyone knows Harrington's sons are as dumb as dirt."

"True, but old man Shamus is still going to hold a grudge," Douglas said. "Mountain men do when one of their own gets shot, and since he has five other sons, you're going to have to be real careful for a long time."

"I'm always careful," Cole boasted. "Now that I think about it, I could go after Ryan, Travis. You've got enough to do without—"

His brother wouldn't let him finish. "No, you're staying here," he said. "Besides, I've got everything all planned out."

"That's right," Douglas said. "He's going to kill three birds with one stone."

Travis nodded. "I'm going to take my papers to Wellington and Smith so everything will be in order when I begin my apprenticeship with their law firm in September, and since Hammond's just a jump away from Pritchard, I'll take care of that business Mama Rose stuck me with, then swing on over to River's Bend, shoot Ryan, pick up the birthday present back in Hammond, and come back here in time for the celebration."

"You owe us ten dollars for Mama Rose's birthday gift," Cole reminded Harrison.

"What are we getting her?" he asked.

"A fancy sewing machine," Douglas said. "Her eyes lit up when she saw a picture of it in the catalog Adam gave her. We're getting her the most expensive model, of course. She deserves the best."

Harrison nodded. "Aren't Golden Crest and River's Bend in opposite directions?"

"Just about," Cole said. "Which is why I think I should go after Ryan, Travis. It would save you—"

Once again his brother wouldn't let him finish. "You've got to lay low," he said.

Harrison agreed and offered an alternative that would save Travis time and trouble.

"Surely you can get a sewing machine in Pritchard and save yourself several days' riding."

"I suppose he could," Cole said. "But Ryan wasn't spotted in Pritchard. He was headed for River's Bend yesterday."

"And how would you know that?" Harrison asked.

"We put the word out to let us know if anyone

10

runs into him," Adam said. "Travis, it's a pity you have to do that favor first. By the time you reach River's Bend, Ryan will probably be long gone."

"I've got it all figured out," Travis said. "It should only take a day of hard riding to deliver this Emily Finnegan woman to her groom in Golden Crest, and if it's dry enough, I can cut through the gully and be in River's Bend the following afternoon."

"You're dreaming," Adam told him. "It's been raining off and on for a month now. That gully's going to be filled. Why, it will take you at least three days to go around."

"Who is Emily Finnegan?" Harrison asked.

"She's the favor I'm doing for Mama Rose," Travis said.

Harrison gritted his teeth. Getting information out of the brothers was an arduous undertaking, but he was tenacious enough to persevere. The Claybornes liked to confuse him with spurious facts, none of which were the least bit relevant. They did it on purpose, of course. They were united in their goal to make him stop "hounding" them, as Cole would say, which meant they didn't want him to question either their motives or their ethics. Three of the brothers still believed they could "out stubborn" him. Adam was the only one who knew better. No one was as stubborn as a Scotsman, and since Harrison had been born and raised in the Highlands, he qualified.

"What's the favor?" he asked Travis again.

"Mama Rose had supper with the Cohens last week, and they happened to tell her about a woman who was stuck in Pritchard. Her escort up and died on her, and she's been trying to get someone to take her on to Golden Crest, but hasn't had any success."

"Why doesn't the man she's going to marry ride down to Pritchard and get her?"

"I asked Mama Rose that very question, and she told me it wouldn't be proper. The preacher's waiting in Golden Crest, and it's up to Miss Emily Finnegan to get there on her own. Mama Rose offered my services."

"She must have thought Hammond was right next door to Golden Crest," Douglas said.

"Why can't someone from Pritchard escort her?" Harrison asked. "It's a good-sized town. Surely she can find some willing couple there."

"People are mighty superstitious in Pritchard," Cole said.

"What does that mean?" Harrison asked.

"It means Miss Emily spooks them," he explained.

"It seems poor Miss Emily has gone through quite a few escorts," Douglas said.

"How many?" Harrison wanted to know.

"Too many to keep track of," Cole answered, deliberately exaggerating. "Rumor has it a couple of them died. Travis, you'd better take something with you for luck," he added with a nod in his brother's direction. "I'd give you my lucky compass, but then I don't have it, now do I, and all because that sneaking, no good son of a—"

Harrison cut him off before he could get riled up again. "You can't know if the compass will

12

bring you luck or not, Cole. You've never seen the thing."

"Mama Rose chose it for me, didn't she? That makes it lucky."

"You're as superstitious as the folks in Pritchard," he muttered. "Travis, do you think you'll have trouble with this Miss Emily?"

"No," he answered. "I'm not superstitious, and I don't believe half of what they're saying about her either. How bad can she be?"

Two

The woman was a walking plague.

They hadn't even gotten out of town before Travis was punched, kicked, tripped, and shot at, but not by anyone from Pritchard. No, it was Miss Emily Finnegan who tried to do him in, and even though she swore on her sainted mother's grave that it had all been a terrible misunderstanding, Travis didn't believe her. Why would he? He had it on good authority from his friends the Cohens that Miss Emily's mother was still alive and probably dancing an Irish jig with Mr. Finnegan back in Boston, now that the two of them had unloaded their ungrateful daughter on a poor, unsuspecting stranger living in Golden Crest.

Admittedly, Miss Emily was a pretty little thing. She had hair the color of sable that curled softly around her ears, and big hazel eyes that

13

were brown one minute and gold the next. She had a real nice mouth too, until she opened it, which, Travis was quick to notice, was most of the time. The woman had an opinion about everything and felt compelled to share it with him so that there wouldn't be any future misunderstandings.

She wasn't a know-it-all, but she sure came close. He formed his opinion just five painful minutes after he'd met her.

It had been suggested by Olsen, the hotel proprietor, that they meet in front of the stage coach station. Travis spotted her from way down the street. She was standing directly behind the hitching post, holding a black umbrella in one hand and a pair of white gloves in the other. There were at least six satchels lined up in a neat row in front of her on the boardwalk, entirely too many to drag up the side of a mountain.

Miss Finnegan was dressed to perfection from head to toe in white linen. He assumed she hadn't had time to change out of her Sunday best church clothes. Then he remembered it was Thursday.

They didn't exactly start out on the right foot. She was standing at attention with her shoulders back and her head held high, watching the commotion across the street. Although it was still early in the morning, a rowdy crowd had already gathered in Lou's Tavern and were making quite a ruckus. Perhaps that was why she didn't hear him come up behind her.

He made the mistake of tapping her lightly on her shoulder to get her attention so that he could tip his hat to her and introduce himself. That's when she shot at him. It happened so fast, he barely had enough time to get out of the way. The little derringer she had concealed under her gloves went off when she whirled around. The bullet would have gotten him smack in his middle if he hadn't spotted the gleaming barrel and leapt to the side in the nick of time.

He was pretty certain the gun housed only one chamber, but he wasn't taking any chances. In a flash, he grabbed hold of her wrist and twisted her arm up so that her weapon was aimed toward the sky. Only then did he move close so he could give her a piece of his mind.

And that's when she whacked him with her umbrella and kicked him hard in his left kneecap. It was apparent that she was aiming for his groin, and when she missed her mark the first time, she had the gall to try again.

He made up his mind then that Miss Emily Finnegan was crazy.

"Unhand me, you miscreant."

"Miscreant? What in thunder's a miscreant?"

She didn't have the faintest idea. She was so taken aback by the question she almost shrugged in response. Granted, she didn't know what a "miscreant" was, but she did know that her sister, Barbara, used the word whenever she wanted to discourage an overzealous admirer, and it had always been very effective. What worked for her conniving sister was going to start working for her. Emily had made that vow on the train from Boston.

"You only need to know that it's an insult," she said. "Now, let go of me."

"I'll let go of you after you promise to stop trying to kill me. I'm your escort to Golden Crest," he added with a scowl. "Or was, until you shot at me. You're going to have to get up there on your own now, lady, and if you kick me one more time, I swear I'll—"

She interrupted him before he could tell her he'd toss her in the water trough.

"You're Mr. Clayborne? You can't be," she stammered out, a look of horror on her face. "You aren't . . . an old man."

"I'm not young either," he snapped. "I am Travis Clayborne," he added, but because his knee was still throbbing from being kicked by the bit of fluff, he didn't bother to tip his hat to her. "Give me your gun."

She didn't argue. She simply placed the weapon in the palm of his hand and frowned up at him. She didn't apologize either. He noticed that slight right away.

"I swear I'm going to be limping for a week. What have you got in your shoes? Iron?"

Her smile was dazzling, and heaven help him for noticing, she had a cute little dimple in her right cheek. If he hadn't already decided he didn't like her, he would have thought she was a might better than simply pretty. She was downright lovely. He had to remind himself the crazy woman had just tried to kill him.

"What a silly thing to suggest," she said. "Of course I don't have iron in my shoes. I'm sorry I kicked you, but you did sneak up on me."

"I did no such thing."

"If you say so," she said, trying to placate him.

16

"You were teasing me about changing your mind, weren't you? You wouldn't really abandon a helpless lady in her hour of need, would you?"

The little woman had a sense of humor. Travis jumped to that conclusion as soon as she told him she was helpless. She'd said it with a straight face too, and, honest to Pete, it didn't matter that his shin was still stinging from her wallop of a kick; he still felt like laughing. He couldn't wait to be rid of her, of course, but he was in a much better frame of mind.

Mr. Clayborne was taking entirely too long to answer her question. The thought of once again being stranded in the middle of nowhere sent chills down her spine. She let out a little sigh and decided there was only one thing to do.

God help her, she was going to have to flirt with the scoundrel. With a little sigh she pulled out the useless little pink-and-white painted fan she'd purchased in St. Louis for entirely too much money, flipped it open with the dainty turn of her wrist she'd practiced for hours on the train, and held it in front of her face. She was deliberately concealing her cheeks so he wouldn't see her blush of embarrassment when she did something she considered utterly ridiculous.

She wasn't just going to try to flirt; she was also going to be coy. She drew a quick breath to keep herself from groaning, then batted her eyelashes up at him in imitation of her sister's tactics. Barbara had always looked very coy; Emily was pretty certain *she* looked like an idiot. God only knew, she felt like one.

She realized her practical, down-to-earth

nature was trying to reassert itself and immediately tried to squelch it. She had vowed to change everything about herself, and she wasn't about to give up now, no matter how foolish she felt.

Travis watched her flutter her eyelashes at him for a long silent minute. No doubt about it, she was crazy all right, and he suddenly felt a little sorry for her. She was definitely out of her element, dressed as she was for a Sunday social in the center of the dirt and grime known as Pritchard, trying her best to be painfully correct in her manners.

He knew she was trying to manipulate him now and decided to have a bit of sport with her.

"Maybe you ought to see Doc Morganstern before you go anywhere, ma'am. He might have something to help stop your eyes from twitching. I don't mean to be indelicate, but it's got to be bothering you."

She slapped her fan closed and let out a loud sigh. "You're either as completely thickheaded as a tree, Mr. Clayborne, or I still haven't perfected it yet."

"Perfected what?" he asked.

"Flirting, Mr. Clayborne. I was trying to flirt with you."

Her honesty impressed him. "Why?"

"Why? So that you would do what I want you to do, of course. I'm not much good at it though, am I?"

He didn't answer the absurd question. "The twitching's stopped," he drawled out, just to get her dander up.

"I wasn't twitching," she muttered. "There

isn't anything wrong with my eyes, thank you very much. I was simply practicing my technique on you, that's all. Shall we go and collect Mrs. Clayborne and be on our way? I do hope she's more pleasant than you are, sir. Please stop gawking at me. I want to reach my destination before dark."

"There isn't any Mrs. Clayborne."

"Oh, that won't do."

He leaned down close to her. "Will you please say something that makes sense?"

She took a step away from him. The man was entirely too good-looking for her sensibilities. He had the most wonderful green eyes. She'd noticed the color while he was growling at her with obvious irritation and asking her such rude questions. She'd noticed what a masculine, fit fellow he was too.

Travis Clayborne was tall, on the thin side, but with muscles galore on his shoulders and arms. She didn't dare look any lower, or he'd get the notion she was going to try to kick him again, but she was certain his legs were just as well-endowed.

No doubt about it, he was an extremely handsome man. Women probably chased after him all the time. Foolish females would be helpless against those beautiful green eyes of his. His smile could cause considerable havoc too. Why, he'd just smiled at her once and for the barest of seconds, but it was still quite enough to make her heartbeat quicken. He probably had broken hundreds of women's hearts already, and she wasn't about to be added to his list. She had already learned that painful lesson, thank you very much.

Miss Finnegan was suddenly glaring up at him, and he couldn't figure out what had caused the sudden change. "I asked you why I have to be married to escort you to Golden Crest."

"Because it wouldn't be at all proper for me to go riding into the wilderness with such a handsome man. What will people think?"

"Who cares what people think? You don't know anyone here, do you?"

"No, but I will get to know them, once I'm married to Mr. O'Toole. If Golden Crest is just a day's ride away, I'll probably be doing some of my shopping here. Surely you can understand my reservations, sir. I must keep up appearances."

He shrugged. "If you can't go with me, then I've fulfilled my promise to offer my services. Good day, ma'am."

He tried to walk away. She was clearly appalled by his behavior. "Wait," she called out, chasing after him. "You wouldn't leave me alone, would you? A gentleman would never abandon a lady in distress . . ."

"I guess I'm not a gentleman," he told her without pausing in his long-legged stride down the walkway. "And I'm certain you aren't a lady in distress."

She grabbed hold of his arm, dug her heels in to stop him from taking another step, and found herself being dragged along in his wake.

"I most certainly am in distress, and it's vile of you to contradict me."

"I was handsome a minute ago, but now I'm vile?"

"You can be both," she told him.

He suddenly turned around to look at her. He knew he couldn't leave her stranded in Pritchard, not if he ever wanted to look his Mama Rose in the eyes again, and so he decided that the only way he was ever going to maintain his sanity while he led the woman to Golden Crest was to strike some sort of a bargain with her.

"I wouldn't consider it a compliment," she announced with a blush he had to admit was downright attractive.

"Consider what a compliment?"

"Being handsome. I thought Randolph Smythe was handsome too, and he turned out to be a hideous creature."

Don't ask, he told himself.

"Don't you want to know who Randolph Smythe is?"

"No, I don't want to know."

She told him anyway. "He's the man I was supposed to marry."

She went and pricked his interest with that statement. "But you didn't," he said.

"No, I didn't. I was ready to though."

"How ready?"

Her blush intensified. "Are you going to escort me to Golden Crest or not?"

He wouldn't let her change the subject now that it had gotten downright interesting.

"How ready?" he asked again.

"I waited at the altar for him. He didn't show up," she added with a quick nod.

21

"He jilted you? Well now, that was a real mean-spirited thing to do," he said in an attempt at kindness. "I can't imagine why he'd change his mind at the last minute."

He wasn't telling her the truth. He was pretty certain he knew exactly why good old Randolph had changed his mind. The man had come to his senses. Travis wondered if Emily had ever tried to shoot him. That would have been enough to send any man with half a mind running in the opposite direction.

"So there wasn't any wedding," he remarked for lack of anything better to say. She was staring up at him with such an earnest, hopeful look on her face, and he guessed she expected him to say something a bit more sympathetic.

He gave it his best shot. "Some men just don't cotton to the notion of being tied down to one woman. Randolph was probably like that."

"No, he wasn't."

"Look, lady, I'm trying to be nice about it."

"Don't you want to know why he didn't show up at the church?"

"You shot at him, didn't you?"

"I did no such thing."

"I really don't want to know his reasons. All right? Suffice it to say, there wasn't any wedding."

"Oh, there was a wedding all right. Did I mention my sister didn't show up at the church either, Mr. Clayborne?"

"You're joking."

"I'm perfectly serious."

"Your sister and Randolph . . ."

"Are now legally married."

22

He was appalled. "What kind of family do you come from? Your own sister betrayed you?"

"We were never close," she assured him.

He squinted down at her. "I can't help but notice you don't appear to be overly distraught about it all."

Travis shook his head. He couldn't understand why the story intrigued him so. He didn't even know Randolph Smythe, yet he still felt like punching him in the nose for doing such a cruel thing to Emily. Come to think of it, he didn't know Emily Finnegan either. Why in thunder did he care?

She saw the pity in his eyes and promptly glared at him. "Don't you dare feel sorry for me, Mr. Clayborne."

She looked as though she wanted to kick him again. Any sympathy he felt for her vanished in a heartbeat.

"It was probably your own fault."

If looks could kill, they'd have been measuring him for a coffin now. Travis didn't back down after making his statement, but added a nod to let her know he meant what he'd said.

"And how is that?" she asked, and then accidentally whacked him with her umbrella when she folded her arms across her chest. Because he'd just made such a rude comment to her, she didn't apologize.

He thought she'd done it on purpose. He grabbed the umbrella, tossed it on top of her satchels, and then answered her.

"You chose an unfit, unscrupulous man; that's

23

why it's your own fault, and you should realize by now that you're better off without him."

He had just redeemed himself in her eyes. He wasn't being cruel when he blamed her; he was only being honest. He was right too. She had chosen an unscrupulous man.

"Are you going to take me to Golden Crest or not?"

"What happened to the couple who was escorting you?"

"Be more specific, please."

"More specific?"

"Which couple are you referring to?" she asked.

She got his full attention. "How many were there?"

"Three."

"Three people or three couples?"

"Couples," she answered.

He noticed she quickly lowered her gaze to the ground and looked uncomfortable. The topic was obviously a sore one. Then he remembered that his brother Cole had told him how the superstitious folks in Pritchard were spooked by Miss Emily Finnegan. He really should have paid more attention to the conversation, he decided, realizing that it was a little late to be worrying about it now. Still, he should get all the particulars before he took the woman anywhere, just to be on the safe side.

"You went through six escorts?"

"It was a very long trip, Mr. Clayborne."

"What happened to the first couple?"

"The Johnsons?"

"All right, the Johnsons," he agreed to get her to continue. "What happened to them?"

"It was really quite tragic."

He had had a feeling she was going to say that. "I bet it was. What'd you do to them?"

Her spine stiffened. "I didn't do anything to them. They became ill on the train, and I believe it was something they ate that made them sick. Quite a few of the other passengers became ill too," she added. "The Johnsons stayed in Chicago. I'm sure they're fully recovered by now."

"What happened to the second couple?"

"Do you mean the Porters? It was also quite tragic," she admitted. "They also became ill. The fish, you see."

"The fish?"

"Yes, they ate the fish too. I believe it had gone bad, and I did warn Mr. Porter, but he wouldn't listen to reason. He ate it anyway."

"And?"

"He and his wife were carried off the train in St. Louis."

"Bad fish can kill a man," he remarked.

She gave a vigorous nod. "It killed poor Mr. Porter."

"What about Mrs. Porter?"

"She blamed everyone else for her husband's illness, even me. Can you imagine? I did warn him not to eat the fish, but he was most determined."

"Then why'd she blame you?"

"Because the Johnsons got sick. She didn't believe it was the food. She thought I was making everyone ill. You needn't fret about it, sir. If you don't eat any fish, I'm certain you'll be fine."

"Did the third couple eat fish too?"

She shook her head. "No, but it was still quite . . ."

"Tragic?" he supplied for her.

"Yes, tragic," she agreed. "How did you know? Have you heard what happened to Mr. Hanes then?"

"No, I was just guessing. What happened to Hanes?"

"He got shot."

"I knew you shot someone."

"I did not," she cried out. "Why would you think I'd do such a terrible thing?"

"You tried to shoot me," he reminded her.

"That was an accident."

He decided to humor her. "All right, then. Did you accidentally shoot Mr. Hanes?"

"No, I didn't. He and another man were playing cards, and suddenly one of them—I can't remember which one it was—accused the other of cheating. A fight ensued and Mr. Hanes was shot. He wasn't mortally wounded, and the other man could just as easily have been the one injured because they were both shooting their pistols at each other. It was very uncivilized. I ruined my best hat when I scooted under my seat with Mrs. Hanes so I wouldn't be struck by a stray bullet."

"Then what happened?"

"The conductor patched up Mr. Hanes's arm, stopped the train outside Emmerson Point and left him and his wife in the care of the town's doctor."

"And you came the rest of the way by your-self?"

"Yes," she said. "I'd go up to Golden Crest by myself too if I knew the way. The hotel proprietor told me I needed a guide, and so I've been looking for one. Then you offered your services. You are going to escort me, aren't you?"

"All right, I'll take you."

"Oh, thank you, Mr. Clayborne," she whispered. She clasped hold of his hand and smiled. "You won't be sorry."

"You may call me Travis."

"Very well. I appreciate your kindness, Travis, in escorting me."

"I'm not being kind. The way I see it, I'm stuck with you, and the sooner we get started, the sooner I'll be rid of you."

She pulled her hand away from his and turned to her luggage. "If I hadn't just remembered I'm not going to be honest and forthright anymore, I would tell you I think you're an extremely insolent and hostile man."

"You've been nothing but honest and forthright since you started talking, haven't you?"

"Yes, but I only just remembered not to be."

"I'm not going to ask you to explain this time," he muttered. "Wait here while I get the horses. And by the way, Emily, you're only taking two satchels up the mountain. O'Toole will have to come and fetch the others. You can leave them in the hotel now. Olsen will make sure no one steals them."

"I'll do no such thing," she shouted so he could hear her. The rude man was already halfway down the street. "I'm taking every one of my bags, thank you very much."

"No, you're not, but you're welcome, anyway."

She gritted her teeth in frustration. She watched him stroll down the boardwalk, noticed how his shoulders and hips seemed to roll with each stride he took, and found his arrogant swagger most appealing. He was a striking fellow, all right. It was a pity he was also obnoxious.

With a sigh, she forced herself to look away. She was engaged to marry Mr. O'Toole, she reminded herself, and she shouldn't be noticing how fit any other man was.

She wasn't the alley cat in the family; Barbara was. Emily was the reliable and practical one, like an old but comfortable pair of shoes, she thought. No—she had always been reliable and practical in the past. She wasn't anymore.

Travis was just about to cross the street when she called out to him.

"Travis, I should warn you. I'm not at all reliable."

"I didn't think you were," he called out. "You don't have any sense either."

She smiled with satisfaction. That reaction stopped him dead in his tracks.

"You don't think I have any sense?"

Honest to God, she seemed thrilled by his assessment of her. Didn't the woman realize she was being given an insult?

No, not an insult, he qualified. Just the blunt truth.

"Emily?"

"Yes?"

"Does O'Toole know he's going to marry a crazy woman?"

Three

Emily was holding a grudge. Her glares and her stony silence were vastly amusing, but Travis didn't dare laugh or even crack a smile. She'd know then he thought her behavior was humorous, and he'd never hear the end of it.

She didn't speak to him again until they stopped in midafternoon to rest their horses. At least that was the excuse he'd given her. She seemed to believe the lie too. He really called a halt so that she could rest her backside. She wasn't much of a horsewoman, and the way her bottom kept slamming against her saddle, added to the pained look on her face, told him she was taking quite a beating.

The poor woman could barely stand up straight when she finally managed to get down to the ground. She wouldn't let him help her and didn't think his exaggeratedly wounded expression was the least bit funny.

Because they'd ridden a good distance up the steep mountain path, the air was much colder. He took the time and trouble to start a campfire so she could shake off the chill. They ate a sparse lunch in silence, and just when he was beginning to think the trip wasn't going to be completely miserable, she went and ruined it.

"You did it on purpose, didn't you, Travis? Admit it, then apologize to me, and I just might forgive you."

"I didn't do it on purpose. You were supposed to hook your right leg over the pommel, remember? You were the one who insisted on riding sidesaddle. How was I to know you'd never done it before?"

"Ladies in the South ride sidesaddle," she announced.

He could feel a headache coming on. "But you're not from the South, are you? You're from Boston."

"What does that have to do with the price of pickles? Southern ladies are more refined. Everyone knows that, which is precisely why I've decided to be Southern."

He could feel the throbbing behind his temples. "You can't decide to be Southern."

"But of course I can. I can be anything I want to be."

"Why Southern?" he asked in spite of his better judgment.

"The little drawl in a lady's speech is considered very feminine and musical. I've done a complete study of it, and I assure you I know what I'm talking about. I believe I've perfected the drawl too. Would you like to hear me say—"

"No, I would not. Emily, not all southern ladies ride sidesaddle."

The glare she gave him made him sorry he'd brought up the subject of saddles again.

30

"Most southern women do," she said. "And just because I have never ridden sidesaddle before doesn't mean I couldn't have managed it if you hadn't interfered. You deliberately threw me over that horse, didn't you? I could have broken my neck."

He wasn't going to take the blame for her ineptness. "I merely gave you a hand up. How was I to know you'd keep on going? Is your shoulder still sore?"

"No, and I do appreciate the fact that you rubbed the sting out of it for me. Still, my dress is now covered with dirt, thank you very much. What will Clifford O'Toole think of me?"

"You've been wearing a pair of gloves with a large bullet hole through them. He'll probably notice that before anything else. Besides, if he loves you, your appearance won't matter to him."

She took a bite of her apple before she made up her mind to set him straight.

"He doesn't love me. How could he? We've never met."

He closed his eyes. Conversing with Emily was proving to be as difficult as trying to win an argument with his brother Cole. It was hopeless.

"You're going to marry a man you've never met? Isn't that kind of odd?"

"Not really. You've heard of mail-order brides, haven't you?"

"You're one of those?"

"Sort of," she hedged. She was, of course, but pride kept her from admitting it. "Mr. O'Toole and I have corresponded, and I believe I've come

31

to know him quite well. He's an eloquent writer. He's a poet too."

"He wrote poems to you?" he asked with a grin.

Her chin came up a notch. "Why is that amusing?"

"He sounds like a . . . pansy."

"I assure you he isn't. His poems are beautiful. Will you quit grinning at me? They are beautiful, and it's apparent to me that he's a very intelligent man. You may read his letters if you don't believe me. I have all three of them tucked inside one of my satchels. Shall I fetch them for you?"

"I don't want to read his letters. You still haven't explained why you're so determined to marry a stranger."

"I tried marrying someone I knew, and look how that turned out."

"You decided on this course of action after you got jilted, didn't you?"

"Let's just say that it was the last disappointment I was going to suffer."

"Is that so?" he remarked, wondering how she was going to prevent further disappointments.

She seemed to read his thoughts. "I stayed up all that night . . . my wedding night," she said.

"Crying?" he asked.

"No, I didn't cry. I spent the entire night thinking about my circumstances, and I finally came up with a plan that I believe will change everything. I've always been forthright and honest. Well, no more, thank you very much."

"How come you're being honest with me?"

She shrugged. "I shouldn't be, I suppose. Still,

I won't ever see you again after today—at least I don't think I will—so it doesn't matter if you know I'm a fraud. No one else will."

"Trying to be something you aren't will only make things worse."

She didn't agree. "Being me didn't do me a lick of good, and once I figured that out, I decided to reinvent myself. I was sick and tired of working hard and being so boringly practical all the time."

"You're overreacting, that's all." *And crazy,* he silently added. "Your pride was wounded, but you'll get over it."

His cavalier attitude irritated her. "I know exactly what I'm doing, and pride doesn't have anything to do with my decision. Working hard hasn't gotten me anywhere. Shall I give you an example?"

She didn't wait for his answer, but plunged ahead. "Randolph was studying to become a banker. He was just beginning his last year at the university when we became officially engaged. His studies were difficult for him, and because of his grades, he was worried he'd be asked to leave. I told him that if he wouldn't accept every social invitation that came to him, he would have time for his studies, but he wouldn't listen to me. He asked me to help him with his research, and because I was such a ninny and wanted to please him, I ended up writing several lengthy papers for him. He was supposed to use the papers as his study guide, but I later found out he put his name on the top of the first page and handed them in to his professors. It was a dishonest thing to do, of course, and do you know what his punishment was? He took honors for his last year's work and was hired by one of the most prestigious banks in Boston. He started out making an impressive salary, and that was when my sister became interested in him. Ironic, isn't it? If I hadn't helped him, he wouldn't have gotten such a fine position, and my sister would have left him alone.

"I've learned from my mistakes though, which is why Mr. O'Toole and I are going to do well together. Randolph broke all the promises he made to me, and I won't let Mr. O'Toole ever break his word."

"How are you going to stop him?"

She ignored the question. "He might not be as rich as Randolph is, but almost, and he lives out here, in this beautiful, wild, untamed land, and that makes him just as appealing to me. I really hated living in the city. I could never seem to fit in. I know you don't understand because you've lived here all your life, but I felt as though I were suffocating. The air's dirty, the streets are crowded, and everywhere you look are buildings so tall you can't see the sky."

"Weren't you willing to live in Boston with Randolph?"

"He promised we would move west after one year of marriage. Father was horrified. He thought Randolph's handsome salary at the bank was far more important than my suffocation problems."

"Money isn't more important. I still remember what it was like living in New York."

Her eyes widened with surprise. "You lived in the East?"

"Until I was around ten or eleven years old."

"Why did you move?"

He was only going to answer her question and tell her a very little bit about his past, but she was such an easy woman to talk to, he got carried away and told her far more than he'd intended. He wasted a good half hour telling her about his brothers, his sister and her husband, and his Mama Rose. She seemed fascinated by his family and smiled after he mentioned he was going to become an attorney. He could have sworn tears came into her eyes when he told her Mama Rose was finally home.

"You're very fortunate to have such a loving family."

He nodded agreement. "What about you?"

"I have seven sisters. It's my hope that one day some of them will come and visit Mr. O'Toole and me. He has a grand house with a curved staircase. He told me so in one of his letters."

Travis didn't care about the house she was going to live in. "You'll be sorry if you marry a man you don't love."

She didn't show any reaction to his remark. He watched her thread her fingers through her hair. No matter how much she messed with it, the curls floated back around her face. She could be a real charmer all right. She was also an amazingly feminine creature, and if she could only learn to be a little less crazy, she'd be just about perfect.

He decided to tell her so. "You know what your problem is?"

"Yes, I do," she replied. "I should have learned from my sister. Barbara doesn't have a practical bone in her body. She doesn't have any common sense either. She pretends to be helpless too, and she's a marvelous flirt."

"No man wants a helpless woman, but a practical one is real handy to have around out here."

He stood up before she could start arguing with him, stretched the muscles in his neck by rolling his shoulders, and then began to gather stones to put the fire out.

She surprised him by helping. It took only a couple of minutes to finish the task, and he was suddenly anxious to get going. He'd spent entirely too much time talking about himself and his family. He didn't understand why he'd told her so much, because it wasn't like him to ever tell an outsider personal facts.

He didn't consider Emily an outsider though. She was . . . different. He couldn't put his finger on what it was about her that got to him, but affect him she did, and in such a strange way his instincts warned him to keep his distance. His body had other ideas. He'd already had several fantasies about making love to her. He'd tried to picture her without her clothes on, which took quite a bit of imagination on his part, since she was covered from her chin to her toes.

He had a feeling she'd be spectacular. The way she filled out the top of her dress, the tiny waistband, and the narrow hips all suggested to him that she was well put together and that he wouldn't be disappointed. The woman had all the right curves and in all the right places.

Still, thinking about it and doing something about it were two different kettles of fish. He wasn't about to give in to his urges, but he didn't feel at all guilty picturing it in his mind. She was a sensual woman, and he appreciated a good-looking female as much as every other man living in the wilderness.

No, he wasn't concerned about his physical attraction to her. He could easily deal with that. What bothered him was the fact that he was actually beginning to enjoy her company, though why he liked being around a woman with such strange notions was beyond him. Emily made him smile, but only because she said the craziest things.

He enjoyed looking at her. Nothing wrong with that, he told himself. Why, it would have been wrong for him not to look. He was a healthy man with normal inclinations, and she was getting prettier by the minute. That didn't mean he was smitten with her.

He felt better once he'd analyzed his situation. He quit frowning too. He watched her feed the rest of her apple to her horse, thought it was a sweet, practical thing to do, and wondered if she had any idea how difficult it was going to be for her to keep up the pretense of being helpless around Clifford O'Toole.

He waited by the horses while she went to the stream to wash. He got a peculiar little catch in the back of his throat when she came running back to him. Her cheeks were rosy from washing in the cold mountain water, and she was smiling with pleasure over what she declared was a glorious day. He thought about kissing her then and there, and it took a good deal of discipline to keep his hands off her.

"I'm ready to go now, Travis."

He was suddenly all business. "It's about time. We've wasted almost two full hours here."

"It wasn't wasted time. It was . . . enjoyable."

He shrugged. "Do you want me to help you get up on your horse?"

"And get tossed over the top again? I think not."

She hopped about for a minute or two while she tried to anchor her foot in the stirrup, and just when he was going to demand that she let him assist her, she made it up into the saddle on her own. She gave him a victorious smile. It didn't last long.

"A helpless woman would have requested assistance," he said.

He was smiling as he swung up into his saddle. He must be crazy too, he decided, because he was beginning to really like Miss Emily Finnegan.

Four

They didn't speak until they reached the gully he had hoped to use to shorten their journey, but just as Adam had predicted, it was flooded.

"You don't want to cross the river here, do you? Surely there's a bridge we could use."

"There aren't any bridges up here," he answered. "And this isn't a river, Emily. It's just a gully."

Her mount obviously didn't like being so close to the water's edge and began to prance about. Travis reached over, grabbed hold of the reins, and forced her horse closer to his side so he couldn't rear up.

"He must think he has to go in the water. He doesn't, does he?"

He could hear the worry in her voice. "No, he doesn't," he assured her. "We can't cross here."

His leg was rubbing against hers. She noticed, of course, but though she could have moved away, she didn't. She liked being close to him. He made her feel safe and yet uneasy too. What in heaven's name was the matter with her? She didn't seem to know her own thoughts anymore.

"We can't cross here." She repeated his words while she patted her horse in what Travis assumed was an attempt to reassure the animal.

"Now what?" she asked him.

"Your journey to Golden Crest has just been lengthened by at least two more days, maybe three."

It took all she had not to shout with relief. God help her, she was actually weak with it. It certainly was a peculiar reaction to hearing she wouldn't have to meet and marry Mr. O'Toole for at least two more days. She should have been disappointed over the news, shouldn't she?

Then why did she feel as though she'd just been given a stay of execution?

"Cold feet," she whispered.

"What did you say?" Travis asked.

She shook her head. "Nothing important," she said.

She wasn't about to tell him the truth. She wouldn't look at him either because she was certain he would be able to see the relief in her eyes. Travis already thought she was out of her mind to want to marry a complete stranger, and, honest to Pete, she was beginning to think he might be right.

Perhaps she was having before-the-wedding jitters. Some brides did, didn't they? Yes, of course they did, and all she needed to do now was read Mr. O'Toole's letters again. She was sure to feel better then. The man she was going to marry had poured his heart out to her and had proven beyond a doubt that he was a sensitive, caring man who would love and cherish her until death did they part. What more could she ever want from a husband?

Love, she admitted with a sinking heart. She wanted to love him as much as he claimed to already love her.

"You aren't getting sick on me, are you, Emily?"

"No, I never get sick. Why do you ask?"

"You're awfully pale."

"I'm just disappointed," she lied. "You must be disappointed too. It seems you're stuck with me for a couple of days. Will you mind?"

"No. Why are you so anxious to get to Golden Crest?"

"I should be, shouldn't I?"

"Did you love Randolph?"

40

The question jarred her. "What made you think of Randolph?"

He shrugged. "Did you?"

"I might have."

"What kind of answer is that? Did you like the way he kissed you?"

"For heaven's sake, it isn't appropriate for you to ask me such personal questions. It's going to rain soon, isn't it?"

"Yes, it is," he agreed. "Answer my question."

She let out a loud sigh to let him know she was becoming irritated with him before she finally acceded to his request.

"I didn't like or dislike them. His kisses were all right, I suppose."

He laughed.

"What did I say that you find so amusing?"

He didn't explain. Her answer had pleased him though. She hadn't liked being touched by good old Randolph if his kisses were just "all right."

"Where will we stay tonight?" she asked, trying to turn his attention so he wouldn't ask her any more personal questions.

"We'll have to backtrack a couple of miles and stay at Henry Billings's way station. The food's bad, but the beds are clean and dry, and if we hurry, we should get there before the rain starts. What are you staring at, Emily?"

"Your eyes," she blurted out, blushing because she'd been caught in the act. "They're very green. Did your brothers tease you when you were a little boy?"

"Tease me because of the color of my eyes?"

"No, because . . ." She realized what she was

41

about to say and felt her face burn with mortification. Lord above, she'd almost asked if he'd been teased because he was so absolutely perfect. There'd be no living with him if she said that, she realized, and the rest of their journey would be filled with one vexing remark after another. She had already noticed he had a tendency toward arrogance.

"Tease me about what?" he asked again.

She stared up at him while she tried to come up with a suitable and impersonal remark.

"Being tall," she said.

He looked exasperated. "I wasn't tall when I was a child. I was short. Most children are."

"If you use that condescending tone in the courtroom, you're going to be a dismal failure. It's just a suggestion," she added when he frowned at her.

"Emily, if you keep looking at me like that, I'm going to get the notion you want me to kiss you."

"I don't."

"Then stop staring at my mouth."

"What would you like me to stare at, Travis?"

"The water," he snapped. "Stare at the water. You sure you don't want me to kiss you?"

The conversation was doing strange things to her. She couldn't seem to catch her breath. She knew she was daring the devil, but she couldn't make herself look away from him. She wasn't at all interested in staring at the water; she wanted to continue to stare at him. What was the matter with her?

"It probably wouldn't be proper for you to kiss me. I'm going to be married soon."

"You have no business marrying a stranger, Emily."

"Why do you care what I do?"

He didn't have a ready answer for the question. "I get bothered when someone does something I consider stupid."

"Are you calling me stupid?"

"If the hat fits . . ."

Five

Neither one of them said another word until they reached Billings's way station. Henry came outside the rectangular log cabin to meet them. He was a middle-aged man, as bald as a rock, and just about as talkative. He greeted Emily— at least she thought he did—but he mumbled so, she couldn't make out a word he said. He wouldn't look at her either. He motioned her to follow him inside and showed her where she would sleep by pointing toward a closed door.

The main room had bunk beds lined against every wall. A long wooden table with benches on either side was in the center near a potbellied stove.

Travis acted as though he and Henry were good friends. During supper, he filled him in on all the latest news. Emily didn't say a word. She sat close to Travis's side at the table and tried to eat the foul-smelling soup she'd been offered. She couldn't get any of it down though, and since the proprietor wasn't paying any attention to her, she ate the brown bread and goat's milk instead and left the soup alone.

She excused herself as soon as she finished, but when she reached the door to her bedroom, she turn back to Travis.

"Will we reach Golden Crest tomorrow?"

He shook his head. "No, the day after," he said. "We'll stay with John and Millie Perkins tomorrow night. They rent out rooms in their home."

She told both men good night then and went to bed. Travis didn't see her again until she came outside the following morning with her satchel in her hands. She was wearing a pink dress with a matching sweater. The color suited her, and damn, but she was getting prettier and prettier.

He wanted to kiss her. He frowned instead and made a silent vow not to get near her today. He would keep the talk impersonal, no matter how much she provoked him.

The day's journey turned out to be extremely pleasant. Emily obviously didn't want to argue either, so the topics they ended up discussing were of a philosophical nature.

She confessed to being a voracious reader. He suggested she read *The Republic*. "It's all about justice," he explained. "I think you'll like it. I did. Mama Rose gave me a leather-bound copy along with a journal, and they're my most prized possessions."

"Why did she give you a journal?"

"She told me it was for me to fill with my accounts of all the cases I defend. She said that when I'm ready to retire, she wants me to be able to hold *The Republic* in one hand and the journal of my experiences in the other. It's her hope that the two will balance."

"Like the scales of justice," Emily whispered, impressed by the wisdom of Travis's mother.

She began to question him about Plato's work, and they debated justice and the law well into the afternoon. He thoroughly enjoyed sparring with her, so much so, he was sorry when the discussion ended.

It was his fault. He made the mistake of getting personal again.

"You're a contradiction, Emily. You've obviously been well educated, and I know you're smart . . ."

"But?" she asked.

"You're doing something that isn't smart at all. In fact, it's just plain stupid."

His bluntness got her all riled up. "I don't believe I asked for your opinion."

"You're getting it anyway," he replied. "You just gave me a passionate argument about honesty and justice, and surely you can see that the pretense you're thinking about pulling on your unsuspecting groom is downright dishonest."

It was the beginning of an argument that lasted until they reached the yard behind the Perkinses' house.

Travis did most of the talking. He gave her at least twenty reasons why she shouldn't marry

45

O'Toole, but he believed his last reason was the most convincing one.

"You won't ever be able to keep up the charade of being a delicate little flower in need of pampering, Emily."

"I am delicate, damn it."

He snorted with disbelief. "You're about as fragile as a grizzly bear."

"If flinging insults is the only way you can argue your position, heaven help your clients."

Travis dismounted, then went to Emily's side and lifted her off her horse. His hands stayed around her waist much longer than necessary. "A good marriage takes effort, and honesty is a definite prerequisite."

"How would you know? You've never been married, have you?"

"That isn't relevant."

"Is flirting honest?"

He was caught off guard by her question and had to think about it for a minute before he answered. "Sometimes it's honest. Flirting is part of the courting ritual, but I personally think it's only honest when a woman flirts with the man she's set her cap on."

"Set her cap on? Are you telling me you think she should only flirt with the man she's already decided to marry?"

"That's what I'm saying all right."

"That's ridiculous. Flirting is the first step in a long process of finding the right man or woman. Men flirt too, you know. They just don't do it the same way women do."

"No, we don't."

Arguing with him was proving exasperating. "It's all a game, isn't it, that's played out between men and women. It's harmless too. Besides, men like women who flirt with them," she added, remembering how Barbara had always been able to get every available man at a party to flit around her as though she were their queen bee.

"No, we don't like women who flirt with us," he insisted. "We're much more intelligent than you think we are, and we sure as certain don't like being manipulated."

"You needn't use that superior tone with me. I've patiently listened to you argue your position for the past hour, and I never once scoffed at you. Granted, I wanted to, but I didn't. Now it's my turn. It's too bad I can't prove my point to you."

"What point?"

She knew he was deliberately trying to frustrate her and refused to cooperate. She stared at the buttons on his shirt so she couldn't be distracted by his smile, and said, "If the circumstances were favorable, I'd prove to you right this minute that a delicate little flower gets far more attention than a practical one."

"You really believe a helpless little woman who flutters her eyelashes and hangs on a man's every word will get his full attention?"

"I do."

"You're as nuts as a tree full of acorns."

She ignored his criticism. "I've done a complete study on this subject, Travis."

"What makes the circumstances favorable?"

he asked, latching onto an earlier remark she'd made.

"Boston," she answered. She waved her hand toward the Perkinses' house as she continued. "I'm not about to draw any attention to myself in front of a crowd of strangers here because it would be foolhardy and perhaps even dangerous to do so. The men in Boston are more refined and know how to conduct themselves as gentlemen around ladies. There are rules, after all, and they abide by them. I can't say the same for the men who live out here because I don't know any of them."

"Most of the men out here are gentlemen, but there are a few who would think nothing of trying to drag you off with them. The way I see it though, being your escort means I'm responsible for your welfare, and I don't like the notion of getting into a fight just because you acted silly.

"Furthermore, we're about to eat, and I don't want to have to shoot anyone afterwards. It's bad for the digestion."

It was such an outrageous thing to say, she struggled to force herself not to laugh.

"Indigestion is the only reservation you have about shooting someone?"

"Just about," he told her.

"I don't believe you. You're teasing me, and a gentleman would never do such a thing."

"Now, Emily, we've been though this before. I know I mentioned I wasn't a gentleman. Fact is, you should be thankful I'm your escort."

She was so surprised by his matter-of-fact

remark she didn't bother to push him away when he put his arms around her waist.

"Is that so? Why exactly should I be thankful?"

"Because if I weren't escorting you, I'd probably be one of the few who would drag you off with me."

She thought that was a lovely thing to say to her. He wasn't really serious. She shook her head at him to let him know she wasn't so gullible, then began to laugh. She stopped when she noticed he wasn't even smiling.

"We both know you aren't serious. Stop tormenting me. You wouldn't really . . ."

"You wouldn't have to flirt with me either."

"I wouldn't want to," she admitted. "Why are you holding on to me?"

"It makes it easier."

"Makes what easier?"

He slowly bent his head toward hers. "Kissing you."

He caught her whispered "Oh," as his mouth covered hers. His tongue swept inside to leisurely explore the sweet taste of her. She wrapped her arms around his neck and leaned into him. The last thought that fluttered through her mind was that she was going to insist that he let go of her just as soon as she finished kissing him back.

All that mattered now was Travis. She could feel his hard muscles under her fingertips and was a little overwhelmed by the sheer strength of him, yet he was being so incredibly gentle. She loved his masculine scent too. It did crazy things to her heart. She could feel it beating frantically now.

Lord, but he did know how to kiss.

He didn't understand why he suddenly felt the need to kiss her, but once the thought came into his mind, he couldn't get rid of it. He wasn't going to let passion get the upper hand, however, and as soon as the urge to become more aggressive entered his mind, he pulled away from her.

Damn, she was seductive.

Emily had a bemused expression on her face, but quickly came to her senses.

"You really can't kiss me whenever the mood strikes you."

To prove her wrong, he kissed her again. She let out a little sigh of pleasure when he lifted his head again.

"That was the last kiss you'll get from me," she announced, groaning inside over the shiver in her voice. "I mean it. You mustn't ever kiss me again." She added a frown to let him know she meant what she said.

"You were a willing participant," he said. "Or wasn't that your tongue inside my mouth?"

She turned scarlet within a heartbeat. "I was being polite."

He burst out laughing. "You are a piece of work, Miss Emily Finnegan. If I were the marrying kind, I'd give good old Randolph a run for his money."

She knew something was wrong with the comment he'd just made, but it took her a full minute to figure out what it was.

"Clifford O'Toole," she said then. "Randolph is the man who married my sister."

"Ah, that's right. The man who jilted you."

"Must you use that word?"

"No need to get in a huff about it," he told her.

Even though they were a good distance away from the barn, Travis could hear the squeak of the door as it was being opened from the inside, and he instinctively moved closer to Emily so he could shove her behind his back if he needed to. He didn't think he was being overly cautious, for he had learned from past experience that a few of the folks who visited the Perkinses' establishment lived like animals up in the high country and were a crude and uncivilized group who didn't abide by any man's laws.

Travis relaxed his guard as soon as he saw the man strutting toward them. It was ornery Jack Hanrahan, whom everyone called One-Eyed Jack for obvious reasons. He was a fright to look at, with long straggly brown hair that hadn't been washed in years and a permanent scowl on his face that was mean enough to make a person think Jack was going to tear him apart. He was also downright vain about his godawful appearance and didn't bother to wear an eye patch. He thought a patch made him look sissified.

Every time Travis looked at Jack, he inwardly blanched. Other men weren't quite as restrained. They let Jack see their reaction, and that, according to old man Perkins, made Jack all the more vain. He got a kick out of terrorizing people.

Travis suddenly came up with one hell of a brilliant plan to make Emily come to her senses and realize how crazy her notions about men were.

"Maybe there is a way you can prove your point to me," he told her.

"There is?"

She tried to turn so she could see what Travis was staring at, but he put his hands on her shoulders and wouldn't let her move.

"Do you really want to show me how effective acting helpless can be around a man?"

"I would if I could. I've done a complete study on this topic, and I assure you I know what I'm talking about."

"Yeah, yeah. You studied it. How about proving it with the very next man you see?"

"You don't think I can do it, do you? Well, I can, Travis."

"You're that sure of yourself?"

"Yes, but only because I've watched it over and over again. My sister Barbara could turn all the men in a ballroom into a pack of fleas hopping around her, just like that," she said and snapped her fingers.

The comparison of Barbara to a dog made Travis laugh. "God help your husband if he ever does anything wrong. You sure do know how to hold a grudge."

"And just what does that mean?"

"Never mind." He gloated with satisfaction over what was going to be a well-deserved victory for all men everywhere. "Want to make it interesting and wager on the outcome?"

Although it wasn't proper for a well-bred lady to gamble, she was so certain she would win, she couldn't resist the temptation. Granted, she hadn't had much practice turning a man's head by acting helpless or coy, but she had observed the ladies traveling on the train who had blatantly flirted with several men, and she had also watched the master, Barbara, and therefore had complete confidence that she could pull it off.

"How much would you like to wager?"

"A dollar."

"Shall we make it more interesting and wager five dollars?"

"Five dollars, it is," he agreed.

"I want you to know I wouldn't agree to this if I thought the gentleman I'm going to give my attention to would end up with hurt feelings, but what I'm about to do is harmless. Wouldn't you agree?"

The thought of Jack Hanrahan getting his feelings hurt made Travis choke on his laughter. "Yes, it's harmless. Have we got a bet, then?"

"As long as it isn't dangerous," she hastily qualified.

"I won't let it be dangerous."

"What are the rules?"

"No rules," he replied. "Just a time limit. Is ten minutes enough time to turn a man into a blithering simpleton, or do you need more time?"

"Ten minutes will be just fine. Are you sure you don't want to set some other rules? I don't want you to accuse me of not playing fair."

"No other rules," he insisted. "Just flirt with the very next man you see," he told her before he slowly turned her around.

He heard her indrawn breath and was a little surprised she didn't scream. She took a step back toward him.

"You want me to flirt with . . . him?"

"His name's Jack Hanrahan, and he was the next man you saw, wasn't he?"

"Yes, but . . ."

Her shoulders were now pressed against his chest. He leaned down close to her ear and drawled out, "Did I happen to mention Jack's an avowed woman hater?"

She closed her eyes. "No, you did not. Is he dangerous?"

"He won't hurt you, or any other female, for that matter, but he sure won't be nice to you either. Folks say he has the personality of a rattlesnake, but I think that's a rotten thing to be saying about snakes. They're much sweeter. Do you want to admit defeat now, give me your five dollars, and be done with it?"

It was the combination of arrogance and laughter in his tone that swayed her. She straightened her shoulders and her resolve. Come hell or high water, she was going to get the man who looked like a barbarian to hang on her every word.

"He will be my finest challenge," she announced. "Stay here, Travis, and observe."

"Wait a minute. How will I know you've won?" he asked with another chuckle he couldn't contain, for the possibility of Jack being swayed by a woman was downright hilarious.

"Trust me. You'll know when I've won." She adjusted the folds of her skirt, straightened the collar on her blouse, and then took a deep, God-help-me breath.

Travis kept right on grinning as he watched her drag her feet toward her prey. He knew she had to be worried. Jack did look like a hungry bear who had just come out of his cave. He usually smelled like one too, and Travis couldn't help but think Emily was actually courageous to try to win him over. She was also being foolish and stubborn, of course, because she refused to admit that men were too intelligent to be taken in by a helpless woman.

"Be sure to do that thing with your eyes, Emily," he called out, pretending to be helpful.

She turned around. "What thing?"

"That twitching thing you did when we were in Pritchard. Jack will love that."

She wasn't amused. She whirled around and hurried toward the man she was determined to tame. By the time she reached him, her heart felt as though it was lodged in the back of her throat.

Whatever it was she was saying wasn't working. Jack kept right on scowling, God love him, and Travis could have sworn he heard him growl each time he shook his head at her.

Although ten full minutes hadn't passed, Travis decided to suggest to Emily that she give up. It really was hopeless, after all. He was just about to call out to her when One-Eyed Jack did the most vile, hideous thing. He smiled.

Six

Travis blanched, blinked, and then looked again. The ugly smile was still there. He watched in

55

disbelief as Jack thrust his arm out to Emily. She immediately hooked her arm through his and started walking by his side toward the house, smiling up at her escort.

Travis didn't think he could stomach much more. He did a double take when the mismatched pair reached him and he heard her chattering away in the most horrendous imitation of a southern drawl he'd ever heard.

"I declare, Jack, you're such a gentleman."

"I try to be, Miss Emily. I sure do like the way you sing your words."

"How sweet of you to say so," she replied with a flutter of her eyelashes that made Travis lose his appetite.

"May I introduce you to my guide, Mr. Travis Clayborne, of Blue Belle?"

Jack quit grinning like a demented man long enough to flash his usual scowl at Travis. "I know you," he accused. "Didn't I shoot you a time or two, Clayborne?"

"No, Jack, you didn't."

"I recollect I did."

The set of his jaw indicated he was getting riled up. She quickly turned Jack's attention. "My, but I'm all tuckered out. Mr. Clayborne and I have been riding for hours and hours, and I'm not at all strong like you are, Jack. I'm too delicate for such strenuous activity."

Jack became solicitous once again. "Of course you're delicate. Anybody can see you ain't got much meat on your bones. Clayborne oughtn't to have set such a hard pace. Want me to shoot him for you, Miss Emily?"

The question so appalled her, she answered in a near shout. "No."

"You sure? I wouldn't mind none."

"I'm sure, Jack, but I thank you for offering. I'll be fine as soon as I sit down. I just need to rest for a spell."

"I'll get you settled in a comfortable chair in just a minute, Miss Emily. You sure do smell nice," he added in a rush.

"I declare, Jack, you'll spoil me with your compliments."

She didn't need to say another word or bat another eyelash. Travis listened as Jack promised to build her a fire so she could warm her feet, fetch her a drink so she could cool her parched throat, and bring her supper so she could regain her strength.

Travis wanted to shoot him. He felt justified too, because Jack had just disgraced every other man in the territory. Come to think of it, shooting was too good for him. Travis glowered as he followed the pair around the corner to the front stoop. The horses would have to be taken care of, but not until Travis knew who the other guests inside were and made certain Emily would be safe.

Jack opened the door for Emily and then, true to his nature, tried to kick it closed before Travis could come inside. It was a childish prank and one Jack so thoroughly enjoyed, he had to snicker about it.

John Perkins was standing in the hall waiting for them. He was a heavyset man with a triple chin, a potbelly, and a ready smile. He looked soft, but he was as tough as any other mountain man and didn't allow any nonsense inside his establishment. Any disputes that arose had to be settled outside, and from the number of unmarked graves on the hillside behind the house, it was apparent there had been a number of those fights in the past.

John usually greeted his guests. He couldn't seem to find his voice now, however, and appeared to be in a stupor as he stared in stunned disbelief at One-Eyed Jack.

John had apparently never seen Jack Hanrahan smile either.

"It's chilling, isn't it, John?" Travis remarked as he strolled past him on his way into the dining room.

John's wife, Millie, let out a little screech when she spotted Jack grinning. Travis thought that was an appropriate reaction.

The dining room was deserted. Still, Travis insisted that Emily sit in the corner next to him with her back against the wall. One-Eyed Jack straddled the chair across from them, but he kept nervously glancing behind his shoulder to make certain no one was trying to sneak up on him.

John came to his senses before his wife did. He hurried to the table, his shotgun cradled in his arms, and stopped when he reached Travis.

"It's good to see you again," he remarked with another quick glance in Hanrahan's direction. "Millie, quit twisting your apron and come meet Travis's woman. Did you go and get yourself hitched?"

"No, Jack. I didn't get married."

He introduced Emily to the older couple and then suggested they both join them.

As soon as Millie had gotten over her reaction to seeing Jack smile, her attention moved to Emily. She seemed mesmerized by her, nervous too; Travis noticed the way she was fiddling with her hair and smoothing her apron.

When Millie was younger, she was quite attractive, and her good looks helped to soften her abrupt way with people. Age had made her features more angular and harsh, but the sparkle was still in her eyes.

"We might as well eat with our guests, Millie, seeing as Travis is a friend," John said. "If you can stop gawking at his woman long enough to fetch our supper."

Millie didn't budge. She gave her husband a look Travis interpreted to mean John was going to catch hell later for teasing her.

"My hair used to curl the way hers does," Millie told her husband. "Might be it still would if it weren't so long."

"Expect you'll cut it, then?" John asked

Millie didn't answer her husband. She simply continued to give Emily her close scrutiny.

"Mr. Perkins, are you expecting trouble?" Emily asked, pretending not to notice that his wife was watching her every move.

"I always expect trouble," he replied. "That way I'm never taken by surprise."

"John started carrying a shotgun when he married Millie because he knew men would try to steal her away from him," Travis said.

"That was years ago," Millie interjected. "I was pretty then."

"You're prettier now," Travis told her. "John's still carrying his shotgun, isn't he?"

Millie blushed with pleasure and hurried out of the room.

"What are the two of you doing up in high country?" John asked with yet another worried glance at One-Eyed Jack.

"I'm escorting Emily to Golden Crest. She's meeting someone there."

Emily was relieved he hadn't given Mr. Perkins any other details.

Travis couldn't stomach looking at One-Eyed Jack's infernal grin another second.

"Emily, tell Jack to stop smiling. He's giving me the chills."

"I think his smile is charming," she replied. She reached across the table and patted Jack's hand. "Don't pay any attention to him, Jack. He's just in a contrary mood."

"Want me to shoot him for you, Miss Emily?"

The question didn't faze her this time. "No, Jack, but thank you for offering."

Travis decided to ignore both Emily and Jack. He turned to John again and remarked, "You're light on guests tonight."

"We won't be light for long," John replied. "Ben Corrigan stopped by on his way home from River's Bend to visit with Millie and me for a spell, and he told me five men from Murphy's outfit are headed this way. They'll expect to spend the night, but if they give me any back talk at all, I'm tossing them out. They're all low-

60

down, thieving troublemakers." He turned and raised his voice so his wife could hear him in the kitchen. "Millie, you'd better hide the money you've got tucked inside the cookie jar." Turning back to his guests, he said, "Travis, I'd keep an eye on your woman if I were you."

Travis nodded agreement. He didn't bother to correct John's misconception that Emily was his woman and, in fact, had to admit he kind of liked the sound of it.

The realization made him frown. She was soon going to be O'Toole's woman, he reminded himself, and he would probably never see her again.

"Looks like I won't be getting much sleep tonight," he said, accepting what he was going to have to do to keep Emily safe.

"Why is that?" Emily asked.

He doubted if she'd get any sleep either if he told her what Murphy's men were capable of, and so he decided not to answer her question and changed the subject instead.

"What other news did Corrigan have to tell you?"

"He mentioned there was a United States marshal poking around up here."

Jack Hanrahan's head snapped up, and he was suddenly mighty interested in the conversation. "What for?" he muttered. "The law ain't no good in these parts."

Jack was wrong, but neither John nor Travis felt inclined to tell him so.

"The marshal's searching for some men, and from the rumors Corrigan heard, they're about as bad as men can be. Word has it they've killed a woman and a child. The little girl was just three years old, and the bastards ought to hang for that. The marshal wants to haul them back to Texas to stand trial."

"The marshal's from Texas?"

"That's what Corrigan told me."

"Did he mention his name?"

"I don't recollect that he did. Why are you so interested in the marshal? I'd stay away from him if I were you. Corrigan said that when he was introducing himself to him, he was suddenly feeling real thankful he'd led such a law-abiding life. The marshal gave him the shivers, all right, with those cold blue eyes staring down at him. Corrigan told me he hopes he never runs into him again. That's what he said, all right."

"I'm looking for a man who goes by the name of Daniel Ryan. He stole something from my mother, and one way or another, I'm going to get it back. All Mama Rose remembers about him is that he's big, he has blue eyes, and he's from Texas."

"You aren't thinking the marshal's the man you're after, are you?"

John didn't give Travis time to answer him, but continued on. "It could be just a coincidence. Lots of men have blue eyes," he reasoned. "Maybe the gang he's after comes from Texas too, and one of them could have blue eyes."

"Mama Rose told me Ryan was very refined. They were close to our territory when they parted company at the train station, but he had already mentioned to her that he was headed north."

"I don't suppose the men the lawman's searching for are refined. Still, you could be climbing up the wrong tree, thinking the marshal's the thief. There might be other Texans roaming through these hills. You know how they like to bring their cattle up to graze on our land."

Travis shook his head. "None of them would bring their herds this high up the mountain. Besides, the man I'm looking for was spotted in River's Bend a couple of days ago, and didn't you say Corrigan had just come from there?"

"I did," John replied. "It sure looks like Corrigan met up with the man you're wanting, all right. If the Texan keeps to the northwestern trail, he'll have to come through this area, and you just might run into him too. If you don't mind my asking, what'd he steal from your mother?"

"A compass she was going to give to one of my brothers."

"A compass don't seem valuable," Jack said. "Is it?"

"It is to my brother," Travis told him.

"Maybe I'll steal it off the Texan and keep it for myself," Jack boasted. "Which brother was supposed to get the compass?"

"Cole."

"Never mind, then," Jack hastily decided. "I don't want him trailing me."

"You don't want any of the Claybornes trailing you," John said, clearly exasperated. "Not if you want to live to be an old man."

He turned back to Travis again and shook his head. "It isn't unheard of for a lawman to turn bad, but it sure makes me sick to think about it. It just isn't right."

"John, it's real doubtful the marshal is the man I'm looking for. I can't imagine a lawman putting his reputation on the line for such a petty crime. The compass is valuable, yet it's insignificant compared to the gold shipments and banknotes the marshal has surely recovered in the past."

Emily had listened to the discussion and couldn't resist offering her opinion. "If the marshal has your mother's compass, I'm sure he'll bring it back to her."

Travis couldn't resist teasing her. "That's what Mama Rose believes, and it's going to break her heart when she finally realizes she's been duped. The Texan has had plenty of time to bring it back. He's keeping it, all right. Still, I'm not certain the marshal is Daniel Ryan."

"I sure wish I'd gotten his name from Corrigan," John interjected.

Emily was becoming passionate about the matter. She shook her head at both men and said, "If the marshal accidentally took the compass, returning it is probably the last thing on his mind. Remember, he's searching for criminals."

"If he accidentally took it? What kind of an argument is that, Emily? No one accidentally steals anything."

"It could happen," she argued. "You're making assumptions based on nothing but a few paltry coincidences. Surely you can see that I'm right."

He hid his smile. Emily was filled with right-eous indignation as she defended the man she had never even met. She was correct about jumping to conclusions, of course, but he wasn't going to tell her so. The debate would end then, and he was having such a good time arguing with her, he wanted to continue on. He liked the way her eyes sparkled whenever he said something she took exception to, and she found it impossible to make a point without waving her hands around, a trait he thought was delightful, even though he had to dodge getting hit a couple of times. He also liked the way her voice turned so earnest and trembled with her demand that he be reasonable.

Come to think of it, he liked just about everything about her. She was going to be difficult to leave in Golden Crest, and handing her over to another man was going to be almost impossible. The smile left his eyes as he pictured her in the arms of Clifford O'Toole.

With a good deal of effort, he was able to block the dark thought and turned back to John. "Did you ask me a question?"

John nodded. "I was wondering if the Texan told your mother he was a lawman."

"No, he didn't tell her what his occupation was."

"That's odd, isn't it?"

He saw Emily roll her eyes heavenward and decided to goad her by agreeing with John. "Yes, it sure is odd. I can't help but wonder why he'd hide it from her."

"You cannot know if he deliberately kept his occupation a secret or not," she cried out, her frustration apparent. "Neither one of you is being the least bit reasonable. I suggest that you stop

65

believing the worst and have a little faith in the man.

"What for?" Travis asked. "He robbed my mother."

"It sure sounds like he did," John agreed.

"We take care of our mothers out here," Travis said.

"You're right about that," John said, and even Jack had to grunt his agreement.

"No one dupes our mothers and gets away with it," John said.

Emily gave up. There simply wasn't any way she could make them see how illogical they were being.

The men continued to discuss the situation for several more minutes, and then Travis asked John to keep Emily company while he saw to the horses.

"You don't need to worry about that chore. I hired a new hand, Clemmont Adam's boy, and I saw him through the window leading your horses into the barn. He'll take care of them and bring in your baggage too."

Emily wanted to wash before supper, and since Travis wasn't about to let her out of his sight, he went with her and made her wait while he washed up too. By the time the two of them returned to the dining room, Millie had already served the food and was sitting at the end of the table.

There was thick stew with biscuits and jam, coffee for those who wanted it, and cow's milk for those who didn't.

"I like to sit by myself when I eat," Jack told Emily. He lowered his head and stared hard at her when he added, "Then I got to get down to Cooper's place before dark."

She gave him a wide smile. "You've been very patient, Jack."

She turned to Travis and put her hand out to him with her palm up.

"I believe you owe me five dollars."

He was surprised she wanted to be paid her winnings in front of Hanrahan and Perkins. While he dug through his pocket for the money he owed her, he glared at Jack for disgracing him. From the curious look on John's face, Travis knew he was going to want to know why he owed her the money, and if Emily told him, Jack would know he'd been taken in by a woman.

There'd be real trouble then.

He put the money in her hand and was just about to tell John any questions he had would be answered later, when Emily turned his attention.

She handed the money to Jack. "Here you are, and thank you so much for your assistance."

"It wasn't too bad," Jack muttered. "Can I stop smiling now?"

"Yes, you may."

He looked relieved for a second or two before his scowl was back in place. Then he shoved his chair back, stood up, and carried his plate and his cup to the table at the opposite end of the room. Like Travis, the mountain man preferred to sit with his back against the wall so he could watch people coming and going without fear of being caught unaware.

Jack hunched over his plate and began to eat his stew with his fingers, but Travis noticed his full attention was centered on Emily. He seemed so taken with her he missed his mouth twice. The man had the manners of a pig, and Travis knew he wouldn't be able to eat his supper if he continued to watch him. He turned back to Emily.

"Let me get this straight. You told Jack what our bet was?" he asked, trying to sound outraged.

"Yes, I did tell him."

"Then I can only conclude you didn't think you could pull it off without his cooperation."

"I most certainly could have, but I didn't want to," she replied. "It wouldn't have been right to use Jack to win the bet. The men in Boston expect women to flirt with them, but Jack wouldn't have understood. No," she insisted, "it wouldn't have been right."

"Aren't you changing your tune?"

"No."

"Is that right? What makes Jack any different from Clifford O'Toole?"

"Let's leave him out of this, shall we?"

"Who is Clifford O'Toole?" John wanted to know.

"The man Emily's supposed to marry. Stop kicking me," he told her. "She hasn't met him yet."

"That doesn't seem right to me," Millie interjected. "Why would you marry a man you don't know when you're wanting another?"

"I don't want any other man," Emily said.

Millie snorted. "It's as clear to me as a clap of thunder that you're taken with Travis. Are you blind, girl?"

Emily could feel herself turning red with embarrassment. "You're mistaken, Millie. I barely know him. He's just my guide to Golden Crest."

Millie snorted again. Emily quickly tried to turn the topic back to the wager. She refused to look at Travis until she was certain he wasn't thinking about Millie's remarks.

"I won fair and square," she announced.

"You broke the rules."

She forced a laugh. "There weren't any rules, remember? You made that choice, not me."

"What was the wager?" John asked.

Travis paused to glare at Emily for kicking him again before he answered. He explained their argument and how he wanted to prove she was wrong.

"It was a foolish wager," Emily said. "But I did win, and it's all your own fault, Travis. You should have been more specific, like the money-lender in a story I read called *The Merchant of Venice*. Have you ever read it?"

"As a matter of fact, I have."

"I don't recall reading the story," John said. "Of course, I don't know how to read yet, and that could be why I don't recollect it."

"I don't recollect it either, John," Millie said. "But I'm wanting to hear about it."

"It's a wonderful story," Emily began. "A gentleman borrowed money and made an agreement to pay it back within a certain amount of time. He also agreed that if he wasn't able to repay, then he would give the moneylender a pound of his flesh."

John's eyes widened. "That would kill a skinny man, wouldn't it?"

"It would kill any man," Travis told him.

Out of the corner of his eye, he saw Jack get up and move to a table in the center of the room. It was apparent he was trying to get closer so he could hear every word Emily said, and he was also trying not to draw any attention to himself. It took all Travis had not to laugh, but, honest to God, seeing the savage up on his tiptoes really was comical. His brothers weren't going to believe him when he told them about it.

"Don't leave my John hanging for the rest of the story," Millie said in her usual abrupt tone. "It seems mighty foolish for a man to make such a rash promise, doesn't it, John?"

"Yes, Millie, it does seem foolish. Now, if the moneylender gave him time to put some weight on around his middle, well then, I'm thinking that promise wasn't so rash after all. Did he give him time?" he asked.

Emily shook her head and tried not to laugh. "No, John, he didn't give him time."

"He never should have made that promise," Millie insisted with a shake of her head. "He obviously wasn't from around these parts. Men out here would never do such a foolish thing."

"He was desperate," Emily explained. "And he was certain he would have the money in time to repay. He didn't though."

"I had a feeling that's what happened. Did he get cut up?" John asked.

"He died, didn't he?" Millie asked at the very same time.

"No, he didn't get cut up, and he didn't die," she answered.

"He welshed, didn't he? It just doesn't seem right to me," John said. "A promise made is a promise that's got to be kept. A man's word is sacred, after all. Isn't that right, Millie?"

"Yes, John, a man's word is all he's got in these parts. How did he get out of his promise?" she asked Emily. "Did he go into hiding?"

"No," Emily answered, smiling over the Perkinses' enthusiastic response to the story.

Travis was also smiling. Although he had read the Shakespearean play at Adam's insistence, he liked hearing Emily tell it much better. Her animated expressions made the characters seem real.

He happened to glance over at One-Eyed Jack then, saw what he interpreted to be a genuine smile on his face, and knew that Emily really had won the bet fair and square after all. The proof was hanging on her every word. Hanrahan was definitely smitten.

"If he didn't run away, what happened to him?" Millie asked.

"He refused to give a pound of flesh, and the moneylender refused to let him out of his promise or give him any more time, and so a trial was held to determine the outcome."

John slapped his hand down on the tabletop. "Leave it to the law to interfere."

"An attorney saved the man, of course," Travis said.

"Who just happened to be a woman," Emily reminded him. "Her name was Portia."

She and Millie shared a smile over that interesting fact before she continued.

"I'm wanting to know what in tarnation happened to the man who borrowed the money," Millie said. "What did the judge have to say?"

"He decided the agreement was legal and binding and that the moneylender was entitled to his pound of flesh."

"I knew it, Millie. Didn't I tell you a promise made is a promise that's got to be kept?"

"Yes, you did, John."

"But," Emily hastily added before she was interrupted again, "it was also ruled that while the moneylender could take his pound of flesh, he couldn't take a single drop of blood."

John rubbed his jaw while he mulled the judgment over in his mind. "Well now, I don't believe you can take any flesh without taking some blood."

"It's a fact you can't," Emily explained. "If the moneylender had been more specific," she said with a meaningful glance at Travis, "the outcome might have been different, but he wasn't specific, and neither were you with our wager, Travis. I won fair and square."

He admitted defeat, told her there were no hard feelings, and even suggested that she gloat if she felt like it.

"Want me to kiss you to prove I'm not mad?"

He realized he'd embarrassed her as soon as she lowered her gaze to the tabletop and shook her head at him. He reached over and put his hand on top of hers.

"You've got a lot in common with Portia," he

whispered. "But I don't think she blushed when she won her case. You have her passion though."

Emily was pleased by the compliment. She wasn't given time to thank him, however, for a loud thumping sound interrupted all of them.

Someone was trying to break through the front door. John jumped up and ran to the entrance. Travis was right behind him.

"Are the men from Murphy's ranch here, Millie?" Emily asked.

"From the way they're banging on my door, I'd have to say it's them all right." She hurried over to Emily's side and latched onto her elbow. "You can finish eating in the kitchen tonight. You'll feel much safer, and Travis will make sure the ranch hands stay in my dining room. I don't know how I'm going to get you up those stairs though, but I'll let John worry about that. Come on, girl. This isn't the time to dally. Lord, I sure hope they aren't all liquored up. There's nothing worse than a drunk," she added with a shiver. "And if any of them steal my valuables, I swear I'll shoot them myself. Oh, I hope they aren't drunk."

Millie really was frightened. Emily wasn't about to take any chances. She picked up her plate of stew, followed Millie into the kitchen, and then offered to help her get the ranch hands' plates ready.

"You sit on down at the table and eat. I'll see to the chore after I put some more biscuit dough into my oven. After you've finished, you can scrub my frying pan if you have a mind to. It's been soaking in the basin long enough."

Emily was happy to have something to do. She quickly ate, then rolled up her sleeves and attacked the pan with a vengeance, smiling to herself as she tried to picture her mother's reaction if she were watching her daughter now. She would probably have heart palpitations, Emily supposed, for none of her daughters were ever allowed to do common housework—there were maids for that—but after she'd gotten over her initial shock, Emily didn't think she'd be disappointed in her.

"Millie, do you have anyone to help you with your chores?" she asked.

"No, but I'm getting used to the notion of hiring someone. My John's been nagging me to slow down, and lately our house has been packed with guests more often than not. After washing and cleaning and cooking and fetching all day long, by nightfall I'm so weary I can hardly get myself ready for bed."

"Have you ever thought about moving to a town?"

"No, I'd never want to do that. Folks have to come through here to get north or west unless the season's dry and they can cut through the gullies, and even though we have lots of company, we're still isolated enough to feel free. I don't think I could abide having neighbors living right on top of me, knowing my business. John wouldn't like it either."

Emily had lifted the heavy pan out of the soapy water and begun to dry it with the towel Millie handed her when she suddenly noticed the pounding had stopped. She also noticed Millie's hands were shaking.

"Do you think Murphy's men have left?"

"We aren't going to be that lucky. Their kind never gives up."

"Exactly what is 'their kind'?"

"Ignorant drunks who steal anything that will bring a dollar for more liquor and break everything else. Can't reason with a drunk, Emily, but don't fret about it. Your man won't let any harm come to you."

"He won't let anyone hurt you either. He isn't my man though," she said.

"You're wanting him to be, aren't you?"

Her bluntness made Emily smile. "Why would you think that? I'm on my way to marry another man," she reminded her.

"Don't seem right to me," Millie muttered. She shut the oven door and turned so Emily could see her frown. "You seem smart enough, girl. You'd best rid yourself of your pride and tell him what's inside your heart before it's too late."

"But, Millie . . ."

"Won't do you any good to argue with me. There were sparks flying between you two, and anyone with half a brain would know what's going on. Ask him to court you."

Emily shook her head. "Even if I did want Travis to court me, it wouldn't matter. He told me he isn't the marrying kind."

Millie scoffed at the notion. "No man's the marrying kind until the ceremony's over. Don't you go believing that nonsense, girl. I saw how close he sat next to you at the table. Why, he had

75

you squeezed up nice and tight against his side. I saw him take hold of your hand too, but I didn't see you pull away. You didn't mind one little bit, did you?"

Emily's shoulders sagged when she said, "No, I didn't mind. I don't know what's come over me. Mr. O'Toole's letters were very nice, and when he suggested—"

"Hogwash," Millie muttered. "Are you going to ruin your life because of some letters?"

"It wasn't supposed to get complicated," Emily said. "I made up my mind to take charge of my destiny, and now I think that maybe Travis was right. He told me it was my pride being wounded that made me act so rashly. Millie, I don't know what to do. I like Travis, but I'm certainly not in love with him. Why, I've only known the man for a couple of days, and we've spent most of our time together arguing about this and that."

"Love can happen quick," Millie told her. "I took one look at my man, and I knew I was going to nab him."

Emily didn't want to "nab" anyone. The conversation was making her agitated, for Millie was forcing her to think about things she would rather ignore. Emily wanted to convince herself that she was simply getting cold feet again, but she quickly recognized the lie. Dear God, what was happening to her? She didn't know her own mind anymore.

"You're very fortunate to have found John," she said. "How did you meet him?" She added

76

the question in hopes of turning Millie's attention away from her conflicting feelings about Travis.

Millie was just about to answer her question when the back door flew open and slammed against the kitchen counter, causing both women to jump in reaction. Two of the scruffiest looking creatures Emily had ever seen came sauntering inside. Millie let out a very unladylike blasphemy that so surprised Emily she turned to look at her.

The creatures quickly recaptured her full attention, however.

"No one's keeping us out," one of the men said. He let out a loud belch before he added, "Ain't that right, Carter?"

The other creature was too busy staring at Emily to answer his friend. "Look at what we got here, standing in front of the cabinet John hides his liquor in, Smiley."

Emily was trying hard to blend into the wall. The men reeked of foul whiskey and were swaying on their feet as they gawked at her, and she knew it would only be a matter of minutes before they both passed out. She decided to humor them until then, or until Travis and John came into the kitchen and tossed them out.

She tucked the frying pan behind her while she stared back at them. She couldn't make up her mind which one was uglier. Smiley's teeth were so rotten they'd turned black in spots, which made his smile all the more repulsive. He drooled too.

Carter wasn't any prize either. His head appeared to be too big for his squat body, and there was a stench about him that was so horrid, Emily actually gagged.

Compared to these two, One-Eyed Jack was a ladies' man.

Millie's profanity hadn't made much of an impression on them. Neither one even bothered to glance her way.

"I'm wanting at that whiskey," Smiley muttered.

"Me too," Carter agreed. He licked his thick lips in anticipation, then made a smacking noise that Smiley found so comical he started chuckling, and if the raucous noise the two of them were making wasn't bad enough, watching the spittle from Smiley's mouth dribble down his chin was simply more than Emily could stomach.

Lord, they were vile.

Emily was simmering with anger. She wasn't going to let her temper get the upper hand though. Caution was prudent now, she decided. It would be foolhardy to provoke them, for even though she had never seen a drunken man up close, she had heard that they were all unpredictable, and Millie had just told her it wasn't possible to reason with a drunk.

She really wished she had a weapon close-by, then realized she was gripping one in her hand. The frying pan could do enough damage to send them running, and she wouldn't have the slightest qualm about using it if either one of them tried to steal so much as a speck of dust.

"Please leave. You're frightening Millie."

"We ain't going nowhere until we're good and ready," Carter muttered.

Smiley snorted agreement.

"I'm wanting at that liquor," he whispered to Carter loud enough for both women to hear. "If I got to toss the woman out of my way, I will. No one comes between me and my whiskey."

Carter vigorously nodded agreement. The movement must have made him dizzy, because he started swaying in a circle.

"I'm wanting the money tucked inside the cookie jar," he told his cohort. His gaze searched the room before he added, "Millie went and hid it on us."

"Guess we got to tear the place apart to find it then."

Carter snickered. Millie straightened her shoulders but continued to give away her fear by twisting her apron. "You get on out of here, both of you, or I'll shout for John."

Carter pulled his bowie knife from his waistband and waved it at her. The stupid man was so drunk Emily was amazed he could hold on to the weapon.

"You keep your trap shut, or this here knife is going in your belly," he hissed.

Millie's complexion turned as white as the dishcloth. Seeing her fear fueled Emily's anger. How dare they come into this dear woman's home and threaten her?

Emily took a deep breath. Oh, what she would have given to have John's shotgun now. She'd shoot both of them for upsetting poor Millie. She wouldn't kill them though; she'd just make it painful for them to walk for a long time.

"Let's get the pretty little heifer out of our way," Smiley suggested to his friend.

Emily blinked. In the space of Millie's loud indrawn breath, she went from anger to fury.

"What did you just call me?" she asked, her voice a strained whisper.

Her eyelid began to twitch while she waited for him to repeat the insult.

"A pretty little heifer," Smiley told her.

She drew herself up to her full height and glared at the men. Caution be damned.

"Millie? I can't seem to make up my mind. Which one do you think is uglier? The one with the black teeth or the one with the fat head?"

Millie let out another gasp. Her eyes looked as though they were about to pop out of her face. "Are you trying to get them mad, girl?"

Smiley took a step toward Emily. "She's Travis Clayborne's woman," Millie cried out. "If you touch her, he'll kill you."

"We ain't got no quarrel with Clayborne," Smiley muttered. "He won't know what happened until it's too late. He's busy with the others out front, and we'll be long gone with our whiskey and money before he comes inside. Ain't that right, Carter?"

"We can ride fast when we got to," his friend boasted. "Go and push the little heifer clear into the dining room. I'll back you up."

Millie started to slowly edge her way to the table, hoping she could duck underneath to protect herself from Carter's knife while she screamed for her husband. Out of the corner of her eye she noticed Emily wasn't trying to back away from the man stalking her.

"Run," Millie cried out.

Emily shook her head. "Not until I help you take the garbage out."

The remark made Smiley stop. He swayed on his feet, staggered backward, then turned to Carter. "Is she talking about us?"

"What's come over you?" Millie whispered.

"Anger. I don't appreciate being called a cow; I don't like being threatened, and I hate the way they're scaring you," Emily answered. She kept her gaze on the drunks. "Millie has asked you to leave. Please do as she says."

Smiley snorted. He put his arms out at his sides and tried to rush her. He was so drunk, he bounced against the counter twice and lost more distance than he'd gained.

"Get behind my back," Millie shouted.

Emily was too busy at the moment to explain she wasn't about to do such a cowardly thing. Timing, after all, was everything. She nervously waited until Smiley was just about two feet away from her, then swung her arm in a wide arc and slammed the frying pan up against the side of his head.

Spittle went flying every which way as Smiley staggered backward, screeching like a wounded rooster, before he finally collapsed in a heap on the floor.

Carter was so taken aback by her attack he dropped his knife. "You knocked him stupid," he bellowed.

"No," Emily corrected in what she believed

was a reasonable tone of voice. "He was already stupid. I knocked him out."

Her heart was frantically pounding, and her hand shook as she lifted the hem of her skirt, stepped over the prone man, and continued on toward his cohort. She had to get to him before he remembered he'd dropped the knife, or both Millie and she were going to be in real trouble.

Carter wasn't as drunk as she thought he was. Quick as a pistol shot, he squatted down, scooped up his knife, and snarled at her like a mad dog.

Emily took a hasty step back. Millie tried to help her by throwing everything she could get her hands on at Carter. He ducked the cup and saucer she hurled at him, but the copper kettle clipped him on his shoulder.

He let out a howl of pain, his gaze shifting back and forth between his two adversaries. Emily thought he was trying to decide which one to go after first. Millie drew his attention when she started screaming her husband's name over and over again. Emily seized the opportunity and slammed the frying pan into his elbow. She let out a yelp of dismay, for she'd tried to knock the knife out of his hand and had missed by an arm's length.

Carter shouted with rage, and from the look in his eyes, she knew his intentions had just turned deadly.

Seven

He never touched her. One second she was staring at his ugly expression and the next she was looking at Travis's broad back. He seemed to have appeared out of thin air, and though she didn't have the faintest idea how he'd managed to get in front of her without making a sound, she was so happy to see him she patted his back.

The odds, after all, had just improved considerably. Emily moved to his side just in time to see his fist strike Carter below his chin. The force behind the blow was so powerful it sent him flying out the doorway through the screen. He landed on his back in the grass with his legs draped over Millie's butter churn.

Travis wanted to hit him again. He was so furious he was shaking. When Jack told him there were two men in the kitchen threatening Emily, Travis became enraged. He got scared too, and that enraged him all the more. His heart felt as if it was going to jump out of his chest as he raced toward the house. When he saw the son-of-a-bitch waving a knife in Emily's face, something snapped inside of him, and he suddenly wanted to tear her attacker apart limb by limb.

The idea still appealed to him. For a full minute he kept his attention on the man he'd knocked senseless, willing him to get up so he could hit him again, but the drunk didn't cooperate. He was out cold, and Travis finally accepted the fact that he wasn't going to be able to beat the hell out of him.

He turned around, put his hands on Emily's shoulders, and asked her to look up at him.

"Are you all right?" His voice was a rough whisper. "He didn't hurt you, did he?"

"No, he didn't hurt me," she answered, surprised at how weak her voice sounded.

He noticed the iron pan in her hand then, took it away from her, and put it on the counter.

Emily suddenly needed to sit down. Now that the danger had passed, the reaction hit with a vengeance. Her knees went weak and she was suddenly shivering with cold. She turned away from Travis, pulled out one of the kitchen chairs, and plunked herself down on the seat.

John came running into the kitchen. He looked at his wife first, saw that she was all right, and turned to survey the damage. His gaze shifted back and forth between the remnants of the screen door and the man sleeping spread-eagle on his floor.

Emily watched him shake his head as he pulled his wife into his arms and hugged her. Emily wished Travis would put his arms around her, hold her tight, and comfort her in much the same way John was comforting his wife. Did the Perkinses know how fortunate they were to have found each other?

John placed a kiss on Millie's forehead before once again turning to the unconscious man littering his floor.

"What happened to him?"

Millie joined Emily at the table before she answered him. She sat down with a loud, weary sigh, and then said, "She's what happened to him." She pointed at Emily to emphasize the fact. "John, I don't know what came over her. One minute she was trying to squeeze herself into the wall, and the next minute she was banging my best frying pan up against his head. It was something he said that set her off."

Travis leaned against the counter, folded his arms across his chest, and stared down at Emily. He watched her lower her gaze to her lap and noticed a faint blush cover her cheeks.

He couldn't understand her timidity now. "Emily, are you embarrassed about something?"

She answered with a dainty shrug of her shoulders. He didn't have the faintest idea what that gesture was supposed to mean. She'd acted like a wild mountain cat moments before, ready and willing to do as much damage as she could with her frying pan, and though Travis had kept his attention on the drunk threatening her with a knife, he had noticed the determined glint in Emily's eyes when he'd moved to stand in front of her.

Now she was acting like a woman who could swoon at the drop of a hat.

John put his hand on Millie's shoulder and gave her an affectionate squeeze. "I'm going to put a strong bolt on that door before I go to bed. I don't know what I'd do if anything happened to you."

"I'm not embarrassed. I'm ashamed. I deliberately provoked them."

85

Travis was the only one who heard Emily's whisper. "How did you provoke them?"

"I lost my temper. I shouldn't have though, because I put Millie in danger."

"How'd you do that?" John asked.

"She did no such thing, John," Millie said.

"Yes, I did. I incited them," Emily argued. "I deliberately made them angry by telling them how ugly I thought they were."

Travis squatted down beside her and took hold of her hands. "Look at me," he ordered.

She lifted her gaze to his. "I should have tried to placate them, but they made me so angry. One of them called me a heifer."

A hint of a smile crossed his face. "A heifer?"

"That's what did it, all right," Millie interjected. "She got that mean look in her eyes right after that one named Carter called her a 'pretty little heifer.' "

Emily straightened her shoulders. "No woman likes to be called a cow," she announced in her haughtiest voice.

Travis and John both tried to hide their grins. Millie shook her head. "I think he was complimenting you in his own vile way. He didn't call you a cow, Emily. He called you a pretty heifer," she reminded her.

"Correct me if I'm wrong, but aren't they the same thing? Travis, I don't believe I've said anything amusing. Why are you smiling?"

"Your indignation," he replied.

John insisted on hearing every detail, and Millie was happy to oblige. Travis listened as he dragged Smiley out of the kitchen and shoved him into the grass next to his friend. His attention kept returning to Emily, and after he'd finished his chore, he leaned against the doorframe and blatantly stared at her.

She had been shivering a few minutes before, but under his close scrutiny, she was feeling uncomfortably warm in no time at all. She was also having difficulty drawing a deep breath.

John drew her attention when he pulled out a chair and sat down next to his wife. Emily watched him put his hand on top of Millie's, and it was that simple, little gesture of affection that proved to be her own undoing. She was suddenly so consumed with such hot, painful longings for Travis, she wanted to weep. She couldn't understand what was happening to her. She had never had lustful, carnal thoughts before, but she was certainly having them now, and how was that possible? Why was she yearning for something she had never experienced?

Emily made the mistake of looking at the man who was responsible for her misery. The sight of him only intensified her erotic thoughts, and she hurried to look away.

She wasn't quick enough though. Wanting him was bad enough. What made it worse was that she was certain he knew it. The dark look in his eyes told her so.

She jumped to her feet, nearly overturning her chair in her haste. She needed to get busy, she told herself, to take her mind off her outrageous daydreams. She decided to clean up the mess around her, but Millie paused in her story to insist that Emily sit back down.

She was simply too agitated to sit anywhere, and so she stood by the entrance to the dining room instead. She was deliberately trying to put as much distance between herself and Travis as possible. She didn't dare look at him again, so she pretended grave interest in Millie's every word.

And, Lord, it was hot in the kitchen.

"John, what took you and Travis so long to get in here?" Millie asked.

"We had our hands full; that's what took us so long," he replied. "Corrigan told me five men were heading this way, but he was wrong about the number. There were eight of them out front trying to get inside, and all but two were stinking drunk. We didn't know a couple of others were sneaking up on the back door. I sure did itch to shoot them, Millie."

"What held you back?" she asked.

"Four of them decided to take Travis on, and all at the same time. They came at him from every direction, putting him right in the thick of it."

Emily's eyes widened, and she couldn't stop herself from looking at Travis. "You were in the thick of it? You don't have a mark on you."

"His fists have got to be tender," John interjected. "I had to keep my shotgun trained on the other hooligans so they wouldn't try any nonsense on me. It was a real fracas, I'm telling you, and One-Eyed Jack was the only one enjoying himself. He looked like he was having a mighty fine time. As pretty as you please, he sat himself down on my front stoop, until he remembered seeing two of the men going around back. We would have

gotten here sooner if Jack hadn't been so preoccupied."

Emily enjoyed the way John painted a story.
She could picture Jack slapping his knee in
amusement while he watched the fight, and she
almost burst into laughter then. The contrary
mountain man was unlike any other man she'd
ever met.

"I'm glad he finally remembered," she said.

"Didn't you hear me shout for you, John?"

"Now, Millie, with all the commotion going
on out front, how could I hear you?"

"If you hadn't come inside when you did, I
don't know what would have happened," Emily
admitted.

"You were holding your own," he told her.

"Millie, I'm so sorry I scared you."

"You didn't scare me. You sure did surprise
me though. I forgot all about the frying pan until
you whacked it upside his head."

"We'd better put her in the corner room, don't
you suppose, Travis?" John asked. "No one can
get to her through the window, and I imagine
you'll hear anyone coming down the hall. I don't
suppose those two sleeping it off in my backyard
will sober up enough to come after Emily, but
we shouldn't be taking any chances."

"Are you going to let Murphy's men sleep
inside tonight?" Emily asked.

"Just the two who aren't drunk," John
explained. "I'll put them at the opposite end of
the house, so you don't need to worry. Travis
will be in the room next to you."

John's last remark wasn't at all comforting.

Having Travis so close seemed as dangerous to her as having Smiley in the next room. Travis wouldn't hurt her, of course, and he wouldn't force himself on her either, but then he wouldn't have to, would he? The mere thought of being alone with him did crazy things to her heart, and she could hear the warning bells ringing loud and clear in the back of her head.

Travis moved away from the door. "I'll show her where her room is," he remarked, completely ignoring Emily shaking her head at him.

He caught hold of her hand and continued on into the dining room. She tried to pull away from his grasp, but he tightened his hold to let her know he wasn't letting go.

Jack hovered near the front door, waiting for Emily. "I'm wanting to leave now," he announced.

Emily smiled at him. "Thank you again for going along with my game, Jack."

"I'm wanting to shake your hand before I leave," he muttered. "Unlatch her for a minute, Clayborne. I'm not going to steal her."

Travis let him have his way. He watched the two of them shake hands and couldn't help but notice the surprised look on Emily's face.

Jack leaned close to her, whispered something into her ear, and then pulled away. "I might be running into you again real soon," he predicted. He shoved his hat on his head, turned around, and stomped out the front door.

Emily hurried to get around Travis before he tried to grab hold of her again. She bent down to pick up the hem of her skirt and then went upstairs.

Travis stayed right behind her. "What did he say to you?"

She reached the landing, turned around, and held out her hand.

Travis saw the five dollars and started laughing. "I knew Jack was taken with you, but I never thought he'd give you your money back."

"He's a dear man."

He looked exasperated. "No, he isn't. He's a cantankerous old goat. He smells like one too. He sure does like you though."

"I like him too," she assured him.

Because he stood on the step below her, they were almost eye-to-eye. All she could think of was moving into his arms and kissing him. Emily realized then that she was staring at his mouth. Dear God, he was bound to know what she was thinking. It was all his fault, she decided. If he weren't such a handsome rogue, she surely wouldn't be having such impossible thoughts now.

"I'm tired tonight," she blurted out.

"You should be tired. You had your hands full with those drunks in the kitchen."

"I was scared."

"There isn't anything wrong with being scared. You used your wits."

Where in thunder were her wits now, she frantically wondered. Travis was turning her into a nervous twit, and if she didn't get away from him soon, heaven only knew what she would do.

She quickly turned around. "You don't need to follow me to my room. I'll find it by myself."

If he noticed her voice trembled, he didn't say anything about it. He caught hold of her hand and led her down the dark hallway to the door at the end of the corridor.

His arm brushed against hers as he leaned past her to open the door. "Your bags are probably inside."

"Yes, they probably are," she replied for lack of anything better to say.

Travis glanced inside and then nodded. "They're in the corner by the window."

"Your satchels," he explained when she gave him a puzzled look.

She shook herself out of her stupor and hurried inside. Travis stayed in the doorway. He knew he should pull the door closed now and walk away. He couldn't make himself move though, and, God help him, he couldn't stop staring at her either.

She was standing entirely too close to the bed, and he was rapidly coming up with all sorts of possibilities.

His voice dropped to a whisper. "If you need anything, let me know."

"Thank you."

"Good night, Emily."

"Good night, Travis," she whispered back.

And still he didn't move. She took a step closer to him. "It's hot in here, isn't it?"

"Are you hot?"

"Yes."

"Me too."

"Where are you sleeping?"

"Close-by," he answered. "I'll hear you if you call out."

"I won't."

"But if you do . . ."

"You'll hear me."

"Yes."

"I'll try not to bother you."

His smile was devastatingly appealing. "I'm already bothered, Emily, and from the way you're looking at me, I'd say you're real bothered too."

She didn't try to pretend she didn't know what he was talking about. She took another step toward him just as he moved toward her. And suddenly she was in his arms and she was kissing him with all the passion she had inside her.

One kiss wasn't enough. Frantic to get as close to him as possible, she wrapped her arms around his neck. Her fingers gripped his hair while his mouth ravaged hers.

He couldn't get enough of her. He lifted her up so she was pressed tight against him, but the feeling he wanted was dulled by their clothing.

He groaned in frustration and began to take her clothes off, but his mouth never left hers. She was so hot and willing, and God, but she tasted wonderful to him. He unbuttoned her blouse, tore it free of her waistband, and then pushed the straps of her undergarment down over her shoulders. His hand moved beneath the fabric and began to stroke her breast.

The feel of her smooth skin against the calluses on his hands pushed his control further away. She made him so hot for her, he could barely think now. He wanted her more than he'd ever wanted any other woman before.

Travis kicked the door shut with his foot, forced himself to pull back from her, and then told her in no uncertain terms what he wanted to do to her.

He had to hold her up when he was finished. "Yes or no, Emily?" he demanded.

She didn't want to make the decision. He was forcing her to be accountable for her own actions, and she would much rather have been swept off her feet instead.

Admitting the truth helped her come to her senses. She pushed away from him and shook her head. "No, we can't. I want to, Travis, but it wouldn't be right."

She was panting now and still couldn't seem to draw a deep breath. She threaded her fingers through her hair in acute frustration.

His own frustration made him sound angry. "Because of O'Toole?"

"Who?"

He clinched his jaw tight. "The man you're going to marry."

She noticed her blouse was open and frantically rebuttoned it. "I used to have morals until I met you, Travis. I don't know what's happened to me."

"Lust happened. That's all there is to it, Emily."

"Don't be angry with me."

"I'm not angry with you. I never should have let it go this far." He pulled the door open, then turned back to her. "You wanted me, didn't you?"

"You know I did."

He saw the tears in her eyes and was heartless to them. "You know what I think? When you're in bed with O'Toole, you're going to be thinking about me."

The door slammed shut on his prophecy.

Eight

She hated him because he was right. She was never going to be able to forget him, and if she married Clifford O'Toole, every time he touched her, she would be thinking about Travis.

Their marriage would be a mockery, of course. Mr. O'Toole was bound to be miserable and so was she, though probably no more miserable than she was now.

She tossed and turned in the double bed for several hours while she thought about the mess she'd made of things. She wanted to blame Travis for complicating her plans, but she was honest enough to admit it was her own wounded pride that had landed her smack in the middle of this mire. When Randolph left her wilting at the altar, Emily had been so mortified and embarrassed she'd run headlong into another engagement. She wasn't devastated by Randolph's betrayal. She had never loved him, and it was her own stupid pride and stubbornness that had kept her from admitting it.

What a fool she'd been. She remembered boasting to her parents that she was the one who was responsible for her own future and no one else. She had truly believed that she could control her own destiny and had diligently tried to do just that, with disastrous results. In less than one short week, everything had gotten all twisted around on her, thanks to Travis.

Her destiny had definitely run amuck, and all because she was falling in love with the wrong man. How could such a thing happen so quickly? Love was supposed to build slowly over time, wasn't it? No one ever really fell in love at first sight. Why did she have to be different? Well, her attraction to Travis didn't matter. She wasn't about to let it go any further and tried to convince herself that it was merely an infatuation on her part and nothing more. He'd called it lust, she remembered, and she thought she'd like to bang Millie's frying pan up against his thick head right this minute for believing such a thing. Perhaps then he would have an inkling of the pain he was causing her.

She was appalled by her own shameful thoughts. She had never had violent notions in the past, but then she hadn't known Travis either, and the two did seem to go hand in hand. It was all his fault that she was so miserable, for not only was he trying to steal her heart, he was also turning her into a shrew with criminal inclinations. Why, by the time Travis had left the bedroom tonight, she'd entertained the notion of shooting him in the backside, where, she was certain, his brain was located.

Emily threw off her covers, got out of her bed, and began to pace around the room. What in heaven's name was she going to do about Mr. O'Toole? She couldn't marry him, of course, but how was she going to tell him? She considered writing a letter to him to explain her change of heart, then decided that a cold, impersonal note was a cowardly way out. She certainly hadn't appreciated getting a note from Randolph and Barbara, and she sincerely doubted Mr. O'Toole would appreciate one either. Like it or not, she was going to have to face him when she told him, and all she could do now was fret about it and pray that she could come up with the right words to use so he wouldn't feel she had betrayed him.

Whispers coming from the hallway turned her attention. She tiptoed over to the door, leaned against it, and then heard what sounded like a gun being cocked. There were at least two men in the corridor, perhaps as many as three. One of them was Travis, for she recognized his whisper. Whomever he'd spoken to left in quite a hurry and didn't try to be quiet about it. His boots pounded on the wooden floor as he retreated.

She heard a door slam then. She didn't hear Travis leave though. She battled her curiosity for a long minute and then decided to find out what he was doing.

She was slowly turning the doorknob when he spoke to her.

"Go back to bed, Emily."

She let out a yelp and jumped a good foot. She

97

pulled the door open wider, forgetting for the moment that she was clad in only her nightgown, and when she saw Travis, she took a step back.

He was right outside her door, sprawled on a chair. He looked comfortable. His head was resting against the doorframe with his legs stretched out in front of him, one ankle crossed over the other.

She didn't have to ask him what he was doing. She already knew, and, dear God, how could she not love him? He was staying up all night just to make certain she was safe.

"Travis, I have a bolt on my door. You don't have to worry about me."

"Go back to bed."

"Will you please turn around and look at me? I'm trying to explain that—"

He didn't let her finish. "Are you in your night-gown?"

The question gave her pause. "Yes."

"You won't be wearing it for long if I turn around. Do you want me to be more specific?"

"No. Good night, Travis."

"I thought you'd see it my way."

She shut the door and leaned against it as the tears began to well up in her eyes. She couldn't cry, she told herself. She'd make too much noise, and then he'd know or at least suspect the awful truth.

She was in love with him.

Emily didn't get much sleep that night, yet she felt refreshed when she came downstairs the following morning. She had made several momentous decisions about her future during the black hours of the night, and for the first time in a long while, she felt as though she were in control again. Ever since the fiasco with Randolph, she'd jumped into one rash thing after another, but fortunately she had finally come to her senses.

She was relieved because she'd realized in time the terrible mistake she would have made if she married Mr. O'Toole. She was also heartsick, because she knew she was going to have to leave Travis.

He was never going to know how she really felt about him. He wasn't the marrying kind, and if she told him she loved him, she would only make him feel uncomfortable. He might also feel sorry for her, and that possibility horrified her.

Come hell or high water, she was going to be cheerful around him. She could cry as much as she wanted once she was on the stagecoach and headed for home. Travis, however, wasn't going to see a single tear.

"Isn't it a fine day, Millie?" she called out as she walked into the kitchen. "Good morning, Travis," she added when she saw him coming in the back door.

He scowled back at her and mumbled something that might have been a greeting. He was obviously in a foul mood, and she decided to pretend she didn't notice.

Millie placed a large bowl of oatmeal on the table for her. Emily sprinkled it with sugar and ate every bit of it. She drank two full glasses of milk too.

Millie wasn't in a very good mood either. Her

gaze darted back and forth between Emily and Travis, and every now and then, she'd mutter something to herself and shake her head.

The second Travis left to saddle their horses, she sat down beside Emily.

"Are you still hell-bent on going to Golden Crest?"

Millie's colorful use of words made Emily smile. "Yes," she answered. "But I—"

"For the love of the Almighty, stop being so stubborn. You're in for a life of heartache if you marry the wrong man."

Emily reached over and patted her hand. She found Millie's outrage and concern endearing. "I'm not going to marry Clifford O'Toole."

Millie's head snapped up. "You're not?"

"No, I'm not, but I owe it to him to tell him so face-to-face."

"Hogwash."

"It's the right thing to do," Emily insisted.

"Does Travis know about this?"

She shook her head. "I'll tell him later, when he's in a better mood. Besides, if I tell him now, he might not take me to Golden Crest, and I really owe it to Mr. O'Toole to explain my reasons for changing my mind."

John came into the kitchen with her satchels in his arms. "I'll just give these to Travis," he remarked as he hurried out the back door.

Emily spotted Travis leading the horses out of the barn. She stood up and turned to Millie.

"Thank you for worrying about me."

"That's what friends do for one another, don't they?"

Emily became teary-eyed. "Yes," she agreed. "Will you stop by on your way back?"

"I'll try," she promised.

Millie patted her on her shoulder. "You've got a good heart, girl. Don't let anyone tell you different."

Emily felt as if she were leaving her best friend. She hurried out the door before she started crying, stopped long enough to thank John, and then ran to Travis.

The couple stood side by side as they watched Emily and Travis leave.

They'd been riding for almost an hour before Emily broke the silence to ask Travis a question. "How long will it take to get to Golden Crest?"

"A while," he answered. "Are you in a hurry?"

"Yes," she began. She was going to tell him that the sooner they got to their destination, the sooner they could leave, but Travis's blasphemy distracted her.

"Hell."

"I beg your pardon?"

"Hell," he muttered once again.

His mood obviously hadn't improved. She waited several minutes before speaking to him again. "I'd like to ask a favor of you."

"No."

She ignored his reply. "When we get to Golden Crest, I would appreciate it if you wouldn't contradict me. No matter what I say to Mr. O'Toole, please go along with it. All right?"

"You're going to pull your helpless act again, aren't you? If he isn't a complete idiot, and I have my doubts about that, he'll see right through your little charade."

She let out a loud sigh in frustration. "Will you try to get along? And don't you dare call me crazy again," she added when he turned in his saddle to give her a hard, you're-out-of-your-mind look.

"If the petticoat fits, Emily . . ."

"Oh, and please don't call me Emily in front of him."

"The petticoat fits all right."

She refused to argue. She thought about telling him what her plan was, then decided that because he was in such a horrible mood, he would just have to wait to find out. Besides, in his present frame of mind, she was pretty certain that if she admitted she was going to tell Mr. O'Toole the wedding was off, Travis would turn the horses around and head back to Pritchard. He wouldn't understand how important it was for her to explain in person instead of sending a note. She could never be so cruel to anyone. She knew firsthand how it felt.

Emily spent the rest of the journey worrying. She hoped Mr. O'Toole didn't have a temper, for the thought of having an out-and-out confrontation with him made her stomach ache, and by the time they started the climb up the last hill to the crest, she was so nervous, her hands were visibly shaking.

When they rounded the curve, Travis saw the shotgun trained on the two of them through the branches in the trees.

She saw the dilapidated shack leaning precariously to one side in the center of the dirt yard at the very top of the crest and frowned in reaction. Where was Mr. O'Toole's grand house? He had told her in his letters that his home was nestled in the clouds at the very tip, and since she and Travis couldn't possibly climb any higher without falling off the mountain, she could only come to one conclusion. Travis had obviously taken a wrong turn and Mr. O'Toole's fine house was on the other side of the crest.

"Emily, move closer to my right side. Do it now."

The tone of his whisper didn't suggest she dally. She nudged her horse forward into the narrow opening between the rock ledge and Travis, but she didn't really become alarmed until she glanced over and saw his dark expression.

"Is something wrong?" she whispered back.

"Maybe."

He was staring intently at a clump of trees to the west. Something fascinated him, all right. Emily leaned forward in her saddle, peeked around him, and gave the area a thorough once-over. She still couldn't see anything amiss and decided then that he was just being overly cautious.

She turned back to the shack just as the front door opened with a loud groan and a ridiculously attired man came hurrying outside. Her eyes widened, for, honest to Pete, she'd never seen anyone like him. He was tall, skinny, and so filthy he could have blended into the dirt if he hadn't been wearing a ludicrous formal black top hat and red satin suspenders over a stained undershirt and brown pants.

She watched him adjust the straps as he moved toward her. "Good Lord," she whispered.

Travis waited until the man had reached the center of the yard before ordering him to stop. "Tell your friend to drop his shotgun or I'll shoot him."

The stranger didn't like being told what to do. He squinted his eyes into slits and stared at Travis a long minute before he gave in.

"Git on out of them trees, Roscoe," he shouted before turning his attention to Emily.

"Are you the Finnegan woman?" he demanded.

Travis didn't give her time to answer. "Who are you?"

His gaze darted back and forth between the two of them. Emily thought he was trying to decide if he should lie or tell the truth. The disgusting man reminded her of a rodent, and every time he glanced her way, she could feel her stomach tighten.

"O'Toole. Clifford O'Toole. Is she our bride?"

Emily let out a gasp. Dear God, the rodent and Clifford O'Toole were one and the same.

"No, I'm not your bride," she blurted out.

"*Our* bride?" Travis asked at the very same time.

"We're sharing her," Clifford explained in a matter-of-fact voice. "Like brothers do," he added with a shrug, and Emily could have sworn she saw a bug fly out from under his hat.

"How many brothers?" Travis asked in the same mild tone of voice that Clifford had used.

"Just Roscoe and me," he answered before his

gaze settled on Emily once again. "You're her, ain't you?"

She frantically shook her head. "No," she insisted.

It wasn't the answer he was looking for, she realized. His hand moved toward the gun tucked in his waistband. Clifford gave Travis a quick glance, then suddenly changed his mind. His hand dropped back to his side.

"Then who are you?"

She straightened her shoulders, gave him a scathing look, and said, "I'm Mrs. Travis Clayborne."

If Travis was surprised by her lie, he didn't show it. His attention remained on the brother, Roscoe, who was now running toward Clifford.

Emily was too shaken to look at him. The meaning behind Clifford's explanation had finally sunk in. The two brothers intended to share the same woman, and, dear God, just thinking about it made her want to throw up. She continued to stare at the loathsome rodent in front of her, and, oh, how she wanted to lash out at him for lying to her in his letters.

She shook her head. No, he couldn't have written them, she realized. The letters were written by a refined gentleman, and it was apparent that there wasn't a refined bone in Clifford's body. He couldn't have written poetry either, of course, and she sincerely doubted he could even read or write his own name.

What in God's name had she gotten them into?

She made the mistake of looking at Roscoe then. He resembled his brother and was certainly just as filthy. His hair wasn't covered with a formal top hat though. He had a red silk scarf wrapped around it like a turban, and from the way he was grinning up at her, she thought he believed he was quite fashionable.

Emily wanted to leave with all possible haste. She found Roscoe vile and disgusting, but Clifford was worse. He frightened her. There was a mean look in his eyes that made her skin crawl.

Travis also wanted to leave, but at the moment he had his hands full. He knew there had to be at least one more man stalking them, and he was trying to find him and keep his attention on Clifford and Roscoe at the same time.

"If you ain't ours, what are you doing here?" Clifford asked.

"We took a wrong turn," she lied. "Travis, we should leave now."

"Don't go rushing off nowhere," Clifford insisted.

"If she ain't our woman, then where is she?" Roscoe asked his brother.

"You seen a woman going by the name of Finnegan?" Clifford asked her.

She was going to tell them no, then changed her mind. If they thought their bride was on her way to them, they might be more willing to let her and Travis leave in peace.

From the looks on the brothers' faces, she knew it was a remote possibility, but it was all she had and she latched onto it with a vengeance.

"As a matter of fact, my husband and I did meet a lady named Finnegan. Now, what did she tell me to call her? Barbara? No, that wasn't it. Emily," she added with a nod.

"Is she perty?" Roscoe asked.

"Oh, yes, she's very pretty."

"Where'd you meet up with her?" Clifford asked.

"We were just leaving the Perkinses' home when she arrived. Her escort will probably bring her to you tomorrow."

"Just one man riding shotgun with her?" Clifford wanted to know.

Emily nodded. "Yes. I recall his name too. Daniel Ryan. Perhaps you've heard of him."

The brothers shook their heads. "We don't recollect him," Roscoe told her. "Why'd you suppose we would?"

"Because he has quite a reputation," Emily said. She was grimacing inside over the tremor in her voice and prayed they couldn't hear it. If they knew how afraid she was, they might jump to the conclusion that she was lying, and then her game would be over.

"He's a United States marshal."

Clifford scowled. Roscoe spit on the ground. "A lawman coming up here?" Roscoe muttered to his brother. "I don't like the sound of that."

"I don't like it neither," Clifford said.

Travis wasn't paying much attention to the conversation. His gaze continued to scan the trees, looking for the enemy.

"Maybe we can get us two brides," Roscoe whispered loud enough for both Emily and Travis to hear.

Clifford nodded, and it was apparent from the

way he was staring at Travis that he'd already made up his mind.

Travis saw the silver gleam coming from the tree to the east just as Clifford let out a shout.

"Shoot him down, Giddy."

Travis's gun was out of his holster and firing before Clifford had finished bellowing the obscene order. A scream came from the trees, a branch snapped, and everyone but Travis turned to watch the brothers' cohort crash to the ground.

Clifford and Roscoe were smart enough not to go for their weapons. Roscoe dropped the shotgun and put his hands in the air, but Clifford stubbornly kept his hands down at his sides. They were balled into fists.

"He killed Giddy," Roscoe muttered.

"There weren't no call for that," Clifford said.

The two brothers shared a nod and then began to slowly edge apart.

They stopped when Travis cocked his gun.

"Take the lead down the hill," Travis told Emily.

He didn't have to repeat himself. She was so terrified now she almost dropped the reins when she forced her mount to back up and turn around.

Travis hadn't spared her a single glance from the moment he'd spotted the bastard hiding in the trees with his shotgun. He ignored her now while he continued to search for more brothers lurking about, waiting for an opportunity to ambush him, but, damn, he couldn't find them, and time was running out.

He made Roscoe and Clifford remove their guns and toss them in the water trough and then made them do the same thing with their boots. Once they were finished, he ordered them to lie on their stomachs with their hands up over their heads.

He still didn't take his gaze off them, trusting his horse to find his way down the path while he turned in his saddle so he could keep his gun trained on them.

He didn't turn around until the brothers were out of sight, and when he did, he goaded his stallion into a full gallop. He reached Emily's side, slapped her mount on his hindquarters, and sent him flying into a gallop too.

He deliberately stayed behind her so that he could protect her back, and for that reason, he was an easy target. The shot still caught him by surprise. The bullet went into his back, and damn, but it burned. He could feel himself slipping to the side, and with his last ounce of strength, he threw himself forward. He grabbed hold of his horse's mane with his left hand and tried to turn so he could fire his gun with his other hand.

He was too weak to lift his weapon. Emily was stopping now to help him. He tried to tell her to keep going, but all he could get out was one harsh word.

"No."

And then she was by his side and taking his gun away from him. He tried to focus on her, but the blackness before his eyes was making it impossible. He knew it would only be a matter of seconds before he passed out, and he desperately wanted to get her to safety first.

"Get out of here," he whispered.

"Hold on," Emily cried out.

She reached over, took the reins away from him, and forced his stallion to veer with hers toward the cluster of trees near the base of the first incline. Shots echoed around them as they entered the protection of the pines. The horses made another sharp turn before coming to an abrupt stop at the edge of a bluff.

Travis tried to sit up, but realized his mistake when he felt himself falling. He heard Emily scream his name a scant second before the darkness claimed him.

She swung her leg over her horse and leapt to the ground. "Get up, Travis," she begged as she ran to him. "Please, God, don't let him be dead."

He'd landed on his side and was half draped over a boulder. His head had struck the rock, and there were splatters of blood everywhere.

She knelt down beside him and gently turned him so she could see his back. She screamed then, a piercing, agonizing scream, and something seemed to explode inside her. She was filled with such rage she could barely think.

A shot stung the rock beside him. Emily came to her senses in the blink of an eye. She put Travis's gun back in his holster so she could use both her hands, put her arms under his, and began to drag him to safety.

She thought only to get him further into the forest. Then she saw a deep crevice between the rocks at one end of the bluff and turned around to drag him there. No one could get to him from behind, she knew, and they couldn't attack from the sides either. They would have to come at them head-on, and then she would shoot them down like the rabid dogs they were.

She didn't know where her strength came from, but she thought that maybe God was lending her a hand now. She tucked Travis into the crevice, rolled him on his side, and then took his gun in her hands again.

Roscoe came at them first. She shot him in the thigh. He yelped in fury and hopped back out of sight.

"The bitch got me, Clifford," he roared. "I got to kill her now."

"You hit bad?" Clifford shouted back.

"I'm bleeding like a pig, but it's just a flesh nick. I'm gonna kill her, all right."

"Not till we take a turn using her," Clifford shouted. "We'll hurt her good, Roscoe."

The two brothers continued to shout at one another. They were trying to terrify her, as each described in vile detail what he was going to do to her. She was already scared out of her wits, however, and nothing they could say now would make it any worse.

As long as the shouts remained distant, she knew she and Travis were safe. She put his gun down on the ground next to her, lifted her skirt, and ripped her petticoat so she could fashion a bandage for him. There was blood on the front of Travis's shirt on the left side. She tore his shirt free, saw the small hole in his skin, and realized the bullet had gone straight through. His back was covered in blood. She pressed the cloth to the injury and used another long strip of her petticoat to wrap around him.

The shouting suddenly stopped. Emily grabbed the gun and waited. A second felt like an hour. Roscoe poked his head out through the branches of a tree. He moved back before she could aim.

"She's tucked in tight between the rocks," he shouted to his brother. "The only way we can get to her is head-on. She'll kill us then."

"Don't you worry none. We'll get her," Clifford called back.

She didn't believe she could become more terrified. Then Rosco shouted to his brother. "We going to starve her out of them rocks?"

"No, we'll rush her during the night. She won't see us coming at her in the dark."

She began to pray again. She knew their chances of surviving were almost nonexistent, but if God could please send them some help, she would be most appreciative. If He wanted one of them to die, then please let it be her. All of this was her fault, not Travis's, and he was just a good, decent man. He didn't deserve to die this way.

God didn't answer her prayer for what seemed like hours, and during that time she was taunted by the hoots and shouts of Clifford and Roscoe.

He did answer her though, and she realized then she should have been a little more specific with her request.

He sent her One-Eyed Jack.

"Miss Emily, are you all right?"

She heard the whisper coming from below the bluff.

"Who is it?" she whispered back.

No one answered until she repeated her question a second time.

"It's me—Jack."

"Jack? Is that really you?"

"I just said it was."

"Are you below Travis and me on the rocks?"

"I skittered out on a ledge. Don't worry; no one can get any higher without pitching off into the canyon."

"Jack, the O'Toole brothers are trying to kill us."

"I figured as much as soon as I heard the gunshots. I can't get to you, Miss Emily."

"Could you please go and get help? Travis was shot in the back."

"He's a goner then," Jack whispered.

"No," she screamed in denial.

"No call to shout at me."

She heard the stubborn edge in his voice and knew he was getting his back up. God, she didn't have time for this. Didn't Jack realize how dangerous their situation was?

"I'm sorry," she whispered. "Oh, Jack, I'm so scared. Thank you for following us."

"I didn't do it for him. I did it for you. I'm taken with you, Miss Emily, and I've come to declare my intentions."

"Jack, now isn't the time," she cried out. "Please go and get help for us."

"It'll cost you. I'm wanting the five dollars back and five more so I can buy me some fancy courtin' clothes. Don't go getting the notion I'm wanting to marry you though. I got something else in mind."

She squeezed her eyes shut. She didn't want him to waste time talking, but she knew Jack well enough to understand he couldn't be pushed. He would leave to get help when he was ready and not a second before.

"Don't you want to know what I'm wanting?"

"Yes, Jack, tell me what you want." She sounded frantic. She couldn't help it.

"I'm wanting you to have supper with me down at the dining room in the Pritchard hotel. You got to latch onto my arm and let me walk you in too, and you can't get up and leave 'fore I do. Is it a deal?"

"Yes, it's a deal."

"I'll be leaving then."

"Hurry, Jack, and be careful."

Travis groaned then, but Emily couldn't take her attention away from the entrance to their hideaway long enough to see if his eyes were open or closed.

"It's going to be all right, Travis," she whispered.

Clifford came flying across the entrance. She didn't even have time to cock her gun before he reached the other side. She had to put both hands on Travis's gun to keep it steady. Her arms were outstretched in front of her. Tears streamed down her face, but she didn't dare take her hand away from the gun to wipe them away. She needed to concentrate, and most of all, she needed to pray.

Travis opened his eyes and looked at her. He

saw the gun in her hands, heard her sob low in her throat, and wanted more than anything to take her into his arms and comfort her. He couldn't move. He knew something was wrong, yet he couldn't figure out what it was. He thought he must be pinned against something, and whatever it was was burning the hell out of his back.

He tried to focus on his surroundings. Emily was sitting in front of him with her back pressed up against his chest. There were two long lines side by side in the dirt leading up to her, and he had to think about it for a long while before he realized someone had dragged something heavy across the narrow clearing.

She'd dragged him to safety. Dear God, it all came back with startling clarity then. He'd been shot, and Emily was sitting in front of him to protect him. The O'Toole brothers must still be out there, and he'd left Emily to fend for both of them.

She needed to get the hell out of there.

He whispered her name and willed himself to stay awake. "Emily, what are you doing? You've got to leave."

She didn't turn around when she answered him. "It's all right, my love," she whispered. "You can sleep now. I'll keep you safe."

Who was keeping her safe? No, no, it was wrong. He should protect her, he knew, and, Lord, he didn't want to sleep; he wanted to take the gun out of her hands and shoot the bastards because they'd made her cry. Then the black waves were suddenly rushing toward him, and he was once again pulled under into the dark.

She didn't know how long she sat there, hoping and praying. Their situation was becoming hopeless. Dusk was fast approaching, and she doubted help would arrive before nightfall. She reminded God that hopeless situations weren't difficult for Him, and though she didn't know what would happen, she was fully prepared for the worst. Only one thought drove her now. She would die protecting the man she loved.

Nine

The sound of gunfire at close range jarred Travis awake. It took him a long while to find the strength to open his eyes, and when at last he succeeded, he thought he was looking up at the blue sky.

Suddenly the sky began to move. He couldn't understand what was happening. He closed his eyes and tried to concentrate on the whispers floating around him, and when he was able to focus again, he saw a man leaning over him . . . a big man, with blue eyes. Was it Cole? No, he realized, it wasn't his brother. It was someone else.

The stranger was moving him. Travis's head dropped down to his chest, but his eyes remained open. He stared in puzzlement at a gleaming gold object the stranger wore clipped to his leather vest. He thought it was a pocket watch.

He heard Emily whisper. She asked the

stranger if there was still time to get to the Perkinses' home before dark, and it was only when she called the man "Mr. Ryan" that everything clicked into place. His gaze moved from the gold case up to the blue eyes, then back again.

No, it wasn't a pocket watch as he'd assumed. It was a compass.

The bastard pulling him every which way was wearing Cole's compass. Travis became incensed. He let out a low growl and tried to rip his brother's gift away from the stranger, but, damn, he was so weak, he couldn't even lift his hand.

The effort drained his strength. He felt as though someone had put a hand on top of his head and was shoving him under the water again.

And then he slept.

Travis came awake with a start to find Millie Perkins leaning over him with a razor in her hands. Instinctively, he knocked the razor out of her grasp and sent it flying across the room. It landed on the dresser, skated across, and dropped to the floor.

He'd given Millie quite a start. She jumped back and let out a shout. "Lord, you're quick. I see you've finally decided to come back to us."

"How long have I been asleep?"

"Off and on, almost four days now. You needed sleep to get your strength back, at least that's what the doctor told us. He must have been right because the glazed look is gone from your eyes now. I was going to shave you," she added with a nod. "You could sure use it. You're starting to resemble a bear."

Travis rubbed his whiskered jaw. "I'll do it," he said. He yawned, stretched the muscles in his shoulders, and felt only a twinge of fire. "I was shot."

"Yes, you most certainly were," she agreed. "They got you in the back, but more to your side than in the center. The bullet went on through, and the doctor assured us there isn't any chance of an infection now because you didn't catch a fever. You were sure lucky. You had an angel looking out for you."

Travis smiled. "I must have," he agreed. His gaze slowly moved around the room. It was familiar to him, and it took him a minute or two to realize why. He was in the same bed Emily had slept in.

One thought jumped to another. "Where is she?"

Millie seemed hesitant to tell him. "I assume you're asking me about Emily. Do you remember any of the last four days? No, I don't suppose you do," she continued before he could answer. "Emily sat by your bed day and night, worrying and praying about you. Yesterday your sleep turned real peaceful, and when Doc Stanley came back by, he convinced her that the worst was over and that you would be just fine."

"Where is she?" he asked again. He could tell something was wrong from the way she was nervously smoothing down her apron and looking everywhere but at him. He had a feeling he wasn't going to like her answer.

She took a step back before answering. "She's gone."

He immediately threw off the covers and swung his legs over the side of the bed. Millie's hands flew to her eyes, and she turned around so quickly she almost lost her balance. He realized then he didn't have any clothes on, let out a whispered expletive, and dragged the covers back up. He leaned against the headboard and muttered, "Damn, I'm weak."

"You should be weak. You lost some blood, but not too much, according to Doc Stanley. It was the hit you took to your head when you fell off your horse and struck a rock that made you sleep so long."

"I fell off my horse?" He was horrified by the mere thought. Cole would have a heyday with that bit of news if he ever found out. His brother would never let him live it down.

"Millie, you can turn around now."

She was blushing like an old spinster and still smoothing her apron when she did as he suggested.

"According to Emily, you did fall off your horse. She was the angel looking out for you, Travis. She dragged you a good long way to safety, and if you don't mind me saying so, that woman loves you more than any other woman ever will, and you're a fool if you don't go after her."

Travis shook his head. "She was all set to marry O'Toole, remember? And do you know why? Because she was hell-bent on marrying a rich man with a grand house and a curved damned staircase."

The longer he thought about it, the madder he became. What kind of a woman would take off without even bothering to say good-bye first? A damned inconsiderate one, that's who.

Millie, he noticed, was vehemently shaking her head at him. "She was not going to marry O'Toole. She told me so before you took her up to the crest."

"No, she decided against marrying him the second she saw him and his shack."

Millie snorted. "You sure are getting yourself worked up into a lather about it. If I were you, I'd get out of that bed and go after her before it's too late."

"I ought to, just to give her a piece of my mind. It was downright thoughtless of her to sneak out like that. Did she leave in the dead of night?"

"No, of course she didn't. She left in the light of day. She's on her way home to Boston, as a matter of fact. I was telling John that sooner or later, some other man is going to snatch her up. Oh, Emily's made up her mind never to marry because of what happened, but in time some smooth-talking man will be able to convince her. Of course, you won't care about her having another man's children, now will you?"

Travis refused to answer the question. "Why didn't she tell me she'd changed her mind before I took her up there?"

"Because she knew you wouldn't take her, that's why. She was determined to do the right thing and tell that no-good rodent face-to-face that she'd changed her mind."

"Rodent?"

"That's what she called him, all right. Of course, she didn't know he was a rodent before she met him. She believed he was a decent man and that she owed him an explanation."

"Let me get this straight. She thought she owed that bastard, but she couldn't wait around long enough for me to wake up?"

"She admitted it was her own foolish pride that landed her in this pickle and that she had learned a valuable lesson. She didn't tell me why she was leaving though. She knew the stagecoach only goes through Pritchard on Sunday, but she needed to go sooner. Guess you're going to have to go after her and ask her your questions. I can't answer them."

"I'm going back to Golden Crest and shoot those bastard brothers before I do anything else."

"The O'Tooles are already dead. A real nice gentleman shot them for you. It was a fair fight, I suppose, what with them trying to kill Emily and you. And the law's on his side," she added with a chuckle. "No doubt about that."

He didn't understand why she was so amused. "I guess I should thank him. Is he still here?"

She shook her head. "He took off right after he dropped you in that bed, but he stopped by yesterday on his way to Pritchard. Emily asked him if she could ride with him."

"You let her ride off with a stranger?"

"He didn't seem like a stranger to us, Travis. John talked to him a good long while. John was

121

downstairs having an early snort with old man Kiley when they left. My husband was going to take Emily, but he was convinced he should stay here and look out for me. There's a gang hiding in these hills. You remember John telling you about them? They've done a lot of killing and robbing. They even murdered a young mother and her little girl."

Travis closed his eyes. "The man was Daniel Ryan, wasn't he?"

"Yes."

He remembered everything . . . those cold, piercing blue eyes . . . and the gleaming gold compass. . . .

"He was wearing my brother's compass."

"He sure was," she agreed. "Emily asked him to give it to her, but he wouldn't. He let her hold the gold case and showed her how to open the little clasp so she could take the compass out and get a good look at it. Then he made her give it back to him. He told her he had to return it to the lady it belonged to, and Emily understood. Now, Travis, don't look at me like that. That lawman saved your life and Emily's too, because she never would have seen the O'Tooles sneaking up on the two of you in the dark. They would have nabbed her for sure, and you know what would have happened then. Ryan got there in the nick of time."

The thought of Emily being in such danger scared the hell out of him. It also infuriated him. If she had only taken the time to tell him what she planned to do, he never would have taken her up there in the first place and she wouldn't have ended up in such a godawful position.

"That woman doesn't have the sense God gave her."

"I guess it's up to you to find her some, then."

He ignored her remark. "Hell, I can't shoot Ryan."

Millie opened the door before commenting on his outrageous remark. "Of course you can't kill him. Will it make you feel any better to know that Emily shot at him? She thought he was one of the O'Tooles. Ryan told me he sure was surprised."

"I'm not surprised. She shoots at every man she meets," he exaggerated.

Millie let out a loud sigh. "You're a stubborn man, Travis Clayborne. Are you going to go down to Pritchard or not?"

He didn't like being prodded one bit. "I'm buck naked and on my way to shut the door, Millie."

She let out a screech and went running down the hallway. He slammed the door behind her.

Travis was in a foul mood by the time he finished washing and dressing. He cut himself shaving because he wasn't paying any attention to what he was doing. He was too busy thinking about Emily.

He made up his mind on his way down to the kitchen. By God, he was going to go to Pritchard so he could tell the ungrateful woman exactly how he felt. He would get a proper good-bye out of her too.

And that was all he was willing to admit.

Ten

They were the talk of the town. People started gathering in the middle of the afternoon, and within an hour, the Pritchard hotel was packed to capacity. The overflow spilled out into the street, and more lined the walkway on the other side.

Traffic came to a standstill, shops closed early, and chores were all but forgotten. This was a momentous occasion, after all, and no one wanted to miss it.

The clock inside the lobby began to chime the hour, and at six o'clock on the dot on Saturday evening, One-Eyed Jack Hanrahan came sashaying into the hotel, looking just about as fine as a man could look.

Money started changing hands immediately. Some of the men in town had bet Jack wouldn't show up; others had been just as certain he would. Olsen, the proprietor of the establishment, didn't believe in gambling, but he still managed to make a small fortune for himself and his staff because he'd been clever enough to charge admission to enter the dining room. He had fancy placement cards made too, and anyone who wanted to sit close to Jack Hanrahan and Emily Finnegan while they dined had to pay dearly for the privilege. In the event Miss Finnegan didn't keep her promise—and what woman in her right mind

124

would?—the proprietor had a sign propped up on the counter to alert everyone that there wouldn't be any talk about refunds.

Olsen didn't feel at all guilty about fleecing his friends and neighbors, for one simple but important reason: history was in the making that day, and all because Jack had finally taken a bath.

Folks had bet on that too, so there was a fair amount of grumbling from the losers when the shout came echoing down the street at precisely five o'clock that Jack Hanrahan had just been seen entering the bathhouse.

The sight of the mountain man, now all squeaky clean and gussied up, was enough to take the crowd's breath away and was surely worth every penny they'd paid. Why, Jack looked as pretty as you please dressed in a starched white shirt, pale blue tie without a stain anywhere, and black twill trousers with a nice straight crease down each pant leg, exactly where it was supposed to be. His shoes were new and shiny; his hair was all slicked down, and he carried a black suit jacket over his arm, just like a dapper gentleman would on a warm day.

The crowd began to cheer as they watched Jack make quite a production of putting his coat on and adjusting his brand-new eye patch, but one mean look from him was all it took to slam the door shut on that nonsense.

The man had a flair, all right. He also had a temper as big as the territory. Olsen nervously waited behind the counter next to his "No Refunds" sign while Jack easily threaded his way through the crowd. He would have gotten to the proprietor sooner, but he paused twice to glare at offenders in the crowd who dared to get too close to him. Folks were squeezed up so tight against one another, they could barely breathe let alone move, yet like the Red Sea, they miraculously parted to give him room. No one dared touch him because that just might make him mad, and only God knew what he would do then.

Olsen was shaking from head to toe. He didn't want to be around when Jack found out Miss Finnegan had changed her mind—if indeed she had—and so he made one of the servants go upstairs with him to announce her escort's arrival. Olsen didn't plan on coming back down. He'd send the servant with the bad news while he sought out a safe hiding place.

With the thought of survival uppermost in his mind, he motioned to a staff member, told Jack in a stammer he would be pleased to go and fetch Miss Finnegan, and then hurried around the counter.

The boy he'd recently hired met him at the bottom of the staircase, and just as the two of them were about to start up, they spotted Miss Emily at the landing.

Money would have changed hands again if the men could have stopped gawking at the beautiful woman long enough to get the bills out of their pockets. Because of the size of the crowd, the noise should have been deafening. It wasn't though. In fact, no one made a sound. They all stared in wonder, astonishment . . . and relief at the lovely lady above them.

She was stunning. Dressed for a formal ball,

she wore a full-length shimmering gold gown with a modestly revealing neckline meant to entice men and placate women, capped sleeves, and a fitted bodice that showed off her figure to perfection. The skirt was full and fell in soft folds around her golden slippers, and when she moved toward the top step, the fabric sparkled and glittered in the candlelight.

Travis watched her from the entrance to the alcove behind the counter. While the crowd would probably never forget what she wore, he was far more enamored by the warmth that came into her eyes when she found Jack in the sea of faces below her and smiled at him.

Travis moved back into the dark before she turned toward him. He was there only to make certain there wasn't any trouble, and unless it was absolutely necessary, he wasn't going to interfere. The evening belonged to Jack Hanrahan, but tomorrow belonged to him.

He shook his head in amazement when Jack moved to the bottom of the steps and put his hand out to her. The gesture was gallant, and obviously pleased Emily, for her smile widened and her eyes began to sparkle.

Travis was suddenly having difficulty catching his breath. The closer she got to him, the faster his heart beat until it was thundering in his ears. The heat was getting to him, he told himself, and surely that was the reason he was feeling so peculiar. He loosened the collar of his shirt. Odd, but that didn't help at all.

Emily was as regal as a princess as she came down the stairs. Her head was held high and her attention was centered on her escort and no other. She reached Jack's side, placed her hand on his arm, and walked close to him into the dining room.

The crowd was all but climbing the walls to give them enough room.

For the hardworking people in Pritchard, it just kept getting better and better after that. It was indeed a magical night for everyone, for not only did Jack eat with utensils, he also patiently waited after supper for the servants to remove the tables from the center of the room so he and Emily could dance.

They were the only couple on the floor. Jack stunned everyone once again when he took Emily into his arms. The couple glided around the room to the gyrating sounds of Billie Bob and Joe Boy's Band. Jack proved to be light on his feet and, in fact, was far more graceful than any other man there. He oozed charm as well, and Miss Emily Finnegan, the crowd decided, was having the time of her life.

The evening ended at one o'clock in the morning when Joe Boy's arm wore out from sawing his fiddle. Jack escorted Emily to the lobby again. He clasped hold of her fingers, leaned down, and kissed her hand. He whispered something to her too that made her burst into laughter. Jack even managed a grin, and after she kissed his cheek, he actually smiled.

He waited until Emily had gone upstairs, then turned and strutted out of the lobby as content as a man can be. By the time he'd reached the street, the eye patch was on the ground behind him, the jacket was draped over a hitching post, and his tie was in the water trough.

And the Jack Hanrahan they all knew and feared was back again.

Emily had just gotten into bed and pulled the covers up when she heard the scrape of a chair or a crate being dragged along the hallway floor. She bolted upright, threw her covers off, and ran across the room to make certain the latch was properly secured.

She had remembered to turn the lock after all. She leaned against the door for several minutes. Blessedly, the sound wasn't repeated, and she decided then that whoever or whatever it was had gone away.

She returned to her bed and got down to the more important business at hand. She desperately needed to cry, and she fervently hoped that by the time she was finished, she would have gotten Travis out of her mind.

She didn't succeed; crying didn't help one bit.

It was time to go home.

Eleven

She had overslept. She was going to miss the stagecoach if she didn't hurry. There wasn't even time for breakfast, which was fine with her because she was too upset to eat anything anyway. She dressed as quickly as possible, threw her things into her satchels, and ran downstairs to ask one of the staff members to please take her bags to the station.

Her luggage got there a few minutes before she did. Fortunately the street was deserted, so she didn't have to worry about anyone trying to engage her in conversation. She simply wasn't in the mood to be civil today.

She wasn't in the mood to go back home either, but she was still going to do it. She tried to be happy about seeing her family again. She couldn't manage it though. Going back to Boston wasn't her only solution, but it was definitely the safest one, because she knew that if she stayed here, she'd throw herself at Travis in no time at all and become thoroughly ruined. And wouldn't her parents just love that.

Emily's patience was about worn out when the stagecoach came barreling around the corner on two wheels and pulled to a rocking stop in front of her. Dust flew up around her, and she hurriedly moved back behind her satchels to get away from it.

The driver was a tall, lanky man with a curt, no-nonsense way about him. He jumped down from his seat, adjusted his bright blue bandanna around his neck, and tipped the brim of his hat to her.

"I'm running late, ma'am. You'd best get on inside while I fill up my water jug. I'll tell you my rules when I come back out."

He opened the door for her before he went inside the station. A few minutes later, he came out again and began to throw her satchels up on the roof of the coach.

He spoke as rapidly as he worked. "If you hear any gunshots, you hit the floor. Try to curl up under one of the seats. Don't look out the window, no matter how much you want to. I just can't tell you how important that rule is, ma'am, so try to remember. I'm not expecting trouble, but I'm always ready for it. Now, if you're needing to stop for a minute, lean on out the window and shout at me. Unless you hear gunshots first. Then don't lean out. I'm hoping you won't need to stop though, because that will make me even later getting to my next town."

"I won't need to stop," she promised.

He climbed up on top of the coach, tied the satchels, then jumped down and opened the door again.

"You got your ticket ready?"

"Yes." She handed it to him and sat back against the warm leather bench.

He gave her a sharp look. "Is something wrong, ma'am? You got tears in your eyes. It's none of my business, of course, unless you're feeling puny. Then I ought to know about it."

"No, sir, I'm not sick. It's just the dust in the air that's making my eyes water."

"No need to call me sir. My name's Kelley. Now, if you do happen to get sick, well then, just lean on out the window and shout at me. Unless you hear gunshots. Then don't look out. I can't stress enough the importance of remembering that rule, ma'am."

He shut the door and climbed back up on his

131

seat before she could even tell him what her name was much less assure him she wouldn't look out the window.

The coach gently rocked back when the horses turned and started down the main street. They gathered speed as they clipped along, and by the time they'd passed the general store near the center of the street, they were in a full gallop.

Emily folded her hands together in her lap and closed her eyes. The decision to leave had been made; there wasn't any going back, and she was determined to come to terms with the fact that she would never see Travis again. God willing, she might even find a little peace.

A gunshot suddenly rang out. Kelley let out a shout, and Emily was flung forward when he pulled on the reins. The horses skidded to a stop.

Emily landed on the floor with her skirt draped over her head. She quickly got back up on her seat and adjusted her clothing. She saw people coming out of the hotel and couldn't help but notice that none of them looked very alarmed.

She couldn't imagine what was going on. She looked out the window to find out. Unfortunately, Kelley spotted her.

"Ah, now, I told you not to do that," he cried out.

"Mr. Kelley, what's happening?"

"Travis Clayborne's what's happening, ma'am."

She didn't even have time to react to Kelley's explanation before Travis's roar filled the carriage.

"Emily Finnegan, get out of that stagecoach. I want a word with you."

She was so startled by the command, she struck her head when she jumped back against the seat. She only stayed there a second or two. Then she leaned out the window again.

And that was when she saw Travis striding down the street toward her.

She was certain she was going to keel over from heart strain right then and there. He looked wonderful and sweet and adorable . . . and furious.

He walked with his usual arrogant swagger. The man was obviously feeling perky again, and when she considered how close he'd been to dying—at least she thought he'd been close, no matter what the doctor said—his recovery was almost miraculous.

She let out a sigh. As much as she dreaded it, she was going to have to tell him good-bye. She wouldn't cry, no matter how overwhelming the urge, and the sooner she got it said and done, the quicker she could leave.

She decided to meet him halfway. Yes, that was what she should do. She would shake his hand, tell him thank you and good-bye, and be on her way.

She had second thoughts as soon as she opened the door. She noticed the telltale, now-you're-going-to-get-it glint in his eyes, and promptly shut the door again. She thought she knew why he was there. He had gotten out of his sickbed and ridden all the way down to Pritchard from the Perkinses' home just to tell her she was crazy again. He was stubborn enough to do such a foolish thing.

"Mr. Kelley, make him go away."

"Begging your pardon, ma'am, but no one tells any of the Clayborne brothers what to do. You'd best get on out and find out what he wants."

Travis shouted to her again. "Now, Emily!"

She stepped out into the street, shut the door behind her, and started walking toward him.

"Don't you dare leave without me, Mr. Kelley."

"That's sort of up to Clayborne, ma'am."

She shook her head to let him know she didn't agree. She continued on toward Travis, muttering all the while. "If that man makes me cry, I swear I'm going to borrow his gun and shoot him. Just see if I don't."

Kelley heard her. "I'd be real surprised if Travis lets you have his gun, ma'am."

Emily ignored the driver. She stopped when she was about twenty feet away from Travis and put her hand out in a silent demand for him to stop where he was.

He ignored it.

"You were really going to do it, weren't you, Emily?"

"Do what?"

"Leave without saying good-bye."

"Travis, please lower your voice. You're drawing a crowd."

She turned to the boardwalk on her left and waved her hand at the group of men and women gathered there. "You there, move along, please. Go on, now."

When she noticed no one paid any attention

to her request, she added a frown and then turned back to Travis.

"Yes, I was going to say good-bye."

"Is that so? Were you planning to shout it out the window of the stagecoach on your way out of town?"

"No, I wasn't going to shout it. I was going to write a letter to you."

His frown intensified. He didn't like hearing that bit of news at all. "You were going to write?"

She held her ground. For a second or two she thought Travis was going to keep on coming and walk right over her, but fortunately he stopped when he was a couple of feet away. She considered backing away from him, then changed her mind. He was deliberately trying to intimidate her, and she simply wasn't in the mood to put up with his antics today.

She was the one with the broken heart, for the love of God, and he had only gotten shot.

"Let me get this straight," he snapped. "You were hell-bent on going up to the crest so you could tell O'Toole face-to-face that you'd changed your mind and weren't going to marry him, but you didn't think you owed me the same consideration?"

"Millie told you."

"Damned right she told me," he said. "If you had mentioned your change of heart a little earlier . . ."

"You wouldn't have taken me up there."

"No, I wouldn't have. I wouldn't have gotten shot either, and you wouldn't have been in such a dangerous position. And by the way, Miss

Finnegan, you won't be stepping out with any other men ever again, not even Jack Hanrahan. You got that?"

"Murder's frowned upon in these parts, Mr. Clayborne."

"Do you have any idea what would have happened to you if those bastards had gotten hold of you?"

"Yes," she cried out. "I know exactly what would have happened. I also know I almost got you killed. I'll never forgive myself for that. My only excuse is that I was trying to do the decent thing. If I'd known the O'Tooles were rodents, I assure you I wouldn't have gone up there. Oh, get it over with, why don't you? Tell me I'm crazy again. I know you want to."

"Fine. You're crazy. I swear you don't have a lick of sense in you."

"I'm not the one who got out of his sickbed and rode all the way to Pritchard just to tell someone she's crazy."

"That isn't why I came after you."

"Then why did you come here?"

She noticed he was having trouble coming up with an explanation. She also noticed the large crowd now surrounding the two of them. They seemed to have appeared out of thin air, and more were hurrying to join them.

She was appalled. "Don't you people have chores to do? This is a private conversation. Move away, now."

No one budged an inch. Out of the corner of her eye she saw a gentleman leaning against a hitching post. He had a wad of money in his hands, and each newcomer who arrived stopped to give him more before running into the street.

"Well, Travis? Why did you come after me?"

"I thought I wanted to give you a piece of my mind—" he began.

She interrupted him. "I wouldn't if I were you. You can't afford it. Now, if you don't mind, I'd like to get back inside the coach and be on my way. The driver has a schedule to keep. Mr. Kelley, where are you going?" she called out when she saw him running toward the man at the hitching post.

"Just making a friendly little bet, ma'am."

"Damn it, Emily, pay attention to me."

She was suddenly so miserable inside she wanted to scream. "Why should I? Everything is your fault. You made me fall in love with you, and now I'm so upset I can't think or sleep or eat."

She didn't realize what she'd blurted out until a woman behind her let out a little sigh. "She loves him."

Travis was looking outrageously complacent. She put her hand out toward him again to try to ward him off.

"I will recover from this affliction," she said. "Besides, loving you doesn't change a thing, so don't get any foolish notions. I'm going back to Boston."

"No, you're not."

"Yes, I am, and nothing you say to me will change my mind."

"You tell him, girl," a woman called out. "Don't let no man push you around."

"If she loves him, she ought to stay," someone else shouted.

The men in the crowd grunted their agreement. Emily was mortified by the audience. She turned to the woman who had suggested she stay, and whispered, "You don't understand. If I stay, I'll disgrace my parents and become thoroughly wanton."

The woman's head snapped up and her eyes widened. "Do you mean to say you would . . ."

Emily nodded. "That's exactly what I'm saying."

"You've got to go home, then," she stammered.

Travis threaded his fingers through his hair in frustration. The thought of losing Emily terrified him, and he didn't know how to make her stay.

God, she was stubborn.

"You love me, but you're leaving. Have I got that straight?"

"Yes," she answered. "I do love you, and I am leaving. It all makes perfectly good sense to me."

"Of course it does," he snapped.

She refused to argue with him. She turned around, waved for the crowd to get out of her way, and headed back to the stagecoach. She was almost running. Travis stayed right by her side.

The crowd chased after them.

"I vowed never to do another rash thing for the rest of my life, and staying here would not only be rash, it would also be sinful. I'm going home."

Travis was getting madder and madder by the

second. He was consumed with panic and didn't like the feeling at all. He couldn't let her leave him. Didn't she understand how important she was to him? Without her, life wouldn't be worth living.

He didn't want to live without her.

The truth slapped him in the face, and he came to a dead stop. "Son of a gun," he whispered, "I love her."

Emily was sweet and good and loving, and all he wanted to think about now was keeping her by his side for the rest of his life. He was going to have to keep her out of that stagecoach first.

He caught up with her, heard her say something about a "rash" again, and patiently waited for her to finish rambling.

She finally stopped talking and gave him an expectant look. "Don't you agree?" she asked, wondering what had caused the sudden smile.

"Sure I do."

"She's leaving now," someone shouted from the back of the crowd.

"She'd be ruined if she stayed," a woman called out.

"Amen," someone else shouted.

They reached the stagecoach. Travis pulled the door open for her.

She put her hand out to him. "Good-bye, Travis."

"You expect me to shake your hand?"

"It would be the polite thing to do. Why are you smiling?"

"I'm a happy man."

She was crushed by the sudden change in his

139

attitude. Her hand dropped back down to her side. "I'll write to you."

"That'll be nice."

"Will you write back?"

"Sure I will."

There wasn't anything left to say. She turned to get back inside the stagecoach then.

"Just one thing," he said.

"Yes?"

"Kiss me good-bye."

Twelve

She married a crazy man. She was so happy she couldn't stop smiling. She had even laughed out loud several times while she'd been in the bath, for she was filled with such an abundance of joy and love she couldn't keep it all inside.

She was waiting now for her husband to join her. She stood at the bedroom window above the Perkinses' parlor and stared out into the night while she brushed her hair. The moon was beautiful tonight, and the sky was alive with at least a hundred stars. Crickets were singing their nightly song in unison. The scent of pine filled the air, and everything seemed magical.

The long-stemmed pink rose Travis had given her before the wedding ceremony was in a vase on the table beside her. She picked it up and held it against her heart.

She turned around when the door opened.

Travis came inside, bolted the door, and turned to look at her. His breath caught in his throat, and he was suddenly overwhelmed by the beautiful woman he had managed to capture.

She was dressed in a prim white nightgown that covered her from the top of her neck to the bottom of her slippers.

"Good evening, Mrs. Clayborne."

She laughed, and he felt as though he'd just been embraced by her warmth. He leaned back against the door and grinned at her.

"Don't be nervous."

"Why do you think I'm nervous?"

"You just threw your brush out the window."

She laughed again. "I want it to be perfect for you."

"It already is."

It was the most perfectly wonderful thing he could have said to her. Oh, how she loved this man.

He removed his shirt, tossed it on the back of a chair, took off his shoes and socks next, and then came to her.

"You aren't really nervous, are you, sweetheart?"

"Just a little," she admitted. "I know what's going to happen. I'm just not familiar with the how."

"You mean you haven't made a thorough study on the subject?" he teased.

"No, but I imagine you have."

He took the rose out of her hand and slowly trailed the fragrant bud down the side of her cheek. His gaze never left hers, and within seconds, the apprehension she had felt was gone.

"I love you, Emily. And only you," he told her in a rich, gruff voice.

Impatient to take her into his arms, he put the rose back in the vase and carried her over to the side of the bed. She kicked her slippers off on the way.

"Do you want me to explain in detail what I'm planning to do?"

She knew from the tone of his voice that he was teasing her. "No, thank you very much, but I appreciate the offer. I believe I'd rather you showed me."

He gently placed her in the center of the bed and came down on top of her, careful to brace his weight with his arms.

He leaned over her and stared into her eyes, savoring the love he saw there. "I'm going to make a thorough study of you, Mrs. Clayborne. God, I love the sound of that, and when I'm finished, it's my sincere hope you'll thank me very much."

He was tossing her favorite expressions back at her. The way he was looking at her, with such love and desire, filled her with anticipation, and if she had trusted her voice, she would have told him he didn't need to worry about putting her at ease now. She was more than ready to become his wife in the most intimate way. Heaven help her, she was eager.

Shivers raced down her spine when he nuzzled the side of her neck. She wrapped her arms around his shoulders and stroked his back.

He was determined to let her set the pace tonight, and within minutes he was richly rewarded. She tugged on his hair, demanded he stop teasing her and give her a proper kiss. One was all it took for passion to explode between them. By the time he removed her gown and his trousers, she was breathless with excitement and he was having a hell of a time breathing at all.

He knew more about how her body would react to him than she did. His hands were strong yet incredibly gentle as he stroked the fire inside her.

And when at last they joined as one, it was all so astonishingly exquisite, she couldn't contain her cry. She was overwhelmed with the love she felt for this man. He made it so very perfect for her.

He felt her tighten around him, and he gave in to his own climax, shaking now because he had never experienced such splendor before.

It took a long while for either one of them to recover. They lay together in a tangle of legs and arms, and, damn, he was so happy and content he thought he must be in heaven.

She was so happy she needed to cry and laugh at the same time. The satisfied look on his face was comical to her. Then she realized she probably looked the same way.

He kept her in his arms when he rolled onto his back. She stretched out along his side and put her arm across his chest.

"Now, aren't you sorry you made me wait so long?"

She patted his chest while she gently corrected him. "It was only two weeks. You knew that stagecoach was going to leave while you were kissing me, didn't you?"

"Of course. Did you honestly think I would let you go?"

"I honestly think I'm happy you didn't."

He laughed. He was so pleased with her he had to kiss her again. Then he let his head drop back on the pillow and let out a loud, sleepy yawn.

"You put me through hell waiting to get my hands on you."

He was exaggerating, of course, at least she thought he was, and she wouldn't have given up the last two weeks for anything. He had proven to her during that time that he was possibly the most romantic man in the entire world. He'd courted her with what he referred to as a vengeance. She had never had a chance against him—he'd warned her about that—but she had held out for as long as possible to give him time to make certain he wanted to spend the rest of his life with her.

She had been concerned that it was only an infatuation on his part and therefore he saw only the good qualities in her. He had set her straight about her misconception at dinner the night before by cheerfully listing every single one of her flaws. It took him a long time to get them said too, and though she had been aware of a few, he pointed out several more she hadn't even known about. She was still stubbornly insisting that she wasn't stubborn at all.

"Do you know what I think, Travis? That one kiss good-bye led to this night."

He rolled her onto her back again. "I knew before then, and so did you. I love you."

"I love you too."

"Emily?"

"Yes?"

"Kiss me good-bye again."

Book II

ONE WHITE ROSE

One

The little woman was in trouble. Big trouble. No one, male or female, pointed a rifle at Douglas Clayborne without paying the consequences, and just as soon as he could get the weapon away from her, he would tell her so.

First, he was going to have to sweet-talk her into stepping out of the stall and into the light. He planned to keep on talking until he had edged close enough to take her by surprise. He'd rip the rifle out of her hands, unload it, and break the damned thing over his knee. Unless it was a Winchester. Then he'd keep it.

He could barely see her now. She was crouched down low behind the gate, shrouded in shadows, with the barrel of the gun resting on the top slat. A kerosene lamp was hooked to a post on the opposite side of the barn, but the light wasn't sufficient for him to see much of anything at all from where he stood, shifting from foot to foot, a few feet inside the open door.

A hard, driving rain was pelting his back. He was soaked through, and so was Brutus, his sorrel. He needed to get the saddle off the animal and dry him down as soon as possible, but what he wanted to do and what the woman would let him do were two different matters.

A bolt of lightning lit up the entrance, followed by a reverberating boom of thunder. Brutus reared up, let out a loud snort, and tossed his head. The horse obviously wanted out of the rain as much as he did.

Douglas kept his attention on the rifle while he tried to soothe the animal with a whispered promise that everything was going to be all right.

"Are you Isabel Grant?"

She answered with a low, guttural groan. He thought his harsh tone had frightened her and was about to try again in a calmer voice when he heard her panting. At first he thought he was mistaken, but the noise got louder. She was panting all right, and that didn't make a lick of sense. The woman hadn't moved a muscle since he'd come inside the barn, so she couldn't possibly be out of breath.

He waited for the panting to subside before he spoke again. "Are you Parker Grant's wife?"

"You know who I am. Go away or I'll shoot you. Leave the door open behind you. I want to watch you ride away."

"Lady, my business is with your husband. If you'll kindly tell me where he is, I'll go talk to him. Didn't he tell you I was coming here? My name is . . ."

She interrupted him in a shout. "I don't care what your name is. You're one of Boyle's men, and that's all I need to know. Get out."

The panic in her voice frustrated the hell out of him. "There isn't any need to get upset. I'm leaving. Will you tell your husband Douglas Clayborne is waiting in town to give him the rest of the money for the Arabian? I'm going to have to see the animal first, as he agreed. Can you remember all that?"

"He sold you a horse?"

"Yes, he did. He sold me an Arabian stallion a couple of months ago."

"You're lying to me," she cried out. "Parker would never have sold either one of my Arabians."

He wasn't in the mood to argue with her. "I've got the papers to prove it. Just tell him, all right?"

"You purchased a horse you've never seen?"

"My brother saw him," he explained. "And his judgment is as good as mine."

She burst into tears. He took a step toward her before he realized he was actually thinking about comforting the woman, and abruptly stopped.

"I'm real sorry your husband didn't tell you about the horse."

"Oh, God, please, not now."

She started panting again. What in blazes was the matter with her? He knew something was wrong, and he had a feeling her husband was responsible for her tears. The man should have told his wife about the horse. Still, her reaction was a bit extreme.

Douglas thought he should say something to help her get past her misery.

"I'm sure all married couples go through spots of trouble now and then. Your husband must have had a good reason for selling the stallion, and he was probably so busy he forgot to tell you about it. That's all."

The panting got louder before it stopped. Then she whimpered low in her throat. The sound reminded him of a wounded animal. He wanted to walk away but knew he couldn't leave her if she was in trouble . . . and just where was good old Parker anyway?

"This shouldn't be happening," she cried out.

"What shouldn't be happening?" he asked.

"Go away," she shouted.

He was stubborn enough to stay right where he was. "I'm not leaving until you tell me who Boyle is. Did he hurt you? You sound like you're in a lot of pain."

Isabel instinctively responded to the concern she heard in his voice. "You aren't working for Boyle?"

"No."

"Prove it to me."

"I can't prove it to you without showing you the letter from your husband and the paper he signed."

"Stay where you are."

Since he hadn't moved an inch, he couldn't understand her need to shout at him. "If you want me to help you, you'll have to tell me what's wrong."

"Everything's wrong."

"You're going to have to be a little more specific."

"He's coming, and it's much too early. Don't you understand? I must have done something wrong. Oh, God, please don't let him come yet."

"Who is coming?" he demanded. He nervously glanced behind him and squinted out into the night. He thought she might be talking about Boyle, whoever in tarnation he was.

He was wrong about that.

"The baby," she cried. "I can feel another contraction."

Douglas felt as though he'd just been punched hard in the stomach. "You're having a baby? *Now?*"

"Yes."

"Ah, lady, don't do that." He didn't realize how foolish his demand was until she told him so between whimpers. His head snapped back. "Are you having a pain now?"

"Yes." She said the word with a long moan.

"For the love of God, take your finger off the trigger and put the rifle down."

She couldn't understand what he was telling her. The contraction was cresting with such agonizing intensity she could barely stand up. She squeezed her eyes shut and clenched her teeth together while she waited for the pain to stop.

She realized her mistake as soon as she opened her eyes again, but it was already too late. The stranger had vanished. He hadn't left the barn though. His horse was still standing by the door.

The rifle was suddenly snatched out of her hands. With a cry of terror, she backed further into the stall and waited for him to attack.

Everything began to happen in slow motion. The gate squeaked open, but, to her, the sound was a piercing, unending scream. The stranger, a tall, muscular man who seemed to swallow up all the space inside the stall, came toward her. His hair and eyes were dark, his expression was angry . . . and, oh, God, she didn't want him to kill her yet. The baby would die inside her.

Her mind simply couldn't take any more. She took a deep breath to scream, knowing that once she started, she would never be able to stop. *Please, God, understand. I can't do this any longer. I can't . . . I can't. . . .*

He pulled her back from the edge of insanity without saying a word. He simply handed the rifle to her.

"Now, you listen to me," he ordered. "I want you to stop having this baby right now." After giving the harsh and thoroughly unreasonable command, he turned around and walked away.

"Are you leaving?"

"No, I'm not leaving. I'm moving the light so I can see what I'm doing. If you're this close to having a baby, what are you doing in a barn? Shouldn't you be in bed?"

She started panting again. The sound sent chills down his spine.

"I asked you to stop that. The baby can't come now so just forget about it."

She waited for the contraction to end before she told him he was an idiot.

He secretly agreed. "I just don't want you to do this until I find your husband."

"I'm not doing it on purpose."

"Where's Parker?"

"He's gone."

He let out an expletive. "I had a feeling you were going to tell me that. He picked a fine time to go gallivanting."

"Why are you so angry with me? I'm not going to shoot you."

He wasn't angry; he was scared. He had helped a countless number of animals with their deliveries, but he hadn't helped any women with childbirth and he didn't want to help Isabel Grant now. Oh, yes, he was scared all right, but he was smart enough not to let her know it.

"I'm not angry," he said. "You just took me by surprise. I'll help you back to the house, and then I'll go get the doctor." He hoped to God she wouldn't tell him the town didn't have a physician.

"He can't come here."

Douglas finally got the lamp hooked to the post connected to the stall. He turned around and saw Isabel clearly for the first time. She was an attractive woman, even with the frown on her face. She had freckles across the bridge of her nose, and he had always been partial to women with freckles. He'd always liked red hair too, and hers was a dark, vibrant red that glistened like fire in the light.

She was a married woman he reminded himself, and he shouldn't be noticing her appearance. Still, facts were facts. Isabel Grant was one fine-looking woman.

She was also as big as a house. Noticing that helped him regain his wits. "Why can't the doctor come here?"

"Sam Boyle won't let him. Dr. Simpson came here once when I was too far along to go into town to see him, but Boyle told him he'd kill him if he ever tried to come to me again. He'd do it too," she added in a whisper. "He's a terrible man. He owns the town and everyone in it. The people are decent, but they do whatever Boyle tells them to do because they're afraid of him. I can't blame them. I'm afraid of him too."

"What's Boyle got against you and your husband?"

"His ranch is next to ours, and he wants to expand so his cattle will have more grazing land. He offered Parker money for the deed, but it was only a pittance compared to what my husband paid for it. He wouldn't have sold it for any amount of money though. This is our home and our dream."

"Isabel, where is Parker now?" As soon as he saw the tears in her eyes, he had his answer. "He's dead, isn't he?"

"Yes. He's buried up on the hill behind the barn. Someone shot him in the back."

"Boyle?"

"Of course."

Douglas leaned back against the post, folded his arms across his chest, and waited for her to compose herself.

She sagged against the wall and lowered her head. She was suddenly so weary she could barely stand up.

He waited another minute before he started questioning her again. "Did the sheriff investigate?"

"Sweet Creek doesn't have a sheriff any longer. Boyle must have run him off before Parker and I moved here."

"No one wants the job, I suppose."

"Would you?" She wiped a tear from her cheek and looked up at him. "Dr. Simpson told me Sweet Creek used to be a quiet little town. He and his wife are my friends," she added. "They're both trying to help."

"How?"

"They've sent wires and written letters to all the surrounding towns asking for assistance. The last time I saw the doctor, he told me he had been hearing stories about a U.S. marshal in the area. He believed the lawman was the answer to our prayers. The doctor hadn't been able to locate him yet, but he was certain he would come if he knew how many laws Boyle had broken. I try not to lose hope," she added. "Boyle has at least twenty men working for him, and I think it would take an army of marshals to defeat him."

"I'm sure there's a way to . . ." He stopped in the middle of his sentence, for it had just occurred to him that she had gone several minutes without panting.

"Did the pain go away?"

She looked surprised. She put her hand on her swollen middle and smiled. "Yes, it did. It's gone now."

Thank God, he thought to himself. "You're really all alone here? Don't look at me like that, Isabel. You've got to know by now I don't work for Boyle."

She slowly nodded. "I've learned to be very distrustful. I've been alone for a long time."

He tried not to let her see how appalled he was. A woman in her last months of pregnancy should have been with people who cared about her.

Anger began to simmer inside him. "Has anyone from town looked in on you?"

"Mr. Clayborne, I . . ."

"Douglas," he corrected.

"Douglas, I don't think you understand the severity of my situation. Boyle has the route cut off. No one gets in here without his approval."

He grinned. "I did."

The realization that he had indeed gotten through made her smile again. Odd, but she was also beginning to feel more in control too.

"Boyle's men must have gone home as soon as it started raining. I think they go back to his ranch every night when the light fades, but I can't be sure."

She straightened away from the wall to brush the dust off her skirt, and suddenly felt her legs give out. She was horrified. She leaned back again so she wouldn't fall to her knees and turned her face away from him as she explained in a whisper what had just happened.

She sounded frightened and ashamed. Douglas immediately went to her side and put his hand on her shoulder in an awkward attempt to comfort her. "It's all right. It's supposed to break." He tried to sound like an authority on the subject. In reality, he had just summed up everything he knew about childbirth with that one simple statement.

"Something's wrong. The baby's not due for at least three to four more weeks. Oh, God, it's all my fault. I shouldn't have scrubbed the floors and done the wash yesterday, but everything was so dirty and I wanted to keep busy so I wouldn't think about having the baby alone. I never should have . . ."

"I'm sure you didn't do anything wrong," he interrupted. "So stop blaming yourself. Some babies decide to come early. That's all."

"Do you think . . ."

"You didn't cause this to happen," he insisted. "The baby's got a mind of his own, and even if you'd been in bed, your water still would have broken. I'm sure of it."

He seemed to know what he was talking about, and she stopped feeling guilty. "I think my baby's going to come tonight."

"Yes," he agreed.

"It's odd. I'm not in any pain."

They were both whispering now. He was trying to be considerate of her feelings. She was trying to get over her embarrassment. The man was a complete stranger, and, oh, God, she wished he were old and ugly. He wasn't though. He was young and extremely handsome. She knew she would probably die of mortification if she let him help her bring her baby into the world, because she would have to take her clothes off and he would see . . .

"Isabel, you about finished hiding from me? You've got to be practical about this. Come on," he coaxed. "Look at me."

It took her a full minute to summon up enough courage to do as he asked. Her face was burning with shame.

"You're going to be practical," he repeated as he lifted her up into his arms.

"What are you doing?"

"Carrying you back to the house. Put your arms around me."

They were eye to eye now. He stared at her freckles. She stared at the ceiling.

"This is awkward," she whispered.

"I don't think the baby cares if his mother feels awkward or not."

He carried her out of the stall, paused long enough to take the rifle away from her and prop it against the post, and then continued on toward the door.

"Be careful," Isabel told him. "The rifle's loaded. It could have gone off when . . ."

"I unloaded it."

She was so surprised she looked him in the eye. "When?"

"Before I gave it back to you. You aren't going to start fretting again, are you?"

"No, but you're going to have to put me down for a minute. I have to take care of Pegasus first."

"Are you talking about the stallion?"

"Yes."

"You're in no condition to get near him."

"You don't understand. He cut his left hind leg, and I need to clean it before it becomes infected. It won't take long."

"I'll take care of him."

"Do you know what to do?"

"Oh, yes. I'm very good with horses."

He felt her relax in his arms. "Douglas?"

"Yes?"

"You're good with women too. I was wondering . . ."

"Yes?"

"About the delivery. Have you ever helped a woman give birth?"

He decided to ease her worry by hedging his answer. "I've had a little experience." *With horses,* he silently added.

"Will you know what to do if something goes wrong?"

"Nothing's going to go wrong." The authority in his voice didn't leave any room for doubts. "I know you're scared and feeling alone . . ."

"I'm not alone . . . Oh, God, you're not going to leave me, are you?"

"Don't get excited. I'm not going anywhere."

She let out a little sigh and tucked her head under his chin as soon as he stepped outside the barn. The rain was still coming down hard, and he was sorry he didn't have anything to wrap around her. The log cabin she called home was approximately fifty yards away, and by the time he had carried her to the door, she was as drenched as he was.

A single lantern provided the only light inside the cabin. The atmosphere was warm and inviting, but what he noticed most of all was the scent of roses that filled the air. To the right of the entrance was an oblong table covered with a yellow-and-white-checked gingham tablecloth, and in its center sat a crystal vase filled with at least a dozen white roses in full bloom. It was obvious she had tried to bring beauty and joy into the stark reality of her life, and the simple, feminine gesture made him ache for her.

The cabin was spotless. A stone fireplace faced the door, and on the mantel was a cluster of silver frames with photographs. A rocking chair with a yellow-and-white-checked cushion had been placed to the left of the hearth and a tall-backed wooden chair with spindly legs sat on the opposite side. Two knitting needles protruded from a burgundy ball of yarn on the footrest, and long strands coiled down to the colorful braided rag rug.

"You've got a real nice place," he said.

"Thank you. I wish my kitchen were larger. I put up the drape to separate it from the main room. It's always such a clutter. I was going to clean it up after I finished in the barn."

"Don't worry about it."

"Did you notice the roses? Aren't they beautiful? They grow wild near the tree line behind the field. Parker planted more on the side of the house, but they haven't taken root yet."

Douglas's practical nature reasserted itself. "You shouldn't have gone out by yourself. You could have fallen."

"It gave me pleasure to bring them inside, and I'm certain the exercise was good for me. I hate being cooped up all day. Please let me stand. I'm feeling fine now."

He did as she requested but continued to hold on to her arm until he was sure she was steady. "What can I do to help?"

"Would you start a fire? I put the wood in the

hearth, but I didn't want to light it until I got back from the barn."

"You carried wood inside?"

"It is my fault the baby's coming early, isn't it? I carried wood down from the hills early this morning. I went back up again this afternoon to collect more. It gets so cold and damp at night . . . I wasn't thinking, and now my baby's going to—"

He interrupted before she could get all worked up again. "Calm down, Isabel. Lots of women do chores right up to the delivery. I was just concerned about the possibility of falling. That's all."

"Then why did you say . . ."

"Falling," he said again. "That's all I was thinking about. You didn't fall, so no harm was done. Now, stop worrying."

She nodded and started across the room. He grabbed hold of her arm, told her to lean on him, and slowed the pace to a crawl.

"It's going to take me an hour to get to the bedroom if you keep treating me like an invalid."

He moved ahead and opened the door. It was pitch black inside.

"Don't move until I get the lantern. I don't want you to—"

"Fall? You seem terribly worried about that possibility."

"No offense, but you're so big in the middle you can't possibly see your own feet. Of course I'm worried you'll fall."

She actually laughed, and she hadn't done that in such a long time.

"You need to get out of your wet clothes," he reminded her.

"There's a pair of candles on the dresser to your right."

He was happy to have something to do. He felt awkward and totally out of his element. He didn't realize his hands were shaking until he tried to light the candles. It took him three attempts before he succeeded. When he turned around, she was already folding back a colorful quilt on the bed.

"You're drenched. You really need to get out of your wet clothes before you do anything else," he said.

"What about you? Do you have a change of clothes?" she asked.

"In my saddlebags. If you don't need help, I'll start the fire; then I'll go back to the barn and take care of the horses. Have yours been fed?"

"Yes," she answered. "Be careful with Pegasus. He doesn't like strangers." She stared down at the floor with her hands folded together. As Douglas turned to leave, she called out to him, "You're coming back, aren't you?"

She was fretting again. The last thing she needed to worry about now was being left alone. He had a feeling they were in for one hell of a night, and he wanted her to conserve her strength for the more important task ahead.

"You're going to have to trust me."

"Yes . . . I'll try."

She still looked scared. He leaned against the

doorframe and tried to think of something to say that would convince her he wasn't going to abandon her.

"It's getting late," she said.

He straightened away from the door and went to her. "Will you do me a favor?"

"Yes."

He pulled the gold watch out of his pocket, unclipped the chain, and handed it to her. The chain dangled down between her fingers.

"This is the most valuable thing I own. My Mama Rose gave it to me, and I don't want anything to happen to it. Pegasus might get in a lucky kick, or I might drop it while I'm drying down my sorrel. Keep it safe for me."

"Oh, yes, I'll keep it safe."

As soon as he had left the room, she pressed the watch against her heart and closed her eyes. She and her baby were safe again, and for the first time in a long while, Isabel felt calm and in control.

Two

She had turned into a raving maniac. She didn't care. She knew she was losing the last shreds of her control, and somewhere in the back of her mind lurked the realization that she wasn't being reasonable. She didn't care about that either.

She wanted to die. It was a cowardly thought,

but she wasn't in the mood to feel at all guilty about it. Death would be a welcome respite from the hellish pain she was enduring, and at this stage, when one excruciating cramp was coming right on top of another and another and another, death was all she was interested in thinking about.

Douglas kept telling her everything was going to be just fine, and she decided she wanted to stay alive long enough to kill him. How dare he be so calm and rational? What did he know about anything? He was a man, for the love of God, and as far as she was concerned, he was totally responsible for her agony.

"I don't want to do this any longer, Douglas. Do you hear me? I don't want to do this any longer."

She hadn't whispered her demand. She'd bellowed it.

"Just a few more minutes, Isabel," he promised, his voice a soothing whisper.

She told him to drop dead.

Honest to God, he would have liked to accommodate her. He hated having to watch her in such misery. He felt helpless, inept, and so damned scared, he could barely think what to do.

On the surface, he was presenting a stoic facade, but he wasn't at all certain how long he could keep up the pretense. Any moment now she was bound to notice how his hands were shaking. Then she would probably become afraid again. He much preferred her anger to her fear, and if it made her feel better to rant at him, he wouldn't try to stop her.

She accidentally knocked the water basin over

when she threw the wet cloth he'd pressed against her forehead.

"If you were a gentleman, you'd do what I asked."

"Isabel, I'm not going to knock you out."

"Just a little clip under the chin. I need to rest."

He shook his head.

She started crying. "How long has it been? Tell me how long?"

"Just six hours," he answered.

"*Just six* hours? I hate you, Douglas Clayborne."

"I know you do, Isabel."

"I can't do this any longer."

"The contractions are close together now. Soon you'll be holding your baby in your arms."

"I'm not having a baby," she shouted. "I made up my mind, Douglas."

"All right, Isabel. You don't have to have the baby."

"Thank you."

She stopped crying and closed her eyes. She told him she was sorry for all the vile names she had called him. He calculated he had a few minutes left to mop up the water from the floor and go get more towels before another contraction hit. He was pulling the door closed behind him when she called out.

"Leave it open so you can hear me."

She had to be joking. She was shouting loud enough for most of Montana to hear. His ears were still ringing from her last bellow, but he didn't think it would be a good idea to tell her so.

He agreed instead. About three hours earlier, he'd learned not to contradict a woman in pain. Trying to get Isabel to be reasonable was impossible. Oh, yes, it was much easier to agree with everything she said, no matter how outlandish it was.

Douglas carried the porcelain bowl to the curtained alcove Isabel used as a kitchen, grabbed a stack of fresh towels, and headed back. He made it past the hearth before the reality of the situation finally crashed down on him. He had to deliver a baby. He felt the door shift under his feet. He dropped the towels and slammed back against the wall. Doubling over, he braced his hands on his knees and closed his eyes while he desperately tried to face the inevitable.

His brother Cole had taught him a trick to use when preparing for a shoot-out. Cole said to think of the worst possible situation, put yourself smack in the middle of it, and then picture yourself winning. Douglas had always thought his brother's mental game was a waste of time, but it was all he had now, and he decided to give it a try.

I can do this. Hell with that. I can't do it. No, no, it won't be bad, and I can handle it. All right, I'm standing in front of Tommy's Tavern in Hammond. Five . . . no, ten bloodthirsty killers are waiting for me to come inside. There isn't any choice. I have to go in. I know that, and I'm ready. I know the bastards have all got their weapons drawn and cocked. I can beat them though. I'll get five them with the gun in my left hand, and the other five with the gun in my right hand while I'm diving for cover.

It's going to be as smooth and easy as a drink of fine whiskey. Yeah, I can take them all right.

He drew a deep breath. *And I sure as certain can deliver this baby.*

Cole's game wasn't working. Douglas was gulping down air now and letting it out faster and faster.

Isabel could feel the beginning of another contraction. This one felt as if it was going to be a doozy. She squeezed her eyes shut in preparation and was about to scream for Douglas when she heard a peculiar noise. It sounded like someone breathing heavily, as though he'd just run a long distance. Douglas? No, it couldn't be Douglas. Dear God, she was imagining things now. It had finally happened; her mind had snapped.

The contraction eased up while she was distracted. A few seconds later, it gained her full attention with a vengeance. She felt as though her body were being shredded into a thousand pieces, and as the spasm intensified, her whimper turned into a bloodcurdling scream.

Douglas was suddenly by her side. He put his arms around her shoulders and lifted her up against him.

"Hold on to me, sugar. Just hold on tight until it stops."

She was sobbing by the time the contraction ended. And then she was immediately struck with another one.

"It's time, Douglas. The baby's coming."

She was right about that. Ten minutes later, he held her son in his arms. The baby was long of limb, deadly pale, and so terribly thin Douglas

169

didn't think the little one had enough strength to open his eyes ... or last a full day. His breathing was shallow, and when at last he cried, the sound was pitifully weak.

"Is the baby all right?" she whispered.

"It's a boy, Isabel. I'll let you hold him as soon as I get him cleaned up. He's awfully thin," he warned her. "But I'm sure he's going to be fine, just fine."

Douglas didn't know if he was giving her false hope or not. He honestly didn't know how the baby could possibly survive. He was small enough to fit in Douglas's hands, yet he could open and close his eyes and squirm about. Dear Lord, his fingers and toes were so tiny, Douglas was afraid to touch them for fear they'd crumble. He gently shifted his hold and gingerly pressed his fingertip against the baby's chest. He felt the heart beating. How could anything this little be so perfectly formed? It was amazing that the baby could breathe at all. And yet he did.

My God, Douglas thought, *I could accidentally break one of his bones if I'm not careful.* The sheer beauty of God's creation both awed and humbled him. Now Isabel needed one more miracle to keep her son alive.

"You've got to be a fighter, little man," he whispered, his voice thick with emotion.

Isabel heard him. "He'll have help. The sisters told us that every time a baby is born, God sends a guardian angel to watch over him."

Douglas glanced up at her. "I sure hope he gets here soon."

She smiled, for in her heart she knew Parker's guardian angel was already here.

He was holding her son.

It took a good hour to get Isabel and the baby settled. Douglas had to alter the plan to use the cradle her husband had made because when his knee brushed up against the side, the bottom fell out. It was evident Grant had used rotten wood to build the base. Yet even if the wood had been freshly cut, Douglas would still have thrown the contraption out. Nails as long as a man's hand had been driven inward from the outside of the uneven slats, and long, dangerously sharp points angled down toward the bedding. He shuddered to think of the damage those rusty nails could do to an infant.

He was too tired to do anything about it now. He stripped out of his clothes, put on another pair of buckskin pants, and went back to the bedroom to make a temporary bed for the baby. He used the bottom drawer of her dresser and padded it with towels covered with a pillowcase.

By the time he was finished, Isabel was sleeping soundly. The serenity on her face was captivating, and he couldn't turn away. He watched her sleep; he watched her breathe. She was as beautiful and as perfect as her son. Her hair was spread out on the pillow behind her in a tangled mess. She looked like an angel now . . . and not at all like the Beelzebub he had compared her to during her labor.

Another yawn shook him out of his stupor. He

carefully transferred the baby to the drawer and was leaving the bedroom when she called to him.

He hurried to her side, forgetting his state of undress. He hadn't put a shirt on yet or bothered to button his pants, but he was more concerned that she was going to tell him the bleeding had increased.

"Is something wrong? You're not . . ."

"I'm fine. Sit down next to me. I want you to tell me the truth and look me in the eyes so I'll know you aren't just telling me what I want to hear. Will my baby make it?"

"I hope so, but I honestly don't know."

"He's so small. I should have carried him much longer."

"He looks like a fighter. Maybe he just needs to put on a little weight."

She visibly relaxed. "Yes, he'll get stronger. Isn't he beautiful? He has black hair, just like his father's."

"Yeah, he's beautiful." She had already asked this question at least five times. "He's still beautiful."

"Shouldn't you bring the cradle into the bedroom?"

"I couldn't use the cradle. It fell apart."

She didn't seem surprised. "What did you do with my baby?"

"I put him in the dresser."

"The dresser?"

He motioned to the bottom drawer. She only had to lean toward him to see her baby. She fell back against the pillow and laughed. "You're resourceful."

"Practical."

"That too. Thank you, Douglas. You were the answer to my prayers."

"No crying, Isabel," he told her. "You need to sleep."

"Will you stay with me for a few minutes . . . please?"

He shifted his position so that his shoulders could rest against the headboard and his legs could stretch out on top of the covers. "Have you decided on a name for your son?"

"Parker," she said, "for his father."

"That's nice."

She heard him yawn again. He was tired, and she shouldn't keep him up with her rambling, yet she couldn't make herself tell him he could leave. She didn't want the intimacy between them to end. They had shared the miracle of birth, and she was feeling closer to him than she had ever felt toward any other man. Her husband would have understood, she knew, and she pictured him now smiling down from heaven upon his son.

Her thoughts returned to Douglas. She was about to ask him where he was going to sleep when she heard his soft snore. She didn't wake him. She edged closer to his side, put her hand in his, and held on tight.

And then she slept.

Three

Douglas had walked into the middle of a nightmare. He knew Isabel's situation was bad. If what she'd told him the day before was true—and he was certain that it was—then she was in serious trouble. Not only was she being preyed upon by a group of thugs under the direction of a malevolent bastard named Boyle, but she was also completely cut off from town, which meant she couldn't get help or supplies. Last, but certainly just as troublesome, was the fact that she had just given birth. The infant needed her undivided attention, and both mother and son were too weak and vulnerable to be moved.

Then bad got worse. The rain didn't let up. Since dawn, it had alternated between a soft sprinkle and a thundering deluge. He'd become extremely concerned about the weather as soon as he stepped outside in the gray light of day and saw exactly where the log cabin was situated. Last night it had been too dark to see much of anything when he'd ridden down the slope, guided by only a faint flickering light in the field below. He'd already known the cabin was surrounded on three sides by mountains, but what he hadn't known was that her home was sitting smack in the center of the flood floor. Any overflow from the lakes and creeks in the mountains would have to pass through her cabin in order to get to the river below.

He couldn't believe anyone would build a home in such a dangerous spot. Douglas didn't usually speak ill of the dead, but facts were facts, and it was apparent Parker Grant, Senior, had been an incompetent imbecile. Douglas had given Grant the benefit of the doubt when he'd seen the cradle. Some men weren't any good at making furniture. Nothing wrong with that, he'd reasoned. Building a home on a flood path was an altogether different matter.

Still, Douglas didn't want to jump to conclusions. Someone else might have built the place years ago, and Grant might simply have moved his wife inside as a temporary measure until he could build a proper home up on higher ground.

Douglas hoped his guess was right. With any luck—and God only knew she was due for some—Grant had gotten a roof on the new cabin. If it wasn't too far away, Douglas could take Isabel and her son there in a couple of days.

Time wasn't critical yet. Although there were patches of water all over the field behind the house and barn, and the ground was soggy under his feet, he figured he still had some time before they had to leave. There was also the chance that the rain would stop. The usual hot summer sun would quickly dry up the water then, which would give them some additional time.

He needed something to cheer him up, he decided, and so he went to the barn to take care of the horses. He was eager to get a look at the

Arabians again. The stallion was as magnificent his brother had told him he was.

The horse was big for an Arabian, with a beautiful gray coat. Douglas could feel the power in the stallion and the distrust. Isabel had been right, Pegasus didn't like strangers, but fortunately Douglas had always had a way with horses, and once the stallion was used to his scent and his voice, he let him check his injury.

His mate was smaller, somewhat delicate looking, and definitely full of herself. She tossed her head about like a vain woman, which made Douglas like her all the more.

The pair was meant to stay together. As soon as he moved the female into the stall next to the stallion, they nuzzled each other and let Douglas brush them. No wonder Isabel had wanted to keep them. Her husband never should have sold the stallion without first discussing it with her, no matter how desperate he was for money.

The animals' feed was running low. He gave his sorrel and the Arabians as much as they needed, then calculated he had less than a week's ration left.

The supplies inside the cabin were just as sparse. He had only just finished taking inventory when he heard the baby's whimpering. He decided to change him so that Isabel could stay in bed, but when he reached the bedroom door, it was closed.

He knocked twice before she answered him. In a stammer she asked him to please wait until she finished dressing.

"You may come in now."

She was standing by the chest of drawers dressed in a blue robe buttoned to the top of her neck. Parker was nestled in her arms. Isabel was getting prettier by the minute. Douglas realized he was staring at her, glanced away, and noticed then the dress she'd laid out on top of her bed.

"You really should stay in bed."

She finally looked up. The glow of motherhood was still in her eyes, and there was a faint blush on her cheeks. She wasn't looking at him though. Her gaze was directed on the wall to his left.

"Is something wrong?"

"No, nothing's wrong." She sounded nervous. "I want to get dressed and fix your breakfast."

He shook his head. "For God's sake, you just had a baby. I'll fix your breakfast. You sit down in the rocker while I change the bedding."

His voice told her not to argue. She sat more quickly than she should have, and let out a loud moan. "I think I'd better stand up."

He helped her to her feet. She still wouldn't look at him.

"Why are you acting so shy with me?"

Her blush intensified. He shouldn't have been so blunt, he supposed.

"After . . . you know."

"No, I don't know. That's why I asked."

"It's . . . awkward. I was thinking about how I met you and you had to . . . it was necessary for you to . . . when the baby was coming . . ."

He started to laugh. He simply couldn't help it. She didn't appreciate his amusement.

"I was real busy at the time. All I remember is the baby. I was worried I'd drop him."

"Honest?"

"Yes, honest. If it hurts too much to sit down, lean on the dresser until I get your bed ready. The last thing we need now is for you to fall. You've got to be weak."

"Parker's fretful," she stammered out, trying to change the subject.

Douglas leaned closer to her side and peered down at the sleeping infant. Fretful was the last word he would have used to describe the baby.

"He looks real peaceful to me."

They looked at one another and shared a smile. Douglas was the first to turn away, but not before he noticed how pretty her eyes were. They were more gold than brown, and, damn, those freckles of hers were going to keep on distracting him if he continued to stand so close to her.

She had delicate hands too. He had noticed them during her contractions when she tried to choke him because he wouldn't knock her unconscious.

He made quick work of changing the bedding while she listed all the qualities she was sure her son possessed. She started out telling him Parker had already proven how smart he was, and by the time she finished listing his attributes, she had elevated him to genius.

Douglas couldn't figure out how she'd arrived at her conclusions. The baby wasn't a full day old, and all she could possibly know about him was that he slept and he wet.

She was sagging against the chest when Douglas took Parker away from her.

"I could go in the kitchen with you and help you fix breakfast."

"You don't need to," he said. "Is Parker getting enough to eat?"

"He will . . . soon."

"Please, try to get past your embarrassment. I need to know if he's doing all right."

"Yes, he's doing just fine. The doctor spent a long while telling me what to expect. I should be able to feed him by tonight."

He nodded. "If you start bleeding, you'll tell me, won't you?"

"Douglas . . ."

"I'm thinking about Parker," he explained. "Maybe I should go and get the doctor so he can check you. I could sneak him past Boyle's men during the night."

"That isn't necessary. I promised I'd tell you if anything happens."

After he put the baby back in his bed, he helped Isabel out of her robe. Her hands trembled as she tried to get the buttons undone, protesting all the while that she could undress herself. He took over the task anyway.

"I'm not at all tired. I've slept a long time."

She kept on protesting, even after he'd tucked her between the sheets. At her insistence, he checked on her son once more before he left the room, and by the time he pulled the door closed, Isabel was sound asleep.

She ate breakfast early that evening. He fed her burnt toast and lumpy oatmeal sweetened with sugar. He thought it looked pretty good.

She thought it looked awful. Because he'd gone to such trouble to prepare the meal, she ate as much as she could without gagging and thanked him profusely.

After he'd removed the tray, he sat down on the side of the bed to discuss the situation. "We need to talk."

She dropped the napkin onto her lap. "You're leaving."

"Isabel . . ."

"I understand."

Her face had turned stark white. He shook his head. "No, I'm not leaving. I'm going to have to do something about your lack of supplies."

"You are?"

"Yes."

"I could use more flour and sugar. I'm almost out."

"I'm going into town."

"They won't let you come back."

He put his hand on top of hers. "Listen to me. It isn't good for you to get upset. I don't plan to stroll into the general store in the middle of the day. Give me a little more credit than that."

"Then how . . ."

He grinned. "I'm going in during the night."

She looked shocked by the possibility. "You're going to rob Mr. Cooper?"

"We need supplies, and I want to pick up some clothes. I only packed one extra shirt and pair of pants to come here. I'll leave money on the counter."

"Oh, you can't do that. Mr. Cooper will know someone came into the store and he'll tell Boyle.

He tells him everything. It's too risky, Douglas. One of them might guess you're helping me. Wait, I know what you can do. Hide the money under the papers on Cooper's desk behind the counter. He'll eventually find it, and it doesn't matter if he ever figures out how it got there. We'll know we didn't steal, and our consciences will be clear. Yes, that's what you should do."

"Why does Cooper tell Boyle everything?"

"He just does," she replied. "So do some of the others. Only a handful of men stood up to Boyle. Dr. Simpson was one of them. He even lied to him for my sake and told him the baby wouldn't be born until the end of September. He was trying to give me more time to figure out a way to get away from Boyle."

"Good. We'll let Boyle keep on believing the lie for as long as possible. Did the doctor ever come out here?"

"Once."

"Did he tell you where the lookouts were?"

"I remember he told me they were lazy because they stay on the hill just outside town, blocking the road leading here. They take turns going back and forth into Sweet Creek."

"I saw those lookouts on my way here. I was wondering if he mentioned any others posted near you. It was dark when I came down the last hills, and I might have missed them."

"I don't think there are any more. There really isn't any reason for them to watch the cabin. They know I can't go into the wilderness. If I tried to go west, it would take over a week to get to the next town. In my condition, I couldn't risk it. No, the only safe way out is through Sweet Creek."

"If they aren't watching the cabin, that's good news."

"Why?"

"The longer I can go without being spotted, the better, and if they aren't watching the field, I can go back and forth from the barn and exercise the horses. I'll make certain Boyle's men haven't changed their lookout points first."

"When will you leave for the general store?"

"As soon as it's dark. Are you going to be okay by yourself?"

"Yes, but it's dangerous for you to go riding in the dark."

"It won't be any problem," he exaggerated. He tried to pull his hand away from hers, but she held on tight. "Tell me everything you know about the layout of the town."

Her memory for details was impressive. She described each building in detail. She even knew exactly where Cooper had his inventory placed inside his store.

"Now tell me where Dr. Simpson's house is located. I want to find out how many men are watching him.

She did as he asked, and then said, "You won't be able to bring much back with you unless you take the buggy, and it's too dangerous. Boyle's men will hear the squeaky wheels."

"I can fix that. You stop worrying, and don't expect me back before morning. I'll leave the rifle and extra bullets next to your bed . . . just in case

Boyle decides to come by. God, Isabel, I hate to leave you, but I . . ."

She threw her arms around his neck. "Please come back. I know you didn't ask for any of this. I'm so sorry I got you involved, but, Douglas, I really hope you'll come back anyway."

He put his arms around her and held her tight. "Calm down. I'm coming back. I promise."

She couldn't seem to let go. She hated herself for being so dependent on him. She had never depended on her husband, but then she had understood his weaknesses. Douglas was the complete opposite of him. Nothing seemed to faze Douglas.

"Parker needs you until I get stronger."

"I'll be back," he promised once again. "You have to let go of me."

"Can I do anything to help you?"

"Sure. Give me a list of the things you need. I don't want to forget anything."

"There's a list in the drawer in the kitchen. I started it weeks ago." She sounded frantic when she added, "I called it my wish list."

He didn't realize she was crying until she released him and sank back against the head-board.

"Ah, sugar. Don't cry."

"I'm just a little emotional today. That's all."

He had to do something to make her trust him. He checked on little Parker, then picked up his pocket watch, told her what time it was, and put it back on the dresser. When he looked at her again, he saw the fear still in her eyes.

"You know what you need, Isabel?"

"It's all down on my list," she answered.

"I'm not talking about supplies."

"Then, no, I don't know what I need."

"Faith. Try finding a little while I'm gone, or you and I are going to have words when I get back."

The hard edge in his voice didn't upset her. She was actually comforted by it. He would come back, if only to give her a piece of his mind for doubting him. He was arrogant and proud enough to do just that, and, oh, it was so wonderful to have him snapping at her. He acted as though he belonged with her and Parker.

"I didn't mean to insult you."

"Well, you did."

She tried to look contrite. She didn't want him to leave on a sour note. "I'll find some faith. I promise." There was a definite sparkle in her eyes when she added, "You be careful, sugar."

Four

Old habits die hard. Douglas had never forgotten how to pick a lock or get in and out of a building without being seen. He'd spent several years living on the streets of New York City, surviving by his wits and his criminal skills, before he met his three brothers and his baby sister, and headed west. Before that, he'd been in an orphanage. Granted, he'd been only a boy when he'd perfected his criminal technique. But it was like making love to a woman. After you learned how, you never forgot.

His experience as a petty thief came in real handy now. So did the rain, for it kept the night owls inside their homes. Boyle's men weren't a problem, just an inconvenience. Douglas stashed the buggy in a cove near their lair on the hill overlooking Sweet Creek, then crept up on the four men and listened to their conversation in hopes of gaining some useful information about their boss. He didn't learn anything significant. Other than taking Boyle's name in vain several times because he'd assigned them this miserable duty, the men spent the rest of the time boasting to one another about the number of shots of whiskey they could swallow in a single sitting. They were incredibly boring, and after listening to their whining complaints for almost twenty minutes, Douglas hadn't heard anything significant. He was about to make a wide circle around them and continue on when Boyle's men decided to leave their posts and go back into town for the night. Not only had the weather finally gotten to them, but they were also certain their boss would never find out.

Their laziness made Douglas's task easier. He made six trips on his sorrel back and forth from the general store to the buggy with supplies Isabel would need, then headed across town to Dr. Simpson's cottage.

He didn't knock. He went in the back door because, just as Isabel suspected, Boyle was keeping a close watch on the physician. He had a man stationed out front. Douglas spotted the guard leaning against a hitching post across the street with a rifle in one hand and a bottle of liquor in the other. There wasn't anyone watching the back, however. Douglas figured Boyle had ordered one of his men to do just that, but like the complainers up on the hill, he'd probably sneaked home too.

Douglas had forgotten that Isabel had told him Simpson was married. His wife was tucked in nice and tight beside him, sleeping on her side with her back to her husband. All Douglas saw was a puff of gray hair above the covers.

He didn't use his gun to wake the elderly man. He simply put his hand over the doctor's mouth, whispered that he was a friend of Isabel Grant's, and asked him to come downstairs to talk.

The doctor was apparently used to being awakened in the dead of night. Babies, Douglas knew, often came during that inconvenient time. Although the physician seemed wary, he didn't argue with him.

His wife didn't wake up. Simpson shut the door behind him and led Douglas to his study. He pulled the drapes closed and then lit a candle.

"Are you really a friend of Isabel's?"

"Yes, I am."

"And your name?"

"Douglas Clayborne."

"You don't intend to hurt Isabel?"

"No."

The doctor still didn't look convinced.

"I want to help her," Douglas insisted.

"Maybe so, maybe not," Simpson replied.

"You aren't from around here, are you? How do you know our Isabel?"

"Actually, I only just met her. Her husband sold me an Arabian stallion a couple of months ago, but I was expanding my business back then and couldn't come for the horse until I'd hired some extra hands."

"But you're a friend. Is that right?"

"Yes."

Simpson stared at him a long minute, slowly rubbing his whiskered jaw until he had worked out whatever it was that was bothering him, and finally nodded. "Good," he said. "She needs a friend as big and hard-looking as you, young man. I hope to God you are hard when it comes to protecting her. You know how to use that gun you're wearing?"

"Yes."

"Are you fast and accurate?"

Douglas felt as though he were undergoing an inquisition but didn't take offense because he knew the physician had Isabel's safety uppermost in his mind. "I'm fast enough."

"I saw your shotgun on the table in the hall," Simpson said. "Are you also good with that weapon?"

Douglas didn't see any harm in being completely honest. "I prefer my shotgun."

"Why is that?"

"It leaves a bigger hole, sir, and if I shoot someone, I shoot to kill."

The doctor grinned. "I expect that's the way it ought to be," he remarked.

He sat down behind his desk and motioned for Douglas to take a seat across from him.

He declined with a shake of his head.

"How's our girl doing? I sure wish I could see her. I expect she's getting big and awkward about now."

"She had the baby last night."

"Good Lord Almighty, she had the baby? It came much too soon. What'd she have? A boy or a girl?"

"A boy."

"Did he make it?"

"Yes, but he's thin, terribly thin . . . and little. His cry is real weak too."

Simpson leaned back in his chair and shook his head. "It's a miracle he survived. Besides being weak, is he acting sick?"

"I don't know if he is or not. He sleeps most of the time."

"Is he nursing?"

"He's trying to," he answered.

"Good. That's real good," he said. "His mama's milk will fatten him up. Tell Isabel to try to nurse him every hour or so until he's stronger. He'll only take a little each time, but that's all right. If the baby refuses to eat, or can't keep it down, then we've got a real problem on our hands. I don't know what good I could do for him if he gets into trouble. He's too young for medicine. We've just got to pray he makes it. A chill will kill him, so you've got to keep him warm all the time. That's real important, son."

"I'll keep him warm."

"I don't want to sound grim . . . It's just, you

have to understand and accept the facts. There's a good chance the baby won't make it, no matter what you do."

"I don't want to think about that possibility."

"If it happens, you have to help Isabel get through it. That's what friends do."

"Yes, I will."

"How is she doing? Did she have any problems I should know about?"

"She had a difficult time with the laboring. She looks all right now."

"You helped her bring the baby?"

"Yes."

"Did she tear?"

"No, but she sure bled a lot. I don't know if it was more than what's expected. I've never delivered a baby before. I ask her how she's doing, and that seems to embarrass her and she refuses to talk about it."

The doctor nodded. "If she were in real trouble, she'd tell you for her son's sake. Try to keep her calm and be real careful about upsetting her. Isabel's a strong woman, but she's vulnerable now. New mothers tend to become emotional, and I don't expect Isabel to be any different. The least little thing might set her off, and she doesn't need to be fretting about anything. Paul Morgan's wife cried for a full month. She plumb drove her husband to distraction worrying about her. The woman cried when she was happy and when she was sad. There wasn't any rhyme or reason to it. Eventually she snapped out of it. Isabel's got more serious problems to deal with. I don't know how I'd stand it if I had Boyle

189

breathing down my neck. I'm sure worried about her son though, coming early like he did, and I know she must be worried too. If the baby makes it, are you planning to stay with our girl until he can be moved?"

"Yes, I'm staying. How long do you think that will be?"

"At least eight weeks, but ten would be even better if he's slow to put on weight. I'm mighty curious about something, son. How'd you manage to get to Isabel's ranch in the first place?"

"It was dark and I was taking the most direct route, using the moonlight to guide me, until it disappeared and the rain started. I almost ran into Boyle's lookouts by accident then. They were so drunk they didn't hear me. I wondered what they were doing hiding out in the rain," he admitted with a shrug. "But I wasn't curious enough to find out. I'm glad now I didn't stop."

"It was dangerous riding down the mountain path in the dark."

"I took my time, walked some of the way, and the light in Isabel's window provided a beacon for me."

"Are you sure you can get back to her tonight?"

"I'm sure."

"I wish I were younger and more agile. I'd try to get to Isabel in the dark too, but I don't dare chance it at my age. I was never very good with horses. They scare me," he admitted. "I've fallen more than I care to recollect. Now I use a buggy, and my wife helps me rig the horses up every morning. Besides, even if I could get there, Boyle might hear about it and then my Trudy would get hurt. No, I can't chance it, but I thank the Lord you came along."

"You told me there wasn't anything you could do for the baby now," Douglas reminded him.

"I could be a comfort to Isabel. She's like a daughter to Trudy and me. After Parker died, I asked her to move in with us, but she wouldn't hear of it. She's determined to stand on her own two feet. Trudy pleaded with her to at least stay with us until after the baby was born; then Boyle got wind of our plans and put a stop to it. My wife found a nice little cottage down the road from us, and we wanted Isabel to consider moving in there and raising her baby in Sweet Creek. She'd be as independent as she wanted, yet close enough that we could lend a hand every now and then."

The doctor's affection for Isabel made Douglas like him all the more. "I'll take good care of her and the baby," he promised.

"Have you noticed how pretty she is yet?"

Douglas felt like laughing, so absurd was the question. "Yes, I noticed."

"Then I've got to ask you what your intentions are, son."

The question blindsided him. "Excuse me?"

"I'm going to be blunt, and I expect I'll rile you. Still, I've got to ask. After she recovers from childbirth, do you plan on dallying with her?"

He'd never heard it put quite that way before. "No."

Simpson didn't look convinced. He suggested Douglas pour each of them a shot of brandy, waited until he'd given him a glass, and then leaned back in his chair to think about the situation. "It might happen anyway," he remarked

"I've only known Isabel for—"

Simpson interrupted him. "You just promised me you'd stay with her for ten weeks, remember? You're a man of your word aren't you?"

"Yes, and I will stay, but that doesn't mean I'll . . ."

"Son, let me tell you about a man I happened to run into in River's Bend."

Douglas could feel his frustration mounting. He didn't want to hear a story now. He wanted to talk about Boyle and get as much information about the man as he could.

The doctor wasn't going to be rushed, if the way he sipped his brandy and stared off into space were any indication. Age gave the older man the benefit of Douglas's attention and respect, and so Douglas leaned against the side of the desk and waited for the tale to be told.

It took Simpson over thirty minutes to tell his story about three couples who got stranded in a snowstorm and stayed together in a miner's shack for the entire winter. By the time the spring thaw came, the six of them had formed what the doctor called an undying friendship. Yet five years later, he happened to meet one of the survivors and asked him several questions. To the doctor's amazement, the gentleman couldn't remember the name of one of the men he'd spent the winter with.

"That's the point of my story," Simpson said. "Yes, sir, it is. You're going to be living close to Isabel for a long time, and I want you to remember the fella I just told you about. He pledged his friendship, went so far as to call the other two men his brothers, yet once he got on with his life, he plumb forgot about them."

"I understand," Douglas said.

"Do you? Isabel has a good heart, and she sure is an easy person to love. It's the future I'm worried about, after you take care of this business with Boyle and go back home. You are going to do something about the tyrant, aren't you?"

Simpson had finally gotten to the topic Douglas wanted to discuss. "It seems I am," he said. "Tell me what you know about Boyle."

"I know the man's a monster." His voice echoed his disgust. "The only reason I'm still breathing is that he thinks he might have need of my services in the future. He's threatened to kill me, but I don't think he'd do it. Doctors are hard to come by in these parts. He'd hurt my Trudy though. Yes, he would."

"Isabel told me that only a few men in this town have had the courage to stand up to Boyle and that you were one of them. Why won't the others help?"

"Everyone that I know would like to help, but they're afraid. They've seen what happens to those good men who have tried. If one of them so much as whispers about doing something to help Isabel, word gets back to Boyle, and then the instigator gets hurt bad. Both of Wendell Border's hands were broken after he told a couple of men he thought were his friends that he was going to find the U.S. marshal everyone's been hearing glory tales about. The lawman was scouring the territory, looking for some wanted men, but Wendell never got the chance to go hunting for him. Boyle's men got to poor Wendell before he could even leave town. While I was setting his broken hands, I promised him in a whisper that I'd find a way to get help here. I promised him I'd pray too."

"Were you going to go hunting for the lawman?"

"No, I'm too old and worn out to go hunting for anyone. My Trudy, fortunately, came up with a better idea. Twice a week I go into Liddyville to see patients there. It's only two hours away from Sweet Creek by buggy," he added. "My wife told me to use the telegraph office there and send wires to all the sheriffs in the territory. She thinks one or two might want to help us. I took it a step further and sent wires to two preachers Wendell told me about and asked them to help with the hunt for the marshal. I still haven't heard back from anyone, but I've got this feeling that if the Texan hears about our trouble, he'll come, especially if he knows a mother with a brand-new baby needs help. Why, he'll drop everything and come running."

"Why do you think—"

Simpson wouldn't let him finish his question. "If the rumors are true, the marshal accidentally caused some women and children to get killed during a bank robbery in Texas. He didn't know they were inside and being used as shields when he and his men rushed in. From what we've heard about the robbers, they would have killed them anyway, but the marshal still blames himself. Oh, he'll come all right . . . if he hears of our trouble. Sure wish I knew the fella's name. It would make chasing him down easier, I expect."

"You're looking for Daniel Ryan," Douglas told him. "My brothers have been searching for him too." He paused when he heard the creak of the steps behind him. "Did we wake your wife?"

"No, but she's used to snuggling up against me and she must have awakened when she got cold."

"Would you mind telling her to put the gun down?"

Simpson was astonished. "Do you have eyes in the back of your head? Trudy, put that away and come in here. I want you to meet Isabel's friend. He's promised to help our girl."

Douglas turned around and nodded to the woman. "I'm sorry I disturbed you and your husband," he began.

Trudy laid the gun on the desk and rushed forward to shake Douglas's hand. Her grip was surprisingly strong for a woman her size, for the top of her head barely reached his shoulders.

"The doctor and I were praying for a miracle. Looks like we might have gotten one. I know you aren't Marshal Ryan. You're big like we were told he was but you don't have yellow hair and blue eyes, and our preacher gave us a good description of the lawman so we'd recognize him if he came into town. We pray every Sunday that the dear man will hear of our troubles and come here. Could you be a friend of the marshal's? Did he send you here?"

"No, ma'am, he didn't send me here."

195

She couldn't hide her disappointment. "But you're still going to help our little girl?"

Douglas smiled. The Simpsons' affection for Isabel pleased him. God only knew, she needed good friends now, and it was nice to know she had two champions in Sweet Creek trying to look out for her.

"Yes, I'm going to help her."

She squeezed his hand before she let go. "Doctor, I expect I'll go into the kitchen now." She waited until her husband nodded agreement before she looked at Douglas again. "You won't be leaving until I've packed some leftovers for you to take."

"You'll have to work in the dark, Trudy," her husband told her.

"I expect I'll manage. I'll light a candle and put it in the hallway. No one can see inside, doctor."

"Ma'am, I really should be heading back to Isabel."

She shook her head at him and left the library in a near run.

Simpson chuckled. "You might as well relax, son. Trudy isn't going to let you leave without a bag full of her home cooking. Sit on down in a chair, proper like, and tell me why your brothers have been searching for the Texan. Do you have troubles where you come from that need the law?"

"No," Douglas answered. "Ryan helped one of my brothers. The fact is, he saved Travis's life."

"So you're wanting to thank him."

"Yes, but also get back a compass he . . . borrowed."

"Now, that sounds like a mighty curious tale."

"I'll tell you all about it some other time," Douglas promised. "When I was coming here, I noticed your town has a wire service, and I was wondering why you had to go to Liddyville to send your telegrams."

"The only way you could have seen the telegraph office is if you'd been inside the general store. It's in the back room. Why'd you go in there?"

"To get some supplies."

"Did anyone see you?"

"No."

"Good," Simpson whispered. "You broke in, didn't you?"

"Yes."

"Did you snap the lock or break a window?"

Douglas was a bit insulted by the question. "No, of course not. Cooper won't know I was there unless he does a close inventory."

Simpson was grinning with pleasure. "I hope you robbed Vernon Cooper blind. His brother, Jasper, runs the wire office, and both the scoundrels are in Boyle's back pocket. No one in Sweet Creek dares send a wire from here unless they want Boyle to know about it, and that's why I used the wire service in Liddyville. Just on principle Trudy and I get all our supplies there too. We'd rather go without than give either one of the Coopers our hard-earned money."

"If Ryan were to show up and arrest Boyle,

would the man whose hands were broken testify against him?"

Simpson shook his head. "I expect Ryan will have to find another way to get rid of Boyle," he said, "or run his henchmen out of town first. Wendell's too scared to testify. He's got a wife and two young daughters. He doesn't dare say a word against Boyle, or his family will pay the consequences. The poor man. He's got crops that will be ready to harvest in a couple of weeks, and with broken hands he's going to have to watch them rot."

"Won't some of the town help him?"

"They're afraid to do anything that might make Boyle mad."

"Why does he want Isabel's land?"

"He's telling everyone he wants to put his cattle there to graze. He has a lot of land surrounding his ranch house, but he rents that out to some foreigners who buy cattle down in Texas and have them brought up to his land to fatten up. Boyle's made a fortune over the last fifteen years, but he's greedy, and he wants more."

"If he wants to use Isabel's land, why doesn't he do it? She couldn't stop him, and he has to know that."

"He doesn't just want her land, son, he wants her too. He's real blatant about letting everyone know she's going to belong to him. Why, he struts around town like a fat rooster inviting people to the wedding. Folks say he started lusting after her the second he saw her."

"Why is he waiting? He could force her to marry him now."

"You don't understand Boyle the way I do. Pride's involved. He wants her to beg him to marry her, and he figures if he makes her desperate enough, she'll do just that."

"Did he kill her husband?"

"If the bullet hadn't gone through his back, I would have suspected Parker accidentally killed himself. I'm not speaking ill of the dead, you understand. I'm only stating facts, and the fact is that Isabel's husband was about as useful as a kettle with a hole in the bottom. The man had grand notions about all sorts of things. He treated Isabel good though, real good. And he was kind to crazy old Paddy, even though he knew Boyle would hear of it and be furious."

Douglas was intrigued. "Being kind to an old man infuriated Boyle?"

"It's perplexing, isn't it? Paddy came to Sweet Creek straight from Ireland and had lived here for as long as I could remember. Boyle came along about ten years ago and squatted on the land adjacent to where Isabel is living now. Within a year he started building himself a grand three-story house, and when it was finished, it was as fancy as any you'll see in the East, I'll wager you. He filled it with new furniture he had shipped from Europe and then had a big party the whole town was invited to so he could show off the palace. Even Paddy was invited, but something happened that night that started the feud between the two men. No one recollects seeing the two of them together during the shindig, but from that night on, Boyle tormented Paddy with a vengeance. Folks started calling the Irishman crazy then because no matter how often Boyle came after him, Paddy laughed about it. You know what that crazy man told me while I was patching him up one evening? He said he was going to have the last laugh. Can you imagine? The funny thing is, he did."

"How'd he do that?"

"Well now, I'm getting to that, son. Paddy was dying of consumption. He hung on until one Saturday night, because he knew that was when Boyle always went to the saloon to play cards. I happened to be there that night too, and I'll tell you it was the strangest dying I've ever seen. Paddy had dragged himself out of his sickbed, came into the saloon, and then laid down on the floor. He folded his hands together on top of his chest as though he was already in his coffin and announced he was going to die in a few minutes. That's when things turned mighty peculiar. Boyle knocked a chair over running to the old man. He knelt down beside him, waving me and everyone else away, and then he grabbed hold of Paddy's shirt and began to shake him, shouting, 'Tell me, old man. Tell me who it is.'"

"What happened then?" Douglas demanded to know, fascinated by the bizarre story.

"It got even more peculiar, son, that's what happened. Paddy gave Boyle a big toothless smile and whispered something only Boyle could hear. And then he laughed. As God is my witness, Paddy died laughing. Boyle went crazy. He started choking the dead man and screaming vile names at him. Two of his men had to pull him off the Irishman so the funeral cart could come and collect him, and I heard one of his men ask him why he hadn't killed Paddy years ago. Boyle was still reeling from whatever it was the Irishman had said to him, and all he would mutter was that he couldn't kill him without knowing. The following day Trudy and I went to say our good-bye to old Paddy, and I swear to you when I looked in that coffin, that crazy old man had a big smile on his face. Isn't that the darnedest story you ever heard?"

Douglas agreed with a nod. The doctor let out a loud sigh, and then said, "Boyle got over whatever was bothering him as quick as could be and started in pestering Isabel and Parker Grant the following week. No one saw him kill Parker, but everyone believes he did. I expect he thought our girl would fall right into his hands then, being pregnant and helpless and all. That was his big mistake because there isn't anything helpless about Isabel. Naturally she's vulnerable because of the baby, and I figure Boyle, with all his money and power, thought he could snatch her right up."

"Does he have marriage in mind?"

"Oh, he wants her legal," Simpson replied. "Since she hasn't started begging him yet, we think he's waiting for the baby to come along. He's a smart one Boyle is. Most mothers will do anything to feed their little ones. Isabel's a fine woman, but too pretty for her own good. I lied to Boyle, told him the baby wouldn't come until the end of September, and Isabel didn't start showing until she was well into her fifth month, so Boyle has no reason to think I'm lying. I don't

201

know if the extra time will help much, but I'm hoping Boyle will continue to leave her alone until he sees for himself that the baby's here."

"Doctor, the food's packed up," Trudy called from the hallway.

Simpson immediately stood up. "What else can I do to help?" he asked.

"I'd appreciate it if you'd send a wire to my brothers telling them I'll be delayed."

The doctor motioned to some paper and a pen. "You write it all down, and I'll see to it first thing in the morning."

"Do you usually go to Liddyville on Mondays to see patients?"

"No, Tuesdays and Fridays are my usual days, but I could come up with a reason to go early."

"There isn't any need for that. Besides, you shouldn't change your routine."

"Are you planning to bring in some help soon?"

"Yes."

"I expected you would," he replied. "I ought to mention something important first. Boyle's going to be leaving to attend his annual family gathering in the Dakotas. He's never missed one in all the years he's lived here, and everyone expects him to leave real soon. You don't want him to bring more men back with him, and I know he'll do just that if he gets word Isabel has evened out the odds. Besides, it's too risky to move the baby now, and you don't want to be worrying about Boyle's men setting her place on fire. They'll do it as sure as thunder follows lightning if they know you're inside."

"How long will Boyle be away?"

"It varies from year to year. There's just no telling. Last year he was gone six weeks, but the year before he was back in a month. I heard it's a big family get-together he attends, and because he's considered to be the most successful of all the relations, he likes to stay a spell to get their adulation."

"I'm going to write down a second message I want you to send when the time comes, and I want you to promise me that if you hear from Ryan, you'll let me know. I'd like to have a word with him."

"How am I going to get word to you?"

"I'm going to come back every Monday night to check in with you."

"Just to find out if I've heard from the marshal? Son, that sounds like you're getting false hopes up. The chances of locating him are mighty slim."

Douglas shook his head. "That isn't my main reason for checking in with you, sir. If I don't show up, you'll know something's wrong, and that's when I want you to send the second telegram. Do you understand?"

"I do," he agreed. "You'll be careful coming back here?"

"Yes," he promised. "I wish there was a way I could get Isabel and the baby to you and your wife though."

"You'd be bringing trouble to town if you tried. Boyle checks in on her, and I'm sure that one of his men will take over the duty while he's gone. If she isn't where she's supposed to be, they'll tear this town apart looking for her. It won't do any good to take them to Liddyville because he's got friends there too, and there isn't another town close enough to be safe for that newborn. You've just got to stay put, son. If you don't let Boyle's men see you, they'll continue to leave Isabel alone. You don't want that monster coming after you. No, sir, you don't."

Douglas didn't agree. "Just as soon as Isabel and her son are safe, I'm going to want Boyle to come after me. Fact is, I'm looking forward to it."

The doctor felt a cold draft permeate his bones. Isabel's champion had smiled when he made his last comment, but his eyes told another story. They were cold . . . deadly.

Simpson took a step back before he realized he didn't have to be afraid. He followed Douglas into the kitchen and whispered additional advice. "When the time comes, you'll need help, son. There are twenty-four men working the ranch for Boyle, and every one of them is no good riffraff looking for trouble. With Boyle leading them, that makes twenty-five in all."

"I'm not worried. My brothers will come."

Simpson's wife heard the remark. "How many brothers are in your family?" she asked.

"Five now, including my brother-in-law."

Simpson looked incredulous. "Five against twenty-five?"

Douglas grinned. "It's more than enough."

Five

Douglas didn't make it back to the ranch until almost dawn. Before he unloaded the supplies and bedded down the sorrel, he hurried to the cabin to check on Isabel and the baby.

She was standing in front of the fireplace with the rifle up and ready. When he called her name and softly knocked, she ran to the door, unbolted the lock, and threw herself into his arms. She didn't mind at all that he was drenched from head to foot.

"I'm so happy you're home."

Her arms were wrapped tightly around his waist. He felt the barrel of the rifle against his back and quickly reached behind him to take it away from her. She continued to hug him while he leaned to the side and put the weapon on the table.

"I couldn't imagine what was taking you so long," she whispered. "But I never once thought you wouldn't come back."

"I'm glad to hear it," he said. "You're shaking. If you'll let go of me, I'll add another log to the fire. New mothers have to be careful. You don't want to get sick."

She didn't want to let go of him. "I'm not cold . . . I'm just very relieved you're back. Douglas, I was worried about you."

She was trembling almost violently now. He held on to her so she couldn't fall down.

"I was worried about you too," he admitted.

Her face was hidden against his chest. "Did you have any trouble?"

"None at all," he replied. "I got everything on your wish list and a few extras as well. Then I went over to see Dr. Simpson."

"But Boyle told me his men are watching his cottage night and day," she cried out in alarm.

"They never saw me," he assured her. "I met the doctor's wife too. She packed up a bag of food and fresh milk for you."

"Oh, that was nice of her."

"The doctor sent lots of advice."

She was patting his chest. He wondered if she realized what she was doing.

"You're very resourceful, Douglas." *And reliable,* she silently added. "How did you manage to get in and out of the general store and Simpson's house without being seen? Did you break the locks?"

"No, I just jimmied them open."

"Good heavens, how did you learn to do that?"

"I was a thief a long, long time ago."

For some reason, she found his admission hilarious. He didn't know what to make of her reaction. He liked her laugh though. It was filled with such joy.

He forced himself to focus on more practical matters. Pulling away from her, he took hold of her hand and led her back to her bed. "Have you been up long?"

"Most of the night," she admitted. "So was the baby. He just went back to sleep."

"Dr. Simpson wants you to try to feed him every hour or so. Is he nursing yet?"

"Yes," she answered.

"Do you think he got enough milk?"

"Yes," she answered. "He kept it down too."

She sounded proud of her accomplishment, yet also shy about it. He caught her looking up at him, shared a smile, and then told her to go to sleep.

"Couldn't I help you unload the supplies?"

"No."

"Oh, I almost forgot. I fixed your breakfast. It's on the counter."

"I'll eat after I've put everything away and taken care of Brutus."

"Did you remember to leave money for Mr. Cooper? I've never stolen anything in my life, and I'm not about to start now."

"I left exactly what he deserved."

Technically he hadn't lied to her. He hadn't told her the truth either, yet he didn't feel guilty about it. He had left Vernon Cooper what he owed him, which was nothing, not a single penny. Cooper had turned his back on Isabel and joined ranks with Boyle, and as far as Douglas was concerned, Vernon and his brother, Jasper, the disreputable telegraph man, should be run out of town. Only then would they get what they really deserved.

Isabel was too excited to sleep, but she pretended to do just that so Douglas would bring in the supplies. Her excitement increased each time she heard him come back inside. She kept count by how often the floorboard in front of the hearth squeaked. Twelve wonderful times she heard the creaking sound, and that meant six trips to the kitchen and six trips back to the buggy. Were his arms filled, or was he carrying in one bag at a time?

Waiting was blissfully excruciating. Finally, she heard the buggy being driven back to the barn, and she couldn't bear the suspense another second. She threw the covers off, put on her robe and her slippers, and tiptoed into the living room.

She let out a gasp of joy then, for the table and four chairs were stacked high with bags, and there were more on the floor as well. She ran to the table and gasped once again when she saw a large crock of butter, real butter, and another crock filled with coffee. Her fingertips caressed each and every bag and everywhere she turned, she saw something even more wonderful to cry about. There was beef jerky and ham and bacon and four giant pickles wrapped in white paper. Pickle juice was dripping onto the tablecloth, and she thought that was a most beautiful sight, indeed.

She glanced up and saw Douglas watching her. He was standing in the door, and in his arm was yet another bag. She wondered what he was thinking. He had the strangest look on his face, as though he didn't know what to make of the sight, but there was such tenderness in his eyes, she knew she didn't need to worry that he might be angry with her for getting out of bed.

"I didn't know you were there," she said.

"I was watching you. You remind me of a little

girl on Christmas morning." His voice was filled with compassion. How long had she gone without the basic necessities every man and woman were entitled to, he wondered, and did she realize she was hugging a bag of flour? Or that she was crying?

"There's more on the counter."

"More?" she cried out.

It seemed to be too much for her to take in. She stood there frozen with the flour wrapped tight in her arms and stared down at her treasures on the table.

"Come and see," he suggested.

She didn't put the flour down but carried it with her to the alcove. He reached up to push the floor-length drape further to one side on the rope and tried to step back so she could see inside. The kitchen was too narrow for both of them, but she wouldn't give him time to get out of her way. She squeezed herself past him.

Then she gasped yet again. "Salt and pepper and cinnamon and . . . oh, Douglas, could we afford all this?"

She was pressed against him with her face turned up to his. A man could get lost in those beautiful freckles and incredible golden brown eyes.

"Could we?" she asked again in a breathless whisper.

The question jarred him out of his fantasy. "Could we what?"

"Afford all this."

"Yeah," he drawled out. "Cooper was having

a sale." He managed to tell the lie without laughing.

"Oh, that was nice."

They kept staring at each other. He reached over and slowly wiped away the tears from her cheeks with his fingers.

She surprised him by leaning up on tiptoes and kissing him.

"What was that for?"

"Being so good to me and my son. I'm sure I'll get my strength back real soon. I've never really depended on anyone before, not ever. It's very nice though. Thank you."

She turned to leave. He followed her, reached over her shoulder, and took the bag of flour away. "What about your husband? Didn't you depend on him every once in a while?"

"Parker had fine qualities. I'm sorry you didn't know him. I'm certain you would have liked him. He really was a good man, Douglas. Good night."

He watched her walk away. She hadn't answered his question, and he wasn't certain if it had been a deliberate evasion or not. He decided he was too tired to ask her again. He went back to the barn to dry down his sorrel, then used a clean bucket of rainwater to give himself a good scrubbing before he finally headed to bed.

He slept most of the day away on his bedroll in front of the hearth. Parker eventually jarred him awake with a bellow guaranteed to make his mama snap to attention. His cry wasn't at all puny, but forceful. Was the infant already getting stronger?

Isabel's laughter rang out. She was in the kitchen giving Parker his first full bath.

Douglas joined her. "He's louder today," he remarked with a yawn.

"He's angry."

Douglas noticed the baby was shivering and remembered Dr. Simpson's advice to keep him as warm as possible. "I should have kept the fire in the hearth going."

"You needed to sleep."

"Are you about finished? I don't want the baby to get cold."

Her full attention was centered on Parker. "There, he's clean again. Hush now," she crooned to the baby. "It's all over. Douglas, will you grab that towel for me?"

He hurried to do as she asked. He spread the towel over his bare shoulder, reached for Parker, and laid him up against it. Isabel used another towel to pat him dry. A minute later she was securing his diaper when Douglas noticed Parker's lips were turning blue.

"We have to get him warm quick. Unbutton your robe and your gown."

She didn't hesitate. "He feels like ice," she whispered in alarm. "I shouldn't have bathed him. He's so cold, he can't even cry now."

"He'll be warm in a minute," he promised. He wrapped the gown and the robe around her, draped a clean diaper over Parker's fuzzy black head, and stood there frowning down at him. "Tell me when he stops shivering."

She was afraid to move. "It's all my fault. What was I thinking?"

"That your son was rank," he told her. "Next time, we'll bathe him together in front of the fire."

"He stopped."

"Shivering?"

"Yes. I think he's asleep." She let out a happy little sigh.

Douglas lifted the diaper away from Parker's head to see his face. "Yeah, he's sleeping," he whispered.

And his face was pressed against freckles. "He's a lucky man."

"Little man," she corrected. She blushed as she looked up at Douglas. "Yes, he is lucky, and so am I to have you here."

"You aren't going to cry, are you?"

"Oh, I never cry."

He thought she was joking, but she didn't laugh.

"It's very difficult for me to show any emotions. Haven't you noticed?"

"Can't say that I have."

"Could you do a favor for me? A couple of the chairs have wobbly legs, and I'd appreciate it if you would show me how to fix them. I'm not sure if I should nail the legs to the base or if I should—"

"I'll fix them," he promised. "Anything else?"

It turned out she had quite a list of repairs she needed. Although it was foolish for him to fix furniture that she wasn't going to be able to take with her when she left, he decided to do the repairs anyway. He wouldn't discuss the future with her yet, purposely waiting until she was stronger and less emotional, for even he could see that childbirth had left her physically and mentally exhausted. Dr. Simpson had told him she shouldn't get upset. Besides, the chores would keep him busy.

"Are Boyle's men watching the cabin?" she asked.

"They weren't last night, but they could have moved closer by now. I'm not going to take the chance. The doctor suggested I stay hidden during the day and work at night, but I had already decided to do just that. As long as Boyle believes you're all alone, he'll hopefully be content to wait."

"What about the horses? They can't stay cooped inside the barn all the time."

"I'll exercise them during the night. I'll start rebuilding the corral as soon as it's dark. Stop worrying."

"What can I do to help?"

"Get stronger."

She would have argued with him if Parker hadn't demanded her attention.

Cooking wasn't one of Douglas's talents, and so he sliced the ham and bread Trudy Simpson had sent, and opened a jar of pickled beets he'd stolen from the general store. He gave Isabel a full glass of milk. She wanted to save it and would have insisted if he hadn't told her he could easily get more.

She returned to the main room an hour later with Parker up against her shoulder and watched Douglas repair a chair while she paced with the fretful baby. Douglas noticed how exhausted she

213

looked and decided to leave the other chairs until tomorrow night. He washed his hands and then took the baby from her.

"I'll walk with him."

"I don't know what's wrong with him. He's been fed and changed and burped, but he still won't go to sleep."

"He's just being ornery."

She started to turn away, then changed her mind. "I'll sit up with you and—"

"You don't need to," he said. "If I get into trouble, I know where to find you."

"You're certain nothing's wrong with him?"

"I'm certain."

"Good night then."

Douglas sat down in the rocker and began to gently pat the baby's back. He remembered how he used to rock his sister, and Lord, how fast time had moved. Soon now Mary Rose would be rocking her own son or daughter. Douglas used to talk things over with his sister while he rocked her, and he did the same thing now with Parker. The vibration of his voice had calmed Mary Rose, or bored her, into sleep. The reason really didn't matter; the result was always the same. Parker settled down within minutes and was snoring like an old man.

It was dark now and time for Douglas to get some work done. He braced himself for the anger he would feel the second he stepped out the door. Sure as certain, he got mad, because he was again reminded that the cabin was sitting in the center of the flood line. He couldn't seem to move past that appalling realization. It didn't matter to him that her dead husband might not have built the cabin, or that he might have moved his pregnant wife into the quarters as a temporary home while he built a cabin on higher ground. The man had still put Isabel in danger. Why in God's name had he done it? Didn't he care?

Grant's incompetence didn't stop there. He'd built a corral—at least that was what Douglas thought it was supposed to be—but apparently the first strong wind had knocked half of it down. He was pretty certain Pegasus had sustained his leg injury by accidentally brushing up against one of its exposed nails. If that was true, the risk of serious infection increased considerably. Douglas had to find out as soon as possible, so that he could change the salve he was applying to Pegasus if he needed to, but he decided to wait until morning and let Isabel get as much sleep as possible.

It was a little after dawn when she joined him at the table. She had Parker snuggled in her arms.

A fire crackled in the hearth and gave the room a nice warm glow. Douglas stood up and pulled a chair out for her.

She noticed the lumpy oatmeal and the burned toast he'd again prepared.

He noticed how her hair was shining in the light coming from the fire. She wore it in a long braid down her back. Curly red strands had escaped the binding and framed the sides of her face, and damn but she was a fine-looking woman. Motherhood agreed with her.

She realized he was staring at her and grew self-conscious in no time at all. "Parker won't burp." It was all she could think of to say to take his mind off her unkempt appearance.

He threw a clean towel up against his shoulder and took the baby from her. "Can you sit at the table?"

"Yes. I'm feeling better now."

Douglas stood over her while he gently patted the baby's back. Isabel didn't want to hurt his feelings by refusing to eat the unappealing food, and so she forced half of it down with big gulps of water. She wanted to save the rest of the milk for supper.

"You should be drinking milk with every meal. I'll bring more back next Monday."

"We did have two milking cows several months ago."

"What happened to them?"

"I'm not sure. They were here one morning, and gone the next."

"Do you think Boyle stole them?"

She shrugged. "Parker didn't seem to be overly upset about it, and he refused to talk about it much. I think he might have forgotten to close the stall doors. He was a bit absentminded."

"Are you telling me they might have wandered away?"

"The barn door might have been left open too," she said, staring down at the table. She seemed embarrassed, and for that reason, he let the topic go. He turned away from her so she wouldn't see his astonishment. Honest to God, her husband hadn't been worth the price of air.

"What about the cabin? Parker didn't build it, did he?"

"No, he didn't. How did you know that?"

It was well-constructed, and that was how he knew her husband couldn't have built it. He didn't answer her question for fear of upsetting her though, and asked another one instead. "Was he building a home for you up on higher ground?"

"No. What an odd question to ask. We moved in here."

She tried to get up from the table then, but he put his hand on her shoulder to make her stay. "Finish your breakfast. You need to regain your strength. Tell me, how did Pegasus get hurt?"

"Some of Boyle's men were shooting their guns in the air, and Pegasus reared up against the barn door."

"Was it an exposed nail that cut him?"

"No, it wasn't."

The baby drew their attention with a belch worthy of an outlaw. Isabel's smile made Douglas think she believed her son had just accomplished an amazing feat.

"I really can't eat another bite," she protested. "I'll save the food for later." She stood up before he could argue with her. "I'd like to prepare supper tonight. I just love to cook," she exaggerated. "It's . . . soothing. Yes, it's soothing."

He wasn't buying her lie. He burst into laughter and shook his head at her. "The oatmeal's that bad?"

Her eyes sparkled with devilment. "It tastes like cement."

They stared into one another's eyes for what seemed an eternity, and neither one of them wanted to look away.

"You've really got to stop doing that."

The huskiness in his voice made her feel warm all over. "Doing what?" she asked in a breathless whisper.

"Getting prettier every day."

"Oh." She sighed the word.

He realized what was happening before she did. He was also staring at her freckles again and quickly forced himself to look out the window instead. A movement near the tree line suddenly caught his attention. He froze. There was a shadow slowly moving down the path toward the field. He was still too far away for Douglas to see his face, but Douglas knew who was coming. The lone rider had to be Boyle. Dr. Simpson had warned him that the predator liked to look in on the woman he was terrorizing. Oh, yes, it was Boyle all right.

Douglas's first concern was that Isabel not panic. She'd wake up the baby then, and Boyle would move his men in. Douglas continued to stare at the shadow and made his voice sound as mild as Parker's snore when he spoke to her. "Isabel, will the baby sleep for a while?"

"Oh, yes. He was up most of the night. He has to catch up on his sleep today."

She took the baby away from him and headed for the bedroom. He followed her, waited until Parker was all tucked in, and then calmly told her company was coming.

Isabel didn't panic. She began to undress instead. "How much time do I have?" she asked. She threw her robe on the bed and started unbuttoning her nightgown.

"What are you doing?"

"I have to get dressed and go outside."

"The hell you do. You're staying in here."

"Douglas, be sensible. If he sees me, he'll go away. I always go out on the stoop with my rifle. I want him to see me pregnant. I'll need a belt. Will you get one of Parker's out of the box in the corner? Don't stand there. We have to hurry. He doesn't like to be kept waiting."

"You are not . . ."

She ran to him and put her finger over his mouth to stop his protest. "If I don't go out, he'll start shooting his gun in the air. The noise is going to wake Parker. Do you want him to hear the baby? Now, help me get dressed so I can placate the man. Please."

He pulled her hand away from his mouth and held on to her. "It's out of the question. I'm going out and kill the bastard. You got that?"

"No."

"It'll be a fair fight," he promised. "I'll make him draw."

She frantically shook her head at him. "Stop being so stubborn. Boyle won't be drawn into a fight. The man's a coward, Douglas. There isn't time to argue about this. You can protect me just fine from the front window. If he looks like he's going to hurt me, then you can come outside and make him leave. You aren't going to kill him though. Do you understand me?" The set of his jaw told her he didn't understand. "Please? Restrain yourself for my sake. All right?"

"Honest to God, I sure would like to—"

She stopped him cold by touching his cheek. "But you won't."

He wouldn't agree or disagree. "Maybe," was all he would allow.

She rolled her eyes heavenward. "The belt, please. Get the belt."

He took his own off and handed it to her. "You're not wearing anything that belonged to Parker."

The issue seemed to matter to him, and since his pants stayed put on the tilt of his hips, she didn't waste time arguing.

As soon as he went back to the window to check Boyle's progress, she got ready. She was still swollen around the middle, but not nearly enough to look as though she were drawing close to the delivery date she and Dr. Simpson had given Boyle.

She joined Douglas as Boyle was just reaching the flat at the base of the hill.

"Do I look as pregnant as I'm supposed to be?"

"I guess so."

She put her hand on his arm. "You're supposed to look at me before you decide."

He finally gave her a quick once-over. He didn't like what he saw and frowned to let her know exactly how he felt. Isabel was dressed in a white blouse and a dark blue jersey jumper that ballooned out around her middle, and in his opinion, she was too attractive for the bastard to see. Was she deliberately trying to entice him? No, of course she wasn't. She couldn't help being pretty, and unfortunately, he couldn't come up

with any ideas to radically change her appearance
. . . unless she was willing to wear a burlap bag
over her head. He didn't bother to suggest it
though, because he knew she wouldn't do it.

"Button up your blouse."

"It is buttoned."

"Not the top two," he said. He put his gun
back in his holster and took over the chore. "He
isn't going to see any more of you than he has
to," he told her.

His fingers rubbed against the bottom of her
chin. How in heaven's name could any woman
have such silky skin?

"He won't hurt me," she whispered.

His gaze moved to hers. "I'll make certain he
doesn't hurt you. If I have to kill him, I don't
want to hear any argument. Agreed?"

"Yes."

"Come on then. He's coming up to the cabin."

She reached for the doorknob, her attention
on Douglas while she waited for him to get into
position by the window. She didn't wait for him
to give her permission to go outside because she
knew she'd stand there the rest of the day if she
wanted the stubborn man to give her his approval.

"I'm going out now."

"Isabel?"

"Yes?"

"Don't you dare smile at him."

Six

Boyle was as ugly as sin. His face was covered with pockmarks, his eyes were set too close together, and his lips all but disappeared when he closed his mouth. The man looked like a chicken. Douglas wasn't surprised by his appearance though. The fact that he had to resort to terrorizing a woman in order to get married indicated the bastard had a serious problem attracting the fairer sex, and most women who had learned to look deeper would have been sickened by the evil lurking inside.

Douglas willed the man to move his hand toward his gun. Boyle wouldn't accommodate him. He didn't even bother to glance toward the window, but kept his gaze firmly directed on his prey.

Isabel held her own against him. "I told you to get off of my land. Now, get . . ."

"Is that any way to talk to your future husband, girl? And me planning a real party wedding for you. You're looking worried today. Are you getting scared about birthing that thing all alone?"

"You've got ten seconds to leave or I'll use this rifle."

"You'd go to prison if you did."

"No jury would ever convict me. Everyone in

Sweet Creek hates you as much as I do. Now, leave me alone."

He pointed his finger at her. "You watch your tongue around me, girl. I don't like sass. You've still got your fire inside you, and I'm going to have to do something about that after we're hitched. You will beg me to marry you, you know. It's only a matter of time."

She was cocking the rifle when he dug the spurs into his horse and rode away.

"I'll be back," he shouted. The threat was followed by his grating laughter.

Douglas kept Boyle in his sights until he was halfway across the field. Isabel came inside, shut the door softly behind her, and sagged against it.

"Damn, he's ugly," he muttered.

She nodded agreement. "He won't come back for another two weeks."

"Maybe," he allowed. "We're still going to be prepared for anything. Dr. Simpson told me Boyle will be leaving for some kind of family get-together."

"He's going away? Oh, Douglas, that's wonderful news."

"Simpson said he usually stays a month to six weeks with his family in the Dakotas. We aren't going to let our guard down or get lackadaisical."

"No, of course not. May I ask you something?"

He kept his gaze on the shadow starting up the path. "Sure."

"Won't you look at me?" she asked.

"Not until Boyle goes over the rise."

"I don't understand what's come over you. You told me you didn't want to let Boyle see you and that as long as he continues to think I'm all alone, he'll be content to wait. . . ."

"That was before I knew you always went outside to speak to him."

"But—"

"I don't like it."

She rolled her eyes heavenward. "Obviously not," she replied. "I'm still going to continue to go out every time he comes here, like it or not."

"We'll discuss it later. You shouldn't get upset, Isabel. The doctor said it isn't good for you."

"For heaven's sake, I'm not sick. Surely you've noticed I'm getting much stronger every hour. So is my son."

"Eight weeks from the minute Parker arrived," he announced with authority. "That's how long it will take him to get stronger."

"Surely not."

"Eight weeks," he stubbornly insisted.

"When will you be leaving?"

He smiled. "In eight weeks, unless you or Parker gets into trouble. Maybe longer. And by the way, Isabel, you and your son are going with me. I'm getting you out of here."

"No, you're not. I won't be run out of my own home. Do you understand me? No one is going to chase me off of my land."

Too late, he realized he'd upset her. Her voice had taken on a shrill quality, and when he looked at her, he saw the tears brimming in her eyes. He quickly tried to calm her.

"You can do what you want," he lied. "As long as it's eight weeks from now."

"You can't possibly stay here that long. I assure

you I'll be fully recovered sooner than that and Parker will be much stronger. We'll be just fine. We'll miss you, of course." *Desperately so,* she silently added.

He didn't know what compelled him to do it, but he leaned down and kissed her forehead. "You seem to be having trouble grasping numbers, sugar. I'm not leaving for eight weeks. Want me to tell you how many days that is?"

She knew he was teasing her but didn't have the faintest idea how to respond. Her husband had always been terribly serious about everything. He never flirted, nor did she, yet she knew Douglas was now doing just that. She decided to get away from him for a few minutes. She couldn't seem to think when he was so close.

"It's your decision," she said. "I won't be plagued by guilt, and if you don't mind staying, I . . . I mean to say, we . . . I *have* a baby, you know, and we'll be happy to have you around." She knew she was stammering her explanation. She'd also lied to him. She wouldn't be happy if he stayed. She would be ecstatic.

"Why don't you take your nap now?"

He was saying something to her, but she couldn't make herself pay any attention. She was trying to figure out how such a ruggedly hand-some man had managed to remain unattached so long. He had to be close to thirty if her guess was right. Perhaps he wasn't unattached after all. There could be a beautiful young lady patiently waiting for his return. Yes, that was it. She was probably very refined and elegant too, and Isabel imagined she had gold-colored hair that wasn't at all unruly with curls.

"Why did you kiss me?" she blurted out.

"I felt like it. Did you mind?"

"No . . . I didn't mind."

She told herself to snap out of her stupor. It was high time she faced a few important facts. She wasn't a naive young lady with hopes and dreams and yearnings to be loved. She was a widow with a baby who depended on her. She couldn't and wouldn't change her past. She had been blessed to have a dear friend for a companion, and now she had his beautiful son.

Still, there wasn't any harm in daydreaming about a future she could never have, was there? Wasn't it natural to wonder what it would feel like to be loved by a man like Douglas? Thinking about it seemed like a natural curiosity on her part. That was all. He was so strong and hard and sensual, and she'd never known anyone quite like him. Why, even though she was a new mother and didn't physically want him, she couldn't help but notice the erotic, earthy aura about him. Besides, there wasn't anything wrong with appreciating the wonderful differences between them, and, Lord, he was masculine all right.

He'd be a demanding lover, and he wouldn't stop until she had . . .

Good Lord, what was she doing? She forced the outrageous fantasy out of her mind.

"I believe I'll rest for a little while." He looked as if he was amused by her remark.

"Sounds good to me," he teased.

She turned, stumbled over something littering the floor, and yet hurried on. He followed her.

"Are you feeling all right?" he asked.

"Yes."

"You seem a little preoccupied."

"I need a nap, Douglas. I'm a brand-new mother and I must rest."

He leaned against the doorframe and refused to budge when she tried to shut the door.

"I would like some privacy so that I can change my clothes. I'll give you your belt back later."

"It's on the floor in the other room with the towels you used to look pregnant."

She didn't believe him until she put her hand on her waist. Good Lord, when had they fallen, and why hadn't she noticed?

"Want to tell me what you were thinking about a minute ago?"

She could feel herself blushing. "This and that."

"Is that what you call it?" he asked.

"The horses," she blurted out at the very same time. "Minerva and Pegasus. Yes, the Arabian stallion is Pegasus and his mate is Minerva. Didn't I tell you their names already?"

"Just Pegasus."

She really wished he would go away for a little while. The way he was looking at her was making her feel self-conscious and as awkward as a little girl. "What have you been calling my Arabians?"

"This and that."

He slowly brushed the back of his fingers down her cheek. "I think you should know something. I'm real partial to women with freckles. Yours

227

drive me wild." He leaned down and kissed her on the mouth quick and hard. "By the way," he whispered, "I'm having some real wild thoughts about you too."

He stunned the breath out of her, and he knew it. That was why he winked at her before he turned around and walked away. She stared after him until he disappeared into the kitchen; then she shut the door and fell back against it. Dear God, he'd known all the while what she was thinking about, and she was never, ever going to be able to look at him again.

She was mortified. She must have given herself away, but how in heaven's name had she done that? She didn't know, and she wasn't going to ask him. She wasn't going to have another scandalous thought about him for the rest of her life. In fact, she wouldn't think about him at all.

She threw herself down on the bed and groaned. She fell asleep a few minutes later with her feet hanging over the side of the bed, her shoes and stockings on, and one thought flitting through her mind.

He liked freckles.

Seven

He also liked games. He asked her during supper if she happened to have a deck of cards, which she did, and then he suggested they play poker.

"Have you ever played five card stud?"

"Oh, yes. I'm good too."

The challenge was issued. They played five hands before Parker demanded to be fed. It was past time for her to go to bed anyway, because she was looking as though she was about to doze off any minute.

At her insistence, he added up their scores and told her the amount she owed him.

She stood up, yawned, and said, 'I'll pay you back with my earnings tomorrow night when we play chess."

He laughed. "Are you good at chess too?"

"Wait and see."

Chess was his game. The following evening, he proved it to her by destroying her in a matter of minutes. He decided she obviously hadn't played a lot of checkers after he'd won five games in a row. By the end of the week, she owed him over a thousand dollars.

Douglas changed the rules from then on. He told her he had a much better idea. Instead of money, the winner could ask any question he or she wanted. No matter how personal the topic, an answer was required.

Suddenly, her skills improved. She won three games before he caught on to her ploy.

"You were deliberately letting me win, weren't you?"

"Some men like to win."

"Most men like to win fairly. From now on, we both play to win. Agreed?"

"Yes," she replied. "We should probably start all over. I let you win last night too."

He tore up the sheet of paper with the totals

before handing the deck of cards to her. She shuffled the cards like a dealer in Tommy's saloon, drawing a laugh from him.

"You little con."

"I've played a lot of cards," she admitted.

"No kidding."

She proved how good she was by winning the next game. Before he had even showed her his pitiful hand consisting of two jacks, she asked her question.

"You told me you were a thief, remember? I want to know when and where."

"When I was a boy, living on the streets of New York City. I took pretty much anything I wanted."

Her eyes widened in disbelief, yet her voice sounded as though she was in awe of his criminal background. "Did you ever get caught?"

"No, I never got caught. I was lucky."

After she'd won the following game, she asked him to tell her about his family. He explained how he, Travis, Cole, and Adam had joined together to become a family when they found a baby in a trash pile.

Isabel was fascinated, asked him a countless number of questions, and before he realized it, he'd talked for over an hour. By the time he was finished, he'd told her about his sister's husband, Harrison, and Travis's new bride, Emily. He saved the best for last and spoke in a soft voice when he talked about his Mama Rose.

"You know it's kind of odd really, now that I think about it, but Mama Rose is the reason I'm here. She heard about the Arabians and wanted me to come and see them. I was too busy at the time, and so I asked Travis to stop by the auction for me."

"Parker was going to sell Pegasus at an auction? That can't be true. The only time he left Sweet Creek was to go to an attorney's office way up in River's Bend. Paddy went with him, and I'm certain they both came back here right away."

Too late, Douglas realized he'd brought up a sore topic. "They probably stopped to rest their horses, that's all. By the way, Dr. Simpson told me about Paddy. Was he really crazy?"

"No, but everyone in town thought he was. He just had a few peculiarities. I got to know him quite well because he came to supper at least four times a week. He was much closer to Parker though. The two of them would put their heads together and talk in whispers well into the night. It was an odd friendship."

"Did Parker ever tell you what they talked about?"

"No, he was very secretive about it, so I didn't pester him to tell me. He said he'd promised Paddy not to discuss whatever plans they were hatching. I miss the Irishman. He had such a good heart. Did you know he was here before Sweet Creek was even a town?"

"No, I didn't," he said. "Tell me, did Parker keep other secrets from you?"

"If you're thinking he was going to sell Pegasus behind my back, you're wrong. Parker and I grew up together at an orphanage near Chicago, and I know everything there is to know about him. He wouldn't have done such a thing. He knew how much the horses meant to me. The sisters at the orphanage gave them to me so that I would have a dowry when I left them."

"Where did they get the Arabians?"

"They were donated to the orphanage by a man they took in. He was dying, and it was his way of thanking them, I suppose. He didn't have any relatives, and he was terrified of dying alone. The sisters sat with him day and night."

Douglas could see she was getting melancholy and quickly turned the topic. "Have I satisfied your curiosity about my family?"

She stopped frowning and shook her head. "How did Travis meet his wife, Emily?"

Douglas answered her question, and by the time he was finished, she was smiling again. It was obvious she had put the matter of Parker's selling Pegasus out of her mind for the moment.

"Does everyone like Emily?"

There was a yearning quality in her voice he didn't quite understand. Was she worried about the newest member of their family? If so, why?

"Yes, we all like her very much."

"I'm sure I would like her too," she said with a yawn she couldn't contain. "We should probably stop now. Could we play cards tomorrow night?"

"After I repair all the chairs. I still have three more to fix."

"You don't need to worry about that. I already fixed them."

He looked surprised. "Honestly, Douglas, I'm not helpless. I did a good job too. See for yourself."

He didn't believe her until he checked them. "You did a better job than I did."

"I watched you, remember?"

He did remember. He was impressed too that she would take the time and trouble after he had promised to do the task for her.

"Your eyelids are drooping now. You're sleepy, aren't you?"

"Yes. Good night, Douglas."

"Good night, sugar."

The next four weeks didn't drag. Douglas was surprised by how quickly the time passed and how comfortable he became in Isabel's home. He felt as though he were part of a family, and while that was a bit disturbing to him, it was also very, very nice.

He kept busy from sundown to sunup. Once a week he risked being seen during the day to hunt for fresh meat and to fish in a stream he'd found in the mountains west of the ranch. Every night he rode Brutus up into the hills to check on Boyle's lookouts to make certain there hadn't been any changes in their positions or numbers. When he returned to the ranch, he kept up with the ordinary chores, such as cutting wood and cleaning stalls.

His relationship with Isabel underwent a subtle change. In the beginning he'd deliberately teased her to make her feel good and smile. Now he teased her because her smiles made him feel good. He wasn't certain when it had happened, but he wasn't thinking of her as a new mother any longer. She had turned into a wonderfully sexy woman with all the right curves. Everything about her aroused him. He liked the way she spoke, the way she moved, the way she laughed. Dr. Simpson had been right when he'd said that Isabel was an easy woman to love. Douglas recognized that his heart was in jeopardy but couldn't figure out how to stop the inevitable from happening.

Like an old married couple, the two of them played cards every evening until it was dark enough for him to go outside. Several nights Parker joined them, and they took turns holding him while they played. Isabel won more games than he did, until he finally stopped staring at her freckles and started paying attention to what he was doing.

Boyle was way overdue for his next check on Isabel, and Douglas was getting edgy thinking about the bastard. He wanted to put an end to the terror tactics the coward used against her.

"You just won a game. Why are you frowning?"

"I was thinking about Boyle. He's late checking on you. You told me he usually comes here every other week to see you. . . ."

"He usually does," she agreed.

"Then why hasn't he? I know he hasn't left for the Dakotas yet because every Monday night when I check in with Dr. Simpson, that's the first question I ask him. Why is Boyle dragging his feet?"

"I don't know, but I don't want to think about him now. We'll be ready for him if he comes calling. Ask me your question so we can play another hand before Parker wants to be fed again."

"Why did you name the Arabians Pegasus and Minerva?"

"I was fascinated by mythology when I was in school. I used to draw pictures of Pegasus all the time. According to the legends, he was a beautiful white horse with majestic wings. Minerva was the Roman goddess of wisdom, and the sisters at the orphanage were constantly telling me I could certainly use a little wisdom. I didn't have much common sense back then," she thought to add. "Anyway, Minerva caught Pegasus and tamed him. I found that very romantic."

She covered her mouth, sneezed, then apologized.

"You don't need to apologize," he said. "Tell me something. Did Parker catch you the way Minerva caught Pegasus, or did you catch Parker?"

"It wasn't like that with Parker and me. We were best friends for as long as I can remember. The sisters at the orphanage called him their little dreamer. I'm sure they meant it as a compliment, because Parker had such a kind heart. He wanted to change the world, and he was very passionate about social responsibilities."

"Was Parker passionate with you?"

"I've answered enough questions. Deal the cards, please."

He could feel her withdrawing and knew it was because he was pressing her, yet he couldn't seem to make himself stop.

She sneezed again and immediately apologized.

He won a game and asked, "What was it like for you in the orphanage?"

"It was nice, very nice. The sisters treated us as though we were their very own children. They were strict, like I imagine parents would be, but loving too."

"Didn't you get lonely?"

"Not very often. I had Parker to tell my secrets to when we were children. I was fortunate, and so were you because you found a family."

"Yes, I was" he agreed.

About an hour later, he finally won another game.

"Wasn't it difficult marrying your best friend?"

"Oh, no," she answered. "It was very nice. My husband was a wonderful man with many fine qualities. Why, there wasn't anything he couldn't do."

Did she really believe that nonsense? From the look on her face, he thought she did, and so he didn't contradict her. In his opinion, there wasn't anything Parker *could* do.

"Yeah, I know. The man was a saint."

Her chin came up a notch. "He was my dearest friend."

"Which means there wasn't any passion in your bed, was there?"

"You have no business asking me such personal questions."

She was right about that, he told himself, yet it didn't stop him from trying to find out everything he could about her. "What are you afraid of, Isabel? Being honest about your late husband doesn't make you a traitor. We both know it had to have been awkward making love to your best friend."

"Are you suggesting you can't be friends with your mate?"

"No," he replied. "But there has to be another element involved besides friendship."

"What element?"

He leaned forward. "Magic."

She shook her head. "I don't wish to discuss this topic any longer. It's rude of you to try to guess what my marriage was like. You never met Parker."

"I wasn't guessing," he argued. "I've already figured it all out."

"Is that so? How did you manage to do that?"

The sarcasm in her voice irritated him. "It was easy," he snapped. "The way you respond to me . . . it's all new to you, isn't it? I can see it in your every reaction. You're actually frightened by what's happening to you."

Her hands were balled into fists. "Oh? What exactly is happening to me? I'm sure you're just dying to tell me."

He leaned over the table toward her. In a low whisper he said, "I'm what's happening to you, sugar."

She bounded to her feet. "I'm going to bed. It's late."

"Don't you mean it's time for you to run and hide from me?"

"No, that isn't what I mean to say."

She took her time strolling into the bedroom. She wanted to run.

Eight

Parker wasn't putting on weight as rapidly as Douglas had hoped he would. The baby was almost six weeks old, but he still seemed to be as tiny as the day he was born. Isabel disagreed and insisted that her son had gained quite a bit of weight. Parker seemed healthy enough for his size, and he certainly had a good appetite. Dr. Simpson was the expert, and he had ordered that Parker be kept inside the cabin for a minimum of eight weeks. Douglas didn't know why the physician had settled on that specific length of time, but Douglas was going to adhere to the number no matter how anxious he was to leave.

If Parker continued to do well, he and his mother could travel in a little over fourteen days. Douglas hoped to God the weather improved before then. The rain had let up, but it was still cold and damp, and anyone who hadn't kept track of the seasons would have thought it was the middle of autumn. The night air was cold enough to require heavy flannel shirts, and Douglas was worried about keeping Parker warm when he was taken outside. Would the night air be too harsh for him to breathe?

The baby wasn't the only one he was worried about. Honest to Pete, he didn't know how he was going to last another two weeks without touching Isabel. Being in the same room with her was all it took to get him bothered. Her scent was so damned appealing, and her skin was so soft and smooth, all he wanted to think about was taking her into his arms and stroking her.

He was determined not to give in to his natural inclinations. He didn't want any complication in his life, and if he kept busy every waking hour, he was sure he'd be too tired to think about her.

After he finished up the chores in the barn around dawn, he went inside the cabin and found Isabel sitting at the table with her head in her hands. Her hair was tousled; her eyes were bleary, and her nose was bright red. She looked hungover.

"Did Parker keep you up all night?"

She sneezed before she answered. "No, I caught a little cold," she said, and promptly sneezed again.

"Maybe you should go back to bed."

She wouldn't hear of it. She had never coddled herself before, and she wasn't about to start now. After doing the washing and ironing, she cooked supper, but she couldn't eat any of it, so she fixed herself a pot of tea before she headed to bed.

She had changed into her nightgown and robe and had wrapped around her shoulders an old tattered blanket that dragged on the floor behind her. She tripped over the hem and would have dropped the tray if he hadn't grabbed it from her.

"I'll bring it in," he said. "You should probably eat something, shouldn't you? What about some toast?"

Didn't that man know how to fix anything else? "Will you try not to burn it?" she said, trying not to sound surly.

He nodded. "You probably got sick because you work too hard."

"It's just a cold. I hope to heaven Parker doesn't catch it. What will we do if he gets a fever?"

He didn't want to think about the possibility. Parker couldn't afford to stop eating the way Isabel had.

"We'll deal with it," he assured her.

When he came back with the tray, she was just drifting off to sleep. She opened her eyes as he was turning to leave. "I'm awake."

He put the tray on the dresser, propped pillows behind her back, and then moved the tray to her lap.

He'd burned the toast again. He'd also put a white rose on the tray next to her mismatched teacup and saucer. The rose was such a sweet touch her mood improved, and she didn't mind eating the blackened bread at all.

"Is your throat sore?" he whispered.

"No. Please stop worrying."

"Isabel, I want to worry, all right? I'm good at it."

She patted the bed, waited for him to sit, and then picked up the rose. "You may be a worrier, but you're also a romantic at heart."

He shook his head and continued to frown at her. Still, his concern was unreasonable, given the fact that she was only suffering from a stuffy head.

She reached up and stroked his cheek, loving the feel of his rough skin. He hadn't shaved this morning, and the dark growth of whiskers made him look even more ruggedly handsome and somewhat dangerous.

She remembered how afraid she'd been that dark rainy night when they met. Silhouetted against the lightning with the rising wind howling around him and the huge beast of a horse with wild eyes beside him, he was a terrifying sight. She had been certain he was going to kill her . . . until he gave the rifle back to her. She should have realized before then that he would never harm her. The gentle tone of his voice when he turned to calm the animal was one indication. The way he so carefully lifted her into his arms was certainly another. His eyes, filled with such compassion and . . .

"Isabel, you look like hell. Stop daydreaming and drink your tea before it gets cold."

She was jarred back to the present by his brisk order. "Has anyone ever told you how bossy you are, Douglas?"

"No."

"Then let me be the first. You're very bossy. Do you remember the night we met?"

The question was laughable. He shuddered every time he thought about it. "I'll never forget it."

The scowl on his face made her smile. "It wasn't that terrible."

"Yeah, it was."

"Was I difficult?"

"Oh, yes."

"I couldn't have been any worse than any of the other women you helped. I wasn't, was I?"

"I've helped lots of . . . females."

"Yes?"

He shrugged. "Yes, what?"

"Was I more difficult than the others?"

"Definitely."

"How?" she demanded.

"The others didn't try to strangle me."

"I didn't—"

"Yes, you did."

"What else did I do? It's all right. You can tell me. I promise I won't get mad." She picked up the teacup and saucer and took a long sip. "I'm waiting."

"I remember you accused me of a lot of crimes."

The glint in his eyes made it difficult for her to tell if he was being honest or not.

"Such as?"

"Let's see," he drawled out. "There were so many it's hard to keep them straight. Oh, yeah, I remember. You blamed me for getting you pregnant."

The teacup rattled in the saucer. "I didn't," she whispered.

"Yes, you did. You almost had me convinced too. Hell, I apologized," he added with a grin. "I wasn't responsible though. Trust me, sugar. I would have remembered taking you to bed."

Her blush was as red as her nose. She put the cup down on the tray but kept her attention centered on Douglas. He could tell she was trying hard not to laugh.

"What else did I accuse you of?"

"Being responsible for your agony."

"You already mentioned that one."

"Sorry. It's just kind of hard to get past it."

"Please try."

"Let's see. I was also responsible for the rain, and, oh, yeah, this one's a doozy. It was my fault you had an unhappy childhood."

"I didn't have an unhappy childhood."

"Could have fooled me. I apologized."

She burst into laughter. "You do love to exaggerate, don't you? I'm certain the other women you helped were just as difficult."

"No, they weren't."

"Who were these women? Saints?"

He moved the tray to the side table as a precautionary measure before he answered. "They weren't exactly women, at least not the way you're thinking. . . ."

She stopped smiling. "Then what were they?"

"Horses."

Her mouth dropped open. Much to his relief, she didn't become angry. She laughed instead. "Oh, Lord, you must have been as terrified as I was."

"Yes."

"Did you have any idea what to do?"

He grinned. "Not really."

She laughed until tears came into her eyes, then realized the noise would wake Parker and quickly covered her mouth with her hand. "You were so . . . calm . . . and . . . reassuring about it all."

"I was scared."

"You?"

"Yes, me. You got real mean. That was even scarier."

"No, I didn't. Quit teasing me. I remember exactly what happened. I was in control at all times. I do recall raising my voice once or twice so you could hear me in the other room, but other than that, labor wasn't bad at all."

"Isabel, are we talking about childbirth or a tea party you attended?"

"I've never been to a tea party, but I have given birth, and I want you to know that my little aches and pains were insignificant compared to the beautiful gift I received. He's wonderful."

"Who's wonderful?"

She was exasperated. "My son. Who did you think I was talking about?"

"Me."

She would have laughed again if she hadn't started sneezing. He handed her a fresh handkerchief, told her to rest, and finally left her alone so she could.

Much to his relief, she got better in a couple of days, and thus far, Parker still hadn't caught her cold. By late Monday afternoon, Douglas was exhausted. He was drifting off to sleep in the rocker with Parker cradled in his arms when he heard the distinct sound of horses approaching. Isabel was fixing supper. She had spotted the unwanted visitors at the same time that he had heard them, for they met by the table on their way to alert one another. She reached for her son and hurried to get ready.

Douglas went to the window to check their

progress. He muttered every blasphemy he could think of while he watched Boyle and a stranger who he assumed was one of the hired men coming across the yard. Douglas made up his mind to personally greet the two men. No way in hell was he going to let Isabel go outside. The terror tactics were going to stop. He actually smiled as he reached for the doorknob.

She watched him draw his weapon. She didn't have to be a mind reader to know what he was planning to do. There wasn't time to say a prayer for the sin she was going to commit. "Douglas, we're going to have to let Boyle wait. You need to look at Parker. I think he has a fever. Let Boyle wait," she repeated in a much more forceful voice.

She waited until Douglas had bolted the door and gone rushing past her, and then she asked for God's forgiveness as she picked up the rifle and ran to greet Boyle. She had to get outside before Douglas realized she'd tricked him. He was going to be furious.

Boyle was just raising his gun to fire in the air when she stepped outside. She kept one hand behind her back on the doorknob, holding it closed, and propped the rifle under her arm. Her finger was on the trigger.

"What do you want?" she demanded.

Boyle grinned at her. Isabel could barely stomach the sight. The stranger sitting atop a black mount sneered at her. She couldn't see his eyes because the brim of his hat was pulled down low over his brow, but she could feel his gaze boring into her. Like Boyle, the stranger apparently didn't consider the rifle much of a threat. He had both hands stacked on top of his pommel.

"You ain't being very sociable, Isabel, pointing your rifle at me."

"Get off my land, Boyle."

"I'll go when I'm ready. I came here to tell you I'm going to be away for a spell. Don't go getting your hopes up 'cause I'm coming back. I'm going to my annual family get-together, and I expect I'll be away a good six weeks, maybe even longer. Now, I don't want you feeling lonely while I'm gone, so I'm putting my right-hand man in charge of you. His name is Spear."

He turned to his cohort, told him to tip his hat to his future bride, and then turned back to Isabel.

"Spear's going to watch out for you. I've put some of my men up on the mountain yonder to watch over you too. They'll be staying day and night. Are you comforted by my thoughtfulness? I wouldn't want you to think you had to leave while I was gone. Next year you'll be going with me. You understand what I'm saying, girl?"

The mockery in his voice infuriated her. "Go away," she shouted.

He laughed. "I expect you will have had that thing by the time I get back. Your figure should be nice and curvy again by the time we get married. Are you about ready to accept your future, honey bell, and start begging me?"

She answered him by cocking her rifle. Spear's hand went to his gun, but he didn't draw.

Boyle jerked on his reins and rode away. Spear followed. "Didn't I tell you she was full of spit and vinegar?" Boyle shouted. "She'll beg me though, and she'll do it in front of the entire town. Just you wait and see."

Isabel didn't hear Spear's answer. Boyle's laughter drowned it out. She stood there on the stoop for several minutes, watching them leave . . . and gathering the gumption to face Douglas again.

She considered staying where she was for the rest of the day, but Douglas had other ideas. She didn't hear the door open. She did feel herself being pulled backward though, and the grip on her waist, even with the padding, felt like a vice. Fortunately, she had enough presence of mind to put the safety on the rifle before she dropped it.

He caught it before it hit the floor, kicked the door closed, and turned her around to face him before he let go of her.

The padding around her waist dropped to the floor, and she kicked it out of the way. She had already determined the strategy she would employ. From the look in his eyes, she knew he wasn't going to be reasonable, and since her only defense was to retreat or attack, she chose the latter.

She took a step forward, planted her hands on her hips, and frowned up at him.

"You listen to me, Mr. Clayborne. If you had gone outside, you would have tried to shoot both of them, and one of them might have killed you. And just where would Parker and I be then, I ask you? Boyle has friends, remember? If you'd killed him, they'd come looking for him, and we would have to fight twenty-some men off while trying to protect an infant. I'm a good shot, and I imagine you are too, but I'm also a realist, and there's no way we could get all of them before we were killed. Am I getting through to you yet?"

She guessed she wasn't when he spoke. "If he comes here again, you aren't going outside to talk to him."

"I knew you'd be stubborn about this."

"You lied to me, and I want you to promise me you'll never do it again."

"Now you've done it. You woke the baby. You go get him."

"Neither one of us is moving until I get your promise. You have any idea how scared I got when I thought Parker was sick? Damn it, Isabel, if you ever lie to me . . ."

"If it meant saving your hide, I'd lie again. We should be celebrating now, not bickering. Didn't you hear what Boyle said? He's finally leaving. That's wonderful news."

"I'm waiting."

"Oh, all right. I promise never to lie to you again. Now, if you'll excuse me, I'll go to my son."

"I'll get him."

All Parker needed was a dry bottom, and as soon as Douglas changed him, the baby went back to sleep.

Douglas couldn't get Spear off his mind. From the look of him, Douglas knew he was going to be a much more dangerous threat than Boyle could ever be.

Isabel noticed how quiet he was during supper

and asked him to tell her what he was thinking about.

"Spear," he answered. "Boyle doesn't worry me nearly as much as his new hired hand does."

"I disagree. Boyle's cruel and heartless."

"He's also a coward."

"How do you know that?"

"He preys on women, that's how I know. He isn't going to be a problem to get rid of now that I know what his biggest flaw is."

"He has at least a hundred flaws, but you still can't kill him. You'd spend the rest of your life in prison . . . or hang, God forbid."

"I won't kill him. I've thought of something worse. I'm kind of looking forward to his day of reckoning too."

"What are you going to do?"

"Wait and see."

"Is it legal?"

He shrugged, then said, "I wonder if Boyle has hired any other new men."

"Do you mean like Spear?"

He nodded. "Since Boyle was nice enough to let us know he has men watching the ranch, I'm going to ride up in the hills every night and listen in on their conversation for a little while."

"Is that necessary?

"Yes, it's necessary," he insisted. "Parker's going to be eight weeks old soon and Dr. Simpson said he would be strong enough to move."

"He also said ten weeks would be better."

"Is Parker putting on any weight?"

"Of course he is."

Douglas wasn't convinced. "Every time I pick

him up, I realize how fragile and tiny he is. He doesn't feel any heavier to me."

"Do you forget how big you are? No wonder he doesn't feel heavier to you. He is getting stronger every day, but it's still too soon to take him out in the cold night air."

"We might have to chance it," he argued.

"I won't put him in jeopardy."

"And staying here isn't doing just that?"

"I really don't want to talk about this now."

"Too bad," he snapped. "We're going to talk about it. You have to listen to reason. My brothers will help protect you and Parker, and it's best if we leave while Boyle's away. I'll make sure he really left town before . . ."

She was vehemently shaking her head. "Parker's too little to be taken out."

"If the doctor thinks we should risk it, will you be reasonable then?"

She had to think about it for a long while before she finally agreed. "As long as you don't change his mind for him. Don't try to talk him into it, Douglas."

He agreed with a nod. "Do you have any idea what you want to do when you leave here?"

She still hadn't made up her mind about the future. She could either move back to Chicago and teach at the orphanage or stay in Sweet Creek and secure a teaching position in town or in nearby Liddyville.

The future didn't frighten her. It was leaving the past behind that made her ache so. She was a realist and she knew she had to leave the ranch because of the dangerous spot where her late husband had insisted their home be built. Eventually the flood waters would wash the cabin away. Yes, she knew she had to leave, yet the idea of packing up and walking away made her feel like such a failure. The land and the home were the fulfillment of Parker's dream. He had died protecting it, and, God help her, where was she going to get the strength to leave his dream behind?

Douglas wouldn't understand the anguish she felt, and she didn't want to explain it.

"I don't want to discuss it now."

"You're going to have to face the future sooner or later."

She got up from the table and hurried into the kitchen. "I have time to decide, now that Boyle's leaving."

"No, you don't have time, unless you've lost your mind and believe anything that bastard tells you."

"Do you like cake? I thought I'd bake one and you could have some when you get back from town."

"For the love of God, you've got to face facts, not bake."

She pushed the curtain back so she could see him. "I want to bake now." Each word was said in a slow, precise monotone. "I work problems out in my mind when I bake. Do you like cake or not?"

She looked mad enough to shoot him if he told her no. He gave up trying to make her be reasonable. "Sure."

Douglas left the ranch a few minutes later. He

checked on Boyle's lookouts before he headed into town and didn't arrive at Simpson's house until midnight.

The doctor was waiting at the kitchen table with a steaming cup of coffee in one hand and his pistol in the other.

"You're late tonight," he remarked. "Sit down and I'll get you some coffee, son. How's the baby doing?"

Douglas pulled out the chair, straddled it, and told the doctor not to bother with coffee.

"Parker's doing all right, but Isabel's recovering from a cold. What should we do if the baby catches it?"

"Keep him warm. . . ."

"We've been keeping him warm. Isn't there anything else we can do? What if he gets a fever?"

"Douglas, it won't do any good to snap at me. The baby's too small for medicine. We just have to hope and pray he doesn't get sick."

"I want to get them both out of that death trap she calls home. If I'm real careful, couldn't I . . . ."

He stopped trying to plead his case when Simpson shook his head at him.

"It's a miracle that baby's surviving, and that's a fact, coming early the way he did. Do you realize how you'd be tempting fate by taking him out at night? And where are you thinking you'll take them? Boyle will turn Sweet Creek upside down searching for them, and you don't dare risk going to Liddyville because you won't know who Boyle has in his hip pocket. I know we've been over this before. Boyle's got friends in Liddyville too, and someone will hear about your arrival. Folks gossip with one another. I'm telling you, it's too dangerous."

Douglas could feel a pounding headache coming on. "What a mess," he muttered.

"Is Isabel anxious to leave?"

He shook his head. "She knows she has to, but she won't talk about her future yet. She keeps putting it off. It's damned frustrating."

"I know it is. I've got some more bad news for you," Simpson said. "Boyle went and hired himself a new man. He goes by the name of Spear, and he's got a real mean look about him. I nosed around to find out what I could and heard that Boyle met Spear when he was on one of his annual trips back to family in the Dakotas. By the way, Boyle's leaving tomorrow morning. I heard him telling Jasper Cooper he was putting Spear in charge while he's gone." The doctor took a drink of his coffee, and then said, "No one in town suspects Isabel's gotten help. Time's on your side because you've got at least another month to fatten that baby up and get him thriving before Boyle comes back."

"You told me the baby could be moved when he was eight weeks old."

"I also told you ten would be better."

"If I could bring help in now, couldn't—"

"Think it through, son. You don't want to put Isabel and her son in the middle of a war, do you? No, of course you don't. Look on the bright side," he suggested. He ignored Douglas's incredulous look and continued on. "You've done fine for over seven weeks now, and I'm sure you can hold out a little longer without any trouble at all. Then you can send for help and get Isabel and her son out of there. I still don't cotton to the notion of taking that baby out at night, but the more weight he has on him, the better his chances will be. With Boyle away, it should get easier. Do you see? It isn't all grim, is it?"

"Hell, yes, it is."

Simpson chuckled. "She's getting to you, isn't she, son?"

Douglas shrugged but didn't say a word.

"I can see it plain as day. Are you thinking about falling in love with our girl?"

"No." He gave the denial with passion and conviction.

It wasn't a lie because he wasn't "thinking" about it. He already was in love with her.

Nine

Douglas's life was miserable. He had never experienced such acute frustration before, and needless to say, he didn't like it at all. He was also angry with Isabel most of the time. Fortunately, she didn't know how he felt, and he was certain she didn't notice how he stared at her whenever she was in the room. The doctor was right when he'd told Douglas that she was too pretty for her own good.

He tried to stay away from her as much as possible. He vowed to stop trying to get her to acknowledge the physical attraction between them. It was wrong to do so and he knew it. Besides, it was apparent that she wasn't ready to admit that her marriage had been less than satisfactory or that Parker had had a few glaring inadequacies. If she was determined to elevate the man to sainthood, that was just fine with Douglas. From now on, no matter how ignorant, incompetent, and foolish he personally believed the man had been, he would keep his opinion to himself. What right did he have to criticize the dead anyway? And why did it bother him that she was so devoted to Parker's memory?

Because she obviously still loved Parker.

Douglas recognized he wasn't being logical. The issue bothering him was loyalty. He had always liked people who proved they were loyal, especially when it wasn't easy. They were several notches above everyone else in character. Like his family . . . and Isabel. Yes, Isabel. She continued to be loyal to her dead husband, and the truth was, Douglas didn't expect less from her. Still, did she have to be so blindly loyal? She had given Parker her faith, her love, and her undying loyalty, and he had failed on all counts.

It wasn't going to matter to Douglas any longer. Just as soon as the baby put on a little more weight, he would get the two of them out of Sweet Creek, take care of Boyle and his hired gunslingers and then go back home, where he belonged. Until that day arrived, he planned to be polite but distant with Isabel.

That was easier said than done.

The days were unbearable, for as soon as he

fell asleep, his mind was filled with erotic dreams about her. He couldn't control his thoughts when he was at rest, and he soon got to the point where he dreaded closing his eyes.

She'd made it worse for him by demanding that he stop sleeping on his bedroll and use her bed. She had a valid argument. She was awake during the day, and if he moved little Parker's bed into the outer room, Douglas could sleep without interruption.

The problem wasn't the noise. He didn't want to be surrounded by her light, feminine scent, but he'd go to his death before he told her so. She wouldn't understand anyway, and because he didn't want to hurt her feelings, he tossed and turned, gritted his teeth, and wondered how much torture a man could take before he snapped.

The baby was the only joy in his life. Parker was slowly putting on weight and seemed to be getting stronger with each passing day. Although it didn't seem possible, he grew louder as well. Douglas didn't think infants developed personalities until they were much older, around five or six months, but Isabel's son proved to be as extraordinary as his sister, Mary Rose, when she'd been a baby.

Parker was thinner than Mary Rose, but he was still able to exert his power over both adults by simply opening his mouth and screaming for service.

Douglas had given his heart to the little tyrant. Admittedly there were times when he was pacing back and forth in the middle of the night with the baby up against his shoulder that he wanted to pack cotton in his ears just to get a moment of blissful silence. Yet there were also times when Parker had his fist wrapped around one of Douglas's fingers, gripping it tight. Douglas would look down at the baby sleeping so peacefully in his arms and feel the tremendous bond that had formed between them. He had helped bring Parker into the world and, like a father, he longed to watch him grow.

Oh, yes, Parker was a joy to be around. His mother wasn't. The physical attraction to her kept getting stronger, and though he tried to convince himself that she was untouchable, the pretense didn't work. After living together so intimately for eight weeks, the tension and frustration had become palpable.

Isabel had a different point of view. She was certain Douglas couldn't wait to be rid of her. He could barely stomach being in the same room with her, and no matter how she tried to get his attention, he blatantly ignored her. If she accidentally touched his arm, or not so accidentally moved closer to him, he became tense and out of sorts.

His attitude upset her more than she wanted to admit. Heaven help her, she was even having indecent dreams about him, and in every single one of them, she was always the aggressor. She couldn't understand why she wasn't dreaming about her late husband. She should be, shouldn't she? Parker had been her dearest friend. Douglas was a friend too, but he was the complete opposite of her husband, for while Parker had been sweet and gentle but somewhat impractical, Douglas was passionate, sexy, incredibly virile, and practical about everything from childbirth to politics. He was filled with confidence, and for the first time in her life, she felt as though she had someone who could, and would, do his part. Until Douglas had come along, she had carried the burden alone.

She wanted him in a way she had never wanted her husband, and that was painfully difficult for her to admit. Mating with her husband had been a necessary duty to produce a child, which both Isabel and Parker wanted, but neither one of them joined together with any enthusiasm. She had been overjoyed to realize she was pregnant, but she'd also been relieved. After Dr. Simpson confirmed the diagnosis, neither she nor her husband ever again reached for the other during the night.

Isabel ached over the loss of her dear friend, but she didn't miss what she had never experienced . . . until Douglas came into her life.

She wanted to dislike him just to stop herself from having such inappropriate daydreams about him, yet she also dreaded their eventual separation.

She wasn't the only one filled with confusion. She was certain she was confusing God as well. She prayed that Douglas would leave. She prayed that he would stay. Hopefully, God would be able to sort it all out.

Late one afternoon Douglas caught her bathing. She had assumed he was sound asleep, since the bedroom door was closed and she'd been as quiet as a mouse while she filled the metal tub with water she'd heated over the flames in the hearth. She didn't want to awaken him, so she had eased into the water and washed every inch of her body without making a single splash or once sighing out loud. She had just retied the ribbon holding her hair atop her head, leaned back, and closed her eyes, when she heard the telltale groan of a floorboard.

She opened her eyes just as Douglas walked out of the bedroom.

They both froze. Too stunned to speak, she could only stare up at him in true astonishment. He looked thunderstruck, making it more than apparent he hadn't expected to find her stripped bare, sitting in a tub of water with her shoulders and toes peeking out at him.

He didn't have all his clothes on. She noticed right away. His legs were braced apart. He was barefoot and wore only a pair of snug buckskin pants he hadn't bothered to button. Dark curly hair covered his chest, and when her gaze began to move lower, she forced herself to close her eyes.

She finally found her voice. "You forgot to button your pants, for heaven's sake."

She had to be joking. He wasn't stark naked; she was. He didn't look at her for more than a second or two, but it was still long enough for him to see golden shoulders, pink toes, and damn near everything in between.

Ah, hell, she had a sprinkle of freckles on her breasts.

He got even with her for her inadvertent torture

the only way he could. He turned around, stomped back into the bedroom, and slammed the door behind him.

The noise awakened the baby, infuriating her. She was suddenly so angry with Douglas there wasn't room for embarrassment, and if she hadn't regained her wits in the nick of time, she would have chased after him wrapped in only a thin towel so that she could tell him she was sick and tired of being treated like a leper.

The baby had other ideas. By the time she dried herself off and put her robe on, he had worked himself into a rage. He was tearing at his mouth with his tiny fists while he screamed for his milk. The drawer was on the table, and as she lifted him into her arms, her anger intensified. Her sweet baby shouldn't have to sleep in a dresser drawer for the love of God, and just why hadn't Douglas done something about it?

After she had changed Parker's diaper and gown, she sat in the rocker and fed him. She whispered to him all about Douglas's transgressions. Parker's eyes were open, and he stared up at her until he had taken his fill. Before she'd even moved him to her shoulder, he let out a loud belch, closed his eyes, and went back to sleep.

She held him in one arm and rocked him until she got dizzy and realized how fast she was going.

Douglas came out a minute later. She didn't dare speak to him while she was so angry. She needed to calm down first.

She handed the baby to him without bothering to look up, changed the bedding in the drawer, then reclaimed her son and put him down for the night.

Supper was almost ready. She'd made a big iron kettle of thick stew and only needed to move the drawer, set the table and warm the biscuits.

He didn't stay inside long enough to eat. He told her he had chores to do, and left. She knew he was as angry with her as she was with him, but he wouldn't lose his temper no matter how much or how often he was provoked, and if that wasn't the most frustrating trait in a man, she didn't know what was. Did he have to be so stoic all the time? Come to think of it, he never ever lost his control, and that simply wasn't human, was it?

He exhibited amazing restraint. The longer she thought about that horrible flaw, the angrier she became. Then she burned the biscuits, and, honest to heaven, that was the last straw. He was going to eat them anyway, she vowed, even if she had to force them down his throat. He was also going to eat the stew she'd spent hours preparing.

Isabel knew she wasn't being reasonable. It didn't seem to matter. It felt good to be angry and frustrated and know that she could blow up at him and still remain perfectly safe. Yes, safe. He made her feel safe, and so gloriously alive, even when he was acting like a bad-tempered boar.

She decided to behave like an adult. She would take his supper to him in the barn as a peace offering. That act of thoughtfulness would surely get him out of his contrary mood. After he'd eaten, she would demand that he tell her what was bothering him and why he'd become so impossible to live with lately. If he wanted specifics, she had plenty.

She checked on Parker one last time, tied her hair back with a white ribbon, and then carried the tray to the barn. She practiced what she would say to him on the way. "I was sure you would be hungry by now, and so I . . ."

No, she could do better than that. She wanted to sound blasé, not timid.

"I'll leave the tray by the door, Douglas. If you get hungry, help yourself," she whispered. Yes, that was better, much better. Then she would suggest they sit down and talk when he was finished.

She straightened her shoulders and went inside. She spotted Douglas at the opposite end of the barn. He had his sleeves rolled up and was pouring a large bucket of water into a metal vat. Two empty buckets were on the floor next to him. He straightened up, rolled his shoulders to work the stiffness out, brushed his hands off on a towel he'd draped over a post, and went to Pegasus's stall.

She walked forward so she could see the stallion. She could hear Douglas whispering to the animal, but she couldn't hear what he was saying. She saw him stroke the stallion's neck, and Pegasus was letting him know how much he liked the attention by nuzzling Douglas's shoulder.

He knew she was there watching him. He'd have to be dead and buried not to hear all the racket she was making. She'd talked herself into the barn and was now obviously having difficulty holding on to the tray. She was either nervous or making the noise on purpose to get him to notice her. The glass was banging against the plate, and out of the corner of his eye, he could see the utensils bouncing up and down.

He wanted to get past his irritation before he spoke to her. If he so much as looked at her now, he knew he'd lose his temper, hurt her tender feelings, and then feel rotten about it.

"Douglas, how long are you going to ignore me?"

He finally turned around. "I thought I'd try to figure out why you broke your promise to me. You remember, don't you? I'm sure I asked you to give me your word that you would stay inside at night because I can't keep watch over you and be in the barn at the same time."

She put the tray down on the seat of the buggy to her right before answering him.

"Yes, I remember, but I thought you might be hungry, and I—"

He deliberately interrupted her. "Do you also remember why we thought it might be dangerous?"

"Douglas, you don't have to treat me like a child. I know exactly what I promised. I know why you were so insistent too. I told you that once . . . just once, some of Boyle's men got all liquored up and rode down the hill during the night, and that was when you suggested I stay inside."

"You left something out."

"I did?"

He gave her a look that let her know he didn't

believe she'd forgotten. "You told me they tried to break into the cabin. Remember?"

She knew he was right. She shouldn't have taken the risk. She should have stayed inside the cabin with her son. It was her duty to protect him. Oh, Lord, the Winchester! She'd left the rifle by the window.

"I wasn't thinking. There, are you happy? I admitted it. I've been preoccupied lately. Now, if you'll excuse me, I'll go back to my son."

She turned around and hurried out of the barn. "Isabel, where's the rifle?"

She didn't answer. He knew good and well where it was, since she hadn't had it in her hands when she'd come into the barn. He'd asked the question just to make her feel like an idiot. She certainly felt like one, and that made her angry with herself. If she hadn't been so distracted by Douglas, she would never have done such a foolish thing.

Douglas strode past her and checked on Parker. The baby was sleeping soundly in the drawer on the table. He would have moved him back to the bedroom, but his hands were greasy, and he decided to wait until he had washed first. Isabel stood by his side, looking down at her son. Douglas didn't say another word to her. The two of them were past due for a long discussion about her future, he decided, and just as soon as he had cleaned up, he planned to sit her down and force her to make a few decisions.

He grabbed a thick, clean towel, a bar of soap, and headed back to the barn to take a bath.

He scrubbed the dirt from his body, but the

cold water didn't rid him of the fever he'd felt for weeks now, every time he thought about Isabel. Unfortunately, that was most of the days and nights. No, cold water didn't help. He could have washed in snow and still burned inside to touch her.

He needed to get away from her as soon as possible, but he couldn't do that until she told him where, in God's name, she wanted to go. She had procrastinated as long as he was going to allow. Before the night was over, she was going to make a decision. Douglas knew he needed to get a grip on himself. He knew how too. All he had to do was get the hell away from Isabel, because she was turning him into a raving animal.

Things were going to change from this moment on. He put on clean clothes, turned down the lantern light, and went to have the long overdue talk with Isabel.

She was waiting for him.

He took the tray with the untouched supper to the kitchen. "We need to talk," he whispered so he wouldn't disturb the baby. "First, I'll put Parker away."

"Back in the dresser?" Her voice was brittle.

"This isn't the time to get into one of your moods Isabel. We need to . . ."

"One of my moods? I can't believe you just said . . . Leave the drawer on the table and come with me. I want you to see something."

She hurried into the bedroom so he wouldn't argue with her. As soon as he came inside, she shut the door and then dramatically pointed to the bedroll on the floor next to her bed.

"Would you mind explaining why you slept on the floor today when there was a perfectly good bed a foot away? I think I know why, but I want to hear you tell me anyway."

"Why do you think I slept on the floor?" he hedged.

"Because the thought of getting into my bed was so repulsive you chose the hard floor instead. I'm right, aren't I?"

"No, you aren't."

He had the gall to scowl, and that infuriated her.

She moved to the other side of the bed to put some distance between them. "You don't have to deny it. I know you don't like being here. You can barely stand to be in the same room with me. What did I do to make you feel this way, Douglas? No, don't answer that. I think the time has come for you to leave. That's what you were going to talk about, wasn't it?"

He couldn't believe a woman could be this naive. She'd twisted everything around, and, honest to God, he couldn't figure out how she had come up with such outrageous conclusions. Hadn't anyone ever told her how pretty she was?

"You really don't have any idea what I'm thinking, do you?" He was astonished by the revelation.

She took a deep breath, ordered herself to stop criticizing him, and then apologized. "I'm sorry I snapped at you. If it weren't for you, I don't know what Parker and I would have done. I felt so powerless then. I should be thanking you for your help, and my only excuse for acting like a shrew is that I haven't been feeling myself lately."

"Why is that?"

"Why? Take a look around, Douglas. My life is in shambles. I don't know how—"

"Now, Isabel, it isn't that bleak."

He was going to remind her she had a handsome son who was getting stronger every day, but she didn't give him time to get another word in.

She wasn't in the mood to be reasonable and didn't particularly like being contradicted. Her voice became shrill when she continued on.

"Of course it's bleak. My son is sleeping in a dresser drawer, for God's sake, when he should have a proper cradle, and I shouldn't have to be terrified every time it rains. Don't you think I know where Parker had the cabin built? Everyone in town tried to talk him out of it, but he was determined to prove them wrong. There, are you happy? I've admitted he wasn't perfect. Neither are you, Douglas. You're rude and cold and so horribly reasonable all the time you make me want to scream."

"You are screaming, sugar."

"Don't you dare start being sweet. Don't you ever lose your composure?"

"Is it my turn yet? You keep asking me questions, but you don't let me answer them."

He sounded cool and collected, as always. It drove her to distraction. "Don't you have any idea how much you frustrate me?"

"You want to talk about frustration?" He let out a harsh laugh and came toward her. "You're looking at it, Isabel. You've got to be blind or just plain nuts not to know what the mere sight of you does to me."

Once he got started, the words poured out and he couldn't make himself stop.

"I sleep on the floor because your scent is on the sheets, woman, and it makes me so damned hot I can't sleep. All I want to think about is making love to you. Now do you understand?"

He was suddenly pressing her up against the wall and glaring down at her. "Are you getting scared yet? Or have I stunned you speechless by shocking your sensibilities? What the hell are you smiling about, Isabel? I want to take you to bed. Got that? Now aren't you frightened?"

She slowly shook her head. "Isabel, I'm begging you. Tell me to leave."

"Stay."

"Do you understand . . ."

"Oh, yes, I understand," she whispered.

She threw her arms around his neck.

He gently cupped the sides of her face and slowly leaned down. "I tried to stay away from you. . . ."

"You did?" she asked with a long, breathless sigh.

"I wasn't strong enough to resist you. It was those sexy . . ."

"Freckles?"

"Yeah, freckles. A man can only take so much temptation before he's got to take a bite out of the apple, sugar, and when I saw you bathing, I . . ."

"Douglas, are you ever going to kiss me?"

She had barely gotten her question out before his mouth came down on hers. It wasn't perfect; it was much, much better. Her reaction was instantaneous. Her entire body responded to his kiss, and when his tongue brushed against hers, she imitated his action and kissed him with all the pent-up passion inside her.

He kept her glued against him while he continued to try to devour her. It would be over before he'd even begun to do all the things he wanted to do if he didn't get her to slow down, yet the thought of stopping so he could explain was simply too much for him to accept.

Neither one of them remembered undressing the other or getting into bed. Douglas thought he might have thrown her there in his haste to cover her with his body. Then again, she might have thrown him down. She seemed to have acquired an amazing amount of strength in the past few minutes as she forced him to let her kiss every inch of his chest.

He didn't give her any resistance. Dear God, how he loved her. She was everything he had ever wanted in a lover.

The feel of her warm skin against his own was incredibly arousing. She was so perfect everywhere. He loved the way her breasts fell against his chest, and the way she gasped each time he moved against her drove him wild. She didn't try to conceal the fact that she was as hot for him as he was for her, and so he let go of his control and his inhibitions.

He kissed her neck, her shoulders, her breasts, and then slowly moved lower.

"What are you doing?" she whispered, her voice raw with passion.

"I'm kissing every freckle on your body."

She thought those were the most romantic words she'd ever heard. "Oh, my," she whispered, over and over again, each time he touched or kissed or stroked her.

He overwhelmed her senses until she was incapable of thought. She thought he asked her to tell him if he did anything she didn't like, and she really tried to answer him, to tell him that nothing he did could be wrong, but every time she tried to speak, he did something more wonderful to her, and she couldn't get more than a sigh or a whimper out.

If he meant to drive her crazy, he succeeded gloriously. When at last he finally came to her, she felt a twinge of pain as he slowly moved inside her, and then he was part of her and holding her so tenderly, and there wasn't any pain, only pleasure.

He savored each whisper, each movement, and when at last the need to find release became unbearable, he forced her fulfillment by increasing the rhythm and tightening his grip.

Ecstasy such as she had never experienced before began with a ripple, then increased within a heartbeat to an explosive climax. She clung to him as the world fragmented into a thousand brilliant stars, the wonder of their lovemaking filled with beauty and joy.

It took several minutes for him to recover. He held her close to him, nuzzling her neck and lazily stroking her.

"Are you all right?" he whispered.

She didn't answer him, but she did sigh against his ear, and he knew, before he found enough strength to lift his head and look at her face, that she was happy.

He was arrogantly satisfied to know that he had exhausted her. She fell asleep clinging to him, her long legs entwined with his, her face nestled in the crook of his neck, and for this moment in time, she belonged completely to him.

It would have to be enough to last a lifetime.

Ten

Lying in the darkness with Isabel in his arms, Douglas was plagued with guilt. Making love to her had been a terrible mistake. He had taken advantage of her when she was most vulnerable and totally dependent on him to protect her and her son. He hadn't been honorable. What in God's name had he been thinking? Hell, he hadn't been thinking at all, at least not with his head, or he would never have reached for her. His sin was unforgivable, and yet he knew that he would never forget how she had felt in his arms. The memory of her was going to haunt him for the rest of his life.

Now he was going to hurt her by making her face reality too. Circumstance had thrown them together, but in another time and place, she would never have chosen him. When she returned to the outside world, she would realize it.

He was the complete antithesis of her late husband. Parker had been a dreamer. Douglas was a realist, and until recently, he had also been a reasonable man.

The baby's demand for attention forced Douglas to put his grim thoughts aside. He changed Parker's diaper, and then rocked him while he explained the torment he was going through. The baby stopped fretting for several minutes and stared up at him with what Douglas interpreted as intellectual curiosity.

He felt as though he would soon lose his son. From the moment Parker had come into the world, Douglas had loved and cherished him as though he were the boy's father.

The baby was lulled back to sleep. Douglas kissed his forehead, told him in a whisper that he loved him, and put him back in bed.

He gently shook Isabel awake. She put her arms around his neck and tried to pull him down into bed with her. He kissed her brow, insisted she open her eyes, and promised she could sleep just as soon as he returned from his nightly ritual.

"Do you have to check on Boyle's men every night?"

"Yes."

She was too sleepy to argue with him. She followed him to the front door so that she could secure the lock after he'd left.

"How long will you be gone?"

"Same as usual," he answered. "I'll listen to

their conversation for a little while, and then come back."

"They haven't said anything important yet," she reminded him.

"I'm still checking."

She yawned, assured him she would stay awake, and kissed him. "Be careful."

The lure of her soft body was difficult to resist. An hour later he was thankful he'd kept to his routine, for Boyle's men were in a talkative mood. As usual, they were also drunk. The topic was different tonight, because they weren't railing against Boyle for making them stay out all night. The target for their resentment was Isabel. Their anger was fully directed on her. If she weren't such a stubborn woman, she would realize how rich and powerful Boyle was and do as he ordered. Their boss wanted her to get down on her knees and beg him to marry her, and it was the unanimous opinion of the hired hands that it was only a matter of time before she did exactly that.

Douglas had heard all the complaints before, but never with such venom. Then one of the men suggested they all go along with Spear's plan to break into Isabel's home and take her over to Boyle's ranch.

"Spear's wanting to impress the boss, and he's sure that putting the woman in his bed ought to do the trick. He thinks Boyle will give him a big bonus, and if everyone goes along with the plan, he promised to share some of the money with us."

Two of the men were dead set against the plan.

One harped on the fact that they hadn't been paid for the last month's work because Boyle was making them wait until he returned from the Dakotas.

It soon became apparent to Douglas that even the men who were against Spear's plan feared him. It would be only a matter of time before they became too frightened not to agree.

Hearing what the men said about Isabel infuriated Douglas, and he was only able to control his rage by forcing himself to remember that Isabel and Parker came first. When they were safe, Boyle and his men were all going to be fair game.

God, how Douglas looked forward to it.

Time had run out. Douglas made the decision to send for his brothers, and continued on to the physician's house.

As he expected, Simpson argued with him, but Douglas wouldn't listen to a word he said.

"Boyle might not be back for another week or two, and that baby needs every extra hour you can give him before you uproot him and take him out into the wild. He's too fragile to go anywhere yet."

"Do you know what will happen if Spear comes down to the ranch? I'll kill him, and then Boyle will come running with at least twenty men. Parker won't have any chance at all if a war starts. You know I'm right. Send the damn telegram tomorrow."

"God help you, son."

★   ★   ★

In the past, Douglas had always been blunt to a fault, and when he talked to Isabel the following morning, he reverted to his old ways.

He paced in front of the hearth until she joined him. She had her sewing basket in her hands and hurried to put it on the table so she could hug him.

He told her to sit down, and still, she didn't have any inkling of what he was about to say to her until she looked at his face.

"What's wrong?"

"We're what's wrong."

Her eyes widened in disbelief. "No."

"Yes," he insisted. "I shouldn't have taken you to bed last night, and I want you to try to understand. I took advantage of you, and that was wrong. For God's sake, don't shake your head at me. You know I'm right. I could have gotten you pregnant, Isabel. It can't happen again."

She was stunned by his cruel words and the anger in his voice. "I won't understand," she cried out. "Why are you saying these things to me? Don't you realize how much you're hurting me?"

"Please don't make this any more difficult than it already is. I could give you a hundred reasons why it was wrong."

"Give me one reason that makes sense."

"You felt obligated to me."

"Of course I felt obligated to you, but that isn't why I wanted to make love to you. Don't do this. What happened between us wasn't wrong . . . It was beautiful . . . and loving. . . and . . ." She couldn't go on. Tears gathered in her eyes as she turned away from him. Did the hours they'd shared together mean so little to him? No, she wouldn't believe that. She couldn't.

"Once you've rejoined the outside world, this interlude will—"

"Interlude?" she whispered. "For the love of God, will you stop being so practical all the time and listen to your heart?"

"Stop being practical? Damn it, woman, if I'd been practical, I would have gotten you and Parker the hell out of here a long time ago, and I would have kept my hands off of you."

"I wouldn't have left. It would have been dangerous for my son. It was prudent to stay, and last night I wanted you as much as you wanted me."

She ran to him and tried to put her arms around him. He pulled back and shook his head.

"Will you try to understand? We were thrown together by circumstances beyond our control. You were desperate, and so thankful for my help you've mistaken gratitude for love. It's a bad foundation for a lasting commitment, and with time and distance, you'll realize I'm right. You must go forward with your son, Isabel. That's the way it has to be."

"Without you?"

"Yes."

He was through discussing the matter, and she was too devastated to try to make him change his mind.

She walked toward the bedroom, praying that

he would follow her and say something that would give her hope for a future with him.

He didn't say a word. She turned back to him to plead one last time, but the words became trapped in her throat. The sight of him was as heartbreaking as his harsh words had been. He was standing in front of the hearth with his head bent, his hands braced on the mantle. The lines of his face revealed the anguish within.

He looked grief-sticken. Had he just told her goodbye?

"Douglas, does it matter that I love you?"

His silence was her answer.

Eleven

Isabel and Douglas avoided each other as much as possible for the next two days. She was lost in her thoughts about a future without him and was desperately trying to accept his decision to leave her and Parker. He, on the other hand, was considering the more practical matter of keeping them all alive until help arrived.

He still hadn't told her about the plan he'd heard Boyle's men discussing, nor had he told her the wire had been sent to his brothers, but, God help him, it hadn't been for lack of trying. Each time he broached the topic, she turned away from him and walked out of the room to attend to her son.

He kept busy each day until it was dark enough

for him to ride up the hills to check on Boyle's men.

She baked. By early evening of the second day, there were four pies and two cakes on the table. She was still at it when he got ready to leave.

"Could you stop stirring that dough long enough to listen to me?"

"Of course."

He realized it would be asking too much of her to request that she look at him. He knew how hurt she was, and he wondered if she had any idea how hard she was making this for him. He didn't ask her, for he had no wish to get into another discussion. If she cried again, it would kill him. His mind was made up, and he was convinced that he was doing the right thing. In time, and with distance separating them, she would understand.

"If you're not too tired by the time I get back, I think it would be a good idea for you to pack a few things to take with you when we leave."

"I'm not too tired."

"Bolt the door after me."

"No one's going to be watching the cabin tonight because of the rain."

"I'm still going to check."

"I love you, Douglas." She blurted the words out before she could stop herself. "I'm trying to understand why you would—"

He cut her off. "You're too upset to talk about this. When you can be more . . ."

"Practical?"

"Yes."

She came close to throwing the biscuit dough

at him. She put the bowl down on the counter before she could act on the urge and followed him to the door.

Then she waited for him to kiss her good-bye, knowing full well that he wouldn't. As soon as the lock was latched, she burst into tears. Love wasn't supposed to be this painful, was it? How in God's name could she make him understand that what they had was real? Why was he throwing it away? She knew he loved her and that he believed with all his heart that he had acted dishonorably and taken advantage of her. He was wrong, but he was also a proud and stubborn man, and she didn't know how to change his mind. With time and distance would he come to his senses, or would he continue to believe he had done the right thing by leaving?

Please, God, don't let him leave Parker and me. Help him realize we were meant to be together.

The thought of a future without Douglas was unbearable, and within minutes she was doubled over and gasping for breath between heart-wrenching sobs.

She didn't hear Boyle's men until their horses came galloping into the yard. In less than a heartbeat, gunshots were fired and the cabin was riddled with bullets. The men were circling her home, shouting vile threats and obscenities at her while they continued to empty their guns.

Dear God, the baby . . . She had to get to her baby and protect him. She ran to him, frantic now to keep him safe. She was whimpering low in her throat as she lifted her son into her arms. She hunched over so that her body protected him and turned to an inside wall. A stray bullet would have to pass through her before it could get to him.

The noise was deafening. Gunshots were ricocheting off the walls, men were shouting, Parker was crying, and all she could think about was finding a safe place where she could hide her son.

There wasn't time to comfort Parker. He needed to be safe.

SAFE. . . Dear God, help me keep him safe. . . help me . . .

The wardrobe. Yes, the wardrobe was on an inside wall. Isabel ran to it, jerked the doors open, dropped to her knees, and frantically shoved the shoes out of her way.

"Hush now, hush now," she whispered as she reached up and ripped her thick robe off the hanger and pulled it down to cover the hard wood. She placed Parker on top, jumped back up, and pushed the doors together, leaving only a crack so that air could get inside.

Less than a minute had passed since the first gunshot was fired, but her mind was screaming at her to hurry, hurry, hurry. She ran back into the living room, doused the lights, and cocked her rifle her back against the wall, she slowly began to edge toward the curtains so she could look outside.

The front window suddenly exploded into a thousand fragments. Glass shattered across the room as more and more bullets pierced the walls and the floor. A candlestick bounced across the mantel, crashed to the rug, and rolled into the fireplace.

And then there was silence, and that was far more terrifying to her than the noise had been. Were they finished with their game, or were they reloading their weapons? If they were drunk, they'd get bored quickly and leave.

Please, God. Please, God. Make them leave.

She edged closer to the gaping hole that once was her window. With the tip of the rifle barrel, she lifted the shredded drape and looked out into the night.

It was as dark as death outside. Thunder rumbled in the distance as rain pelted her face and her neck. She strained to hear every little sound and waited for one of them to come toward her.

Suddenly the sky was lit up by a bolt of lightning and she saw all six of them clearly. They had formed a line in front of her door and were less than twenty feet away from her son.

Spear's face loomed out at her, and in the gray, crackling light, his skin had taken on a ghoulish tinge, and his eyes, oh, God, his eyes, were as red as a demon's.

She threw herself back against the wall and took a deep breath so she wouldn't scream. She would kill him first.

A voice lashed out at her with the force of a bullwhip slicing through the stillness.

"Remember me, bitch? My name's Spear, and I'm in charge now. I'm through waiting on you. You hear me? I'm going to count to ten, and if you don't want me to hurt you, you'll get outside before I'm finished."

His voice was cold, deliberate, and filled with

hate. He didn't sound drunk, and that made him all the more dangerous. Liquor wasn't ruling his actions; evil was.

"One . . . two . . . three . . ."

"Wait, Spear," one of the others shouted. "Is that a baby bawling?"

"Son of a bitch," someone yelled. "She went and had the baby."

Douglas slowly turned the corner of the barn and moved up behind Spear. He was in such a rage now, he had to keep telling himself to take his time.

"One of us ought to go inside and take the baby. Then she'll follow us," the man on Spear's left suggested with a nervous giggle. "Go and get it, Spear. I ain't going in there and taking on that hellcat. You do it."

"I'll go get both of them," his friend said. "I'm not afraid." His boast was promptly followed by his scream. "I've been bit," he cried out. "I've been bit up my leg."

"What are you crying about, Benton? There aren't any snakes out tonight. You're just spooked, that's all."

Spear dismounted. "Both of you be quiet so I can hear the woman when she calls out."

"You think she's gonna invite you inside?" one of the men asked with a snicker.

Benton turned his mount and headed for the hills. Douglas could hear him sobbing as he rode away. He wondered how long it would take for the drunken fool to realize he had a knife lodged in the back of his thigh.

Spear was standing next to his mount, obviously trying to decide if he wanted to go inside or not.

Douglas hoped to God he'd try. Douglas wasn't going to let him get near that door, and if that meant killing him, Douglas wouldn't suffer any qualms. The bastard had terrorized an innocent mother, partially destroyed her home, and now believed he could drag her and her baby away with him. The mere thought of any of them touching Isabel or Parker sent Douglas into a black rage.

Move, Spear. Move.

Spear pulled his gun out of his holster, and that was a fatal mistake. He had taken one step toward the stoop when Douglas shot his right leg out from under him.

Damn, it felt good.

Spear didn't think so. He screamed as he went down to his knees. He frantically staggered back to his feet, whirled around, and swung his gun up to shoot.

Douglas shot the other leg out from under him. Spear fell forward, his gun clutched in his hand, and landed face first in the mud.

"Anyone else want to limp for the rest of his life?"

The venom in Douglas's voice, added to Spear's screams, was enough to convince the others to give up the fight.

Spear was wiggling around in the mud like a pig trying to keep cool. He shouted to his men to kill Douglas, as he rolled to his side, lifted his head, and took aim with his gun.

Douglas shot him in the center of his forehead.

One of his friends went for his gun, but his hand never reached his holster. Douglas's next bullet cut deep into his shoulder. The man cried out and slumped forward.

"Throw your weapons on the ground," Douglas ordered.

He waited until they'd obeyed his command before he called out to Isabel. "It's over now. Are you and the baby all right?"

He could hear the fear in her voice when she answered him. "Yes, yes . . . we're fine."

A few seconds later, light from the kerosene lamp spilled out into the yard through the window.

"We've got friends waiting up in the hills, mister," one of the captives boasted. "If you've got any sense at all, you'll leave before they come riding down here and kill you."

"I'm guessing he's all alone," his friend whispered.

"Guess again, jackass."

The voice was Cole's. Douglas was so happy to hear it he began to laugh. He didn't have to turn around to know that his brothers were standing behind him. He hadn't heard them approaching and would have been disappointed if he had, for any sound would mean that they had gotten lazy. Being lazy in the West would get a man killed.

"What the hell took you so long to get here?"

"I had to round up the others before we could leave," Adam answered.

"Are you going to kill these men? You might as well since you've got your gun drawn and all."

284

"He isn't going to kill them, Cole."

"Glad you could make it, Harrison," Douglas said.

"You should let us go, mister. Benton already got away, and he'll tell the others."

"Lord, they're stupid," Adam said.

"I assume the man with the knife in his backside is Benton," Harrison said. "Travis went after him. He figured you'd want your good knife back."

Douglas tossed his shotgun to Cole. "Tie them up inside the barn."

The cabin door suddenly flew open and Isabel came running outside with her rifle in her hands.

Douglas moved forward into the light. He took the rifle away from her so that she wouldn't accidentally shoot one of his brothers. He knew she'd seen them because she'd come to an abrupt stop and was staring beyond his shoulder, but after giving each one of them a quick glance, she turned her attention to Boyle's henchmen.

"Where is he?" she asked, her voice shaking with anger.

"Who?" Douglas asked.

"Spear. Did you kill him? Never mind. I don't care if he's dead or not. I'm going to shoot him anyway."

Douglas wouldn't let her have her rifle back. He made sure the safety was on, then threw it to Adam. "You don't want to shoot anyone."

"Yes, I do. I want to shoot all of them."

She grabbed hold of his shirt and held tight. "I'm going to shoot someone, Douglas. They . . . woke . . . my . . . baby . . . and they . . ."

She couldn't go on. The horror of what she had just gone through suddenly struck her full force. She collapsed against him and began to sob.

"We'll leave here, Douglas. I won't fight you any longer. We'll leave . . . We'll leave."

Twelve

The Simpson kitchen was crowded with Claybornes. Trudy Simpson was making a fresh pot of coffee for her honored guests. She was thrilled to have the men at her table and wanted to prepare a feast to show her appreciation. The brothers had come to Sweet Creek to help Isabel, and that made them exceptional.

The men spoke in whispers to one another so that Parker wouldn't be disturbed. He was sleeping peacefully up against Cole's shoulder.

The doctor joined them a few minutes later. He dropped a large packet of yellowed papers tied together with a pink ribbon on the table in front of Douglas.

"I took these away from Isabel. It's after one in the morning, and I found her poring over them when she should be sleeping. Why don't you go through them for her? One of the papers has to be the deed to that useless land, and when you find it, I think we ought to burn it, for all the good it's done."

"How is she feeling, Doctor?" Trudy asked.

"She's tuckered out, but otherwise just as fit as can be. You needn't be worrying about our girl."

"It's a miracle this little boy made it," she remarked. She put a platter of ham on the table and turned back to the counter to fetch the biscuits. "Why, he's no bigger than a minute. I don't believe I've ever seen a baby so tiny."

The doctor squeezed a chair in between Adam and Harrison and sat down. "He's not as small as I expected him to be, but he's got to stay put until he has more weight on him. Do you understand what I'm saying, Douglas? Isabel and her boy have got to stay here. Now, since you brought them to us, I'm wanting to know what you're planning to do when trouble comes calling."

"Meaning Boyle and his gunslingers?" Harrison asked.

Douglas had already told his brothers everything he knew about Boyle, and by the time he'd finished giving the details, they were all anxious to meet the man who had single-handedly terrorized an entire town. Cole was the most curious. He was also the most determined to end the tyrant's reign.

"I'll make certain the fight doesn't come into town," Douglas said.

"How are you going to do that?" Dr. Simpson wanted to know.

"Mrs. Simpson, will you please stop staring at me?" Cole asked. "You're making me nervous."

Trudy laughed. "I can't help it. You look just like I expected Marshal Ryan to look. You've got the same color of hair and eyes, and you're as big as he's supposed to be."

"But you've never seen Ryan, have you, ma'am?" he asked, his exasperation apparent.

"It doesn't make any difference. The minister gave us a fine description of the lawman, and almost every Sunday during his preaching time he's told us another story of Ryan's courage."

"Shouldn't he be preaching parables or something from the Bible? Why would he talk about Ryan?" Adam asked.

"To give us hope," Trudy answered. Her eyes got misty with emotion. "Everyone needs to have hope. And when Cole came strutting into my kitchen, I just naturally assumed he was Ryan. That's why I grabbed hold of him and kissed him."

"Ma'am, I don't strut. I walk. And I don't much like being compared to Daniel Ryan," Cole said.

"Why not? The man's a legend, for heaven's sake. Why, the stories we've heard about him, the tales of glory—"

"Begging your pardon, ma'am, but I don't think it's a good idea to tell Cole any of those stories now. He doesn't like the marshal. Fact is, he doesn't like him at all," Adam said.

Trudy's hand flew to her throat. "Oh, no, that can't be. Everyone likes him."

Douglas wasn't paying any attention to the conversation. He stared at the bundle of papers Parker Grant had left his wife. He didn't want to go through them, because every time he thought about her late husband, he became angry. Parker had subjected Isabel to hardships no woman should have to endure.

He shoved the packet across the table to his brother Adam. "You go through them. Pull out the important documents."

Adam immediately pushed the packet in front of Harrison. "You're the attorney. You go through them."

"Why does this have to be done now?" Harrison asked.

"Isabel wants to find the registration for the Arabians. She's got a mind to do something with the papers, but she won't confide in me. She can be stubborn, and you know how women can get a bug up their—"

"Doctor, watch your language please," Trudy reminded him.

"I was only going to say women get a bug up their sleeve, Trudy."

She snorted with disbelief. Her husband quickly changed the subject to avert an argument. "What did you do with those Arabians?" he asked.

"Travis had something in mind. We left it up to him," Adam explained. "Those sure are fine horses," he added with a nod.

Harrison was hunched over the table, reading documents. Douglas was explaining the change the doctor would have to make in his routine until Boyle was taken care of.

"You're going to have to stay here until this is resolved," he said.

"And just what will happen if anyone gets sick

in the meantime? I have to go where I'm needed," the doctor argued.

"Then two of my brothers are going to go with you. Cole, you stay in town with Adam and make certain no one gets near this house."

"That's going to mean killing some of Boyle's men," Cole said.

"Then that's what you'll do."

"Who is Patrick O'Donnell?" Harrison asked.

The question caught the doctor's full attention. "Why in heaven's name would you be asking me about crazy Paddy Irish? Did you know him?"

"No, sir, I didn't know him, but his will is here, and his name is on this deed. I was wondering—"

Simpson wouldn't let Harrison continue. "Well now, son, I've got to tell you the story, just like I told Douglas, about Paddy Irish having the last laugh."

Douglas motioned for Harrison to hand him the will and the deed so he could read them while the physician retold the bizarre story about the crazy old Irishman.

The brothers were fascinated by the tale. Douglas was fascinated by the documents he held in his hands. He was rereading the description of the property Parker Grant had inherited from Patrick O'Donnell but still couldn't accept what he was seeing until he'd read the deed a third time.

Simpson had just finished his story when Douglas began to laugh. He tried to explain why he was so amused, but every time he began to speak, he was overcome with laughter again.

"Son, you're making me think you're as crazy as old Paddy Irish. What's got you so tickled?"

Douglas handed him the papers. Moments later, Dr. Simpson was also overcome with laughter.

"Good Lord above, there's justice in this sorry world after all," he said as he wiped the tears away from his eyes.

"What's gotten into you two?" Trudy asked.

Cole stood up and began to pace around the kitchen with Parker. The baby had been awakened by all the commotion. "Lower your voices," he snapped. "Parker doesn't like it."

Adam got up and took the baby away from his brother. "You've had him long enough. It's my turn."

"Paddy wasn't crazy, Trudy. Fact is, he was a very clever man."

"And so was Parker Grant," Douglas acknowledged.

He leaned back in his chair and shook his head. "Paddy filed a claim on a piece of land years before Boyle came along and settled here."

The doctor picked up the story then. "Boyle never did give the law a second thought. He liked to take what he wanted. He still does," he thought to add. "Well now, I reckon he'd only been here a little while when he decided to build himself a grand house on the top hill just outside of town.

"Everyone thought it was kind of peculiar the way Paddy would go out there every single day, rain or shine, to watch the progress being made. It took more than a year to finish it, almost two. Yes, sir, it did. The house was three stories high and had every fancy gadget inside you could ever imagine. A chandelier hanging in the dining room came all the way from Paris, France. Oh, yes, it was a palace all right, and Boyle meant to show it off."

"Where did he get the money to build such a grand house?" Adam asked.

"He rented out most of the land to those foreign barons who have gotten into the cattle business because it's so profitable. The cattle were driven up from Texas to graze on sweet Montana grass. He's made a bloody fortune over the years collecting his rent money."

"Only it wasn't his rent money. It was Paddy's. Paddy owned the land Boyle built his home on," Douglas explained.

"He must have told Boyle the night of the party, because that's when the beatings began. I had to patch Paddy up so many times I lost count."

"Why didn't Boyle simply kill Paddy?" Cole asked.

"Paddy must have gone to an attorney and had a will drawn up. He was smart enough not to taunt Boyle without having some sort of legal protection, and knowing how that crazy Irishman liked to have his fun, I imagine he refused to tell Boyle who would inherit the land after he died. He certainly wouldn't have told him where the will could be found. Paddy was a shrewd one all right."

"Who did inherit?" Adam asked.

"I don't know who he was going to leave everything to when he first had the will drawn up, but you can see from this amendment that he had the will changed after he met Parker and Isabel. Probably because they showed him such kindness, he gave it all to them."

"Then Isabel owns Boyle's house and all the land?" Travis asked.

"Yes," the doctor answered.

"The money Boyle collected from renting the land to the barons belongs to her too," Harrison interjected.

Douglas nodded. "Either Paddy told Boyle right before he died who the land would go to, or Parker told Boyle after Paddy had died. Either way, it was a mistake. Whoever it was should have used the law to force the claim."

"Boyle wouldn't have listened to the law," Simpson said.

Harrison disagreed. "A good attorney would have gotten a judge to confiscate the accounts at the bank. Boyle would have had to go into court and win before he could get his hands on the money again. He would have lost, of course, and poor men can't hire gunmen to do their dirty work."

All of a sudden, the Clayborne brothers were up and moving. Douglas and Cole both pulled out their guns at the same time and headed for the back door. Adam disappeared into the hallway with Parker, while Harrison stood in front of Trudy Simpson with his gun out.

Everyone waited in silence. Trudy jumped when a low whistle sounded from just outside the window.

A second later, Travis came strolling inside,

looking weary but happy. He slapped Douglas on his shoulder as he passed him, tipped his hat to Mrs. Simpson before removing it altogether, and then sat down at the table.

Introductions were made, and Trudy did her best to make the latest addition to her table feel welcome.

"Are you hungry, young man? I believe I'll fix you a bite to eat."

"I don't want you to go to any trouble, ma'am."

Trudy had already turned away to fetch her skillet. The doctor poured Travis a cup of coffee and then sat down again. "You're going to eat, son, so you might as well accept it. My Trudy's got her mind set and her frying pan out."

"Yes, sir. I'll eat."

"Did you get my knife back for me?" Douglas asked.

"Yes. I tied Benton to a post inside the barn so he could drive the others crazy with his crying. I've never seen a man weep like that. Honest to God, it was disgusting."

Cole laughed. "We heard you coming up to the door, Travis. You're getting sloppy."

"I wanted you to hear me."

Adam came back into the kitchen with the baby. "Parker's hungry," he remarked.

Douglas immediately got up, took the baby into his arms, and headed for the steps.

Trudy chased after him. "Now, hold on, Douglas. You can't go barging into Isabel's room. It wouldn't be proper."

"Trudy, he delivered that baby," her husband

called out. "I don't believe it's going to matter if he sees her in her nightgown now. He's been living under her roof for over two months."

"That was then, and this is now," Trudy said. "Douglas, you had to deliver that baby because there wasn't anyone else around to do it. Things have to be more proper now though. I'll take the baby up."

She wiped her hands on her apron before taking the baby away from Douglas. He didn't give her any argument, for he knew that it would probably be better for Isabel if she didn't see him again. He had hurt her by making her face reality. In time, she would realize he had taken advantage of her, and he hoped to God that when that day came, she wouldn't hate him.

He leaned against the wall, folded his arms across his chest, and stared off into space as he tried to imagine what his life was going to be like without ever seeing Isabel or Parker again.

Harrison pulled him out of his bleak thoughts. "You delivered the baby?"

"Yes."

"Sit down and tell me what it was like."

"Why?" Adam asked.

"I want to be prepared for my son or daughter's birth. I'm a little . . . nervous about it. I don't like the idea of my wife having pain."

Douglas was thankful for the diversion. He straddled the chair to face Harrison. "You're nervous? I didn't think anything ever got to you."

Harrison shrugged. "Tell me what it was like," he demanded.

Douglas decided to be completely honest. He leaned forward and whispered, "Sheer hell."

"What did he say?" Cole asked.

"He said it was sheer hell," Adam repeated. "Stop joking, Douglas. Harrison's turning gray."

The brothers found that fact hilarious. Douglas thought he had pretty much summed up the experience, but upon reflection he realized it had only been hell for a little while.

"It wasn't bad," he said. "I was scared at first, and then I was too busy to think about everything that could go wrong. Isabel did all the work, and when I held Parker in my hands . . ."

The brothers were waiting for him to finish. Douglas shook his head. He didn't want to share the memory. It belonged to Isabel and him, and it was all he would be able to take away with him when he left Sweet Creek.

"It was pretty miraculous, Harrison," he admitted. "So stop worrying. Besides, you won't have to do anything. Mama Rose will help with the delivery."

"I plan on being with my wife when the time comes."

Trudy returned to the kitchen for the coffeepot, then circled the table refilling their cups.

"Thank you," Cole said. "You know what I don't understand?"

"What?" Adam asked.

"The folks in Sweet Creek," Cole said. "How can so many cower to one man?"

"One man with twenty-some gunslingers working for him," the doctor said. "There aren't any cowards in Sweet Creek, but most of the men

296

are ranchers. None of them could hold their own in a fight because they don't have the expertise. Just ask poor Wendell Border."

"What happened to him?" Adam asked.

"Wendell was coming out of church with his wife and two little girls when some men grabbed him. They forced him to kneel down in front of Sam Boyle. Wendell wouldn't beg for mercy, and that was when Boyle ordered them to break both of his hands. Folks tried to stop what was happening, but the hired thugs had their guns out and threatened to kill anyone who got in their way. Poor Wendell's family had to watch. It was a sorry day all right."

"Now do you understand why I was so overcome with joy when I thought you were Marshal Ryan, Cole?" Trudy asked. "You seemed to be the answer to our prayers."

Travis's eyes widened. "I bet you just loved being mistaken for Ryan," he said.

"Everyone in town is going to make the same mistake I made," Trudy insisted.

It was this innocent remark that gave Douglas his plan. Dr. Simpson was excusing himself when Douglas turned to him.

"Doctor, is there a jail in Sweet Creek?" Douglas asked.

"Yes. It's at the opposite end of town, near the stables. No one's been inside since the old sheriff put his badge on his desk and left town. Why do you want to know about the jail?"

"Cole's going to be using it," he replied. "I don't think you'll want to hear any more details, sir. It could get you into trouble with the law."

"All right then," the doctor agreed. "Come on, Trudy. The men need some privacy now. I've got a feeling tomorrow's going to be a hard day for all of us. We might as well get some sleep now while we can."

Douglas waited until the elderly couple had gone upstairs before he told his brothers what he wanted to do.

"Mrs. Simpson told me that everyone in town has been praying for Daniel Ryan to come and save them."

"And?" Cole asked.

Douglas grinned. "Tomorrow, their prayers are going to be answered."

Daniel Ryan, or rather Cole Clayborne masquerading as Daniel Ryan, came riding down the main street of Sweet Creek on Friday morning at precisely ten o'clock. He went directly to the telegraph office, where it was later reported he held a gun to Jasper Cooper's forehead to gain his cooperation in sending a wire to Samuel Boyle, informing him that his accounts had been confiscated.

At that very same moment, Harrison went inside the bank and presented to the officers in charge an impressive-looking document ordering them to remove all the money in Boyle's account to the bank of Liddyville, where it would remain until the court determined ownership. The document was signed by a judge, but none of the officers could quite make out the signature.

The bank president, as it turned out, wasn't one of Boyle's followers. He didn't look too closely at the papers and didn't waste a minute transferring the money to Liddyville. He did do quite a bit of laughing though and, like Daniel Ryan, seemed to be having the time of his life.

Two of the cashiers helped print up a large sign, which they nailed to the hitching post outside the bank, notifying everyone that Boyle's money was gone.

Word spread like free whiskey, and within two hours at least fifteen of the twenty-five hired hands had left town for parts unknown. Their loyalty ran out with the money. Those who were determined to wait for Boyle to straighten out the situation were arrested by Marshal Ryan and two deputies, and duly locked in the jail.

None of what the Claybornes were doing was legal, a fact that Harrison pointed out at least a dozen times. Cole could get twenty years of hard labor for impersonating a lawman, and Harrison would be sharing the cell with him for falsifying documents.

Cole refused to worry about the consequences. It was his fervent hope that Ryan would hear he had an impersonator and come looking for him. Then Cole would finally get back the compass the lawman had taken from Mama Rose.

Douglas went after Boyle. He wouldn't let any of his brothers go with him and refused to give any details of what he planned to do. He asked Dr. Simpson to tell Wendell Border to bring his family to church the following Sunday, and to step outside at exactly eleven o'clock. There would be a surprise waiting for him.

Needless to say, that day the church was

packed to the rafters. The Reverend Thomas Stevenson was thrilled to have a full house and decided to make the most of it. He threw out the sermon he'd prepared and preached about the fires of hell instead. He ranted, he raved, and he threatened. Anyone who failed to attend his church on a regular basis was doomed to spend eternity burning in hell. Oh, the reverend worked himself into a fine lather all right, screaming and pounding his fists on his pulpit while he worked the congregation into a frenzy of guilt and put the fear of God into their hearts.

He was right in the middle of screaming the word "damnation" when Wendell Border and his family stood up.

The preacher stopped in mid-shout. "Is it time then, Wendell?"

"It's going on eleven," Wendell called back.

The crowd waited in breathless silence for Wendell to leave his pew and lead the way outside. His wife held on to her husband's arm and walked beside him, while their two little girls skipped along behind.

In their wildest speculations, none of the townspeople could have guessed what was going to happen.

Coming down the center of the street toward the church was Sam Boyle. Douglas walked behind him and prodded him forward with the barrel of his shotgun.

Folks started laughing. Boyle didn't look so fierce now. He was dressed in dirty long underwear and nothing else. He hopped from bare foot to bare foot with his head down, and even though the laughter drowned out all other sounds, everyone could see that Boyle was crying.

No, he didn't look like much of a threat to anyone now, not even to the children. The bully had been revealed at last, and only the coward remained.

Dr. Simpson told Isabel later that Douglas had found something better than death to punish Boyle with. He'd used his pride to destroy him.

Boyle cried all the way to the steps, then knelt down in front of Wendell and begged his forgiveness. Wendell wasn't in the mood to give it, and so he remained stubbornly silent.

The law-abiding citizens of Sweet Creek chased Boyle out of town. No one expected him to ever return, but if he did, they would measure out justice once again. His mantle of power had made him seem invincible to those he terrorized, but now the town had seen him for what he really was and stopped being afraid.

Peter Collins, the stableman, stepped forward to offer his services as sheriff. Cole, still masquerading as Daniel Ryan, took the time and trouble to swear him in.

The Claybornes left town a few hours later. Douglas left his heart behind.

Thirteen

Getting on with life wasn't easy. Douglas kept busy every waking hour so that he wouldn't have time to think about Isabel. Business was booming, and folks from as far away as New York City came to Blue Belle to look over the magnificent horses the Clayborne brothers raised.

Douglas broadened his operation by purchasing additional land adjacent to the main ranch. The wild horses Cole and Adam captured were taken to the green pastures and trained there before they were also put up for sale.

The stable in Blue Belle was also expanded, as was a second stable Douglas had purchased on the outskirts of Hammond.

He worked from sunup to sundown, but time, distance, and backbreaking labor didn't ease the ache he felt whenever thoughts of Isabel intruded.

He told himself over and over again that he had done the right thing. Why then did it hurt so much?

His brothers stayed out of his way as much as possible. Adam dubbed him "The Bear," which, it was unanimously agreed, fit Douglas's gruff personality these days. He snapped at everyone but his Mama Rose and his sister, rarely smiled, and stubbornly refused to tell anyone what was bothering him.

His brothers had already figured it out, for they had met Isabel Grant, and after spending five minutes in the same room with her and Douglas, it had become apparent to them that their brother had fallen in love with the beautiful woman. She was soft-spoken, sweet-natured, and obviously much more intelligent than Douglas was. She didn't make any attempt to hide how she felt about their brother, which made them like her all the more. Douglas, on the other hand, was determined to act like a mule's backside. If *they* knew he loved Isabel, they figured *he* had to know it too, and just when was he going to come to his senses and do something about it?

Cole predicted it would take three months for Douglas to act and wagered five dollars that he was right. Travis bet it would only take two months, met Cole's five-dollar wager, and upped the ante to ten dollars. Adam thought it was disgusting that his brothers were wagering on Douglas's misery. He also thought it would take his brother four months to go after Isabel and matched Travis's twenty-dollar bet.

Douglas didn't know about the wagers. Six weeks had passed since he'd left Sweet Creek, and not a single day had gone by that he hadn't thought about Isabel and Parker. He didn't know how long he'd last before he gave in and went back.

He was just leaving Hammond to go up to an auction in River's Bend when he received a telegram from Adam telling him to come home.

Douglas assumed his sister had gone into labor early. Mary Rose had made all of her brothers promise to be there for the delivery of her first-born. She didn't need them to comfort her but was, in fact, far more concerned about her husband. It was up to her brothers to keep Harrison calm.

He arrived at Rosehill around three in the afternoon. The sun was beating down on his shoulders; he hadn't shaved in two days, and all he could think about was getting a cold drink and a hot bath.

He spotted Pegasus as he was riding down the last hill. The Arabian stallion was prancing about inside the corral. Douglas squinted into the sunlight and saw Adam and Cole sitting in the shade of the porch with their feet propped up on the railing.

He slowed his sorrel to a walk as he passed the corral. The barn door opened as he was dismounting, and Travis led Minerva outside.

"Isn't she a fine-looking horse?" Travis called out.

Douglas was numb with disbelief. His voice was hoarse when he called out, "How did they get here?"

Travis shrugged. "You'll have to ask Adam," he suggested. "He probably knows."

Douglas headed for the house. Before he could ask any questions, Adam offered him a cold beer.

"You look parched," he remarked.

"I think he looks kind of sickly," Cole said.

"How did they get here?" Douglas demanded.

"How did who get here?" Adam asked.

"The Arabians," he muttered.

"They probably walked some," Cole said.

"Probably galloped some too," Adam told his brother.

They shared a smile before turning back to torment their brother a little longer.

Douglas was leaning against the post, staring into the hall through the screen door. The agony Adam saw in his eyes made him feel guilty.

"Maybe we ought to tell him, Cole."

"I think he ought to suffer a little longer. He's been hell to live with for the last month and a half. Besides I lost the bet, or will, just as soon as he sees her."

"She's here, then?"

"She was," Adam said.

"Where is she now?"

"You don't need to yell at us. We can hear you just fine," Adam said.

"Isabel Grant is a contrary woman," Cole remarked. "She looks so sweet and innocent, but she's got a dark side to her, Douglas, which is why I'm so partial to her. You need to understand what you're getting into before you go looking for her."

"What are you talking about. Isabel doesn't have a dark side. She's perfect, damn it. She's good and kind and . . ."

"Generous?" Adam asked.

"Yes, generous."

"I agree with you," Adam said. "But I also agree with Cole. The woman does have a dark side all right. She wants you to have the two Arabians because you were so helpful to her, and that makes her a downright generous woman. Don't you think so, Cole?"

"Sure I do," his brother said. "But she also came here to kill him," he reminded his brother. "She seems real determined too. Maybe I shouldn't have loaded the shotgun for her, Adam."

"Nope. I don't suppose you should have."

"Is she still here?"

Douglas was moving toward the door when Adam answered. "Yes, she's here."

"If she kills you, we still get the Arabians," Cole called out. "Isabel promised us."

Douglas had already gone inside. He searched the upstairs, looked in the parlor, the library, the dining room, and then went into the kitchen. Mama Rose was standing at the stove. She turned as he entered the room, and that was when he saw Parker in the crook of her arm.

He came to a dead stop and simply stared at the baby.

"Isn't he about the sweetest little thing you've ever seen, Douglas? Why, he smiles all the time. Just look at him. He's smiling now."

Douglas reached out to touch the baby. The tips of his fingers brushed over the top of his head.

Parker looked up at him and smiled.

"Where's his mother?" he asked, his voice rough with emotion.

"She was headed for the barn," Mama Rose said. "I'd be careful if I were you. She's upset with you."

Douglas was suddenly smiling. "So I heard."

He went out the back door, turned the corner of the house, and ran toward the barn. Cole called him back with a shrill whistle.

He turned around, and there was Isabel. She was standing on the top step watching him.

He suddenly forgot how to walk. He couldn't believe she was here. She looked as mad as a hornet and was, without a doubt, the most beautiful woman he had ever seen . . . or loved.

Honor be damned. Right or wrong, he was never going to let her go. He took a step toward her. She lifted the hem of her skirt and started down the stairs, but Cole stopped her.

"Don't forget your shotgun, Isabel."

"Oh, yes, thank you, Cole, for reminding me."

She picked up the weapon, turned around, and continued on. She stopped when she was about fifteen feet away from Douglas and put her hand up.

"Stop where you are, Douglas Clayborne. I have something to say to you, and you're going to listen."

"I've missed you, Isabel."

She shook her head. "I don't think you missed me at all. I waited and waited, but you didn't come for me, and I was so sure that you would. You hurt me, Douglas. I needed to come here and tell you how cruel you were to leave me. Everything you said to me before you left . . . Do you remember? I remember every word. You told me I had to rejoin the outside world and that I would eventually forget all about you. Well, you were wrong about that. I'll never forget you. Will you forget me?"

"No, I could never forget you. Isabel, I was going to—"

She wouldn't let him finish. "You never told me you loved me, but I know that you do. I told you how I felt. Remember? I loved you then, I love you now, and I will go on loving you until the day I die. There, I needed to say that too. I hope you're as miserable as I am, you stubborn, pigheaded mule."

He took a step toward her. She backed up and put her hand up again. "Stand still, and let me have my say. I've only just gotten started. I've saved all this up for a long time, and you're going to listen. How dare you tell me I took you into my arms and my heart because I felt obligated to you. I was furious that you would believe such a thing, but then, the longer I thought about it, the more I realized how right you were."

He was taken aback by her admission. "No, I wasn't right," he said.

"Yes, you were," she replied. "I did feel obligated to you, and that was surely why I slept with you. Love didn't have anything to do with it."

"Isabel, you can't really believe—"

"Will you stop interrupting me? I need to finish this. After you left, I had plenty of time to think things over, and I realized I also felt obligated to dear Dr. Simpson. Yes, I did, and so I slept with him. Trudy didn't mind. Then I realized I also felt obligated to Wendell Border. The man tried to get help for me, after all; This isn't funny, Douglas, so you can stop smiling."

"Did you sleep with Wendell?"

"Yes, I did," she said. "His wife was very understanding. The Arabians belong to you. They can't be separated, and Parker did sell Pegasus to you. Besides, I don't have any place to keep them."

"You own half of Montana," he reminded her.

"No, the orphanage owns half of Montana. The sisters should be moving into Paddy's grand house any day now with the children. They'll be self-sufficient and have a nice income from the rents they collect on their grazing land. I made the sisters promise to call their new home Paddy's Place. They wanted St. Patrick's Place, but I got my way."

"You gave it all away? What about your son? How are you—"

"My baby and I will be just fine. I'm going to teach at the school and will make enough money to support the two of us."

"Isabel, I really need to kiss you."

"No," she said. "I haven't finished with my obligations. I realized I was beholden to your brothers. They were very helpful, if you'll recall, and I am going to sleep with each one of them too. It's only fair. When I'm finished, I'm going to come out here and shoot you for being so stubborn." She put the shotgun down and tried to walk away. "Cole? May I have a few minutes of your time?" she called out.

Douglas was laughing when he grabbed her hand and pulled her toward him.

"I love you, Isabel. I loved you then, I love you now, and I'll love you until the day I die. We're like your Arabians, sweetheart. We can't be separated. I've been so damned miserable without you and Parker. I don't want to get over loving you, and the only man you're ever going to be obligated to is me. Ah, sugar, don't cry. I was coming to get you. I couldn't fight it any longer. Being away from you and Parker was making me crazy."

"I'm leaving you this time."

He wrapped his arms around her, leaned down,

and kissed her. "No, you're not leaving. We belong together, now and forever."

She put her arms around him and let him kiss her again. "Are you through being stupid, then?"

He laughed again. "Yes," he promised.

"I'm still going back to Sweet Creek, and you'd better follow me. God help you if you don't. You're going to court me and take me to tea parties and dances. I don't care if you want to or not."

"I've got a much better idea. Marry me, sugar."

Book III

ONE RED ROSE

One

*Rosehill Ranch, Montana Valley,
Spring, 1881*

He found her in his bed.

Adam Clayborne surprised his family by coming home in the dead of night two days earlier than expected. He hadn't planned to return to the ranch until Friday, but his business was finished, and he was sick and tired of sleeping outdoors. He wanted clean sheets and a soft mattress underneath him.

He knew the house was packed to capacity, for next weekend was Mama Rose's birthday, and his brothers and sister had all agreed to come back to the homestead early to help with the preparations. Most of the town of Blue Belle was invited to the shindig, along with twenty or thirty people from as far away as Hammond. Mama Rose had made a good number of friends since she'd taken up residence at the ranch a little over a year ago. There were more than fifty men and women in her church group alone, and every one of them was planning to attend the celebration.

By the time Adam had bedded down his horse and gotten a cool drink in the kitchen, it was well after midnight. The house was as quiet as a church on Saturday night. He removed his boots in the foyer and tried not to make any noise as he crept up the stairs, went into his bedroom at the end of the hall, and began to undress. He didn't bother to turn up the lamp on the night stand because the moonlight streaming in through the open window was sufficient for him to make out the contours of the furniture.

He tossed his shirt on a nearby chair, stretched his arms wide, and yawned. Lord, it was good to be home. Bone weary and half asleep, he sank down on the double bed to take off his socks— except he didn't actually sit on the bed. He sat down on a very soft, warm, sweet-scented woman.

She let out a loud groan. He let out a blasphemy.

Genevieve Perry had been sound asleep one second and was wide awake the next. She felt as though the house had just caved in on her. Instinctively she shoved the dead weight off of her legs and bolted upright in the bed. Grabbing hold of the sheets, she held them up to her neck and peered over at the huge man sprawled out on the floor.

"What *are* you doing?" she whispered.

"I'm trying to get into my bed," he whispered back.

"Adam?"

"Yes, Adam. Who are you?"

She swung her long legs over the side of the bed and put her hand out to him.

"My name's Genevieve, and it's such a pleasure to meet you. Your mother's told me so much about you."

His eyes widened in disbelief. He almost

laughed, so ludicrous was the situation. Didn't the woman realize he could see her bare arms and legs? She obviously didn't have much on, and that sheet was a paltry barrier at best.

"I'll be happy to shake your hand when you're dressed."

"Oh . . . Lord."

Her reaction told him she'd finally recognized the awkwardness of their circumstances.

"I guess turning the lamp up is out of the question," he said.

"No, no, we can't do that. I'm in my night-gown. You really should get out of my room before anyone finds you here. This isn't appropriate."

"It's my room," he reminded her. "And lower your voice, or you'll wake the entire household. I don't want my brothers running in here to find out what's going on."

"Nothing's going on."

"I'm aware of that, Genevieve." He sat up, untangled his long legs, and braced his arms on his knees. He tried to be patient as he waited for her to explain why she was in his bed.

Her vision finally adjusted to the darkness, and she got a good look at the man she had been dreaming about for the past two years. Lord, he was gorgeous. She had tried to picture him in her mind, had fantasized about him too, but now she realized she hadn't done the man justice. The angles of his face were perfectly sculptured. He looked as though he had been molded from one of the ancient statues she'd seen in the museum back home. Adam had the same square forehead and high cheekbones and the identical straight nose and mouth. His eyes made him even more beautiful. They were the color of midnight. His gaze was intensely focused on her now, and she could feel the heat all the way down to her toes.

She couldn't stop staring at him. He was much bigger than she'd imagined him to be, and far more muscular. He was lean, yet his upper arms were enormous, suggesting amazing strength. She could feel the coiled tension in him and knew, without a doubt, that if he decided to pounce on her, it would happen before she had time to blink. The thought made her shiver. She'd never imagined that he would be dangerous, but then she'd never pictured him frowning, and he was certainly frowning now.

And she looked like a poor, frumpy relative. She was wearing an old, faded nightgown, a favorite she refused to throw away because it was so comfortable. She pulled the sheet up higher to hide the frayed neckline.

She should have been horrified by his intrusion. She wasn't though. She wasn't the least bit afraid. Why, she wouldn't be feeling the most irresistible urge to laugh if she were afraid, would she? Besides, she knew Adam better than anyone else in the whole world, even his brothers, because she had read all the letters he'd written over the years to his Mama Rose.

"You don't have to worry," she whispered. "I'm not going to shout for help. I know who you are and I'm not afraid."

He clenched his jaw tight. "You don't have

any reason to be afraid. What are you doing in my bed?"

"The guest room's occupied, so your mother told me to take your room. I surprised her by showing up without giving her any advance warning. She invited me to come to Rosehill a long time ago, but due to circumstances beyond my control, I couldn't get here until now."

It suddenly dawned on him exactly who Genevieve was. Adam was a big man, but he could be quick when he wanted to be. He was on his feet and halfway across the room before she had time to draw another breath.

She grabbed her robe from the foot of the bed and quickly put it on. She started to stand up but changed her mind almost immediately. She didn't want him to get the notion that she was chasing after him.

"Wait," she called out. "Didn't your mother tell you I was coming to Rosehill?"

"No."

Adam knew he sounded surly. He couldn't help that. He should have known who she was right away. Her southern accent should have been a dead giveaway, and although he'd certainly noticed the soft, musical lilt in her voice, it hadn't occurred to him until this moment that Genevieve was the woman his Mama Rose had told him about.

He was reaching for the doorknob when she called out to him again. "Do you mean to say she didn't explain?"

He slowly turned around. "Explain what?" he hedged.

317

She pulled her robe close about her and moved into the moonlight. He saw her face clearly then, and in that moment, Adam realized the jeopardy he was in. Without a doubt, Genevieve Perry was the most beautiful woman he had ever seen. Her dark hair was cropped short and framed a heart-shaped, angelic face. She had high cheek bones, a narrow nose, and a mouth that could drive a man to imagine all sorts of things. Her skin was flawless, and that innocent smile of hers could cause real havoc.

His gaze moved lower and, Lord help him, her long, shapely legs were as perfect as the rest of her.

He broke out in a cold sweat. She was beautiful all right, and he couldn't wait to be rid of her.

"What exactly was Mama Rose supposed to explain?"

She smiled once again, a heart-stopping smile. Every nerve in his body was warning him to get out of there before it was too late and he was captured in her enchanting spell.

"Adam, I'm your bride."

He didn't panic, but he came close. He nearly ripped the door off its hinges when he opened it, but escape was impossible. His brothers Travis and Cole were blocking the entrance. The two of them came rushing into the bedroom to find out what all the commotion was. Both men were bare-cheated, barefoot, and wide awake. Travis had his gun out and was looking for a target.

"What the . . ." Cole came to a dead stop when Adam gave him a hard shove.

"Put your damned gun away, Travis," Adam ordered.

"We heard a crash in here," Cole said.

"I fell on the floor," Adam whispered.

Both brothers looked incredulous. Travis was the first to smile. "You fell on the floor? How in God's name did you do that?"

"Never mind," Adam muttered.

Travis elbowed his way past his brothers so he could see Genevieve. "Are you all right?"

"Of course she's all right," Adam answered

"What are you doing home so soon?" Cole asked.

"Get off my foot," Adam snapped.

Cole took a step back and then asked, "What are you doing in Genevieve's room?"

"It's my bedroom," Adam reminded him. "No one told me she'd be sleeping in my bed."

Cole smiled. "Well, now, that had to be a real nice surprise."

"Gentlemen, will you please leave?" Genevieve called out.

She was immediately sorry she'd said a word, for she'd inadvertently drawn attention to herself. All three brothers turned to her. She tried to scrunch down under the sheets and disappear.

Cole walked forward. "Adam didn't scare you, did he?"

The brother had almost reached the bed when she bolted upright. "Do you mind, Cole?"

He stopped. "Mind what? You aren't embarrassed, are you?"

"You've got your robe on," Travis reminded

319

her. "And after living with us for a week, you've got to know you're perfectly safe."

"Is anyone hungry?" Cole asked.

"I could eat something," Travis said. "What about you, Genevieve?"

"No, thank you."

Adam gritted his teeth in frustration. He couldn't wait to get his brothers out in the hallway so he could give them a piece of his mind.

"You two haven't been properly introduced, have you?" Travis said. He crossed the room to stand next to Cole. "One of us ought to introduce them to each other, and now is as good a time as any."

"For the love of . . ." Adam began.

"Stop teasing your brother . . ." Genevieve said at the very same time. The laughter in her voice indicated she wasn't the least bit upset.

"This will only take a minute," Travis insisted. "Genevieve, I'd like you to meet the oldest and the meanest of the Clayborne brothers. His name is John Quincy Adam Clayborne, but everyone calls him Adam. Adam, I'd like you to meet Miss Genevieve Perry, who came here all the way from New Orleans, Louisiana. You should get to know her as soon as possible, since the wedding plans are already in the works. Good night, Genevieve. See you in the morning."

"Good night," she replied.

Adam wasn't amused by his brothers' antics. He pushed Cole and Travis out into the hallway, pulled the door closed, and then demanded to know what Genevieve was doing there.

"Mama Rose invited her to come here," Travis explained.

"But that was over a year ago. Why did she decide to come to Rosehill now?"

Cole shrugged. "Maybe it wasn't convenient before or she had something else she had to do first. Does it matter?"

Adam shook his head. Now, he decided, wasn't the time to get into a long discussion. "Where am I supposed to sleep?"

"The guest room's out," Cole said, "unless you want to sleep with our nephew. Parker's teething, and he'll wake you up around four in the morning."

"Why can't the baby sleep in with his parents?"

"Mama Rose thought Douglas and Isabelle could use a little privacy," Travis explained with a yawn. "Genevieve's pretty, isn't she? And don't tell me you didn't notice."

Adam let out a sigh. "I noticed."

He started down the steps, but Cole stopped him with a question. "What are you going to do about her?"

"I'm not going to do anything about her."

"She came here to marry you," Cole whispered. "At least that's what Mama Rose told us, and when she suggested a June wedding, Genevieve didn't argue."

"What a mess," Adam muttered.

"I'm going back to bed," Cole announced.

Travis followed Adam down to the foyer. "We really like her, Adam. If you'll open your mind to the idea, I think you'll like her too. She's got a great sense of humor, and you should hear her sing. She's amazing. If you'll only get to know her before you make any decisions, you'll—"

"I'm not marrying her."

"Adam, you don't have to do anything you don't want to do."

"Why didn't one of you let me know she was here?"

"How could we let you know? You've been camping, remember?" Travis said.

"You had a week to find me."

"Why are you in such a foul mood? No one's going to hold a gun to your head and make you marry her."

"I'm going to bed."

He ended up in the bunkhouse. A half hour later, he was still trying to get comfortable on a narrow, lumpy mattress. He was too big for the bed. His feet hung over the edge, and he couldn't turn over without flinging himself to the floor.

He doubted he would get much sleep anyway, as thoughts of Genevieve kept intruding. He stacked his hands behind his head and thought about the situation. His mother's interference in his life was galling, and what in the name of God was he going to do about the mess she had created? Surely Genevieve didn't really expect to marry him just because Mama Rose had suggested the idea to her. Nowadays, most women balked at an arranged marriage, and what son in his right mind would let his mother choose his bride for him?

Adam knew it was going to be up to him to make Genevieve understand that marriage was out of the question. He would sit her down and have a long talk with her. Yes, that's what he was going to have to do. He would tell her that he had made his mind up a long time ago that he was meant to live alone. He was too set in his ways, liked solitude, and hated distraction of any kind. In other words, he wasn't husband material. Family was the only disruption he allowed. His brothers were rarely at Rosehill now, and since his sister, Mary Rose, had had the baby, Mama Rose spent most of her time with her new granddaughter. Mary Rose's husband, Harrison, had built a home on the edge of Blue Belle to accommodate the three women in his life, and Mama Rose much preferred town life over the isolation of the ranch.

Adam wasn't a recluse. There were always at least twenty hired hands to supervise, so his days were quite busy, and he didn't mind returning to the big empty house at night alone. In fact, he liked it. Admittedly, his life had become a little too structured and orderly to suit most people, but he was content, and that was all that mattered. When he was younger, he'd longed to see the world, but he'd given up on that foolish dream years ago and now traveled from one exotic port to another through the books he read. Cole accused him of acting like an old man. Adam didn't disagree with his brother's evaluation. He had always been happy with his life, and he would be happy again just as soon as he straightened out this misunderstanding.

He decided to wait until after the birthday celebration to talk to Genevieve. He would be kind, but forceful, as he explained his position.

Her expectations were unreasonable, and he hoped that after he'd had his say, she would realize he was right. He didn't want to hurt her, and he certainly wasn't looking forward to a confrontation. He wasn't a cruel man who took delight in breaking women's hearts, but he would do what was necessary to avert a disaster, no matter how distraught she became.

He hoped to God she wouldn't cry or become hysterical. Regardless, he would stand firm. Adam fell asleep convinced that eventually Genevieve would get over him.

Two

She couldn't possibly marry him, and just as soon as she could get him alone for a few minutes, she would tell him so. She wasn't in a position to marry anyone now, not with all the trouble hanging over her head, but she wasn't about to go into a lengthy explanation when she talked to Adam. She would simply tell him that marriage was out of the question. Then she would be on her way.

Admittedly, before things had become so horribly complicated and bleak, she had entertained the notion of marrying him. After she had read all of his letters, she'd even dreamed about it, but then the Reverend Ezekiel Jones came into her life and turned it upside down. Because of her own naiveté and self-involvement, she could no longer consider becoming the wife of such an honorable man as Adam Clayborne.

It was her hope that once she had completed the dreaded duty of explaining her change of heart to Adam, she would gain a little peace of mind. Lord only knew, she was due for some.

She needed privacy for their talk though, and privacy wasn't easily accomplished at Rosehill these days. The two-story house was bursting at the seams with returning family members and their spouses and babies. Adam was constantly surrounded by his relatives, and there was also a steady procession of friends, and strangers too, who stopped by the ranch for a cool drink, a hot meal, and a little conversation. None of the Claybornes ever turned anyone away.

As head of the household, Adam tried to be hospitable. He also tried to avoid her whenever possible. It hadn't taken her any time at all to come to that conclusion, for every time she entered a room he happened to be in, he found a reason to get up and leave. His abrupt departures would have bothered her if she hadn't already surmised from his wary glances that he was as uncomfortable with the situation as she was.

Time was running out and she would have to leave soon. She had made a promise, and she was determined to keep it. She had already stayed at Rosehill much longer than she had originally intended, and she was feeling tremendously guilty about deceiving all of the Claybornes. She had come there under false pretenses to hide, and every time she looked at dear Mama Rose, Genevieve's shoulders slumped a little more from the weight of all her lies.

The Clayborne family had made her feel worse by being so good to her. They had welcomed her into their home and treated her as though she belonged there. Mama Rose constantly sang her praises. She told her family that Genevieve was a sweet, generous person with high moral standards. Genevieve wondered how Mama Rose would feel about her if she knew the truth.

The opportunity to talk to Adam in private finally presented itself on the day of Mama Rose's birthday celebration. As Genevieve was coming down the stairs to the first floor, she spotted Adam going into his library, and, saints be praised, he was all alone. She straightened her shoulders, gathered her resolve, and hurried after him.

Two hours later, she was still trying to get to the library. First she had been waylaid by his sister, Mary Rose, who asked her to please supervise the men putting up the picnic tables while Mary Rose fed and changed her daughter. Over the past week, Genevieve had become very close to Mary Rose, and she was happy to help out. An hour later she had only just completed the task when Adam's brother Douglas asked her to please hold his ten-month-old son, Parker, while he helped construct the platform that would be used by the band Travis had hired.

Parker was a little charmer, and Genevieve certainly didn't mind taking care of him. The baby was persnickety with almost everyone but her. He was going through what his parents referred to as "a shy phase," which meant he usually started screaming whenever a stranger came within ten feet of him. He'd taken quite a fancy to Genevieve though, and much to his parents' surprise, the moment he'd spotted her, he'd put his arms out and demanded with a grunt that she pick him up. She was wearing a colorful necklace at the time, and she was convinced Parker only put up with her so that he could get to the trinket he thought he might like to eat.

Genevieve considered taking the curly-headed cherub with her to the library to talk to Adam, then changed her mind. Parker was fretful and would have been too much of a distraction. With all the pounding and shouting and laughing, she also knew that if she tried to put him in his crib, he'd have none of it. So she carried him out to the porch, sat down in the rocker Douglas had carried out for her, and let the baby rest against her chest and watch the chaos.

A shrill whistle made Parker jump. She soothed him with a gentle pat and a whispered word.

"Harrison, we could use your help," Cole shouted. "Bring Adam with you."

The screen door opened and Mary Rose's husband came out. He had his daughter, Victoria, in the crook of his arm. He looked a bit guilty as he came across the porch to stand in front of her. Genevieve knew what he wanted before he asked. She shifted Parker to the left side of her lap so there would be enough room for his adorable seven-month-old cousin.

"Would you mind holding Victoria for a few minutes while I help build the platform?" he asked in his rich Scottish brogue. "She's been fed and changed. My wife's helping in the kitchen, but if you don't think . . ."

"I can manage," she insisted.

Harrison got his daughter settled next to Parker, patted both babies, then removed his jacket and tossed it on the railing on his way down the steps.

Genevieve had her hands full. Parker was determined to gnaw on Victoria's arm, but Genevieve gently pulled her arm away and substituted his blanket. His thumb immediately went into his mouth, and he began to make loud slurping noises.

Travis came running up the steps. The sight of his nephew and niece snuggled together in her arms made him smile.

"You sure do have a way with babies."

"It would seem so," she agreed. She burst out laughing then, for her little charges looked up at her and smiled. Both babies were drooling.

"They're perfect, aren't they?" she said.

"Yes," Travis agreed. "But it doesn't seem fair that Victoria only has peach fuzz on her head and Parker has all the curls. They're as different as night and day."

She agreed with a nod. "Where are you headed?"

"To the kitchen to get my hammer and then to the library to get Adam to help us. He can do his paperwork later. The band's going to be here by three, and we've got to be ready."

As soon as he had gone inside, Genevieve began to rock the babies. A soft warm breeze, sweet with the fragrance of wildflowers, enveloped the porch, and she stared at the mountains in the distance. She felt as though she were sitting in the middle of paradise.

She began to sing a French lullaby she remembered from childhood days, a favorite because her mother used to sing it to her every night before she tucked her into bed. The lyrics were simple and repetitive, and the melody was innocent and joyful. The lullaby brought back memories of happier, carefree days. Genevieve closed her eyes, and for a few brief, precious moments, she wasn't all alone. She was back in her childhood home, sitting in the big overstuffed chair listening to her mother sing as she pulled back the covers on her bed. The scent of lilacs enveloped Genevieve. She could hear her father's laughter floating up the stairs and feel the peace and contentment of that house. She was once again surrounded by people who loved and cherished her.

Adam stood in the doorway watching her. He was just about to push the screen door open when she began to sing, and having no wish to interrupt her, he had turned to go out the kitchen door. The music pulled him back. The rich, lustrous timbre of her voice, so pure and clear, was surely as perfect as an angel's, yet the look of tranquillity on her face was just as beautiful. The longer he listened, the more magical her voice became. Like a blade of grass drawn to the heat of the sun, he was drawn to the glorious melody. Captivated, he never wanted the song to end. He didn't make a sound, didn't move, and barely drew a breath as he let the music, and Genevieve, enchant him.

He wasn't the only man affected. One by one the crowd of men working in the yard paused to listen. Harrison was bending over to pick up his hammer when her song reached him. He straightened up and tilted his head in her direction. Travis, carrying a stack of two-by-fours across his shoulder, was halfway across the yard when he heard her singing. Like Harrison, he instinctively turned toward the porch, then went completely still and closed his eyes. Sweat dripped off his brow, the sun beat down on his face, but he was oblivious to any discomfort. In fact, he smiled with genuine pleasure.

Douglas had a nail in his mouth and a hammer in his hand and was swinging his arm in a wide arc when he heard Genevieve singing. He slowly lowered his hand and, like his brothers, turned to the sound.

The hired hands were bolder in their reaction. They dropped their tools and moved in unison to the front yard, as though they were drawn by some inexplicable force to the heavenly melody.

The babies were the only ones who weren't impressed. Both Parker and Victoria fell asleep during the first verse. Genevieve finished the lullaby and only then noticed the silence. She was given quite a start when she opened her eyes and saw the crowd watching her. One of the men began to clap, but a hard nudge and a reminder from his friend stopped the noise. However, her audience must have felt she was due some sort of appreciation, and within a few seconds every man there was smiling and tipping his hat to her.

Their grins were a bit unnerving. Embarrassed by their attention, she gave the men a tentative smile, looked away, and found Adam watching her. That was even more unnerving.

He smiled. She was so astonished she smiled back. His usual guarded expression was gone, and the look in his eyes was one she hadn't seen before. He looked . . . happy. He didn't seem so dangerous or fierce to her now, yet her heart was pounding a wild beat. The tenderness she saw in his eyes made him even more handsome . . . and how could such a thing be possible?

The screen door squeaked open, and he walked over to her. She stopped rocking the babies and simply stared up at him. He wasn't smiling any longer, but he still looked pleased. She was feeling flush and in dire need of a fan. She needed to get hold of herself. She was behaving as though a man had never looked at her before. Under his close scrutiny, her usual confidence evaporated, and she was suddenly feeling like the shy, awkward little girl who had made such a mess of things the first time she tried to sing in the church choir. Fortunately, he was never going to know how nervous he made her.

He dropped to one knee in front of her. She couldn't imagine what he was going to do . . . and then he reached for Parker. He was so very gentle as he lifted the sleeping baby into his powerful arms. He stood up, put Parker against his shoulder with one hand splayed against the baby's back and then put his other hand out to her.

She moved Victoria into the crook of her arm and let Adam pull her to her feet. For several heartbeats they simply stood staring at one another. He didn't say a word to her, nor she to him, yet the silence didn't seem awkward. Perhaps the babies made them feel connected to one another for the moment. Adam's fingers were entwined with hers, and she didn't know if she should pull away or not.

He made the decision for her when he turned toward the door. She had to let go of him then. She assumed he was going to put Parker in his crib and wanted her to follow with Victoria.

A few minutes later, both babies were sleeping peacefully in their cribs. She was putting the blanket around Victoria when she looked up to see Adam quietly stepping out of the room.

Oh no you don't, she thought. *You aren't getting away from me this time.*

She glanced over at Parker to make certain he was covered, then picked up her skirts and rushed after Adam.

He was waiting for her on the landing. Unfortunately, she didn't know that. When she came running around the corner, she crashed into him and very nearly sent him flying over the banister. Had he been a couple of inches shorter and a few pounds lighter, she probably would have killed him, and, dear God, he never would have forgiven her then.

He buckled under the impact, let out a low

grunt, and grabbed hold of her to keep her from falling down the steps.

Her sense of humor helped her get past her embarrassment. She burst into laughter in the middle of her apology.

"I didn't want you to get away before . . . I'm so sorry, Adam. I didn't mean to bump into you. Are you all right? I didn't hurt you, did I?"

He shook his head. "Are you always in such a hurry?"

His smile sent her heart racing. She stared up into his beautiful dark eyes and felt herself melting. She knew that if she didn't say or do something soon, she would find herself married to him in no time at all. Why, oh why, did he have to be such a charming man?

"I'm sorry. What did you ask?"

"Are you always in such a hurry?"

"In a hurry? No, I don't think I am."

"We need to talk, don't we, Genevieve?"

She vehemently nodded. "Yes, we need to talk."

"We'll need privacy."

As if to underline that fact, the screen door slammed shut and Cole crossed the foyer below them.

"Yes, we need privacy."

"Is something wrong?" he asked. "You seem a little nervous."

"Nervous? I seem nervous?"

He nodded. She took a deep breath and ordered herself to stop repeating his every word. The man was going to think she was a twit.

"I am a little nervous," she said. "Do you know what I think?"

He didn't have a clue. "What do you think?"

"You and I started off on the wrong foot."

"We did?"

"Yes, we did," she insisted. "It's all my fault. I shouldn't have told you I was your bride. I stunned you with my announcement, didn't I? Well, of course I did. You obviously didn't expect to find me in your bed. You looked so horrified, and you were in such a hurry to get away from me you were tripping over your own feet. I simply couldn't resist tormenting you. I didn't take offense over your conduct, but now that I think about it, I probably should have been insulted, or at the very least . . . Why are you smiling?"

He didn't tell her the truth, that he was amused by her. The play of emotions that had crossed her face as she rambled on and on was comical. She was smiling one second and glaring up at him the next. He felt like laughing, and if she hadn't been so agitated, he probably would have given in to the urge. He didn't want to hurt her feelings though. Genevieve obviously took the matter of their engagement seriously, and he was pretty certain she expected him to do the same.

It really was a hell of a mess, and he had no one but Mama Rose to blame for meddling in his private affairs. He would deal with her later, but now he needed to have a long-overdue discussion with Genevleve.

First things first. He needed to move away from her. He was standing entirely too close. Odd, but he couldn't seem to make himself step back. Her scent so light and feminine, made him think she'd bathed in lilacs. He liked it more than he thought he should. He liked just about everything about her. He even noticed, and approved of, what she was wearing, and he had never been interested in such superficial things before. Still, the starched, high-collared white blouse and white skirt were a nice contrast to her flawless coloring. She looked as prim and proper as a banker's wife, and was as sexy as hell.

He shook himself out of his reflection. "Why don't we go down to the library."

"The library? Yes, we should go to the library."

"Good idea," he drawled out.

She inwardly groaned. She was doing it again, repeating his words. He was going to start calling her a parrot if she didn't get hold of herself and stop thinking about foolish things, such as how deep and rich the sound of his voice was and how clean and masculine his scent was. He seemed to carry the outdoors around with him.

He really had the most devastating effect on her. She let out a little sigh. "I've been dreading this."

"Dreading what?"

"Our private talk," she said. "Shall we go and get it over with?"

She sounded as though she were on her way to a firing squad. He agreed with a nod and walked by her side down the stairs. When they reached the end of the back hall, he moved forward to open the door, then stepped back so she could enter the library first.

The room was musty and smelled of old books.

She found it very pleasing and looked around in fascination and approval. There were hundreds of volumes lined up on cherry wood shelves from the ceiling to the floor, and more books were piled in stacks on the hardwood floor near the windows.

The library had taken on the character of the man who occupied it, she decided. She knew from Adam's letters to his mother how much he loved to read, and she would have wagered every cent she possessed that he had already read every book there. He might even have read them more than once.

He motioned for her to take a seat. She chose one of the two overstuffed leather chairs facing the desk, sat down on the very edge of the seat, with her knees and her ankles pressed together and her back as straight as a ruler, and folded her hands in her lap.

She couldn't sit still long. While he was getting comfortable in his chair behind the desk, she nervously began to tap her heels against the floor. She stared down at her lap so she could concentrate, and rehearsed what she would say to him.

She thought it would be better if she let him speak first, and after he was finished, she would then gently—yes, gently—explain that her circumstances had changed and she couldn't marry him. She would be as diplomatic as a statesman so that she wouldn't injure his feelings or damage his pride.

Adam sat back in his chair and stared at her, patiently waiting for her to tell him what was on her mind. After several minutes passed in silence, he decided it was up to him to begin. He knew exactly what he wanted to say to her, for he'd been thinking about it all week long. Why then was it so difficult for him to get started?

He cleared his throat. The tapping got faster and louder.

"Genevieve, I'm not certain what your understanding with Mama Rose was, but I—"

She jumped to her feet. "Oh, Adam, I can't do it. I just can't."

"You can't what?"

"I can't marry you. I wish I could, but I can't. I wanted to explain right away, but you've been avoiding me all week long, which makes me think you don't really want to marry me anyway, and this personal matter wasn't something I wanted to talk about in front of your relatives. It's all so awkward, isn't it? Your mother put both of us in such a peculiar position. Are we engaged or aren't we? No, of course we aren't. Will it surprise you to know that I do want to marry you, or at least I used to want to marry you? For heaven's sake, don't look so surprised. I'm telling you the truth. Everything's changed though, and I can't possibly marry you now. No, it's out of the question, and even if you did want to marry me, well, eventually you'd find out about the trouble I'm in, and then you'd be horrified you ever entertained the notion. Do you see? I'm saving you from making a terrible mistake. I'm so sorry to disappoint you. Truly I am. You're just going to have to get over me. Broken hearts do mend. There, I've had my say. We can't get married, no matter how much you want to, and I apologize for deliberately misleading you. It was insensitive and cruel of me."

She finally paused long enough to take a breath. She knew she'd made a mess out of her explanation, and even while she had been rambling on and on, she'd kept telling herself to stop, but she couldn't seem to make herself do it. He probably thought she was crazy. His expression didn't give her a hint of what he was thinking, and she could only conclude that he was too stunned to react at all. Some of the words she'd blurted out kept repeating inside her head. Dear God, she'd started out telling him she didn't believe he wanted to marry her, and by the time she'd finished, she was insisting that his broken heart would mend. Oh, yes, he had to think she was demented. Mortified, she turned her attention to the wall behind him, pretending great interest in the framed map hanging there.

"I have to 'get over' you?"

She was relieved there wasn't any laughter in his voice when he asked the question. She gave him a weak nod and said, "Yes, you do."

"I see. You said you misled me. When exactly did you do that?"

She continued to stand and stare at the map while she answered him. "The night we met, I introduced myself as your bride. That was a falsehood."

"Ah, yes, I remember."

She dared a quick look at him. The warmth in his eyes had a strangely calming effect on her, and she began to relax.

"Are you always so self-assured?"

He laughed. "No."

"I think maybe you are. You don't get riled easily, do you?"

"No, I don't. Did you want to rile me?"

"No, of course not. You really do have an odd effect on me. I'm very relaxed around your family, but you . . ."

"I what?"

She shrugged and then decided to change the subject. "Your mother didn't tell me what a nice-looking man you were. It doesn't change anything. I still can't marry you, and I wouldn't marry any man just because he was handsome. I've learned from experience that appearances are misleading."

"Mama Rose didn't tell me how pretty you were. Why don't you sit down and tell me about the trouble you're in. Maybe I can help."

"Trouble? Why do you think I'm in trouble?"

Her voice rose an octave, and she seemed astonished that he would ask her such a question. He held on to his patience. "You just told me you were."

She didn't remember. "I spoke out of turn. I was in such a hurry to get everything said, and I was very nervous. I'm sure you must have noticed. I was talking a mile a minute, but I so wanted you to understand. And I was concerned about hurting your feelings. I didn't, did I?"

"Hurt my feelings? No, you didn't," he assured her with a smile he couldn't quite contain. "I might be able to help you, Genevieve, if you'll tell me what the problem is," he insisted once again.

She shook her head. She didn't want to lie to him, but she didn't want to tell him the truth either, for then he would be involved and could very well end up in trouble too.

"I don't have a problem."

She didn't think she could have been more emphatic, yet from his frown, she knew he still wasn't convinced. Once again she tried to get him to talk about something else.

She nodded toward the wall behind him. "Your mother showed me that map right after she purchased it for you. Why did you frame it and hang it on your wall? That wasn't what she wanted you to do with it. You were supposed to take it with you when you set out to see the world."

He knew she was deliberately evading his question, and that only made him more curious to find out what was troubling her. He wasn't usually intrusive, but she was a guest in his house and a close friend of his mother's, and if she really was in trouble, then he should try to help. He couldn't imagine that she was involved in anything serious though. She was such a sweet, innocent woman, one who undoubtedly had been sheltered by her family. What possible trouble could she have gotten into?

His mind leapt from one possibility to another. "Did you leave a suitor pining after you when you left New Orleans?"

The question gave her pause. "No," she answered. "I wasn't in New Orleans long enough to meet anyone. Why would you ask me such a question?"

"I was just curious."

"Are you always this curious with all your guests?"

"Only the ones I find myself engaged to," he teased.

She hastened to correct him. "You were engaged, Adam, but you aren't any longer."

He laughed again. "That's right," he agreed. "How long were you in New Orleans?"

"Two weeks."

"Just long enough to see the sights?"

"I wasn't there to see the sights. I was singing in a choir, but then I decided it was time for me to leave. Now it's your turn. Answer my question and tell me why you haven't left here to travel the world. I know you wanted to, because I read all the letters you wrote to Mama Rose."

He raised an eyebrow in reaction. "You did? Why would you—"

She wouldn't let him finish. "I love Mama Rose, and I wanted to know everything I could about her family. It was something I could share with her. We met at church," she added. "Then I joined the choir and traveled from place to place."

"You have a beautiful voice. Did you ever think about teaching music?"

"No, but I did think about a career on the stage. Then I came to my senses. I sing in church, and I occasionally sing to babies," she said with a smile. "Now it's your turn to answer a question. Tell me, why haven't you gone out to see the world?"

"I can see the world every time I turn my head

and look at a map, and I can go from port to port by simply opening one of my books and reading."

"It isn't at all the same. You've become too complacent, Adam. Think of all the adventures you could have. What happened to your dream? You've forgotten about it, haven't you? Your mother didn't forget, and that's why she gave you the map. She showed me all the presents she was bringing to her sons and her daughter, and every one of them had special significance. Mary Rose continues the family tradition by wearing her mother's brooch, and Douglas carries his gold watch with him. Travis told me he takes his books everywhere he goes. Why, just last night he was rereading *The Republic.* I haven't seen Cole's compass yet," she added.

Before she could continue, Adam interjected, "He hasn't seen it yet either."

She looked perplexed. "I don't understand. Why hasn't he seen it? Didn't Mama Rose give it to him?"

"Both the compass and the gold carrying case were either stolen or borrowed from Mama Rose."

"Which was it, for heaven's sake? Stolen or borrowed?"

"It depends on who you ask. Cole insists it was stolen, but the rest of us think it was borrowed. I'll admit that when Mama Rose first told us what happened, we all thought it was stolen, but since then most of us have changed our minds."

"Tell me what happened," she insisted. She

sat down, folded her hands together, and waited for him to begin.

"Mama Rose was waiting for a train at one of the stations on her way here. She showed the compass and the gold case to a man who was traveling with her. He was also headed for Montana," he continued. "According to Mama Rose, the two of them became friends and confided in one another."

"Your mother's a good judge of character."

"Yes, she is," he agreed. "She told us that he looked out for her on the journey and was very kind to her."

"He gained her confidence, and after a while, she began to trust him," she said with a nod that suggested she understood what had happened.

"Yes, she trusted him."

Her voice was edged with sadness when she said, "I bet I know what happened then. He betrayed her, didn't he?"

Adam found her reaction to the story intriguing. He had expected her to be a little curious, but she seemed upset about it.

"Cole thinks he did betray her," he said. "Is that what happened to you, Genevieve? Did you trust someone who betrayed you?"

The question startled her. She quickly shook her head in denial. "We're talking about your mother, not me."

"Are we?"

"Yes," she insisted. "I do find the story disturbing," she admitted. "Has anyone notified the authorities about the theft? They might be able to get the compass back."

"So you think he stole the compass?"

"Yes, I do. The gold case is very valuable. I'm telling you, Adam, you just can't trust anyone these days."

He was trying not to smile. She had formed her conclusion without knowing half the facts. She and Cole had a lot in common. Like his brother, Genevieve was willing to think the worst.

"You sound as cynical as Cole."

"I am cynical," she said. "I'll bet the authorities also think the compass was stolen. What did they have to say?"

"It's complicated."

"Why?"

"The man who has the compass *is* the authority." Her hand flew to her throat. "What's this?" she demanded.

"A U.S. marshal has the compass. His name is Daniel Ryan."

She was astounded. "The thief's a marshal? How shameful. Your dear mother must be devastated."

"No, she isn't devastated at all. She's convinced herself that he never meant to keep the compass. There was a crowd trying to get on the train, and she and Ryan were separated. He just happened to be holding the compass and the gold case at the time. She believes he'll bring Cole's gift here as soon as he finishes his more pressing business. Cole thinks Mama Rose is being very naive. From the description we have of Ryan, it does seem peculiar to all of us that he could be pushed around in a crowd. He's a big man with muscle."

344

"Is he as big as you are?"

Adam shrugged. "If the description's accurate, then yes, he is."

She mulled the story over in her mind for a moment and then condemned Ryan. "He stole it all right."

"Then you also believe Mama Rose is being naive?"

Genevieve stood up and began to pace around the room. "She has to have faith in Daniel Ryan, and you should let her."

"Why?" he asked.

"Because otherwise she would have to accept that she had been duped, and that's very difficult for anyone to admit. She would feel foolish and stupid, and blame herself. Yes, she would. She wouldn't be able to sleep worrying about it."

She turned at the window to look at him and knew by his expression that her outburst had been a bit extreme. She took a deep breath and tried to explain herself. "You must think it strange that I would become so passionate on your mother's behalf. It's just that she's such a good-hearted woman and it wounds me to think that anyone would take advantage of her. I wouldn't advise going after Daniel Ryan though, because it will only make matters worse."

"Why would it make matters worse?"

"Because in the end, it would be his word against hers."

"And you think that because he's a marshal, the law would be on his side?"

"Yes, of course," she replied. "It's naive to think otherwise. Ryan holds a position of power and influence over others, and if Mama Rose doesn't use her wits to figure a way to outsmart him, then all will be lost."

Adam stood up and came around the desk. "Tell me something. Did you use your wits to outsmart . . ."

He stopped in the middle of his question when Genevieve headed for the door.

"Don't run away. I'll stop prying into your personal life. I promise."

Her hand was on the doorknob, and he could tell from her frown that she didn't believe him.

"Your affairs are none of my business," he insisted. "I just thought I might be able to help."

"I don't need your help."

He leaned against the desk, folded his arms across his chest, and nodded. "Obviously not."

She took a step toward him. "It was very kind of you to offer. Please don't think I'm not grateful."

"I don't."

She visibly relaxed and moved closer.

"You smell like lilacs. I like it," he said.

She smiled. "Thank you," she said. "And thank you also for offering to help. It was very kind of you, but since I don't happen to have a problem, I don't need your assistance."

She wasn't a good liar. She couldn't quite look him in the eyes when she insisted she wasn't in trouble. He wouldn't challenge her though. He knew she'd head for the door again if he didn't agree with her.

"No," he said. "You don't have a problem, and you don't need help."

"That's right."

"Mama Rose doesn't need help either. She made all of us promise not to go after Ryan, but now that we know where he is, Cole's having a real hard time keeping his word."

"Where is the marshal?"

"About a hundred miles from here, in Crawford," he answered. "He lives in Texas, but he's working out of the office there while he rounds up a gang hiding out in the hills. Word has it, he's determined to take them back to Texas to stand trial."

"Couldn't one of you go to Crawford and have a little talk with him? I'm sure he'd give you the compass once he knows who you are."

Adam shook his head. "We have to wait until he brings it here because we promised we would. I figure he'll get around to it one of these days. Besides, the circumstances changed, and Cole's the only one who still wants to go after him."

"How did the circumstances change?"

"Ryan saved Travis's life."

She was astonished. "Tell me what happened."

He told her the story of Travis's encounter with the O'Toole brothers. "They ambushed him, shot him in the back. If Ryan hadn't gotten there when he did, Travis would never have made it."

"I wish you had mentioned this earlier," she said. "I have to revise my opinion now. Why, he probably didn't steal the compass at all. The man proved that he's honorable by coming to Travis's rescue. Shame on you, Adam, for making him out to be guilty."

The sparkle in her eyes told him she was

teasing. She really was a beautiful woman, and that smile of hers was doing crazy things to his heartbeat. He found himself wondering what she would feel like in his arms. If he kissed her the way he wanted to, he knew he'd shock her sensibilities, but that didn't stop him from thinking about it.

"You made him out to be guilty."

Her remark jarred him out of his daydream. "I what?"

She repeated her statement. He shook his head. "I did no such thing. You drew your own conclusions before I could give you all the details."

She burst out laughing. "I got all riled up for nothing. I won't worry about Mama Rose any longer. I've taken up too much of your time. You're needed outside," she reminded him. She glanced back at the map once again. "You should take the map out of the frame. Your mother doesn't want you to give up on your dreams, and neither do I. You should see all the wonderful places you've read about before it's too late, and if you ever find your way to Paris, be sure to look me up."

She turned to leave. He didn't know what compelled him to do it, but he grabbed hold of her hand and pulled her back.

"You're going to France?"

"Yes. My grandfather lives there, and he's all the family I have left now."

"When will you leave?"

"In a couple of days."

The news that she would be going so far away bothered him, and he couldn't understand why.

He should be happy to be rid of her, shouldn't he? And now that he thought about it, why hadn't he been elated when she'd told him she couldn't marry him? He had intended to say those very words to her.

Adam knew he wasn't making any sense, and that made him angry. He immediately let go of her hand and watched her walk away.

Then he got up and went back to work. His involvement with Genevieve Perry was over.

Three

It had only just begun.

Quite a crowd attended the party, and everyone seemed to be having a good time. Adam and Cole stood near the bandstand watching the couples dance to the gyrating, foot-stomping sounds of Billie Bob and Joe Boy's Band. Isabelle and Douglas came twirling past, and right behind them were Travis and his wife, Emily. If their laughter was any indication, the four of them were thoroughly enjoying themselves. Mama Rose was delighted by all the commotion. She sat at one of the picnic tables, flanked by Dooley and Ghost, two family friends, and all three of them, Adam noticed, kept time to the music by clapping their hands and tapping their feet.

Cole nudged his brother in his side. "Isn't that Clarence riding down the hill?"

Adam squinted toward the mountain. "It looks like him."

"We invited him, but he turned us down because he had to work the telegraph office. Someone has to be on duty all the time. Maybe he's bringing a wire to someone."

"Maybe he got someone else to work for him," Adam suggested.

Douglas and Isabelle came dancing past again. Cole waved to them and then said, "I never thought Travis or Douglas would ever get married, and now look at them."

"They're happy and they found good women. What about you, Cole? Do you think you'll ever get married?"

"No," he replied, his voice emphatic. "I'm not cut out for marriage. You are though. What happened with Genevieve? Did you have your talk with her?"

"Yes."

"I hope you let her down easy. She's a real sweetheart, and I'd hate to see her get hurt."

Adam shook his head. "If you're worried about her feelings, don't be. You've got it all backwards. She talked to me. She doesn't want to marry me either."

"Why the hell not?"

"Her circumstances have changed," Adam said. "Besides, we were never really engaged. That was just Mama Rose's dream. She's hell-bent on getting all of us married."

"You must have been happy Genevieve let you off the hook."

Adam shrugged. He thought about lying to his

brother and then changed his mind. Cole would see right through him, and if anyone would understand, he would.

"I wasn't happy or relieved. My reaction was kind of strange."

"How's that?"

He looked at his brother when he answered. "I got mad."

Cole shook his head. "You really got mad?"

"I just said I did. Genevieve didn't know it though."

"That doesn't make any sense at all. You've been avoiding the woman all week long, and now you're telling me you want to marry her?"

"No, that isn't what I'm telling you."

"Then why did you get mad?"

Adam let out a weary sigh. "I don't know."

Cole let the matter go. "Are you going to dance with her?"

"I hadn't thought about it. I don't even know where she is."

Cole motioned toward the porch. Mary Rose and Genevieve were carrying pies out to add to the dessert table. Both women had on white aprons over their dresses. Mary Rose was wearing her new store-bought blue skirt and blouse, and Genevieve was dressed in pale pink. Standing side by side, they were a handsome pair.

Adam couldn't take his gaze off of Genevieve. She was smiling over something Mary Rose had just said to her.

"Genevieve sure is pretty, isn't she?" Cole remarked.

"Yeah, she's pretty."

"She's tall."

"You think so?"

Adam turned around to watch the band. Cole didn't take the hint. "Mary Rose has to look up at her."

"So what? Our sister has to look up at everybody."

"You don't have to get defensive. I'm not finding fault with Genevieve. I like tall women. Have you noticed how shapely she is?"

"Of course I noticed. What's your game, Cole? Are you trying to make me angry?"

"No, I'm trying to get you to realize women like Genevieve don't come along very often. She sure is sweet."

"Then you marry her," he snapped.

Cole laughed. "You want her, don't you?"

"Damn it, Cole . . ."

"All right," his brother said. "I won't hound you any longer."

Adam started to walk away, but Cole's next remark pulled him back.

"It looks like Clarence is headed for the house."

"Maybe he needs to talk to Harrison," Adam suggested as he watched their brother-in-law step forward to shake Clarence's hand.

"Guess again," Cole said when Clarence turned to Genevieve and tried to hand an envelope to her. She gave the pie she was holding to Harrison, wiped her hands on her apron, and then accepted the wire.

"It's got to be bad news," Cole said.

"Maybe not," Adam said, and even he realized how unconvinced he sounded.

"No one ever sends good news in a wire. It costs too much. It's bad all right. Someone must have died. You ought to go comfort her."

"You go."

"I wasn't engaged to her; you were."

"For God's sake, there wasn't any engagement."

When Clarence turned to go down the steps, Adam saw his expression clearly.

"Clarence looks scared."

Cole nodded. "He sure is in a hurry to leave, isn't he?"

Adam turned back to Genevieve. "Why doesn't she open the envelope? What's she waiting for?"

"Maybe she wants to stare at it a little longer while she gets her courage up. No one's ever eager to get bad news."

"We shouldn't be watching her."

"Why not?" Cole asked.

"It's intrusive. She probably wants privacy."

He watched her tuck the unopened envelope into the pocket of her apron before taking the pie back from Harrison and hurrying down the steps. She put the dessert on the table with the other baked goods, then turned around and walked away from the crowd.

Adam forced himself to turn to the couples twirling about the dance floor, but he kept glancing back at Genevieve.

He saw her stop when she reached the far side

of the corral near the barn. She pulled the envelope out, tore it open, and read the contents.

The news couldn't have been good. Even with the distance separating them, Adam could see how shaken she was. She couldn't stand up straight. She staggered back against the fence and turned away from him, but not before he saw the fear on her face.

"Maybe you ought to go find out what the trouble is," Cole suggested.

Adam shook his head. "She obviously wants to be alone. If she tells us what the news was and we can help, then we will. Quit giving me that look, Cole. I'm not going to intrude into her personal life again, and neither are you."

"Again? What are you talking about?"

"Never mind."

Isabelle was suddenly standing in front of Adam, demanding that he dance with her. Emily grabbed hold of Cole's hand at the same time and pulled him onto the dance floor.

Adam tried to keep track of Genevieve. He saw her crumple up the wire and put it back in her apron, but then the music started and he lost her in the crowd. After the dance ended, he went searching for her. Harrison intercepted him to tell him that Mama Rose was about to open her presents. Since the family was giving her a trip to Scotland, Harrison thought it would be a nice touch if he played the bagpipes. Adam couldn't talk him out of it. He joined his sister and his brothers on the side of the bandstand and tried to appear interested. He nudged Cole and asked him in a low voice if he'd seen Genevieve.

Cole shook his head. He was going to suggest that she was probably inside the house, but then Harrison began to play, and the piercing noise was so deafening, he knew Adam wouldn't hear him.

"He's getting better, isn't he?" Mary Rose shouted.

"No," all four brothers shouted back.

Their sister wasn't offended. She maintained her smile for her husband's benefit and gave Douglas a hard shove when he put his hands over his wife's ears.

Genevieve was standing in the center of the crowd on the opposite side of the bandstand, watching the Clayborne family—the four brothers side by side, Emily and Isabelle leaning back against their husbands. Their expressions were comical, but she thought Adam's was the most revealing. Like his brothers and his sister, he was smiling, yet every time Harrison tried to hit a high note and missed, Adam would visibly flinch.

They were all such good-hearted people and so very loyal to one another. They were united now in giving Harrison their encouragement and support, and though it was apparent from their forced smiles that they thought the music was terrible, she knew they would cheer him when he was finished and never admit to any outsider that the sound had been less than perfect. And that was what family was all about.

God, how she envied all of them. She longed to walk across the dance floor and stand in front of Adam and lean back against him. She wanted to belong to his family, but most of all, she wanted to be loved by him.

It was a fool's dream, she told herself. She whispered a good-bye in Mama Rose's direction, and then turned and walked away.

Four

The party didn't wind down until after midnight. Riders with fiery torches lighted the way back to Blue Belle for those guests who lived in the nearby town and wanted to go home. The guests from Hammond stayed overnight. They slept on cots in the parlor and the dining room, filled the bunkhouse, and spilled out onto the porch. Cole gave up his bed to the Cohens, and Adam let old man Corbett sleep in the bunk bed he'd used all week. The brothers weren't inconvenienced, for they much preferred sleeping outside under the stars, away from the crowd.

Adam left at dawn the following morning with three hired hands to round up the mustangs grazing on sweet grass down in Maple Valley, and he didn't return to Rosehill until late that afternoon.

Cole was waiting for him on the front porch. He handed Adam a beer and sat down on the top step.

He didn't waste time getting to the news. "Genevieve's gone."

Adam didn't show any outward reaction. He

356

took his hat off, tossed it onto a nearby chair, and sat down next to his brother. He took a long swallow of his drink and remarked that it was damned hot today.

"You look tired," Cole remarked.

"I am tired," Adam replied. "Have all the guests gone home?"

"Yes, the last of them left around noon."

"When are you leaving for Texas to bring the cattle up?"

"Tomorrow."

Several minutes passed in silence. Adam stared at the distant mountains and tried to ignore the unease he felt about Genevieve. As soon as Cole had given him the news, his gut and his throat both tightened up on him. Why had she left so abruptly, and why hadn't she told him good-bye? Maybe he shouldn't have hounded her with questions, but damn it, she'd let it slip that she was in trouble, and he had naturally wanted to find out the particulars so that he could help. No, he decided. His few questions wouldn't have made her so skittish that she would pack up and leave.

The telegram had to be the reason she'd taken off. He remembered the fear he'd seen on her face after she'd read the wire. He should have gone to her then and demanded that she confide in him.

He let out a loud sigh. He knew then what he was going to have to do and was already getting angry about it.

"Hell," he muttered.

"What?"

"Nothing. Did Genevieve say good-bye to anyone?"

"No, she didn't tell anyone she was leaving. She just took off. Mama Rose is up in arms about it. She says it isn't like Genevieve to leave without saying her thank-yous. She says she's a well-bred young lady with impeccable manners. I think Genevieve was spooked by that telegram," Cole added. "But Mama Rose thinks you chased her away."

Adam rolled his eyes heavenward. "Genevieve must have left with some of the guests last night. She's too smart to go off on her own."

"Maybe so," Cole allowed. "It's odd though. She was supposed to ride with the Emersons to Salt Lake, and they aren't leaving town until tomorrow."

"Maybe they decided to leave earlier."

"In the dark? They're old, not crazy. Besides, they were here last night."

Adam's unease intensified. Had she gone off on her own? The possibility sent chills down his spine. No, she wouldn't have done that. She was too intelligent to do such a rash, irresponsible thing. She would surely be aware of the danger a woman alone would face in the wild. Women were hard to come by in some of the more remote areas, and pretty women like Genevieve were considered prizes for the taking by some of the less civilized mountain clans.

Cole was watching his brother closely. "You don't seem too broken up over her leaving," he remarked.

Adam shrugged indifference. "It's her life. She can do whatever she wants."

"What if she took off on her own?"

"There isn't anything I can do about that."

Cole smiled. "It isn't working, Adam."

"What isn't working?"

"Your I-don't-give-a damn attitude. You're trying to act like you aren't worried about her, and we both know you are."

His brother didn't deny it. "I wish I knew what was in that telegram. Whatever it was scared her. Maybe someone close to her got sick. That would scare a woman, wouldn't it?"

"That would scare a man too," Cole said. "You don't think she's in any kind of trouble, do you?"

"It can't be anything serious. I was pretty sure that there was something wrong, but she denied it. She looked me right in the eye and told me she didn't need any help. She said it was just a minor inconvenience."

"You think she was telling you the truth?"

"About her problem being a minor one? Yeah, I do. She's led a real sheltered life, and I can't imagine she has any real serious problems."

"I think Genevieve's real smart, but even smart people do crazy things when they're scared."

"Such as?"

"Riding out at night all alone."

Adam refused to believe that she would take such a chance. "I'm sure she got a ride with someone."

Cole didn't argue with him. "Maybe you ought to go into town and have a little talk with Clarence. You can be real intimidating when you want to, and I'll bet you could get him to tell you what was in that wire."

"If he tells me, he'll lose his job. Wires are supposed to be kept confidential."

"So?"

Adam shook his head. "Clarence is too ethical." He spat the words out as though they were foul. He stood up, grabbed his hat, and headed for the door. "I've wasted enough time."

"Where are you going?"

"Back to work as soon as I change my shirt. I'm going to be up half the night catching up on all the paperwork, and tomorrow I've got to start breaking in the mustangs so we can sell them at the auction next month, and I—"

"You're going after her, aren't you?"

Adam gave his brother a look that suggested he wanted to punch him for asking such a stupid question. "What do you think?"

He didn't stay outside long enough to hear Cole's answer. He went upstairs to his room, stripped out of his shirt, and washed the dirt and grime off. He could have sworn the scent of lilacs was on the towel he used, but that was the only reminder that Genevieve had occupied his room.

Her suitcase was gone from the corner. There was an empty space in the wardrobe where her clothes had hung, and the jewelry and hair clips he'd noticed on the dresser yesterday when he'd come in to get clean clothes were also gone.

She hadn't left anything behind. Yet the memory of her smile lingered in his mind, and he knew it was going to take him a long while to forget her.

He decided to get busy. He went downstairs to grab something to eat before he tackled the paperwork. Mary Rose was sitting at the kitchen table with a pen and paper in her hands. She smiled when she saw him.

"You're back early. Are you hungry? I made soup, but it isn't as good as Mama Rose's."

"I thought you went home," he said.

"We're leaving in a few minutes. I wanted to copy down this recipe first. Sit down and I'll get you a bowl. You are going to try my soup, aren't you?"

"Sure," he said.

She stood up and reached for the apron she'd draped over the back of her chair. Adam had only just taken his seat when he bounded back to his feet.

"The apron," he announced.

She slipped the garment over her head and then looked down to see if something was wrong with it.

"It looks fine to me."

"Not yours," he said, his impatience evident in his brisk tone. "The apron Genevieve was wearing. Was it hers?" he asked, wondering if women packed such things when they traveled.

"No, I loaned her one of Mama Rose's. I didn't want her to get her dress—"

Adam cut her off. "Did she give it back?"

"For heaven's sake, of course she gave it back. What's the matter with you?"

"Nothing's the matter. Where is it?"

"The apron?"

"Yes, damn it, the apron. Where is it?"

Her eyes widened in reaction to his bizarre behavior. It wasn't like Adam to ever lose his temper, but he appeared to be on the verge of doing just that. He was usually so calm and in control. Nothing ever riled him.

"Why are you getting so upset about an apron?" she demanded.

"I'm not upset. Now answer me. Where is it?"

She gave him a frown to let him know she didn't appreciate his surly attitude.

"I suppose it's hanging with the others on the hooks in the pantry."

Adam was already halfway across the kitchen before his sister had finished explaining. She followed him to the doorway and stood there watching him sort through the clutter of coats and hats and scarves and bibs, tossing them every which way until most of them were on the floor behind him.

"You're picking all those up," she said. "Adam, what's come over you?"

"Where the hell is it?"

"It's the white one on your left with the two lace pockets," she said. "Why do you want it?"

Adam lifted the apron from the hook and quickly searched the pockets. He felt like shouting with victory when he pulled out the crumpled piece of paper. Just as he had hoped, in her haste to leave, Genevieve had forgotten the wire.

He unfolded the paper, moved into the light, and read the message.

Then he exploded. "Son of a bitch."

"Watch your language," Mary Rose demanded. She moved close to her brother's side and tried to see what he was holding.

She wasn't quick enough. He had already refolded the paper before she could see anything.

"What is it?"

"A telegram."

"That's Genevieve's," she said. "I was standing next to her when Clarence gave the wire to her. Shame on you, Adam. You shouldn't have read it. It's confidential."

Cole came up behind his sister in time to hear her protest and offered his opinion.

"Sure he should read it. Who's it from, Adam?"

"A woman named Lottie."

Adam finally looked at him. Cole could tell from the look in his brother's eyes that it was serious. Mary Rose didn't seem to notice, however

"I know what it says," she announced

Adam turned to her. "You do?"

"Yes."

"And you didn't tell anyone?"

"Don't yell at me," she snapped. "Genevieve told me her friend was expecting a baby and promised to have her husband send a wire to let her know if she had a boy or a girl."

"Is that so?" Adam asked.

Mary Rose nodded. "She had a girl," she said. "I can't understand why you would get so upset over someone else's personal . . ."

She stopped talking when Cole put his hands

on her shoulders and suggested she take a good look at Adam's expression.

Their brother looked furious. "How bad is it?" Cole asked him.

In answer, Adam handed the wire to him. Cole unfolded the paper and read the message out loud.

"Run for your life. They know where you are. They're coming for you."

"Good Lord," Mary Rose cried out.

Cole whistled at the same time. "Son of a . . ."

"How could anyone want to harm such a sweet, loving young lady?" Mary Rose asked.

"I thought you told me she wasn't in trouble," Cole said.

"That's what she told me," Adam muttered.

"She lied."

"No kidding. Of course she lied."

Mary Rose shook her head. "She must have had a good reason not to involve us.

"We are involved if trouble is coming here," Cole replied.

"I thought we had become good friends over the past week. She acted as though she didn't have a care in the world. Are you going to go after her, Adam.

"Hell, yes."

"Mama Rose is going to be beside herself with worry when she hears about this."

Adam gave his sister a hard look. "She isn't going to hear about it. There isn't any reason to worry her."

Mary Rose agreed with a quick nod. "Yes, you're right. I won't tell her."

Adam started for the door, but Mary Rose grabbed hold of his hand to detain him.

"Why are you so angry?"

"It's a hell of an inconvenience to drop everything and go chasing after her, and I don't much like knowing trouble's coming to Rosehill. Cole, you're going to have to put off your trip to Texas for another week or two and stay around here."

"I will," he assured his brother.

"If anyone comes looking for Genevieve—"

"I'll know what to do."

Adam left Rosehill fifteen minutes later. Genevieve Perry was about to find out what real trouble was.

Five

Genevieve was trying hard not to be afraid and failing miserably. She sat in front of her campfire with her legs tucked underneath her, gripping a gun in one hand and a heavy tree branch in the other. There weren't any stars out tonight, and it was so dark she couldn't see beyond the circle of the fire. She had never been bothered by the dark before, not even as a child, but then she'd always lived inside a nice strong house in the heart of the city with locks on every door and a mother and father to look after her. Now she was all alone and sitting in the middle of the forest, where all sorts of wild animals roamed about looking for food. She couldn't see the predators, but she knew they were there because she could hear them, and that made the dark all the more terrifying.

At night, the forest shrieked with life. Every sound was magnified. A twig snapped nearby and she flinched, her heart pounding frantically. She was certain an animal had made the noise, and she began to fervently pray it wasn't anything bigger or more dangerous than a rabbit. God only knew what she would do if a mountain lion or a bear wandered into her camp. The idea of becoming some animal's next meal didn't sit well with her, and she began to imagine all sorts of horrible ways she would die.

She began to hum one of her favorite hymns to take her mind off her dark thoughts until she realized the hymn was about death and redemption. Then she stopped and sagged against the tree behind her. She slowly stretched her legs out, crossed one ankle over the other, and willed herself to stop having such crazy thoughts. She would get through this night the same way she'd gotten through the past two. She would keep her eyes open and her wits sharp. Sleep was out of the question.

She never heard Adam coming. One second she was all alone, and the next he was sitting beside her and had her gun in his hand.

She was so startled to see him she screamed. She jumped back, struck her head against the tree, and cried out again. Her heart felt as though it had just leapt into her throat. How in heaven's name had he managed to drop down beside her without making any noise? As soon as she could find her voice, she would ask him that very question.

He didn't say a word to her. She watched him drop the gun on the ground between them. She stared stupidly at the weapon for several seconds before she turned to look up at him.

She had never been so happy to see anyone in all her life. He didn't look happy to see her though. His anger was more than apparent in the darkening of his eyes and the set of his jaw.

She wanted to hug him. She frowned instead and put her hand over her heart. "Adam, you scared me."

He didn't have anything to say about that. She took another breath and then admitted, "I didn't hear you coming."

"You weren't supposed to hear me."

They stared into each other's eyes for what seemed an eternity without saying another word. He was trying to calm his temper and kept telling himself that he had gotten to her in time, that nothing god-awful had happened to her, and that she was all right—for the moment. Relief intensified his anger, and, honest to God, he wanted to kiss her and shake some sense into her at the same time. He didn't give in to either inclination.

She was so thankful not to be alone any longer, tears welled up in her eyes.

He saw them. "What are you doing out here?"

"I'm camping. What are you doing here?"

"I came to get you."

Her eyes widened. "You did? Why?"

He didn't explain but asked another question

instead. "Why did you leave the ranch so abruptly?"

She turned away and stared at the fire. "I felt it was time for me to leave."

"What kind of answer is that?" he demanded.

"Lower your voice," she whispered.

"Why?"

"I don't want to . . . The animals will . . ."

"What about the animals?"

"If they hear us, they'll know we're here and they might come into camp."

He tried not to smile. "Animals are also directed by scent."

"I heard a mountain lion a little while ago."

"He won't bother you."

"You're sure?"

"Yes."

She visibly relaxed and leaned into his side. Her arm rubbed against his when she turned to him again. "There aren't any stars out tonight."

"Why did you leave in the middle of the night without telling anyone good-bye? Why were you in such a hurry?"

He already knew the answer, but he was curious to find out if she would tell him the truth. If she did, it would be a novelty, he decided. His frown darkened as he thought about what an adroit liar she was.

His scowl was hot enough to set her hair on fire. Her spine stiffened in reaction. "I know you're angry, but—"

He cut her off. "Hell, yes. I'm angry."

"Why?"

He shook his head at her. "Don't you realize

what could have happened to you? A beautiful woman like you can't go riding off in the wild without escorts. Do you have some sort of a death wish, Genevieve? Is that it? I know you're smart, but honest to God, I can't figure out why you would do such a foolish thing. Don't you care about the danger you're in?"

"I'm perfectly capable of taking care of myself, and if you came all this way just to give me a piece of your mind, then it was a wasted trip. Go back home."

She had tried to sound as angry as he had, but she was so rattled at the moment she didn't know if she'd accomplished the feat or not. He thought she was beautiful. The comment, made so matter-of-factly in the middle of his blistering lecture, took her by complete surprise. No one had ever called her beautiful before, and she had certainly never thought of herself that way. She was built all wrong. She was too tall, too thin, and her hair was too short. Yet Adam thought she was beautiful.

He couldn't figure out what had just come over her. She was staring off into space, a dreamy expression in her eyes. A hint of a smile crossed her face, and if he hadn't known better, he would have thought she was daydreaming.

He heard her sigh. It was long and drawn out, the kind of sigh a woman makes after she's been satisfied. Ah, hell, he thought to himself. Now wasn't the time to be thinking about such things.

"You were about to tell me why you left the ranch in the middle of the night without a word," he reminded her in a voice that sounded like a bear growling.

The reminder jarred her out of the fantasy she was having about living happily ever after.

"It wasn't the middle of the night. It was evening, and I wanted to say good-bye, honestly I did, but I was in a hurry and there wasn't time."

"Obviously not," he said. "Do you want to tell me why you were in such a hurry?"

"No."

Her abrupt answer didn't please him. He held his patience and said, "You left something behind."

"I did? What did I leave?"

"The telegram."

She closed her eyes. "You read it, didn't you?"

"Oh, yes, I read it."

She heard a faint rustling and gripped the branch with both hands as she squinted into the darkness. "I think something's out there. Did you hear that noise just now?"

"It's just the wind kicking up the leaves."

"I'm not so sure," she whispered.

"I am," he insisted. "You haven't done a lot of camping, have you, Genevieve?" His exasperation was obvious.

"No, I haven't. It's an adventure for me."

"You're trembling."

"It's chilly tonight. I will admit I was a little nervous before you arrived. I'm not nervous now. I'm glad you're here, Adam, even though you're angry with me."

"There's a town less than five miles from here. The Garrisons are a real nice couple who live on the outskirts. They rent out rooms. If you had asked—"

"I can't afford to spend any more money," she interrupted. "The trip to Rosehill cost more than I had anticipated. Besides, it wouldn't have been an adventure if I took a room for the night. I'm experiencing life. I'm not content to read about it the way you are."

He ignored her barb. "You could probably put that branch down now. What were you planning to do with it?"

She tossed it aside before she answered him. "I was going to swat animals away with it."

He didn't laugh at her, but the look he gave her suggested he thought she had lost her mind. She lifted her shoulders. "It seemed like a good idea at the time."

"You have a gun," he reminded her.

"I know I have a gun. I hoped I wouldn't have to use it. I'm the intruder here, not the wild animals. This is their home."

"Have you ever fired a gun before?"

"No."

Her answer made him angry all over again. It was a miracle that he had found her in one piece. Didn't she have any sense at all?

"You're going to start lecturing me again, aren't you?"

"You have no business being out here on your own. You're totally unskilled. Why didn't you tell me the truth back at Rosehill? Why did you lie?"

"I didn't want to lie to you."

"Then why did you?"

She moved away from him and leaned back against the tree again. "My problems aren't your concern. Your brothers made you come after me, didn't they?"

The question was so ludicrous he felt like laughing. "I'm here because I want to be here. Who wants to hurt you?"

"Besides you?"

"Answer me, Genevieve."

"No one wants to hurt me."

Her hands were clenched in her lap

"Do you ever tell the truth?" he asked.

"Yes, I usually do," she replied. "But this is my problem, not yours, and I don't want you to get involved."

"Too bad. I'm already involved."

She shook her head. He nodded. "You are going to tell me everything."

"No, I'm not, and you have no business trying to interfere in my life. You could get hurt or maybe even killed, God forbid. I can't let that happen. The less you know, the better. My problems aren't your concern."

"According to Lottie, whoever is chasing you is coming to Rosehill. That makes it my concern."

"That won't happen. I left the ranch so they wouldn't track me there. I made sure I was seen leaving Blue Belle, and I left an easy trail to follow when I headed west."

"Then you backtracked to go south."

"Yes."

"Tell me about Lottie. Who is she?"

"A friend I met when she joined the choir. She's very nice, but she tends to overreact."

"Is that so?"

"Honestly, no one wants to hurt me."

His hand dropped down on top of hers. "You are going to tell me all about the trouble you're in, but first tell me who is coming after you."

She was too tired to keep on fencing with him, and he was as relentless as a devil after a soul.

"The preacher is coming after me."

He raised an eyebrow. "The preacher?"

"His name is Ezekiel Jones. It isn't his real name though. One day he decided he had a calling, and he changed his name to Ezekiel to make himself sound more important. He and three others visited the church I regularly attended. . . . I think I mentioned to you that your Mama Rose used to go to that church too. That's where I met her," she thought to add. "I never asked her, but I'm sure she liked Ezekiel. Everyone liked him. He was very charismatic and smooth talking."

A tear slipped down her cheek. Adam let out a sigh, put his arm around her shoulders, and hauled her up against him.

"Why is the preacher chasing you?"

"I sang in his choir."

He squeezed her to get her to continue. She really was an exasperating woman. Getting information out of her was a difficult undertaking, but fortunately he was a patient man. He reminded himself of that fact when the silence continued.

She outlasted him. "He wants to hurt you because you sang in his choir."

"I really don't think he wants to hurt me," she insisted. "He just wants me back."

"Why?"

"I'm his meal ticket. When I sing in his choir, the attendance goes up."

"Ah, now I understand. The donations also go up, don't they?"

She nodded. "People seem to like my voice." She sounded embarrassed to admit such a thing.

"I can see why they would."

She smiled. "You can?"

"Yeah, I can," he said.

"Do you know what, Adam? You make me feel very safe."

He laughed. Now that he knew what her problem was, his anger diminished. The trouble wasn't serious after all. It was just a nuisance, and one he would quickly deal with.

"I make you feel safe? If you knew some of the thoughts I was having about you on my way here, you wouldn't feel that way."

She couldn't tell if he was teasing her or not. "What were you thinking?"

"Never mind. Have you told me everything?"

"Yes, of course I have."

"You didn't leave anything out?"

"Lord, you're suspicious," she said. "I'm not keeping any secrets from you. You know everything there is to know. Truly," she added with a nod.

"If you were telling me the truth—"

"I was," she interrupted.

"Then it's a very simple problem to solve."

"It is?"

The eagerness in her voice made him smile. "Yes, it is," he assured her. "I can't figure out

374

why you didn't tell me about Ezekiel when we were at Rosehill. It would have made things easier."

"I explained why I didn't confide in you. I didn't want you to get involved. Ezekiel Jones isn't a very nice man, Adam. He won't take no for an answer."

"Did you tell him no?"

She rolled her eyes heavenward. "I certainly did."

"And?"

"He locked me in a room."

"Is that so?" he asked in a voice that was soft and chilling.

The look that came into his eyes frightened her, and she realized once again what a dangerous adversary he could be. She was suddenly very happy that he was on her side.

"Yes," she said. She rubbed her arms to ward off the chill and added, "I had to climb out a window to get away from him and his two henchmen. I tore my best skirt."

"I really wish you had said something sooner. If you didn't want to confide in me, you could have told Harrison about Ezekiel. He's an attorney, and I'm sure he could have taken some sort of legal action to discourage the man."

"Could he keep Ezekiel from following me or threatening me?"

"No, but I could," he told her quietly.

"How?"

He wouldn't explain. She worried about his intentions for several minutes and then shook her head. "I don't want you to do anything. Ezekiel can't possibly know where I am now, and when I get to Salt Lake and board the train to New York, I'll be rid of him once and for all."

"Genevieve, if I found you, why do you think the preacher won't?"

"Because you've lived in the mountains most of your life and you know how to track, but Ezekiel has always lived in the city. He won't find me, and he certainly won't follow me to the East Coast just to get me back in his choir."

"Salt Lake isn't right around the corner. You're going to have to go into Gramby, then over to Juniper Falls, turn south again and pass through Middleton, swing east through Crawford, and then it's a straight shot down into Salt Lake. Unless you plan to ride hard, that's a good four days away from here. Jones could catch up to you in any one of those towns."

"If he were following me."

"Would you worry if you knew he was only a day behind you?"

"Yes, I would. He can be a real nuisance. If he were tracking me, would you know it?"

Of course he'd know. After living in the territory for so many years, a man developed a sixth sense about such things. The skin on the back of his neck would begin to prickle, and an uneasiness would settle in his bones until he backtracked to make certain his instincts were right. Adam had done just that while he'd been following Genevieve, and that was how he had known that Ezekiel and two others were following her all right. Jones might not know how to track someone down, but one of his cohorts certainly knew what he was doing. If Genevieve stayed right where she was, the three of them would catch up with her by late tomorrow afternoon.

Adam considered telling her about Jones now, then decided to let her get a good night's sleep first. She looked exhausted and needed rest. She could worry all she wanted tomorrow.

She waited for him to answer her question, but he changed the subject instead.

"You could take the coach from Gramby, and it will take you all the way to Salt Lake. Do you have enough money to buy a ticket? You mentioned you were low on funds," he reminded her.

"I have just enough to buy the train ticket."

"You should ride in the coach. I'll give you what I have with me, but it isn't much. The bank was closed when I left Blue Belle, and I didn't want to wait."

She yawned again, apologized, and then told him in no uncertain terms that she wouldn't take a cent from him. "I've never borrowed anything from anyone, and I'm not going to start now. I'll make do."

Her head dropped down on his shoulder. He was trying to concentrate on the conversation, but she'd cuddled up against him, and her soft, warm body was proving to be one giant distraction. She smelled so good to him, and her skin was just as silky and smooth as he'd guessed it would be. He trailed his fingers down her arm and smiled when he felt her shiver.

She was as warm as a kitten and as stubborn as a mule.

"I'm very happy you came after me, and I'll be sorry to see you leave when we get to Gramby. You will have to escort me that far," she added with a nod.

"Is that right?"

"You'll worry about me if you don't go with me to Gramby. Think of it as an adventure, Adam."

"You like adventures, don't you?"

"Yes, I do."

"Then you should be happy you aren't getting married. You'd have to settle down."

"With the right man, marriage would be the most wonderful adventure of all, and when I find him, I'm never going to let go."

He was sorry he'd brought up the topic of marriage. The thought of any other man having such an adventure with Genevieve irritated him. He felt possessive toward her and couldn't understand why.

"Get some sleep, Genevieve. You're tired."

She closed her eyes. "I haven't slept much in the past couple of days."

"You aren't going to sleep sitting up, are you? Don't you have a bedroll with you?"

"Yes, but I don't want to use it."

"Don't be ridiculous. I'll get it for you."

"No," she told him in a near shout. She put her hand on his thigh to stop him from getting up.

She'd sounded as though she was in a panic. Puzzled by her bizarre reaction, he asked, "Why not?"

"Snakes," she suddenly blurted out.

"What about them?"

"They slither under the cover and curl up against your feet."

"Has that ever happened to you?"

"No, but it could, and I'm not willing to take the chance. I'm very comfortable where I am, and I would appreciate it if you didn't touch my bedroll. I spent over an hour rolling up my dresses just so inside, and they'll get wrinkled if you unroll it."

He gave up trying to reason with her. If she wanted to sit up all night, that was fine with him.

"You're a very stubborn woman."

"No, I'm not. I'm sensible."

He snorted in disbelief. She decided to ignore him and tried to go to sleep.

Adam took care of his horse, then got his own bedroll and put it on the ground on the opposite side of the fire. After adding more wood to the flames, he stretched out on top of his cover, stacked his hands behind his head, and stared up at the black sky while he thought about how he would handle the Reverend Ezekiel Jones and his friends.

"Adam?"

"I thought you were asleep."

"Almost," she whispered. "May I ask you something?"

"Sure. What do you want to know?"

"Did you ever think of marrying me?"

"No, I didn't."

His answer was quick and brutally honest, but she didn't seem to be offended by his admission.

He watched her for a long time. He couldn't figure out why he was so drawn to her, and if he hadn't known better, he would have thought he was acting like a man who was falling in love

The possibility made him uneasy. He was content with his life, he reminded himself, and he wasn't going to change a thing.

He was just drifting off to sleep when she spoke to him again.

"I dreamed about you."

Six

He figured he would have to take her as far as Gramby. It was the least he could do, and there really wasn't any other choice. She was right: he would worry about her if he didn't go along. Besides, he'd never hear the end of it from his family—and he had a sneaking suspicion they'd find out—if he didn't accompany her and make certain she got on the coach. He had considered dragging her back to Rosehill and letting Harrison take some sort of legal action against Jones and his friends to discourage them from harassing her, but he was pretty sure Genevieve would take off again and he'd just end up chasing her.

He felt responsible for her because she was all alone. Like it or not, he was temporarily bound to her, and though it was completely out of character for him to do so, he was determined to interfere in her life.

She'd dreamed about him. He couldn't seem to get past that startling announcement. If she had meant to stun him with it, she'd succeeded magnificently. Speechless, he'd simply stared at her and waited for her to explain why she would have done such a thing She fell asleep instead.

She didn't wake up when he lifted her into his arms and carried her to his bedroll. He got her settled and sat down next to her. After removing his boots, he stretched his legs out, rested his shoulders against a tree, and closed his eyes.

Even in sleep she tormented him. She rolled over and curled up against his side, and just as he was dozing off, her hand dropped down in his lap. He was suddenly wide awake again. He quickly removed her hand, but less than a minute later, it was back, only this time it landed much closer to his groin. He gritted his teeth in frustration and tried to block the impossible thoughts that came into his mind. He could have gotten up and moved to the other side of the camp, but for some reason he felt compelled to stay close to her.

Needless to say, he didn't get much sleep that night.

He was up before dawn; she didn't wake up for two more hours. She was cheerful and refreshed; he was out of sorts and surly. She liked to talk in the morning; he preferred silence.

By noon, Adam had come to the conclusion that they were as different as night and day. When he wanted to get somewhere, he didn't let anything distract him. She wanted to stop and smell every flower along the way.

He rarely smiled; she laughed a lot. Mostly she laughed at him for being so overly protective toward her. She didn't seem to worry about anything and told him she thought he worried far too much.

The biggest difference between them was their attitude toward strangers. He was instinctively wary and distrustful. She was the complete opposite. Her trust in her fellow man astonished him. She greeted everyone she met as though he were a long lost friend, and she spent entirely too much time in conversation.

When they stopped to rest the horses, he reminded her of what she had told him back at Rosehill.

" 'You can't trust anyone these days,' " he said. "Remember telling me that?"

"I do remember, but I meant to say that I can't trust anyone in a position of power these days. How long before we reach Gramby?"

"That all depends on you. If you insist on stopping to talk to every stranger we pass on the road, we won't get there until tomorrow."

"And if I don't talk to anyone?"

"Gramby's about five hours away. If we ride hard, we could be there before supper."

She nudged her horse forward so she could ride beside him. "Do I have a choice? If so, I think I'd prefer to take my time. I like meeting new people and hearing their stories. I think you do too."

He smiled in spite of himself. "I do?"

"Yes," she insisted. "I looked through the books in your library, and I remember seeing quite a few biographies. You obviously enjoy reading about other people's experiences. I like to read about them too, but I also like to hear firsthand about their adventures, and if you show an interest, complete strangers will tell you the most wonderful stories. Of course, you'll have to put them at ease first, which means you're going to have to stop frowning all the time and looking so threatening. People tend to shy away from armed men who look like they're going to shoot them if they say the wrong thing. Do you have any idea how intimidating you are? You're such a big man, and surely you've noticed how strangers back away from you. Maybe if you put your guns away—"

He wouldn't let her finish. "No," he told her in a voice that didn't leave room for negotiation.

She shook her head. "There isn't any polite way to tell you this. You scare people." He laughed. She didn't know what to make of that. "Do you want to scare people?"

"I haven't given it any thought, but, yes, I suppose I do."

"Why?"

"They'll give me a wide berth, that's why. I've learned not to trust anyone, and until I put you on the coach in Gramby, I'm responsible for keeping you safe."

"No, you aren't responsible for me."

He wasn't going to argue with her. "So you would rather sleep outside again tonight?"

"I don't see any reason to rush."

"What about Ezekiel Jones? Aren't you worried about him?"

"No," she answered. "He's given up looking for me by now."

It was the perfect opportunity to tell her that she was wrong and that Ezekiel was indeed following her, but once again Adam was silent. He didn't want her to fret, and if she knew he intended to talk to Ezekiel, she would probably pitch a fit. The preacher scared her, and Adam was determined to put a stop to his harassment as soon as possible.

She had been saying something to him, but he hadn't been paying any attention. The expectant look she gave him now indicated she was waiting for an answer. He had to ask her to repeat the question.

"I said I don't have a schedule to maintain, but you do, don't you? I'll bet you have a hundred things to do when you get back home."

"There's always work to be done."

"Your brothers will run the ranch while you're away. They're probably very pleased that you finally left Rosehill. I know for a fact that you've never gone anywhere outside of the mountains surrounding your ranch."

"And how would you know that?"

"I read all your letters to Mama Rose, remember? You got so busy building the ranch you forgot about your dream. By the way, Adam, I haven't made up my mind if I want to take the coach to Salt Lake or not. It seems like a waste of good money. I have a sound horse," she added. She leaned forward in her saddle to give the mare a pat of affection.

"I was a boy when I wrote those letters, and you are taking the coach."

"You wrote most of the letters when you were

a boy, but there were also some that you wrote just a couple of years ago."

His response was a shrug of indifference. They rode along in silence, each caught up in thought. About fifteen miles outside of town they passed a family traveling on foot, following a wagon laden with their possessions. Genevieve stayed by Adam's side until they had reached the crest of the hill, then abruptly turned her mare around and headed back. He didn't have any choice but to follow her.

He caught up with her just in time to hear her invite the strangers to dine with her. There were five in all, a young couple with two little girls about the age of five or six, and an elderly man Adam assumed was the grandfather and patriarch of the family. The little girls stared up in fascination at Genevieve, but their mother stared at the grandfather while she awaited his decision. There was a look of eagerness and desperation on her face.

The two men were warily studying Adam. The younger one gathered his daughters up and pushed them behind his back. The protective gesture wasn't lost on Adam. If he had had children of his own and a stranger had ridden up to him with a rifle across his lap, he probably would have done the same thing. It was always better to be safe than sorry

The little girls weren't frightened of him though. They didn't give him the time of day. They were giggling as they peeked out to look up at Genevieve.

"Adam, I would like you to meet Mr. James Meadows and his family."

The elderly man stepped forward. He was tall painfully thin, and had snow white hair. Adam judged him to be around sixty-five or seventy years old.

As soon as Genevieve introduced the old man, he moved forward and reached up to offer his hand to Adam.

Adam shook it. "It's a pleasure to meet you, sir."

"Folks back home call me James, and I'd be pleasured if you'd do the same," he said in a voice that was thick with a southern twang. "This here is my son, Will, and his wife, Ellie. Those two little chatterboxes are Annie and Jessie. You can see they're twins," he added proudly. "Jessie's the one missing her front teeth."

Will stepped forward to shake Adam's hand. He was a strapping man with broad shoulders and brawny hands. After sizing him up, Adam decided that Will was used to doing hard labor out in the sun for he had bulging muscles in his forearms and weather-beaten skin.

"Are you a gunslinger?" Will asked, frowning over the possibility.

Adam shook his head. "No, I'm a rancher."

Will didn't look as though he believed him. Genevieve gave Adam an I-told-you-so look before turning back to the Meadows family.

"Adam does look like a gunslinger, but he really is a rancher. He and his brothers own quite a large spread outside of Blue Belle."

"You own the land?" James asked Adam.

"Yes, sir, I do," Adam replied.

James gave his son a quick nod of encouragement. The younger man immediately stepped forward again. He tried not to sound overly eager when he asked, "Would you be looking to hire some extra hands?"

"I can always use more help," Adam said. "Are you looking for a job?"

"Yes, sir, I am," Will answered. "I can put in a long day doing any job you give me, and I won't stop until I get it done. I'm a good worker, sir, and I'm strong, real strong."

"Ranching is hard work," Adam warned.

"I'm not afraid of it," Will replied.

"Then you've got a job," Adam told him.

"We're headed for a new beginning. Jobs have dried up down south," he explained. "Where exactly might this ranch of yours be?"

Adam gave them directions to Rosehill. "It will take you a good two weeks to walk all that way. I should be back home by then, but in the event I'm not, just tell my brother Cole you're there to work."

"We'll make it without any trouble at all," Will promised.

His wife grabbed hold of his arm and hugged him. There were tears in her eyes, and she was frantically trying to blink them away.

"I might be useful for you to hire too," James said. "I've got a few good years of work left in me."

"Why don't we talk about this during lunch?" Genevieve suggested.

James looked as if he was about to decline

the invitation. Adam thought he knew why. The family had obviously hit hard times, and they had probably used up all of their money too. They were dressed in clothes that were so worn they should have been thrown out. The little girls were barefoot, but aside from the dirt on the bottoms of their feet, they were spotlessly clean.

All of them looked in dire need of a good meal.

Genevieve wasn't going to take no for an answer "We were planning to have a picnic," she announced "And we would love for you to join us. There's plenty of food, and I don't want it to go to waste. Isn't that right, Adam?"

The entire family turned to hear his reply.

"Yes, that's right," he said.

"We'd be pleased to join you," James announced with a nod.

Will and Ellie shared a smile. Genevieve beamed with pleasure. Adam knew she was relieved. She had obviously been worried about the family. She had seen the condition of their clothing and had assumed as he had, that they were hungry, but unlike him, she had rushed forward to do something about it. Her generosity and compassion humbled him, and he no longer minded the delay in their journey at all.

They ate lunch by a stream about a half a mile south of the main road. While Adam took care of their horses, Ellie helped Genevieve spread the blanket on the ground and put the food out. There was cheese, salted ham, biscuits, apples, dried bananas, and sugar cookies for dessert. They drank cold water from the stream. Although Genevieve had enough food for all of them, she didn't eat much at all. She seemed content to nibble on a biscuit, and as soon as everyone had eaten their fill, she insisted they take most of the leftover food with them, using the excuse that she would have to throw it away if they didn't.

"How does a man like yourself end up owning a ranch?" James asked.

Adam shrugged. He wasn't used to telling anyone about his personal life. Private to the extreme, he decided to tell them that owning the ranch was a result of hard work and a lot of luck. Genevieve had other ideas. She decided to tell his life story.

He was too astonished to interrupt. She knew everything about him, which really wasn't all that surprising since she had read his letters and Mama Rose would have filled in the gaps. What stunned him was the fact that she remembered so many details that even he had forgotten. She had a way with words, and by the time she was finished, she had romanticized the story until he barely recognized himself. She made him out to be a champion, a warrior, and a hero, and from the look in her eyes as she gazed at him and the sound of her voice as she spoke, he couldn't help but think that she really believed he was all those things.

The Meadowses were captivated by the tale. They stared up at him as though he had just grown a halo over his head. He gave Genevieve a look to let her know she was going to catch hell when they were alone. She smiled back at him.

Adam thought he and Genevieve should head for Gramby. Genevieve thought they should stay and visit for a spell. Will and James were full of questions about Rosehill. While Adam answered them, Genevieve sat by his side. She waited for a lull in the conversation and then suggested that he give Will and James an advance against their wages to secure their positions.

Adam knew what her real motive was. They needed money to replenish their supplies. Realizing how important it was for a man to hold on to his pride, she had come up with a solution that would be acceptable to them. James and Will both protested, and Genevieve must have thought that Adam was going to let them have their way, because she put her hand on his arm and pinched him.

He kept his attention centered on the grandfather while he put his hand down on top of hers and squeezed hard. She let out a little yelp and pulled away.

"If you work for me, you take the advance," he told both men.

"Is that how it's done at Rosehill?" Will asked.

"Yes," Genevieve blurted out.

Adam handed each man twenty dollars. "I expect to see you at the ranch by the end of the month."

He shook their hands to seal the bargain, told Genevieve it was time to leave, and then started to get up.

James Meadows changed his mind with his next remark. "Adam, you've got the same noble look in your eyes that President Abraham Lincoln had when I saw him. Yes, sir, you do."

Astounded, he asked, "You saw Lincoln?"

"I sure did."

Adam wanted to hear every detail. He sat back down, and for the next hour he listened in rapt fascination as James shared his remarkable experience of seeing the man Adam personally believed was the greatest orator and president of all time.

"He was on his way to Gettysburg," James said. "It was a terrible time back then. The war had already taken so many young men. Folks were scared, and rightly so, and when the war finally ended, everyone flooded into the cities looking for work. It was bad for a long spell, but then it got better for a while."

"And now it's bad again," Will interjected.

"Where is home?" Adam asked.

"The prettiest little spot in the whole country," James boasted. "Norfolk, Virginia."

"Rosehill is very pretty too," Genevieve said. "I'm sure you're going to like living there, and soon you'll think of the town of Blue Belle as home."

"I'm sure we will," James agreed with a smile before turning back to Adam and asking him if he had ever been to Gettysburg.

"No, I haven't," Adam replied.

"I walked the fields of battle," James announced.

Adam wanted to hear all about it. He was impressed that James remembered the battles and the dates. He also knew details Adam had never read about.

While the men discussed the war, the twins took turns sitting on Genevieve's lap. She braided their hair and used the pink ribbons from the sleeves of her dress to tie bows for each of them. Ellie sat by her side. She and Genevieve whispered back and forth, and every now and then Genevieve would nod.

Adam kept glancing over at her. He heard one of the twins tell her she was pretty. He silently agreed.

It was going on three in the afternoon when Adam finally pulled Genevieve to her feet and insisted they get going.

James followed them to their horses. "If you don't mind my asking, how long have you two been married? You're newlyweds, aren't you?"

Genevieve laughed. Adam frowned.

"What makes you think we're newlyweds?" she asked.

"The way he looks at you," James replied.

"How exactly do I look at her?" Adam wanted to know.

"Like you haven't quite figured her out. You're puzzled, but you like what you're seeing, and that's about the same way I used to look at my bride, God rest her soul. Come to think about it, I guess I looked at her that very same way until the day she died. I never did figure that woman out, so I guess you could say we were newlyweds for close to thirty-two years."

Genevieve thought that was the sweetest thing she had ever heard. "What a lovely tribute to your late wife," she whispered, fairly overcome with emotion.

"I didn't mean to make you weepy about it," he replied. "If the two of you are considering sleeping outside, you might want to camp over by Blue Glass Lake. It's mighty pretty over there, and peaceful. You two will have all the privacy you could want."

Genevieve waited for Adam to tell James that they weren't married. He didn't say a word, and when she nudged him and looked up at him, he ignored her.

"We're going to stay in Gramby," he said.

"Why is it called Blue Glass Lake?" she asked.

"Because the water looks like blue glass," James answered. "It's deep, but you can see all the way to the rock bottom, and you can sit on the bank and actually see the fish swimming around. Someone tied a rope to one of the branches that hangs out over the water. I expect so you can swing out and drop down in the center of the lake, but my granddaughters are too young and too timid to try, and Will and Ellie weren't inclined."

Genevieve turned to Adam. He was already shaking his head.

"Wouldn't we—"

"No," he interrupted. "We're going to Gramby."

Seven

Blue Glass Lake was breathtakingly beautiful. James Meadows certainly hadn't exaggerated, but Genevieve was surprised he hadn't mentioned the trees, for they were even more glorious. Like towering sentinels keeping watch, they surrounded the lake on all sides. They were so thick in some spots it wasn't possible to squeeze through the openings between the trunks. Long branches arched gracefully across the expanse of water, and like the fingers of a lady's hands, they were elegantly entwined. The sun dappled on the leaves, and in the soft breeze they glittered like diamonds.

Adam told her the oaks were at least a hundred years old. He sat down on the ground with his rifle across his lap and leaned back against a fat tree trunk, smiling as he watched her try to get a foothold so she could climb up to fetch the rope hanging from one of the lower branches.

Her skirts hindered her movements, and after trying several times, she gave up.

"Now, aren't you happy we decided to make the detour?" she asked.

"I'm happy you quit hounding me," he teased.

"Look what you would have missed," she told him. She put her hands up and twirled around in a circle. "It's a paradise."

He silently agreed. He felt as though he had just entered a magical land. Spring's vibrant colors surrounded him, and he knew that if he had seen a painting of this idyllic spot, he wouldn't have believed that it really existed. Yet here it was in all of its perfection, and for a short while the beauty belonged to him.

He stared at Genevieve and decided that she belonged in such a place. Her surroundings enhanced her beauty. The joy in her face, so innocent and pure, made his breath catch in the back of his throat.

"What are you thinking about?" she asked.

She sat down beside him and began to untie her shoelaces, but then glanced up at him when he hesitated in answering.

"I was thinking that you never take anything for granted."

"I've learned not to," she replied quietly.

"How did you learn not to?" he asked.

Her shoulders sagged. She removed one shoe and started on the other. "Family," she whispered. "So many people go through their lives with blinders on. They become self-involved and only want to think about their wants and their desires. They don't leave room for anything else, and then, too late, they realize how important their families were."

"Were you like that?" he asked.

"Yes, I was," she replied. "I was so busy getting where I thought I wanted to go I didn't make time for the people who loved me. Now they're gone."

The sadness he heard in her voice made him want to put his arms around her and comfort her. When she leaned against him, he gave in to the urge and pulled her close.

"I'm sure your family was very proud of you."

"Yes, they were proud of me, but I'm not sure they really knew what to make of me. I rarely came home for a visit, and when I did, I never stayed more than a night or two. I would be all decked out in the latest fashions, and I tried to act so sophisticated. I called them 'mother dear' and 'father dear,' and now that I look back, I realize they exhibited an amazing amount of patience with me. I'm not sure if I was trying to impress them or myself. I never took time to think about it. I was so busy back then chasing fame and fortune." She shook her head and then added, "What a waste of precious time."

"Genevieve, I'm sure they understood."

"Perhaps," she agreed. "I didn't understand them though. My father put in a lovely garden in the front of the house, and every evening after supper he and my mother would tend it. They spent hours there. It was lovely," she added. "They had every flower you could imagine blooming, and on the fence were roses. Red roses. I used to think my parents led such boring lives, and now . . ."

"Now what?" he asked.

"I want to have a garden of my own someday just like theirs. I don't want to waste time. I want to appreciate every minute, and I want to teach my children to do the same thing."

"I thought you longed for adventure."

"Living is an adventure, Adam. Look around you. Being here is an adventure, and we would have missed it if we had hurried to Gramby."

He laughed. "Point taken."

"I love the fact that it's so secluded. Right this minute, this beautiful spot belongs to us and no one else."

He also liked the seclusion, though for a different reason. Blue Glass Lake was so far off the beaten path Ezekiel Jones and his friends wouldn't find them here. On their way to the lake, Adam had led her through a creek bed so that their tracks couldn't be followed, and he was certain no one was going to intrude on them now.

She shrugged his arm off of her. "I'm going swimming if the water isn't too cold. Would you like to join me?"

"Maybe later," he replied.

She turned away from him to remove her socks, then stood up and ran to the water's edge.

"It looks deep," she called out. She lifted the hem of her skirt and tested the water with her toes. It was surprisingly warm and too inviting to resist. Had she been alone, she would have taken her skirt and blouse off and swum in her underclothes. Since Adam was watching her like a hawk, she was going to have to keep everything on.

She turned around to face him put her arms out wide, closed her eyes, and then fell backward.

She could hear him laughing when she came up for air. The sound echoed through the trees around her. She would have laughed with him, but she was too busy trying to stay afloat. Her skirt and petticoats had absorbed quite a bit of water and were weighing her down. She was able to swim, but she stayed close to the bank, and after fifteen minutes or so, she was exhausted.

Getting into the water had been much easier than getting out. She made three attempts before she gave up.

All she had to do was call to him and he was there. He reached down with one hand and pulled her out of the lake with incredible ease.

He didn't let go of her. Honest to God, he

tried, but his hands seemed to have a will of their own. They slid around her waist and pulled her up tight against his chest.

Her clothes were plastered to her, and she was dripping wet. He didn't mind. Her head was tilted back, and all he wanted to think about was kissing every inch of her perfect neck. No, that wasn't true. He wanted to do a whole lot more than simply kiss her.

Her hands were pressed against his chest. She could feel his heart beating under her fingertips, and she had the almost overwhelming desire to caress him. She blamed the urge on him. The way he was looking at her made her shiver with excitement. He was so serious and intense.

She stared into his eyes and felt as though she were drowning under his dark, sensual scrutiny. Was he going to kiss her? He was frowning, and she didn't think he wanted to, but, oh, God, she would die if he didn't.

"Adam?" she whispered. "What's come over you?"

He shook his head. How could he tell her that he thought she had cast a spell on him and he didn't know how much longer he was going to be able to resist her? From the moment he'd met her, she had ruled his every thought.

The infatuation had to end. "You'll be leaving tomorrow," he said, his voice rough, angry.

"Yes, I will," she whispered.

"We'll never see each other again."

"No, we won't," she agreed.

She was making circles on his chest with her

fingertips. The feathery light caress was driving him crazy.

"It's for the best." He was slowly pulling her arms up around his neck.

"Yes, it's for the best," she said.

His frown deepened. "My life's all mapped out, Genevieve. I don't have time for you."

"I don't have time for you either," she told him. *Liar, liar,* she silently chanted. "Adam? Are you going to kiss me?"

"Hell, no."

And then his mouth came down on top of hers, and it was the most amazing kiss she had ever experienced. His mouth was warm and firm and wonderful. He nibbled at her lips until she opened her mouth, and then his tongue slipped inside, and, oh, Lord, that was even more glorious. She clutched handfuls of his shirt and held on for dear life while he slowly, meticulously devoured her.

The kiss seemed endless, and he didn't lift his head away from hers until he had taken every ounce of her strength. She sagged against him and closed her eyes.

Her head rested in the crook of his neck. She sighed into his ear. "Are you going to want to kiss me again?" she asked dreamily.

"No."

"It was very nice," she whispered.

She kissed the side of his neck and felt him shudder. Then he slowly pulled her arms away from him. The moment was over.

"Tomorrow you're going to get on that coach and I'm going to go back home."

"I know," she replied. "I'm going to Kansas."

"No, you're not. You're going to Paris."

"Yes, Paris."

He put his hands on her shoulders and took a step back. She had a bemused look on her face, and damn if he didn't want to kiss her again.

He made himself turn away from her instead. "I shouldn't have kissed you. It won't happen again."

"I wouldn't mind . . ."

"I'd mind," he snapped. He softened his voice when he next spoke. "You're shivering. You should get out of those wet clothes."

"That isn't why I'm shivering."

"I'll build a fire."

Those were the last words he said to her for a very long time. She thought he was probably thinking about all the work he had to do when he returned to Rosehill.

The long day had worn her out. Wrapped in a blanket he had given her, she fell asleep and didn't wake up until the following morning.

After a breakfast of fresh fish, Adam saddled the horses while she put the supplies away. They left paradise a few minutes later. Thunder rumbled in the distance, and the sky became an omen of what was to come.

Eight

Trouble was brewing in Gramby.

The pretty little town was nestled high up in the shoulder of the mountains. Several years ago the population had swelled considerably when rumors circulated that there was gold to be found in the surrounding hills and creek beds. The Pickerman Hotel had been constructed during that booming period, as had countless other buildings, but as luck would have it, the rumors turned out to be false, and as quickly as folks had hightailed it into town, they packed up their belongings and hightailed it out. Now there were more buildings than people to occupy them.

Hard times called for hard measures. The Pickerman Hotel was rarely full, but every once in a while, when he became desperate enough, Ernest Pickerman would join forces with his arch enemy, Harry Steeple, the owner of the neighboring saloon. The two men would pool their money and pay outrageous sums to entice entertainers to come to their town. What made their collaboration remarkable was the fact that Pickerman and Steeple had been trying to kill each other for years. Neither could abide the sight of the other, but business was business, they both agreed, and they could put off feuding until their coffers were refilled.

They had a gentleman's agreement, but since they didn't happen to be gentlemen, the rules governing conduct didn't apply.

Pickerman and Steeple were both skating on thin ice with the rest of the folks of Gramby. Twice in the past month alone the two men had collected money from them to send for entertainers, and both times the entertainers hadn't bothered to show up. It never occurred to either man to give refunds, which made them extremely unpopular fellows with the good citizens, but Pickerman and Steeple were about to redeem themselves by pulling off their greatest coup of all time.

Adam and Genevieve just happened to ride into town on the day that Miss Ruby Leigh Diamond— showgirl extraordinaire, as she was billed—was expected to perform at the Gold and Glitter Saloon. The folks of Gramby were suspicious that they were once again about to be fleeced, but they still paid in advance for tickets on the off chance that Ruby Leigh would show up. Word had spread like smallpox, and folks had flooded into the town from as far as fifty miles away. They were also willing to pay an exorbitant price to get a peek, or gander, depending on where they were seated, at Ruby Leigh's spectacular legs.

The two mismatched entrepreneurs had worked out all the arrangements so that there wouldn't be any problems. Pickerman would personally take Ruby Leigh from the coach to her hotel room. When she was rested and ready, he would escort her halfway down the boardwalk, where Steeple would be waiting, then step back and hand her over to him. Neither man had set foot in the other's establishment in over ten years, and not even a pair of magnificent legs would make them break that important tradition.

Gramby was the turning point for the stage-coach. It came up from Salt Lake City once a week, then turned around and went back. On Tuesday morning, the coach arrived right on schedule, at ten o'clock in the morning. Pickerman was ready. With a flourish and a prayer, he stepped off the boardwalk and prepared to open the door. Sweat dotted his brow and his palms, and saliva filled his mouth in anticipation of being the first man in Gramby to gaze upon Ruby Leigh Diamond's curvaceous legs when she alighted from the coach.

Unfortunately, Ruby Leigh's legs were missing, and so was the rest of her. For a minute, Pickerman refused to accept that she wasn't inside. He stuck his head in to make certain she hadn't gotten stuck in a crevice somewhere. Then he started cursing and spitting. Panic quickly set in as soon as he spotted a number of people hurrying toward the coach. He slammed the door shut, shouted to the driver to move along, and then ran inside the hotel.

An immediate conference was called. The two owners met in the alley between their establishments to decide what to do. They knew they would be strung up from the nearest tree if they didn't produce the goods, and so they furiously tried to come up with an acceptable story.

The pity was that even though they put their

heads together, they still didn't have enough brains between them to think of anything remotely plausible.

And so they lied. Everyone who stopped by the hotel or the saloon that day was told that Ruby Leigh Diamond had already arrived.

By six o'clock that evening, Pickerman had gone through three handkerchiefs mopping the sweat from his brow. Steeple had worn two blisters on his toes from pacing around his saloon in his brand-new two-toned shoes. He decided that the only way he was going to be able to keep that noose from slipping around his neck was to blame Pickerman and shoot him down like a mad dog before the truth came out. Ironically, Pickerman had come up with the very same idea.

They took off with their guns blazing and had each other pinned down outside of town in Tommy Murphy's tomato field. They were so busy trying to kill each other they almost let a golden opportunity ride past. Pickerman just happened to jump up from behind the rock where he had been hiding, with the intention of putting a bullet in Steeple's backside because it was the biggest and easiest target he could find, when out of the corner of his eye he saw a beautiful woman on horseback trotting by.

He called an immediate truce by waving his soggy handkerchief in the air with one hand and pointing his pistol toward the beautiful woman in the distance with his other hand.

Steeple caught on to Pickerman's plan right away. "We've been saved," he shouted.

"She could be our manna from heaven," Pickerman shouted back.

In unison, the men tucked their guns in their pants and ran to intercept her before she got away. They were running so fast the heels of their shoes smacked their backsides. When they came barreling around the corner of the dirt road that led into town, they spotted Adam and immediately stopped dead in their tracks.

Steeple put his hands up in the air to let the big stranger know he didn't mean to do any harm. Pickerman mopped his brow but kept a wary eye on the woman's companion.

"Wait up, miss," Steeple shouted. "We got a proposition for you."

"It's a moneymaker," Pickerman bellowed.

Genevieve reined her horse in. Adam shook his head at her and told her to keep going.

"Aren't you the least bit curious?" she asked while she waited for the two strangers to catch up with her.

"No," he answered.

"He mentioned money," she said. "You have to be low on funds, and I'm completely out. It would be foolish of me not to listen to what they have to say," she added.

Adam was incredulous. "You don't have any money at all?"

"No, I—"

"You gave it away, didn't you?"

"Now, why would you—"

"Did you?" he demanded.

"As a matter of fact, I did. I had to," she cried out. "If you had only seen—"

She was going to tell him about the couple she had encountered on the road the day before yesterday and how desperate their situation was, but Adam didn't give her an opportunity.

"Had to give it away? Were you robbed?"

"No, I wasn't—"

"I cannot believe you would go traipsing—"

"Their need was greater than mine," she interrupted. "And I don't traipse anywhere."

He took a deep, calming breath. "Exactly how were you planning to get to Salt Lake?"

She turned back to him. "I will either ride my horse there or I will sell her and use the money to buy a ticket on the coach. I did think things through," she added.

"And if you can't get enough money to buy a ticket?"

"Then I won't sell the mare."

"What about food and shelter and—"

"Adam, it's ridiculous for you to get angry. I can always find work," she assured him.

Pickerman's huffing and puffing turned her attention. He was the first to reach her side. Steeple was hot on his heels. Adam instinctively moved his rifle across his lap. The barrel was pointed at the men.

He then ordered the strangers to step away from her.

They barely gave him a glance, for both were staring up at Genevieve with expressions of rapture on their faces.

Pickerman made the introductions. "How would you like to earn twenty whole dollars?"

Steeple poked him hard in his ribs and smiled when he heard him grunt in pain.

"You might have gotten her for ten," he muttered.

Genevieve glanced at Adam to see how he was reacting to the pair. His expression showed only mild disdain. The two men were peculiar, she thought, and complete opposites in appearance. One was tall and thin and seemed to have a problem with perspiration. His face was dripping wet. The other man was short and squat. He seemed to have a problem walking, for she noticed he was grimacing and kept hopping from foot to foot.

"What exactly did you have in mind, gentlemen?" she asked.

Steeple answered her. "We just want you to spend the evening entertaining some folks."

Adam exploded. "That's it," he roared. "Genevieve, we're leaving. As for you two—"

Pickerman raised his hands. "It ain't what it sounded like. We're in a bind, a real bind, and if the lady won't help us out, we'll be hanged for sure."

Steeple vigorously nodded. "I own the saloon next to his hotel," he said with a nod toward Pickerman. "I got a real fancy stage, and some-times we get big-name entertainers to come here. Both of us happened to observe what a nice pair of ankles you have, miss, and we're hoping and praying your legs are just as shapely."

"You aren't going to be seeing her legs," Adam snapped.

"Steeple, shut your trap 'cause you're only

making the gentleman mad every time you speak. Let me tell it," Pickerman demanded. He paused to mop his face with his handkerchief and then said, "We're in a real bad way, miss. We've already disappointed folks twice in the past month because the entertainers we sent for didn't show up. Now it's happened again. We collected money and sent for Miss Ruby Leigh Diamond to come and sing and dance at the saloon. We whet everyone's appetite by putting up signs all over town, and wouldn't you know it? She didn't come. In about an hour and a half, folks are going to start getting suspicious. They'll catch on quick when she doesn't come twirling out on stage."

"I expect they will," she agreed.

"All you got to do is pretend to be Ruby," Steeple pleaded.

"Ruby Leigh Diamond? That can't be the woman's real name," she said, trying hard not to laugh.

"Alice," Pickerman blurted out. "Her name's Alice O'Reilly."

"Then she's Irish."

"Yes, miss, she is," Steeple said.

Genevieve smiled. "I'm not Irish," she said quietly. "My ancestors came here from Africa. Surely you noticed. You cannot think anyone would think I'm Ruby Leigh Diamond, for heaven's sake. Have you lost your wits?"

"Begging your pardon, miss, but I don't think you grasp the seriousness of our predicament. We'll lose our necks if we don't find a pretty lady to go out on stage," Steeple whined. "You don't have to be Ruby if you don't want to. We can give you another stage name. How about Opal or Emerald?"

"My name is Genevieve. What exactly am I expected to do on stage?"

"Don't you see? We don't rightly care what you do. You're real pretty, and maybe if you twirl around a couple of times and sashay back and forth, folks will think they got their money's worth."

"Are you about ready to get going?" Adam asked.

She shook her head. "These gentlemen do seem to be in a bind. If I help them out, I could be saving their hides."

"Yes, miss, that's exactly right," Pickerman agreed.

She did feel sorry for them, but she was also intrigued by the possibility of replenishing her funds so quickly. It was an appealing proposition. There was a dilemma however.

"I do sing, but only in church," she explained.

"She sings, Pickerman," Steeple shouted. "It's a sign, I tell you. She was sent to us."

"There you have it," Steeple said. "You sing. That's what you'll do, then."

"Can you twirl?" Pickerman wanted to know.

Adam was shaking his head. She ignored him and asked, "Is twirling important?"

Steeple shrugged. "I expect so," he said. "Folks will want to see your ankles."

She glanced at Adam, saw his dark expression, and knew he'd reached his boiling point.

"I don't think I'll be doing any twirling or sashaying, but I would like to earn thirty dollars.

I'll sing for that amount of money and not a dollar less."

The two men didn't need to discuss the matter. Steeple reached up and shook her hand. "You've got yourself a deal, little lady."

"May I have the money in advance?" she asked.

"As soon as you step out on stage, we'll give the money to your companion," Steeple told her with a nod toward Adam.

"He'll shoot you if you don't pay him," she said sweetly.

Pickerman turned to Adam. "You won't have to shoot anyone. He'll pay."

"Now all we have to do is sneak you in the back door of the saloon so folks won't know you only just got there."

"I've never been inside a saloon," she remarked.

"Well, now, this will be a treat for you," Pickerman said.

Adam's patience was all used up. "Genevieve, I'm putting my foot down. You aren't going to sing for a bunch of drunk men."

"There might be women there too," Steeple promised.

"Adam, have some compassion," Genevieve said. "These gentlemen need my help."

Both Pickerman and Steeple nodded in unison, their chins wobbling like a pair of turkeys pecking at the ground.

"People will understand if they tell them the truth," Adam said.

"We can't tell them Ruby didn't show. They'll hang us," Steeple insisted.

"Don't you have a sheriff in Gramby?" Genevieve asked.

"Yes, miss, we do," Pickerman answered. "But he isn't in Gramby today. He headed over to Middleton as soon as he heard their bank was robbed. Folks over there don't need his help though, because there are three U.S. marshals on their way to Middleton now. They'll catch the robbers quick enough."

"But Middleton's a couple of hours away, and by the time our sheriff comes back home, we'll be swingin' from the trees," Steeple said.

"You took money for tickets, didn't you?" Adam asked.

"We did," Steeple agreed.

"Then give them refunds."

The men looked horrified by the notion. "We couldn't do that," Pickerman said.

"It's bad business," Steeple interjected.

Adam gave up trying to make them be reasonable. Genevieve continued to look sympathetic.

"Miss Genevieve, do you happen to have a nice little something to wear on stage?"

She smiled. "I have just the thing."

Nine

She wore her favorite church dress. It was the color of freshly churned butter and had a matching wide-brimmed hat, wrist-length gloves, and shoes. The dress was long-sleeved and covered her ankles and her neck, and therefore met Adam's stipulations. Nevertheless, he still wasn't happy when he saw her all decked out in her Sunday finery. Neither were Steeple and Pickerman. They took turns begging her to find something else to put on.

Adam had insisted they stay at the boarding-house outside of town, but there hadn't been time to go there to change her clothes, and so she'd ended up using Steeple's storage closet behind the stage. She made Pickerman guard the door, ignoring his protest that he was breaking a sacred vow by entering Steeple's den of iniquity. Adam and Steeple waited near the stage. When she stepped out and asked Adam if she looked all right, he shook his head and told her she would incite men's appetites wearing such a revealing garment. While Steeple pleaded with her to at least roll up her sleeves, Adam moved forward, nudged her chin up, and fastened her two top buttons.

She knew he was angry that he hadn't been able to change her mind. He knew she was nervous, because he could feel her trembling.

"It isn't too late to leave," he whispered.

She moved closer to him and tried to smile. "I am a little nervous," she admitted.

He put his arms around her, but resisted the urge to try to shake some sense into her.

"Then let's go. You don't have any business inside a saloon. You're too refined for such a place."

She thought that was a lovely thing for him to say. "I am?" she asked.

"Let's go."

She shook her head. "It's thirty whole dollars," she reminded him once again. "I could pay you back what I owe you."

"You don't owe me anything."

"I made you give your money to the Meadows family, remember?"

His head dropped down toward hers so that he could hear her whispers over the crowd's shouts coming from the other side of the stage.

"You didn't make me do anything I didn't want to do."

"For the love of God, now isn't the time to be whispering sweet nothings into each other's ears. We got a situation here," Steeple cried out.

"The audience sounds . . . restless," she said.

"It isn't an audience, it's a mob," Adam snapped.

Steeple latched onto Genevieve's arm. "If he'll unhand you, I'll show you where you should wait."

He tugged her away from Adam and then guided her over to the left side of the stage behind the red velvet drape. She had grabbed hold of Adam's hand and wouldn't let go. He kept trying to get her to change her mind, but she was in such a panic now, she could barely hear a word he said.

The noise of the crowd was deafening. Pride kept her from picking up her skirts and running for safety. She had given her word, and she meant to keep it.

She tried to look out at the audience, but Steeple saw what she was about to do and rushed forward to put himself in front of her.

The crowd was getting restless. As one, they began to chant Ruby Leigh Diamond's name and pound their fists on the tables. They hurled their empty whiskey bottles at the walls and the stage.

The noise was frightful. "They sound . . . impatient," Genevieve said when she heard a loud crash.

"Ruby . . . Ruby . . . Ruby . . ." the crowd chanted.

"You still haven't told them Ruby isn't here?" Adam demanded.

"I'm going out there now to tell them," Steeple promised. He turned to Genevieve. "After I introduce you, the band will start playing, and you come on out."

"Wait," she cried when he turned to leave. "What will they be playing?"

Steeple smiled. "Well, now, no one rightly knows. Elvin will be pounding a tune on his piano, and the two fiddlers I hired will figure it out and catch up in no time."

"But what is the song?"

"Is that important?"

"Yes," she stammered.

He patted her arm. "It'll be fine. Just fine," he promised.

Her stomach was doing flips. She thought she might be turning green too. She dared a peek out at the audience and was immediately sorry. There were two men hanging down from the balcony above, and both were pouring bottles of liquor on the cantankerous crowd below.

She jumped back and sagged against Adam's chest. "Oh, dear," she whispered.

Adam had never felt such acute frustration in his entire life. Why must Genevieve be so stubborn? Didn't she know that as soon as the crowd heard that Ruby wouldn't be performing, they would tear the place apart?

"Are you still hell-bent on this foolishness?"

Before she could answer, Pickerman came running. "You'd best get on out there," he told Steeple. "Fargus is swinging from your chandelier and cross-eyed Harry is trying to lasso him with his rope. They're both drunk as skunks."

Adam reached over Genevieve's shoulder and grabbed Steeple by his collar. "If anyone gets near her while she's out there, I'm going to shoot him. Got that?"

Steeple vigorously nodded and then scurried out on stage. She held her breath in anticipation of the crowd's reaction when they heard Ruby wasn't there.

Steeple had both his hands up with the palms out and was waving to the audience to be quiet. An expectant hush followed. Fargus let go of the chandelier and landed on top of the table to take his seat. Cross-eyed Harry dropped his rope and sat down next to his friend. He let out a loud, low belch. The crowd erupted in laughter, but quieted down again as soon as Steeple motioned to them.

"Now, men, I told you Miss Ruby Leigh Diamond would be performing tonight—"

He abruptly stopped. The crowd leaned forward and waited expectantly for him to continue. Steeple didn't say another word for a full minute. He simply stood in the center of the stage, shifting back and forth from one foot to the other, smiling at his audience as he squinted out at them. They squinted back. The seconds ticked by, and the only sound that could be heard was the squeak of Steeple's brand-new, two-toned shoes.

The audience soon grew impatient. A murmur of dissent began in the back of the saloon, and like a wave, it gathered momentum as it worked its way forward.

Just as Fargus turning to the chandelier and his companion was reaching for his rope, a slow, sly smile came over Steeple's face.

"I promised you Ruby Leigh Diamond," he bellowed. "And here she is."

With a flourish, he bowed low to Genevieve, straightened back up, and gave Elvin the signal to start pounding on his piano. Then he ran as though lightning were chasing him to the opposite side of the stage. He ducked behind the curtain, but peeked out to see how the audience was reacting.

Pickerman slapped thirty dollars into the palm of Adam's hand, gave Genevieve a pitying glance and a quick shove toward the stage, and then ran to find a place to hide.

Adam was glaring at Steeple. "I'm going to kill that son of a—"

She interrupted him. "This *is* going to be an adventure," she whispered.

She straightened her shoulders, forced a smile, and inched her way onto the stage.

Adam went with her. He moved out just far enough to be seen by everyone. He slowly lifted his rifle, slipped his finger through the trigger ring, and pointed the barrel at the center of the crowd. His message wasn't subtle. The first man who dared to utter a single word of disappointment over the obvious fact that Genevieve wasn't Ruby was going to get shot. If the weapon wasn't a sufficient deterrent, the expression on his face was. He looked bad-tempered and trigger-happy.

As it turned out, none of his precautions were the least bit necessary.

She took their breath away. The sight of her dressed so primly in her Sunday best stunned them speechless. They stared and they gaped. Elvin stopped playing the piano; the fiddlers dropped their bows, and like everyone else in the saloon, they too stared up in openmouthed stupefaction at the woman on the stage.

She was a nervous wreck. Some adventures were better left unpursued, she thought frantically. She had to be crazy to be doing this. Adam was right. It was foolishness.

She turned to leave and saw him standing there on stage with her, with his rifle up and ready to fire and an expression on his face that would have made the fainthearted shriek.

He wasn't going to let any harm come to her. Her smile widened as she turned back to her audience. Her knees were knocking, her stomach was flipping, and her throat was closing, but all she could think about was that Adam was protecting her.

Was it any wonder why she loved this man?

Something smelled vile. It was the sinful stench of whiskey surrounding her. She looked from side to side and saw all the empty bottles littering the tables and the floor.

Her audience was drunk, shame on them, and she was suddenly too disgusted to be nervous.

The crowd was finally getting over their initial surprise. Some of the men smiled at her; others frowned. She wasn't at all what they had expected, but before any of them could get riled up about Steeple's trickery in substituting one woman for another, Genevieve began to sing.

From that moment on, she held them in the palm of her hand. Adam wouldn't have believed it if he hadn't seen it with his own eyes. Within minutes, she had turned drunken louts into simpering crybabies.

She chose to sing one of her church songs, "Come Ye Sinners, Poor and Needy." The lyrics aptly fit the audience. Her voice was so rich and vibrant it caressed the crowd and soothed the beast within them. One by one the men began to listen to the words and bow their heads. Several pushed their glasses of whiskey aside. Others took out their handkerchiefs and wiped the tears from their eyes.

By the time the song ended, everyone was weeping. Adam moved back into the shadows and lowered his rifle. He wanted to laugh, so bizarre did he find their reaction, but he didn't dare for fear the sound would break the collective mood in the saloon. He knew why she had chosen the song, of course. She wanted to shame the men, and from the way their shoulders were shaking and their heads were bobbing, it was apparent she had succeeded.

The second song was called "My Sainted Mother, Your Hopes for Me" and struck an even greater emotional chord with the crowd. By the time she was finished with the third verse, one man was bawling so loudly his friends had to hush him.

Steeple went into a panic as soon as he noticed no one was buying or drinking his high-priced liquor. He moved forward to get Genevieve's attention, and when she glanced over at him, he started seesawing his arm back and forth and snapping his fingers to let her know he wanted her to pick up the beat.

Adam did laugh then. He simply couldn't contain his amusement any longer. Genevieve smiled at Steeple and then proceeded to sing yet another song about death and redemption and sinners who finally saw the light and changed their sorry ways. Adam suspected she was making up the lyrics as she went along, because none of the words rhymed, but he seemed to be the only one who noticed.

Steeple was tearing his hair out in despair over the amount of money he was losing because she wasn't cooperating. He was doing the two-step on the side of the stage in yet another attempt to get her to sing something a bit more snappy.

She ignored him and continued to work the crowd into a frenzy of regret. One man called out in a weepy shout to please sing that pretty song about his mama once again. Steeple frantically shook his head at Genevieve, but she simply couldn't refuse the request and launched into the heart-wrenching song one more time.

When she finished, they clapped and they wept, and Harry Steeple burst into tears.

Her throat was getting parched, and she decided to sing one last song and then take her leave. She poured her heart and her soul into the sweet, uplifting spiritual. It had always been a favorite of her father's, and her audience responded to the melody and the lyrics in much the same way he had. They stomped their feet and clapped their hands to the beat.

She was just reaching the high note in the last verse when she happened to notice the doors of the saloon open. Three men squeezed their way inside.

One of them was Ezekiel Jones.

She froze. She stopped singing so abruptly it was as though her voice had been cut off in midnote by a blade. She jerked back, her gaze locked on Ezekiel, and she went completely rigid. She was staring into the glowing eyes of the devil himself, but she couldn't turn away, couldn't move, for what seemed an eternity. Fear immobilized her. Her hands balled into fists at her sides, and she could only stand there and watch as Ezekiel slowly threaded his way through the crowd. She kept telling herself to run, run, and finally the frantic thought penetrated her stupor and she turned to Adam and started to run to him, but just as suddenly she stopped.

He saw the panic in her eyes, took a step toward her, and at the same time swung his rifle and scanned the audience looking for the threat.

She shook her head. No, she couldn't go to him. She wouldn't put him in such jeopardy. The jackals were closing in on her, and he would try to protect her. She couldn't risk Adam getting hurt, and she knew without a doubt that Ezekiel was capable of killing him.

Shuddering heavily, she turned toward Steeple and ran. Her hat flew down to the stage behind her. Steeple tried to grab her as she passed him, but she was too quick and he was too surprised by her abrupt departure.

Her satchel was on the chair next to the storage closet. She scooped it up in her arms as she raced by. She went out the back door into the alley, turned one way and then the other as she tried to remember which direction to take to the livery stable.

Adam was tearing the door open when she made up her mind and ran. He shouted her name and knew she heard him because she hesitated before she turned and disappeared around the corner. She was headed for the main street, and he was pretty certain she was going to the livery stable to get her horse and leave town.

He started to go after her, but just as he was about to reach the mouth of the alley, he heard the telltale squeak of the saloon's back door, and he quickly moved into the shadows behind a stack of crates.

Someone in that crowd had terrified her, and he was determined to find out who and why. He wasn't concerned that Genevieve would get away from him, because even if she did leave town, she would be easy to track in the moonlight.

His patience was quickly rewarded. Three of the homeliest and meanest-looking men he'd ever laid eyes on came strutting past. Two of them were big and bulky, and it soon became apparent that they took their orders from the shorter, heavier man dressed like a statesman at a funeral who trailed behind them.

Adam guessed the thugs were in the dandy's employ. When the man stopped at the entrance of the alley to strike a match to a cigar, the other two also stopped to wait for him.

"Do you want me to chase her down for you, Reverend?" the tallest of the three asked.

"No need to rush," the reverend answered in an accent that was as thick as southern maple syrup.

"The bitch won't be getting away from me this time," he crooned. "I've got her now, praise the Lord. I told you, Herman, that God would show me the way. Didn't I?"

"Yes, Reverend, you told me," Herman agreed.

He moved into the moonlight, and Adam got a good look at Herman's face. His forehead bulged out over his brows, his nose was crooked, no doubt from being broken a time or two, and there were scars on his cheeks that Adam thought were the result of a few knife fights. He looked exactly like what he was, a thug, and so did his companion.

"What do you want Lewis and me to do if she refuses to go back with you?" Herman asked.

Before the reverend could answer the question, Lewis stepped forward. "Will you want us to hurt her?" he asked eagerly.

"I expect so," the reverend crooned.

He motioned for his two companions to get out of his way and then walked into the street. "Come along, boys. God helps those who help themselves."

Adam had heard enough. He quietly followed the three men past the saloon and the hotel, but then he turned and took a shortcut between the buildings and shortened the distance to the livery stable by more than half.

He slipped inside without making a sound and bolted the doors behind him. He heard Genevieve before he saw her. She was whimpering low in her throat as she tried to swing the saddle up on her mare.

"Going somewhere?" he drawled out.

She jumped a foot and let out a loud yelp. She whirled around and found him standing right behind her inside the stall.

She felt as if her heart were going to explode. "You scared me."

"You were already scared."

He gently pushed her out of his way and took over the task of saddling her mare. He worked quickly and quietly. She picked up her bedroll and cradled it in her arms while she waited for him to demand an explanation.

He didn't say a word. He turned to her when

he was finished, saw the bedroll, and suggested she leave it behind.

"Good God, no," she cried out.

He didn't have time to get into an argument with her. "Then tie it up behind the saddle."

He went into the adjacent stall and quickly saddled his stallion. She followed him and stood by his side with her bedroll still in her arms.

"You can't go with me," she told him in no uncertain terms.

"Sure I can," he replied. There was a hard edge in his voice, indicating to her that he planned to be stubborn about it.

"Please listen to me. You can't go with me now. You could get hurt."

"What about you?"

"I don't want you to come with me."

"Too bad."

"Adam, please. I'm begging you. Walk away now."

"No," he snapped. "We're staying together. I'm kind of anxious to get going. I just can't wait to get you alone for a few minutes so you can tell me again how you don't have any problems at all. Isn't that what you told me, Genevieve?"

She bowed her head. "I know you're angry with me."

"No, I'm not angry," he replied. "I've gone way past anger."

She started to say something more to him, but he put his hand up in a signal to be silent. Someone was pushing hard on the outer doors. Genevieve was turning toward the sound when Adam reached out and grabbed her. He wasn't gentle as he shoved her behind him and pushed her into the corner of the stall. He grabbed his rifle, cocked it, and then waited.

The doors crashed open, and Herman came running into the stable. Lewis was right behind him. The two men spread out to the opposite sides of the barn and squinted into the shadows.

Ezekiel Jones sauntered inside.

"My, my, it's dark in here. Where are you hiding, girl? I know you're in here. Maybe I ought to light the lantern and have a little look-see. I always liked to play hide-and-seek when I was a lad."

Adam could feel Genevieve trembling. She was also trying to get around him, but he made it impossible by squeezing her further into the corner. He was determined to protect her, even if she didn't want him to, and when she begged him in a whisper to save himself, he shook his head. He didn't dare turn to her, for it was imperative that he keep track of Ezekiel's two companions, who were slowly and methodically checking each stall as they made their way down the aisle.

They were getting closer. Ezekiel waited near the door. "Come out, come out, wherever you are," he called out in a singsong voice.

"Are you scared, girl? You ought to be scared. No one crosses Ezekiel Jones without suffering God's wrath."

"We need some light in here," Lewis called.

Ezekiel struck a match. The sizzling powder sounded like an explosion in the sudden silence. He lit a lantern and left it swaying back and forth on its hook, and then turned and shut the barn doors behind him.

"I wouldn't want any company coming inside to bother us," he drawled out. "And I wouldn't want you to get past me again, Miss Genevieve. There aren't any windows here to climb out, are there?"

Herman had steadily crept forward into the stall next to them and suddenly popped up. He was eye to eye with Genevieve. She didn't have time to shout a warning, but one wasn't necessary. Adam saw him at the same instant she did. He proved to be much quicker than the other man too. He used the butt of his rifle struck him hard on the side of his head. Herman looked stupefied, and then his eyes rolled back into his head and he dropped down hard to the floor.

The noise brought Lewis running. He stopped short as soon as he saw the rifle pointed at him.

Ezekiel took his time strolling down the aisle to stand beside his hired gunman. His expression hardened when he spotted Adam, but just as quickly as his scowl appeared, it was replaced by a smile.

"Who are you, mister?"

"No one you need to know," Adam answered.

"I've got business with the woman you've got behind your back, but I don't have any quarrel with you. If you'll hand her over to me, you can leave, and no harm will come to you."

"I'm not going anywhere, and you're not getting near her."

"I'll make it worth your while."

"No."

There was pure hatred in Ezekiel's gaze as he stared at Adam. His voice lost its gentlemanly tone when he next spoke. "You're harboring a criminal and a sinner. She pulled you into her web of deceit, didn't she?"

Genevieve edged her way to Adam's side. "You're the criminal, not me," she cried out.

He pointed a finger at her. "Jezebel," he shouted.

"Just who the hell are you?" Adam demanded. "And what do you want with Genevieve?"

Ezekiel puffed up like a rooster. He held the lapel of his jacket with one hand and stood poised as though he were having his portrait done.

"I am the Reverend Ezekiel Jones," he announced importantly. "And she has something that belongs to me."

"I don't have anything that belongs to you."

"God will smite you for lying, girl."

"How dare you call yourself a preacher. You're nothing but a petty thief."

"My dear, there isn't anything remotely petty about me."

He looked at Adam again, feigned an expression of remorse, and said, "Like the sainted Paul, I too was a sinner before I was shown the light. I want my money back," he added in a snarl.

"I don't have your money," she cried out.

Lewis took a step forward. Adam fired into the ground in front of him. Dust flew up into his face, and he jumped back and very nearly knocked Ezekiel off his feet.

The reverend shoved him aside. "She took over four thousand dollars from me."

"No," she insisted. "I didn't take any of your money."

"She's lying," Ezekiel roared.

"Adam, you believe me, don't you?"

"You heard the lady. If she says she didn't take it, then she didn't. Now get out of here before I lose my patience and put a bullet in your pompous backside."

Ezekiel stood his ground. "Can't you see how she's blinded you to the truth? She's a jezebel, I tell you, and she'll take you to hell with her if you don't listen to me."

"Why don't we bring in the law and let the sheriff decide who's telling the truth," Adam suggested.

"No," Ezekiel blurted out. "There isn't any need to involve the law."

"Is that so?" Adam said.

"My checkered past still haunts me," Ezekiel confessed. He was trying hard to look contrite and failing miserably. "Otherwise, I'd run to get the sheriff. As God is my witness, I would."

"Get out of here," Adam ordered.

Ezekiel turned away. "This isn't over," he hissed.

Lewis tried to go to his friend, who was still unconscious on the floor in the next stall, but Adam wouldn't let him.

"Leave him be and get out," he ordered.

Ezekiel opened the barn door. "I'll get you, girl," he bellowed. "I know where you're headed, and I'm telling you now, you're never going to get there. Judgment Day is at hand."

And then he disappeared into the darkness. Lewis chased after him.

Genevieve fell back against the wall in exhaustion and relief.

Adam wouldn't let her relax. "We have to get out of here before they figure out how easy it would be to ambush us. Hurry, Genevieve. Ah, hell, now what are you doing?"

She had thrown herself into his arms and burst into tears. "Thank you for believing me."

He allowed himself a moment to hold her. He squeezed her tight, bent down, and kissed her forehead. Then he pulled away.

"Let's go, sweetheart."

She wiped the tears away from her face with the back of her hands and stood there smiling up at him with a dazed look in her eyes.

"Now what?" he asked gruffly.

"You called me sweetheart."

"Yes, I did," he said. "Now move it."

He tried to lift her up into the saddle. She backed away. "My bedroll," she explained.

She turned around and picked it up from the corner of the stall where she'd dropped it, but Adam was quicker. He grabbed one end and swung the bedroll up behind the saddle.

Then he froze and watched in disbelief as a hundred-dollar bill slowly floated down from the bedroll to the floor. It landed between his feet.

He stared at it for several seconds and then bent down to pick it up. He didn't say a word to her, and his expression showed only mild curiosity as he turned to look at the bedroll again. Before she realized what he was going to do, he untied the rope holding the bedroll secure and then flipped it open in front of him.

Hundreds of bills poured down like rain on his feet until he was standing in a pyramid of money. He was pretty certain he knew how much was there, but he decided to find out the exact amount anyway.

His gaze slowly moved to hers. "Four thousand?" he asked quietly.

She shook her head. "Close to five," she said. "Four thousand seven hundred and three dollars, to be exact."

"Ezekiel's money, I assume." His voice blazed with anger.

He was so furious with her he could barely speak, yet he couldn't help but notice she didn't look the least bit guilty or contrite. She didn't appear to be at all worried either.

"Care to explain, Genevieve?"

She folded her arms across her waist. "I didn't steal Ezekiel's money."

He glanced down at the pile and back up at her. The evidence was damning.

"Adam?"

"What?"

"You *will* believe me."

Ten

From the moment he'd met her, she'd done nothing but lie—or so it seemed—and there was

430

absolutely no reason to believe she was telling the truth now. And yet he did believe her. He was either the most gullible man in the world or just plumb crazy. Regardless, he trusted her.

She wasn't a thief. Therefore, there had to be a logical explanation for why she just happened to have all that money with her, and just as soon as possible he was going to sit her down and demand that she tell him everything.

He didn't speak to her again until they made camp about twelve miles south of Gramby. He asked her to get a fire started while he backtracked to find out if they were being followed. By the time he returned to the campsite, she had the bedrolls laid out and a pot of coffee brewing over the flames.

She waited until after he had taken care of the horses and had eaten his supper to bring up the topic she was sure would give him indigestion.

"I don't think it's a good idea to keep the money in my satchel, because that's the first place Ezekiel will look for it."

"Hopefully he won't get close enough to look."

He glanced around the campsite. He remembered dropping the satchel next to the bedrolls, but it wasn't there now.

"What'd you do with the money?"

She pointed to a jagged boulder about twenty feet away from where she was seated. "I hid the satchel behind that rock under some bushes."

He dropped down beside her and added some twigs to the fire. She offered him an apple, and when he shook his head, she put it back in her lap.

"Could you tell if Ezekiel was following us or not?"

"No," he replied. "The clouds were already moving in. If he is, he's going to have a hell of a time seeing our tracks."

"Won't he see the smoke from our fire?"

"With all this mist? No, he won't see it."

"Why is it so damp here?"

"We're close to Juniper Falls," he replied. "Genevieve, what could you have been thinking, carrying all that money? My God, you left it in the stable with the horses."

"No one ever steals an old bedroll," she said. "It was safer there than in the saloon."

He was trying to keep his temper under control. "I think you'd better start explaining. If you didn't steal the money from Ezekiel, then where did you get it?"

"Oh, I stole the money from him all right."

His mouth dropped open. "You what?"

She put her hand on his knee in an attempt to calm him. "Don't get mad until you've heard everything. I did take the money from Ezekiel, but it never belonged to him. I guess you could say I stole from a thief. Yes, that's exactly what I did," she added with a nod.

"Start at the beginning and try to make sense."

"I just hate it when you snap orders at me like that."

"Start talking, Genevieve."

His impatience irritated her. She put the apple back in the burlap sack and folded her hands in her lap.

"I was duped, just like everyone else. I remember telling you that I attended the same church your mother had joined and that I sang in the choir," she said. "Once a year, on Palm Sunday, an assembly of preachers would join the congregation and one would be chosen by our preacher to give the sermon. On one such occasion, the Reverend Thomas Kerriman spoke. He was begging for our help and told us that he was going to lead a large group of families to Kansas to join a settlement there. The families were in a hard way, Adam. They didn't have money or clothes or food, but what they did have was a will to start over again and build a new life. Reverend Kerriman was their Moses."

"And was he like Ezekiel Jones?"

"Oh, no, he's the complete opposite. I knew Thomas before he became a preacher. We grew up together in the same parish, and I know for a fact that he's a good and decent man. He would never dupe anyone."

"So what happened?"

"Ezekiel was also in the congregation that day. He stepped forward and promised Kerriman that he had a sure way to help him. He pointed to the choir and said that if the members agreed, he would take us from town to town to sing, and all the donations would go to Kerriman's cause. He singled me out and said that my voice alone would guarantee large donations." She sounded ashamed.

"You have a beautiful voice, Genevieve," Adam remarked.

"Thank you," she replied. "My father used to tell me that God gives each one of us a special talent and it's up to us to decide if we will use that talent for good or evil. I didn't understand at the time what he meant. I do now."

"Because of Ezekiel?"

"No, because of me. I let him turn my head with all his compliments. I liked being singled out, Adam, and I started dreaming about fame and fortune. He easily drew me into his scheme. I was very full of myself back then, and Ezekiel fed my pride. I'm very ashamed of the person I became. I acted like a spoiled child," she added. "Fame went to my head, and before long the only friend I had left in the choir was Lottie."

"The woman who sent you the wire."

"Yes," she replied.

"So you went from town to town singing and collecting money."

"Yes," she said. "Ezekiel became more and more demanding. I was never allowed to go anywhere by myself or with my friend. He hired men to watch over me . . ."

"Lewis and Herman?"

She nodded. "Ezekiel told me they were there to protect me, but I was more afraid of them than the men they were protecting me from. I still stubbornly clung to my dream of being famous, and then something happened and I saw how shallow and empty my life was becoming."

"What happened?"

"My mother died and I didn't even know about it until two weeks after her funeral. We were singing in Birmingham, and one of her friends come all that way to tell me. I found out later that she had sent a wire to Ezekiel when my mother became ill, but he hid it from me. I will never forgive myself or him."

"If you didn't know—"

"I should have known," she whispered. "I should have gone home more often to see her, but I was so caught up in my own dreams I forgot what was the most important thing of all."

"Family."

"Yes, family."

"Would Ezekiel have let you leave?"

"No, but I could have found a way."

He put his arm around her shoulders and pulled her into his side. "What about your father?"

"He died a year before my mother."

He let out a sigh. "I understand why you want to go to Paris. Your grandfather's the only family left, isn't he?"

"I didn't exactly tell you the truth about my grandfather. He is in Paris . . ."

"But?"

"He died a long time ago. I'm going there to pay my respects."

"Why did you let me think he was alive?"

She glanced over at him. "If you had thought I was all alone in the world, you would have felt sorry for me, and I didn't want that to happen."

The tenderness in his eyes made her want to curl up in his lap and cling to him. She turned away, resisting the lure, and said, "Lots of people are alone, so stop looking at me like that. Now, do you want to hear the rest of this or not?"

"Yes, I want to hear the rest of it."

He was gently rubbing her arm. She never

wanted him to stop, and as soon as that thought came into her mind, she pushed his hand away.

"When I heard my mother had died, I wanted to go home, and that's when Ezekiel started locking me in my room. I heard him tell Lewis I was his meal ticket. It was a horrible time. The shock of losing my mother put everything in perspective. I knew I was chasing a fool's dream and didn't want fame or fortune. I kept thinking about my father and what he'd told me. I could use my talent for good or bad. The choice was up to me. I made up my mind that I would only sing for money when it was absolutely necessary."

"You sang for money in the saloon."

"Yes, but I did so out of necessity, not vanity, and I only sang hymns. We needed money for food and shelter."

"You have almost five thousand dollars," he reminded her.

"But that isn't my money. It belongs to Reverend Kerriman and his families."

He nodded to let her know he understood. "Tell me how you managed to get the money away from Ezekiel."

"One afternoon when we were in New Orleans I was sitting in the garden of a lovely old church and I happened to see Thomas in the courtyard. He was talking to Ezekiel, and I could see how upset he was. Ezekiel wasn't upset though. He was laughing and mocking Thomas."

"Where was your guard?"

"Lewis was assigned to me that day. I let him lock me in my room, and then I snuck out."

"Through the window."

"Yes, I went out through the window and ran back to the courtyard. I heard Ezekiel boast that he had collected over four thousand dollars and that he wasn't going to give Thomas one cent."

"And what did Thomas do?"

"He threatened to go to the authorities, and Ezekiel went into a rage. He told him he'd kill him if he said a word to anyone. Thomas didn't believe him at first, but Ezekiel told him he'd killed before and he could kill again.

"Lewis and Herman started beating Thomas. He fell to the ground, and then Ezekiel kicked him over and over again. I was so terrified for him I couldn't even scream. I ran toward him to make them stop pounding him, but some other people got there first. Lewis and Herman ran. Ezekiel didn't run though. As arrogant as ever, he turned around and strolled back to the church."

"And that's when you decided to steal the money from him, isn't it?"

"Yes. I went to his room and found it right away under his mattress. The stupid man slept on it every night. I put it in a satchel, and then I left."

"To go to Rosehill?"

She shook her head. "Thomas was taken to the hospital, and I hid in New Orleans and waited for him to recover so I could give him the money. I didn't dare go and visit him because I was afraid of being spotted by Ezekiel's men, and when I finally got up enough courage to sneak in during the night, I found out he'd already left for Kansas."

"And that's where you're headed now, isn't it?"

"Yes," she answered. "When I left New Orleans, I was going to go directly to the settlement in Kansas, but then I started worrying about Ezekiel. He knew I had seen what he and his men had done to Thomas, and he had to have figured out why I took the money. I was afraid he would follow me, and I didn't like the idea of being ambushed along the way."

"So you came to Rosehill."

"I thought the ranch was a perfect place to hide for a little while, and I was so sure Ezekiel wouldn't follow me there."

"I wish to God you had told me all of this when we were in the library together."

"I didn't want you to get involved. It was my problem, and I had to take care of it. If I had confided in you, you would have insisted on taking the money to Thomas for me, which would have put you in danger. Isn't that so?"

"Yes," he agreed.

"I don't want anyone else to give Thomas the money. It's important to me that he know I wasn't involved in Ezekiel's scheme."

"I'm sure he already knows that."

"I also want to tell him how sorry I am, but I have to be realistic. Ezekiel isn't going to give up, is he?"

"No, he isn't," he said. "Five thousand dollars is worth his trouble."

"Will you promise me something?" She pushed his arm away and turned to face him.

"If anything happens to me, or if we should get separated, will you take the money to Thomas?"

"I'm not going to let anything happen to you."

"Adam, the money's important to those people. It will buy food and clothes and peace of mind. Promise me," she demanded.

"I promise."

She bowed her head. "I can't imagine what you must think of me. I was so naive and stupid and vain and . . ."

He stopped her from berating herself by tilting her chin up and kissing her. His mouth brushed over hers in a gentle, undemanding caress.

"You're good-hearted," he whispered gruffly.

She pulled back. "I can't let you think that. I'm not good-hearted. If I hadn't been so full of myself, I would have seen through Ezekiel right away. I acted like a fool, but I've learned my lesson. Now do you understand why I've become so cynical?"

Because she was being so earnest, he didn't dare laugh. He couldn't contain his smile though. "I understand you might want to be cynical, but, sweetheart, you haven't quite mastered it yet. There isn't anything cynical about you. You're one of the most trusting souls I've ever met. You have a beautiful heart Genevieve."

"You did it again," she whispered.

He was slowly pulling her onto his lap. She didn't resist and, in fact, put her arms around his neck.

She stared into his eyes and thought that he was the most amazingly perfect man in the whole world. How would she ever have the strength to leave him?

"What did I do?" he asked.

"You called me sweetheart," she told him in a breathless whisper. "You mustn't do that anymore."

"Why not?"

"Because I like it," she stammered. "And now you're going to kiss me again, aren't you? And you really shouldn't. When the time comes for us to go our separate ways, it's going to be very difficult for me, and if you keep kissing me, I'll end up miserable. I have to go to Paris, and you have to go back home. We should just be friends, shouldn't we? But, Adam, I think I really want you to kiss me now. Just one, last kiss, and then we . . ."

"Shake hands?" he suggested dryly.

"Yes, or you could give me a peck on the cheek, the way friends do."

She wanted friendship and nothing more? Didn't she understand they had gone way past that stage? Maybe it was his fault, he decided. He hadn't told her how he felt about her. He hadn't allowed himself to think about it, much less discuss it. He knew he cared for her, but as he did with everything else, he wanted to think about all the ramifications before he told her.

His voice was deceptively mild when he said, "I think you need to get something straight in your head. I don't kiss my friends, I don't peck my friends, and I sure as certain don't call my friends sweetheart."

"We can't become involved."

She really was an exasperating woman. "We *are* involved."

She looked miserable. "We're all wrong for each other. You do realize that, don't you? You want peace and quiet. I'm a troublemaker."

"No, you're not. You're aggravating and as stubborn as can be, but you aren't a trouble-maker, and I'm definitely not your friend."

She was slowly pulling back from him. He wasn't about to let her get away. He jerked her hard against his chest, ignoring her startled cry of surprise. His hand cupped the back of her head, and as he was moving toward her, he whispered, "I never had a chance, did I?"

She didn't understand what he meant, and he was too busy kissing her to explain.

His mouth was warm and firm against hers. It wasn't a friendly kiss. He made sure of that. He coaxed her mouth open, and his tongue swept inside to mate with hers. She began to respond, timidly at first and then with growing passion. He melted away her inhibitions in a matter of heartbeats, and, Lord, she tasted as sweet and fresh as he remembered. He couldn't get enough of her. Passion flowed between them as his mouth slanted over hers again and again, and when at last he forced himself to pull back, he couldn't seem to draw a proper breath. Her own shortness of breath was music to his ears.

The hell he was her friend.

"Now do you want to shake my hand?" he asked, driving his point home.

His sarcasm was lost on her. She was blissfully content snuggled up against him. Her head rested in the crook of his neck and her eyes closed in sweet surrender to the moment.

He held her for a long while in his arms. His hands tenderly caressed her back, and all he wanted to think about was her soft body. Unfortunately, thoughts of Ezekiel Jones kept intruding.

"What are you thinking about?"

"Ezekiel Jones," he said.

"I knew it had to be something unpleasant. You're squeezing the breath out of me, and your muscles have become rigid."

He forced himself to relax and loosened his grip on her. "Is that better?"

"Yes," she answered. "I should probably get off your lap, but I don't want to move," she admitted. "I was also thinking about Ezekiel. Do you think he was telling the truth when he said he had gotten away with murder? Or was he just trying to scare us?"

"I think he was telling the truth, and I'd sure be interested in finding out the particulars. You told me Ezekiel changed his name. Do you know what his real name is?"

"Henry Stevens," she answered. "I heard Lewis call him by his full name once. Ezekiel became furious and threatened dire consequences if he ever called him by his real name again. The stupid man was yelling so loud most of the choir heard him."

Adam filed the information away. Henry Stevens. He wouldn't forget the name again. Had Ezekiel changed his name because he was a wanted man, or had the crime gone unreported? Adam decided to find out as soon as possible.

"When we get to Salt Lake City, I think I'd like to pay a visit to the marshal's office."

"I doubt anyone's there. Don't you remember Mr. Steeple told us that three U.S. marshals were in Middleton, investigating the bank robbery?"

The plan came to him all of a sudden, and he found himself smiling in anticipation. His idea was perfect, and if it worked, it would be well worth the risk. Ezekiel would get what was coming to him, and Adam wouldn't have to kill him. There were a lot of *ifs* involved. If he could find a safe place for Genevieve, and if he could trick Ezekiel into following him to Middleton, and if the marshals were indeed there, then Adam would lead the bastard right into their hands.

"I think we should split up," she said.

She'd spoken his thought aloud. "Is that so?" he asked.

"Yes," she said. "One of us should lead Ezekiel north, while the other takes the money to Kansas."

He shook his head. "The money should go in a bank until I've dealt with Ezekiel and his friends."

"Are you crazy? There are bank robbers roaming these hills. They'll steal it. My plan makes sense."

"I've got a better plan. We'll find a safe place for you, and I'll take care of Ezekiel."

"It's out of the question. This is my problem and I have to solve it."

"No, it's our problem, but I'm going to solve

it. You aren't going with me. I would be worried about you the entire time, and I wouldn't be able to concentrate on what I needed to do."

"Such as?"

"Putting an end to Ezekiel's terror tactics."

"It's very sweet of you to be worried about me, but, Adam, I won't be left out. Do you expect me to sit quietly in a parlor somewhere while you put yourself in such danger? I won't hear of it."

He smiled. "I wasn't thinking of putting you in a parlor. I have another place in mind where I can be absolutely certain Ezekiel won't go near you or the money."

"There isn't any such place."

He kissed her again just to get her to stop arguing with him. "Trust me, Genevieve. I've thought of the perfect place."

Eleven

He put her in jail. Even though she had to admit it was a perfect place to keep the money safe, she still wasn't happy about Adam's choice, because she knew he expected her to stay inside while he went gallivanting after Ezekiel and his men. If she had had a few minutes alone with him, she would have let him know just how unhappy she was, but the jail was crowded with lawmen, and she wasn't about to criticize Adam in front of strangers. She did glare at him though when he

444

suggested she might be more comfortable inside one of the empty cells.

She sat down in a chair next to Sheriff Norton's desk, put her satchel on her lap, and folded her hands on top. Adam stood behind her. After removing a stack of papers from his chair, the sheriff sat down and tilted back against the wall. He was an older man with a big belly and melancholy eyes. His face reminded Genevieve of a hound dog's. His jowls extended past his chin, and when he smiled—which seemed to be most of the time—the folds of extra skin on either side of his face wrinkled up to his ears. He was very kind to her and Adam, and she liked him immensely. His voice radiated fatherly concern when he asked how he could be of help, and he listened patiently without interrupting once while Adam explained why they were there.

Two U.S. marshals leaned against the wall and listened. The men were so similar in appearance and attitude they could have been brothers. They were about the same height, nearly six feet, and had the same worn and world-weary expressions. The more muscular one was named Davidson, and the other was called Morgan.

Their presence should have been a comfort, but they made her nervous instead. Their gazes seemed to bore right through her. There was an air of danger about them as well. She couldn't even begin to imagine the horrors they must have seen that would have turned them into such frightening men. Her mind conjured up one horrible possibility after another, and before long she was fighting the urge to jump up and leave.

She really wished they would stop staring at her. She kept expecting one of them to pounce on her, and she glanced over at them every other minute just to make sure they hadn't moved.

Adam must have sensed her unease because he put his hand on her shoulder and gave it a little squeeze.

After he had finished explaining their circumstances to the sheriff, including details she wished he hadn't mentioned, Marshal Davidson suggested that Genevieve look through the posters of wanted men to see if Ezekiel was one of them.

The sheriff pointed to a knee-high stack of papers on the floor in the corner behind him. "There they are, but I'll wager you it will take you the rest of the day to sort through them."

"Adam, are you certain Jones and his friends are following you?" Morgan asked the question but watched Genevieve all the while.

"Yes, I made sure they could easily follow my tracks to Middleton."

Davidson took a step toward her. She visibly jumped and then became angry.

"Gentlemen, what are you staring at?" she demanded.

The marshals glanced at one another before turning back to her. Davidson raised an eyebrow and looked a little sheepish, but Morgan maintained his glacial expression. She didn't think the man had blinked in the past five minutes.

"I was looking at you, ma'am," Davidson said.

"I wish you wouldn't," she said. "I swear to heaven you make me want to confess to a crime just to get you to stop."

"Did you have a particular crime in mind?" Morgan asked. A hint of a smile crinkled the corners of his eyes.

The marshal became human to her. She began to relax. "No," she answered. "I would have to make one up. Do you know how intimidating you are? Yes, of course you do. That's how you interrogate criminals, isn't it?"

"Genevieve, what are you talking about?" Adam asked.

"You wouldn't understand even if I tried to explain. You do the very same thing."

Davidson burst into laughter. "Ma'am, did you really impersonate Ruby Leigh . . . ?"

"Diamond," Morgan supplied with a grin.

"You sure don't look like the kind of woman who would go by such a name," Davidson remarked.

She frowned at the marshal. "How exactly do I look?"

"Refined," Davidson answered. "You're a lady, and I'm having trouble picturing you up on a stage in a saloon."

"I didn't impersonate anyone, at least not on purpose. Mr. Steeple tricked me. Adam, you really didn't need to tell the marshals I sang in a saloon."

He squeezed her shoulder again. Davidson came to his defense. "He was telling us how he first spotted Ezekiel, so he had to mention the saloon."

"I assure you I'm not in the habit of entertaining drunken men, and I only sang church songs."

"Did you really make all of those men cry?" Morgan asked.

"Not on purpose."

Her answer made them laugh again. Her embarrassment intensified. She waited until the noise died down before suggesting in a righteous stammer that they tell her what they were going to do about Ezekiel and his friends.

Norton reached over to pat her hand. "Don't you be worrying about it, little lady."

His condescending tone of voice didn't sit well with her. "Sheriff, Ezekiel Jones is coming after me. I have to be worried about him, and I also have to be worried about Adam. He's determined to go after all three of those horrible men. Please stop squeezing my shoulder," she added with a quick glance up at Adam. "I don't want you to get hurt."

"My mind's made up," he told her in no uncertain terms.

She turned back to the marshals. "Well?" she demanded.

"Well, what?" Davidson asked.

"I'm waiting for one of you to tell Adam he can't take the law into his own hands."

Morgan shrugged. His response wasn't what she was hoping for. Neither was his reply. "He seems real determined, ma'am, and I don't think anything I say will change his mind. I don't blame him for wanting to go after Jones. If the woman I loved were being threatened, I sure as certain would put a stop to it."

She didn't know if she should correct the marshal's assumption or not. Adam didn't love

448

her; he was simply being compassionate by helping her. That was all.

"If Ezekiel's wanted for murder or any other crime, I'd be real interested in talking to him," Morgan continued.

The marshal's casual attitude drove her to distraction. "I don't want you to talk to him. I want you to lock him up. If the murder he committed wasn't reported, then I shall press charges against him."

"On what grounds?" the sheriff asked.

"The man locked me in my room."

"Begging your pardon, but it's your word against his, and I don't think he's gonna admit locking you up," the sheriff told her.

"The sooner you go through the posters, the better," Davidson suggested.

"Yes, of course, but in the meanwhile, I want you to arrest Ezekiel and his two friends. I'll be happy to give you their descriptions."

"Now we're right back where we started," the sheriff complained. "As I was telling you before, you just got to have grounds to make an arrest."

"Such as?" she asked.

The sheriff pondered the question a long minute before answering. "If one of them happens to take a shot at you, well then, we could nab him for attempted murder."

Davidson grinned. "I know it's frustrating, ma'am, but the law's the law. Maybe we could talk to him and scare him into leaving you alone."

"We ought to ask Ryan to have a word with Ezekiel," Morgan told his friend.

"Adam, what do you think?" Genevieve asked.

She turned to look up at him and only then discovered he was gone. "When did he leave?"

She was on her feet and turning toward the door before the sheriff could answer her.

"He took off a few minutes ago," he said. "Sit back down, ma'am. You got to start looking through the posters. These here are the latest ones, but if you think Jones might have committed a crime a while back, then I got to take you into the storeroom. I keep every poster I receive. Some go back as far as ten years."

"While you're looking through them, Morgan and I will stop by the telegraph office and send a couple of wires asking for information. Adam gave us a good description, and we should hear something back real soon. In the meantime, you're in good hands," Davidson said.

"Are you boys headed back up the mountain?"

Morgan nodded. "Ryan's going to stick close to the doctor's house as long as there's a chance our witness will make it. If you run into any trouble, he'll lend a hand."

Genevieve watched the marshals leave and then turned to the sheriff and asked, "Mr. Steeple told me there were three marshals in Middleton. Ryan's the third one, isn't he?"

"Yes, ma'am. Morgan and Davidson are taking orders from him, and I heard Morgan say Ryan was senior man in charge. He's also the youngest."

"Is Ryan's first name Daniel by any chance?"

"It sure is," he replied. "I don't expect I'll ever be calling him anything but marshal or sir. He ain't the type to get friendly with. Fact is, he scares just about everybody in town, and I imagine that's why Morgan suggested Ryan be the one to talk to Ezekiel Jones or Henry Stevens or whatever in tarnation his name is."

"What did Morgan mean when he said that Marshal Ryan was staying close to the doctor's house?"

"He's over at Doc Garrison's house, waiting to see if poor old Luke MacFarland is gonna up and die on him. He's the only witness we got to the terrible trouble we had here the day before yesterday. What started out as a plain old bank robbery turned into a massacre. Luke was outside and saw what happened through the bank window. Before he passed out on us he told Ryan and me he could identify the leader.

"The folks working at the bank handed the money over as meek as could be and then put their hands up to let the robbers know they weren't gonna be heroic and go for their guns. There weren't no call to shoot them down, no call at all, but that's what the robbers did. Frank Holden, the president of the bank, had six bullets in his head. There was blood splattered all the way up to the ceiling. It was a cold, vicious act, and five good men I called friends died like dogs."

Genevieve was sickened by the story. "Those poor souls," she whispered. "If they didn't put up a fight, why were they killed?"

"They would have been witnesses, that's why. Luke and Nichols were watching all of it. Both of them got shot. Luke took a bullet in his gut, and that means he don't have much hope of lasting, which is a crying shame for his family.

He's got a wife and four boys to feed, and if he dies, I don't know what will happen to them."

"What about the other witness?" she asked.

"Nichols took a bullet through his heart. Doc said he probably died standing up."

"I hope the marshals catch the men and lock them up for the rest of their lives."

"I'd ruther they strung them up," Norton said. "You can understand now, can't you, why Davidson and Morgan are letting Adam take care of Ezekiel? They got their hands full trailing the gang. None of the marshals have had much sleep lately."

"Do you think they'll find the gang?"

"Maybe, and maybe not. There's over a hundred caves in these mountains, and they could be hiding out in any one of them. Eventually they'll get caught because they're bound to make a mistake. The five of them have been on a killing spree for over a year now. The man in charge is a clever devil to be able to elude Ryan for so long. The bastard always makes sure there ain't no witnesses, just in case he gets caught."

The sheriff stood up and stretched his arms wide. "If you don't mind being alone, I'd like to go over to the doc's house and see how Luke's doing."

"I don't mind," she replied. "But if you happen to run into Adam, will you please tell him I'd like him to help me go through the posters?"

"I doubt I'll see him anytime soon," the sheriff responded. "We both know he went looking for those fellas. Why, he's probably waiting by the hill outside of town. That's what I'd do if I wanted to nab someone coming from Gramby. The only way into Middleton is over that hill beyond the stable. I got a feeling he'll come back empty-handed by nightfall 'cause if you heard there were three marshals here, this Jones fella probably heard the same thing."

Genevieve shook her head. "I don't think Ezekiel was in town long enough to talk to anyone. At least that's what Adam hopes. Sheriff, I'm worried about him. Ezekiel is terribly bold, and the two men riding with him wouldn't think twice about shooting a man in the back."

"I don't want you sitting in here fretting," the sheriff told her. "Maybe I will mosey on up the hill and have a look around for Adam. He probably don't need my help though. From the looks of him, I'd say he could hold his own in any fight, even against three."

He showed her where the storeroom was located and then left her alone. At first sight, she thought the task was hopeless, for there were papers stacked everywhere. They lined the shelves to the ceiling, and more were on the floor. The dust made her sneeze, and some of the old posters crumbled when she touched them.

It wasn't as chaotic as she'd first thought though. The sheriff had separated the posters by the year they were received. She ignored the latest notices and, starting with the year-old fliers, worked her way back.

After three hours of searching, she was stiff from sitting on the floor, hungry, and covered with dust. When she stretched her legs out to get rid of a cramp in her calf, she knocked over a pile of posters she had yet to look through. With a sigh, she leaned forward to straighten them up, and then let out a whoop of joy. Ezekiel Jones's ugly face was staring up at her.

The drawing had done Ezekiel justice, because it captured the evil essence of the man right down to the detail of his beady, squinty eyes. He was wanted for murder and extortion, he was considered armed and dangerous—and she could certainly testify to those two facts—and there was a hundred-dollar reward for his apprehension. Several of the aliases he had used were listed at the bottom of the sheet, and in bold letters across the top was the notice that he was wanted dead or alive.

She was so excited with her discovery she could barely think what to do. Adam needed to see the poster as soon as possible. Surely then he would realize what a dangerous adversary he was up against. My God, the man really had committed murder. She had heard him boast of the heinous crime, but a part of her hadn't believed him. The poster removed all doubt. Ezekiel was a killer. Hopefully, after Adam had seen the poster, he would agree to let the authorities take over the hunt.

She grabbed her satchel and hurried to the front door and then decided it was foolish to carry Thomas's money with her. She ran back to the jail cells and locked the satchel inside one of them. She wasn't about to leave the keys behind, and so she slipped the heavy metal ring over her wrist and wore it like a bracelet. The keys jingled and jangled with each step she took down the board-walk.

The streets and the boardwalk were crowded with people coming and going. She wasn't quite sure where Adam was, but she hoped he was waiting for Ezekiel near the base of the hills behind the livery stable. The sheriff had told them that the main road from Gramby led into Middleton from the north, and if Ezekiel was coming after them, he would probably use that route. Earlier she had hoped that Ezekiel hadn't heard that U.S. marshals had converged on Middleton, but now she prayed he had indeed heard, so that he would stay away. The thought of Adam taking on not one but three blackguards frightened her. He played by the rules. He would never shoot a man in the back. Ezekiel would.

The possibility terrified her, and before she realized what she was doing, she started running down the boardwalk toward the livery.

A shot rang out. The noise so jarred her she stumbled. She grabbed hold of a hitching post to keep from falling and dropped the poster. She scooped it up, folded it, and shoved it in her pocket as she squinted into the sunlight to see who was firing his gun. Someone shouted to her, but the words were drowned out by a hail of gunfire. The noise was explosive, the sound rico-cheting from building to building. The men and women who had been strolling down the main thoroughfare ran for cover, and within seconds, the streets and boardwalk were deserted.

She was frozen with panic. She saw a man running down the center of the street toward the sound, his gun drawn. He was moving so fast into the sunlight he was almost a blur.

A yellow-haired woman poked her head out of the general store a few feet in front of Genevieve and shouted to her. "Get on inside here before you get yourself killed."

"The gang who robbed the bank came back, and now we're all gonna die," another woman screeched from behind the first.

Genevieve turned to go inside. Then she stopped. Why would the robbers come back? They already had the money from the bank. What if it wasn't the gang . . . ?

Adam. A chill went down her spine. Oh, God, what if Adam was in trouble? She had assumed he had gone in search of Ezekiel, but what if he had returned to town? She pictured him pinned down and surrounded by Lewis and Herman and Ezekiel, and, dear God, what if he had already been shot? She had to find out. She just needed to get close enough to see for herself that Adam wasn't involved.

She picked up her skirts and ran. The noise seemed to be coming from between two buildings on the next street. The sun was blinding her, and fear was making it hard to breathe. Panting, she raced forward as though his life depended on it. She was leaping off the boardwalk between the alley and the next building when she heard someone whisper her name. She stumbled as she turned to see who was there.

And then she screamed.

Twelve

He had them right where he wanted them. Adam pressed back against the brick wall facing the street and quickly reloaded his gun. He was on the left side of the entrance to an alley that dead-ended, and he was feeling damned smug because he was certain he had all three of the bastards pinned inside.

His mood wasn't friendly. One of them had tried to ambush him behind the livery stable just as he had been dismounting, and if he hadn't thrown himself off his horse and to the ground in the nick of time, he would have taken a bullet in the back.

He wanted to get even, and though he fancied the notion of killing all of them, he knew he would have to settle for wounding one or two. It was his fervent hope that Ezekiel would become desperate enough to try to rush past him. There wasn't any other way out of the alley, and if Adam had to spend the rest of the day waiting to nab him, then that's what he would do.

He spotted a man running toward him from across the street. The stranger was wearing a badge, and Adam assumed he was the third marshal he'd heard about. The lawman was tall, thick-shouldered, and had blond hair and blue eyes.

He seemed familiar, but Adam couldn't

remember where he had seen him before. Adam nodded to him and was just turning away when he spotted a gold chain dangling from the marshal's vest pocket. What looked suspiciously like a gold compass case dangled from the end of the chain.

Recognition was immediate. "Son of a . . ." Adam whispered. The lawman was Daniel Ryan.

"Drop your gun," Ryan roared.

Adam shook his head and went right on reloading.

The marshal aimed his gun at him and was repeating his command when a shot rang out. The bullet roared past Ryan's left shoulder. He dove for cover on the opposite side of the entrance, and like Adam, pressed his back against the wall.

His gaze was directed on Adam. "Who the hell are they?" he roared.

Adam quickly explained. When he was finished Ryan asked him how many there were.

"Ezekiel was leading the way and his two hired guns were following him. When I turned the corner, I saw one of them run into the alley. I'm certain all three are there. They must have thought they could cut through, and now they're trapped. When they run out of bullets, they'll come out."

Ryan nodded. "I'll handle this. Just stay out of my way."

"No," Adam answered. "You stay out of my way. You're Daniel Ryan, aren't you?"

"Yes. Who are you?"

"Adam Clayborne."

Ryan raised an eyebrow in surprise, and then a hint of a smile lifted the corners of his mouth. "You're Rose's son."

"Yes," Adam agreed. "Nice compass."

"Yes, it is."

"The compass belongs to my brother Cole."

"It sure does," Ryan agreed.

Before Adam could demand that he hand it over, Ryan shouted to the men in the alley. "Drop your weapons and put your hands up, or you're going to die."

A hail of bullets whizzed past in response. Ryan leaned in, shot twice, and then jerked back.

"How's your mother doing?" he asked in a voice as mild as the afternoon breeze.

"She's fine," Adam replied a scant second before he moved forward, took aim, and shot. One of the men let out a loud wail of distress.

The sound made Adam smile. He pressed back against the wall and grinned. "One down, two to go."

"Stay out of this."

"No way."

"What's Cole up to these days?"

"Ranching."

"You ready to give it up?" Ryan bellowed. "This is the last time I'm gonna ask you."

"Go to hell," one of the men shouted.

Ryan let out a sigh. "Seems like they want to die," he drawled out.

Adam nodded. "It seems so."

"Less paperwork involved," Ryan remarked. "So I might as well accommodate them."

"Ezekiel Jones is mine. If anyone's going to shoot him, it's going to be me."

Ryan shrugged. "Does Rose like living in Montana?"

"Yes, she does. She speaks highly of you, and she seems to think you're going to bring the compass you borrowed back to her," he added, deliberately stressing the word "borrowed."

Ryan laughed. "I didn't borrow it. I took it."

"Give it back."

"I will when I'm ready. I've got some business to discuss with Cole, and as soon as I've finished up here, I'm coming to Rosehill."

"You'd better come armed then. You've made Cole angry enough to shoot you on sight."

Ryan smiled. "He doesn't have a problem killing, does he?"

"No, none at all."

"Good. That's what I heard. He's just the man I need."

"Need? What do you need him for? You can't possibly think he'd go to work for you."

"That's exactly what I think. I can be real persuasive."

The conversation was interrupted by gunshots from the alley. Ryan and Adam returned the fire. The sound was deafening. Both men fell back against the wall and reloaded.

"What exactly do you want Cole to do for you?"

"Kill some vermin."

Before Adam could question him further, one of Ezekiel's men shouted at them.

"We're coming out. Don't shoot."

"Drop your weapons and put your hands up," Ryan shouted.

After giving the order, he motioned for Adam to stay where he was, and then Ryan moved back at an angle into the street.

Herman came strutting out of the alley first. He was closely followed by Lewis, who was limping. The two men had just reached the entrance when Lewis, using Herman as his shield, fired at Ryan and missed. The marshal shot the gun out of his hand a scant second before Adam slammed the butt of his gun up against the side of his head. Lewis crumpled to the ground.

In one fluid motion Herman dove for the ground and reached behind his back for his weapon. He was swinging his arm up with a gun in his hand before he hit the ground.

Ryan shot to kill. The bullet sliced through Herman's chest, propelling him backward. He died before his head struck the edge of the board-walk.

Adam moved into the alley to search for Ezekiel. The bastard wasn't there. Muttering curses under his breath, he reholstered his gun and turned around. Ryan had moved to the center of the street and was staring at something in front of him. He looked as though he was ready for a shoot-out. His legs were braced apart, his back was rigid, and his hand hovered just above the hilt of his gun.

"Let her go," Ryan shouted.

Adam ran forward, ignoring the signal the lawman gave him to stay where he was. Adam was about ten feet away from Ryan when he saw the two of them. Genevieve—his sweet, loving Genevieve—and Ezekiel.

The bastard had the barrel of his gun pressed against the side of her head and was slowly moving toward a covered buggy someone had hitched to the post in front of the general store.

Adam felt as though he'd just been run over by a train. His knees almost buckled, his heart seemed to drop, and he was filled with rage.

"No." The word was issued in a low, guttural moan.

Ryan was slowly edging toward Ezekiel. His attention was fully directed on him. Adam also moved closer, but his focus remained centered on Genevieve.

He knew she had to be terrified, but she was valiantly trying to hide her fear from him. Then he saw the tears in her eyes, and his rage became uncontrollable.

He wanted to kill the bastard with his bare hands.

He first had to get rid of the gun threatening Genevieve. Ezekiel's left arm was wrapped tightly around her waist, and he was using her as his shield as he slowly pushed her forward to the side of the buggy. His right hand held the gun up against her head, and his finger was on the trigger.

"It's going to be all right," Adam whispered so low she couldn't possibly hear him.

As if by some unspoken joint decision, both Adam and Ryan began to fan out in a V as they continued toward their prey. They were about fifteen feet away from Ezekiel when he shouted an order to stop.

"If you take another step, I'll kill her," he screamed.

Adam could hear the panic in his voice and see the wild, frantic look in his eyes. Like a cornered rat, he was ready to strike. Adam didn't want to do anything that would provoke him into accidentally squeezing that trigger.

He'd never been so damned scared in his whole life. He hadn't told Genevieve he loved her, and, God, he needed to say the words at least a million times. He wanted to grow old with her and tell her each and every day for the rest of their lives how much she meant to him.

"Let her go, Ezekiel," Adam pleaded.

"I'm getting out of here, and no one's going to stop me," Ezekiel screeched. "I've got nothing to lose, and if you want her to live, you won't follow me."

"I can't let you take her with you," Ryan shouted.

Ezekiel turned his head toward the marshal. "I'll kill her," he yelled. "If my hand starts shaking, this gun's going to fire, and it'll be your fault. Both of you throw your weapons down and turn around."

"No." Genevieve screamed. "He'll shoot you in the back. Don't do it, Adam."

"Shut your trap," Ezekiel hissed. "You brought this trouble on yourself. If you hadn't stolen my money . . ."

"It's Thomas's money, not yours. I'm taking it back to him."

"From your grave?" Ezekiel taunted. "You don't think I'll let you live, do you? You're a naive fool, Genevieve. Stop struggling," he snapped when she tried to push his arm away.

"Let her go," Adam implored.

The anguish she heard in his voice broke her heart. "I'm so sorry," she whispered.

"I told you to drop your guns," Ezekiel demanded once again.

"I can't do that," Ryan called out.

Adam was slowly advancing to the left while Ryan angled to the right. The lawman extended his arm and aimed his gun at Ezekiel and Genevieve. Adam knew what Ryan was going to do. His blood ran cold. He looked at Ryan and saw that his blue eyes had turned as cold as frost.

"Don't do it," he shouted.

"I can take him."

"No."

Ryan ignored him. He kept moving forward, trying to get a clear shot. He knew he'd get only one chance, and if Ezekiel's death wasn't instantaneous, Genevieve would also die.

"Stay where you are," Ezekiel warned. His eyes darted back and forth between Adam and Ryan as he slowly pushed Genevieve closer to the buggy.

"This is your last chance," Ryan called out. "Let her go now, or I swear to God I'll drop you where you stand."

Adam now wanted to kill Ryan. How dare he gamble with Genevieve's life? Adam didn't care that Ryan was right. He too knew Ezekiel would kill her as soon as he had the opportunity, but if Ryan's shot missed, or if Ezekiel's finger flinched, Genevieve would pay the price.

He couldn't let that happen. If keeping her safe

meant that he had to die, then that was what he was going to do.

Adam started running toward the buggy, deliberately trying to draw Ezekiel's fire, and when he was about five feet away, he went for his gun.

The bastard fell for his ploy. Adam had made himself an easy target, and the temptation was too great for Ezekiel to resist. He swung his gun away from Genevieve and took aim.

Ezekiel was dead before he could squeeze the trigger. As soon as the barrel moved away from her head, Ryan fired. The bullet cut through the center of his forehead. Adam's bullet entered Ezekiel's forehead a hair's width away from Genevieve's.

The force lifted Ezekiel off his feet and hurled him backward. Genevieve was thrown to one side. She screamed as she fell and then began to sob.

She had thought that Adam was about to die when he put himself in front of Ezekiel, and the terror and desolation she had felt in that terrifying moment had nearly destroyed her.

Adam gently lifted her up. She threw herself into his arms and continued to sob uncontrollably.

He held her tight and tried to get rid of his rage so that he could comfort her.

Both of them were shaking. "I thought I had lost you," he whispered gruffly.

"It's all my fault. You should have stayed at Rosehill. . . . I almost got you killed, and if you had died, Adam, I couldn't have gone on. I . . ."

"Hush, sweetheart. It's over now."

She jerked away from him. "How dare you take such a chance," she cried out. "How dare you . . ."

She couldn't go on. Her sobs were heart-wrenching. He pulled her back into his arms and hugged her tight. He never wanted to let go.

"Don't cry, my love. Don't cry." He bent down and kissed the top of her head. "You were very brave."

"No, I wasn't. I was scared."

"I was scared too," he admitted.

She looked up at him, her eyes wide. "You? Scared? I don't believe you. Nothing scares you."

He laughed. The sound was harsh to his ears. He used his thumbs to wipe the tears away from her cheeks and laughed again. "My hands are still shaking. I swear to you, Genevieve, no one is ever going to hurt you again."

She was safe. He kept telling himself that in hopes that he would get over his anger. He was still so furious with Ryan he could barely control himself.

She knew she would never be able to stop crying if she didn't move away from him, but she wanted to cling.

"I almost got you killed," she said again. "Ezekiel was right. He told me I was a naive fool, and I was, Adam. I've been nothing but trouble to you. No man deserves such heartache."

He grabbed hold of her chin. "You didn't make me follow you," he reminded her, and before she could argue the point, he kissed her.

She promptly burst into tears again. He was

such a good man, and he was being so terribly sweet to her.

She looked down at Ezekiel and cringed inside. Adam took her hand and pulled her away. He was staring at the lawman who had helped him only minutes ago.

"Is he Daniel Ryan?" she asked.

"Yes."

"Does he still have Cole's compass?"

Adam nodded. "He told me he'll bring it to Rosehill," he said.

"Why are you glaring at him?"

"He took a terrible risk with your life. If he had missed . . ."

"Don't think such thoughts. I'm thankful, and I must go to him and tell him so."

"No."

"Ezekiel told me he was going to kill me because I had caused him so much trouble."

"Ryan should have waited," he stubbornly insisted.

The marshal heard his comment. "I knew what I was doing, Adam."

"The hell you did. You should have let me—"

Before he could continue, Ryan cut him off. "You were too emotionally involved. I wasn't."

"You're a coldhearted bastard."

Ryan stepped closer. "Damned right I am."

"You could have killed her. If Ezekiel had moved an inch or flinched, you would have gotten her."

"I waited for my shot."

"The hell with that logic."

Genevieve couldn't figure out what was

happening. The two men who had worked together to save her life just moments ago were now acting as though they wanted to kill each other. It didn't make any sense. "Gentlemen, if you will please calm down and—"

"You didn't care if she lived or died. What kind of marshal are you? You're supposed to protect citizens, not shoot at them."

Adam shoved Ryan in the chest. Ryan shoved back. "I cared about her, but I don't happen to love her, and you obviously do. Understand the difference? Look at your hands. I'll bet they're still shaking."

"They're shaking all right, with the need to put my fist through your face. I swear . . ."

Out of the corner of his eye Adam saw Lewis, the man he'd struck unconscious, come up on his knees. He also saw the gun in his hand. At the same instant, Ryan spotted the flash of metal. Both men turned simultaneously and fired.

Adam's bullet shot the gun out of Lewis's hand. Ryan's bullet blasted a hole in his chest. Lewis swayed backward, then pitched forward to the ground.

Genevieve's hand flew to her throat. It happened so fast she didn't even have time to scream. Neither Adam nor Ryan seemed much perturbed by the interruption. They both watched Lewis for several seconds to make sure he wasn't going to move, then turned back to each other and resumed their heated debate as though nothing out of the ordinary had happened.

She took a step back from them and bumped into Sheriff Norton.

"How can they be so callous? They just killed a man." Her voice shook with emotion, and she was trembling from head to foot.

"It seems to me that man needed killing. He would have gotten one of them if they hadn't shot him, so you shouldn't be fretting about it."

"Why are they arguing?"

"Ah, it's just their way of letting off steam. I saw the whole thing from Barnes's porch. You had both of them real scared, ma'am. If that gun had gone off up against your head, it would have been a real mess."

The sheriff nudged Ezekiel's leg with the tip of his boot. "He don't look so dangerous now, does he?"

Genevieve wouldn't look at the dead man. She turned back to Adam just in time to hear him tell Ryan he should have tried to negotiate with Ezekiel.

"I never negotiate with criminals," Ryan countered. "You can get as mad as you want, but after you calm down, you'll admit I was right to do what I did. I told you I wouldn't miss. I didn't, did I?"

"You're that cocksure of yourself?"

"No, I'm that good," Ryan boasted. "You made it easy by becoming his target. That was a stupid move, by the way."

Adam took exception to his comment. He shoved Ryan again. The lawman didn't budge.

Genevieve desperately needed to sit down for a few minutes. Her heart was racing, and her legs were so weak she could barely stand up. She headed back to the jail with the sheriff at her side.

"I almost got Adam killed," she confessed in a pitifully weak voice.

The sheriff latched onto her arm. "You're trembling like a leaf," he remarked. "It weren't your fault your man almost got shot."

"Yes, it was my fault. He was living a peaceful, safe life on his ranch until I came along. I've caused him a considerable amount of trouble."

The sheriff awkwardly patted her. "Now, now, there ain't no call to cry. You weren't the trouble-maker. That dead man stiffening up on my street caused all the trouble."

"He was wanted," she cried out, remembering the poster. She pulled it out of her pocket and handed it to the sheriff.

"You were personally involved with the lady," Ryan accused loud enough for Genevieve to over-hear.

"Hell, yes, I'm personally involved," Adam roared. "I love her, but that doesn't mean I couldn't have gotten the job done."

She whirled around. "You love me?" she cried out.

Adam didn't even spare her a glance. "Stay out of this, Genevieve. You're wrong, Ryan. You gambled with her life. I could kill you for that."

"You can't love me. I'm going to Paris."

Both Ryan and Adam turned to look at her. She turned around and ran to the jail. Her mind was made up. She would get her satchel and leave for Kansas immediately. As soon as she had given

Thomas his money, she would catch the next train to the coast.

She was in such a hurry she didn't give the sheriff time to open the door for her. She ran ahead, but when she reached the cell, she discovered she didn't have the ring of keys with her. She must have dropped it along the way.

She didn't realize she was still crying until the sheriff handed her a handkerchief.

"There ain't no need to carry on so," he said.

"I lost your keys," she wailed.

"I've got them right here," he said. He moved forward and reached for the lock. "I found them in the middle of the street where you dropped them. I sure don't understand why you needed to lock up your clothes though. Did you think someone would steal them?"

She shook her head, then nodded. Neither she nor Adam had told the sheriff the money was in the satchel, and she was too weary now to explain much of anything.

The front door opened then, and Adam came inside. He had to duck so he wouldn't bump his head on the doorframe. He was frowning, but it didn't make any difference. He was still the most beautiful man she had ever seen.

"Make him go away," she whispered to the sheriff.

"I've got to have a reason to make him go away, ma'am," he replied as he swung the cell door open.

She ran inside to get the satchel but turned when Adam spoke to her.

"What's come over you? Why are you so upset?"

She couldn't believe such an intelligent man could be so obtuse. She stared up at him through the bars and tried to make herself stop crying.

"You almost got yourself killed because of me. You were willing to die for me, weren't you? You're good and noble, and I'm not worthy of your love. Your mother would never have forgiven me if anything had happened to you."

"Nothing happened, sweetheart."

She wiped the tears away with the back of her hands. "It's time for us to go our separate ways. Go home, Adam."

"Genevieve . . ."

She ignored his warning tone of voice. "My mind's made up."

Adam smiled. She should have known then that he was up to something, but she was too distressed to think about it. She sat down on the cot and folded her hands in her lap. She had just been through a horrible ordeal, and every time she thought about Adam putting himself in the thick of it, she was overwhelmed with tremors.

She didn't think she would ever recover.

Adam shut the door and turned the lock. Then he leaned against the bars, folded his arms across his chest, and smiled at her again.

"I've got you now, Genevieve."

"I won't love you."

"It's too late. You already do, or at least I think you do. That's why you were scared, isn't it? You thought you were going to lose me, and it scared the hell out of you."

"How do you know how I felt?"

"Because I was going through the same thing."

"Love isn't supposed to be painful."

"I love you, sweetheart."

She shook her head. "It could never work. We're so different from one another, and I'd drive you crazy in no time at all. I'll never forget you," she whispered.

He laughed. "Since we're going to be living together for the rest of our lives, I don't suppose you will forget me."

"I've got to leave."

"I'll follow you."

"You want peace and quiet, and I like adventures."

"We'll compromise and have a little of both."

Tears streamed down her cheeks. "Sheriff, let me out of here. I have to catch the coach."

"The sheriff went outside. He can't hear you, and I'm not letting you out until you promise to marry me. We'll go to Paris for our honeymoon, and then we'll settle down at Rosehill and you can plant your garden. I want to grow old with you, Genevieve."

She gripped the bars with her hands. He reached over and trailed his fingers across her knuckles.

"This is an adventure," he drawled out. "You can tell our children how their father locked their mother in jail."

The sparkle in his eyes was mesmerizing. She stared up at him in wonder. He loved her, and how was that possible?

"Our children?" she whispered.

"Yes," he replied. "We're going to have lots of children, and, God willing, every one of them will be as adventurous as you are. You do love me, don't you, sweetheart?"

"I love you. I've always loved you."

He unlocked the door and pulled her into his arms. He kissed her long and hard, and when he lifted his head and looked into her eyes, he saw the love there.

"You're the man of my dreams, Adam."

He smiled. "And you, my love, are my greatest adventure."

Epilogue

Daniel Ryan was Adam's best man at the wedding, and Sheriff Norton was given the honor of escorting Genevieve down the aisle of the cottage-sized church on the outskirts of Middleton. She wore the white linen dress that her mother had made for her the year before she died, and in her hand she carried a lovely bouquet of red roses.

Adam could barely catch his breath at the sight of her. His voice shook when he said his vows, but then, so did hers. When the preacher blessed the union, Adam leaned down and kissed her.

They left Middleton an hour later and spent their first night as man and wife in Pickerman's fancy hotel. Adam had a particular fondness for the town of Gramby, and the town now had a great fondness for his wife. They called her Ruby Leigh, and after trying to explain over and over again, she finally gave up and began to answer to the name.

She was as nervous as all brides are on their wedding night. Her robe was buttoned up to the top of her neck, and its sash was double-knotted. From the look on her face, he guessed it would be easier to break into the U.S. Mint than to get her undressed.

He shut the bedroom door behind him and leaned against it. She moved to the far side of the double four-poster bed, her gaze locked on his.

"Do you want to hear something funny?"

"What's that?"

"I'm scared to death."

His smile was filled with tenderness. "I noticed."

She took a step toward him. "You aren't nervous are you?"

"Maybe just a little. I don't want to hurt you."

"Oh."

The way he was looking at her made her weak all over. Her heart was racing, and she was having trouble breathing. Loving Adam was going to kill her. The thought made her smile.

"Do you want to go to bed now?" he asked.

"You go ahead," she whispered. "I'll join you in a little while."

He tried not to laugh. "Sweetheart, what I have in mind requires your attendance."

She could feel herself blushing. "Yes, I realize that. Did you mind giving away the reward money?"

The switch of topics didn't faze him. "No, I didn't mind at all. As soon as Sheriff Norton told you about that injured man's family being so hard up, I knew what you would want to do. You have a very kind heart, Genevieve Clayborne. No wonder I love you so much."

She watched him take off his shirt and then bend down and remove his shoes and socks. He was still standing by the door, and she suddenly realized he wanted her to come to him when she was ready.

Tonight had to be perfect for her, and if it took her an hour to cross the room, he would patiently wait.

She made it halfway to him before she stopped again. "Wasn't it nice of Mr. Steeple to send champagne?"

"Yes, it was," he agreed. "He and Pickerman are already hatching up another plan to get you to sing again."

"But I made everyone cry."

"He's hoping you won't sing your church songs again."

"I will though."

He burst out laughing. "I know."

She ran to him and threw her arms around his neck. "I love you so much."

"And I love you."

She sighed deeply and then stepped back and began to remove her clothes. He found it difficult to swallow, and when she pulled the nightgown over her head and dropped it on the floor behind her, his heart began to slam inside his chest. She was perfect.

He drew her into his arms, and the feel of her soft skin against him was as wonderful as he knew it would be.

"You make me feel beautiful."

"You are beautiful," he whispered. "Ah, Genevieve, how did I exist before you?"

He kissed her deeply, passionately, lingering over the task of seducing her, and in between his ardent kisses, he told her over and over again how much he loved her. He stroked her back, her arms, and her breasts, and within minutes, her shyness was gone.

She took hold of his hand and led him to the bed. After he removed the rest of his clothes, he eased down on top of her and shuddered with desire.

"I want tonight to be perfect for you, Adam."

"It already is," he whispered.

"Tell me what to do so I won't disappoint you."

He nibbled on her earlobe. "You could never disappoint me."

Their lovemaking was magical, and so intense she thought she would go out of her mind. He knew just where to stroke her to drive her wild. She was awkward touching him, then eager, and when she couldn't stand waiting another second, he moved between her thighs and swiftly entered her. The pain of his invasion became all tangled up in ecstasy. He was so incredibly patient. He moved slowly at first until she was writhing in his arms, and then he increased the pace. He felt her tighten around him, knew she was about to find fulfillment, and allowed his own surrender.

She whispered his name. He shouted hers.

Spent, he collapsed on top of her and buried his face in the crook of her neck. The scent of lilacs surrounded him, and he was certain he had just died and gone to heaven.

She kept sighing. The sound made him arrogantly pleased with himself.

He finally found the strength to lift his head. "Did I hurt you, sweetheart?"

"I don't remember." Her hands dropped down

to her sides, and she sighed once again. "It was wonderful."

"Then you wouldn't mind if we made love again?"

She knew he was teasing because of the sparkle in his eyes. "Now?" she asked.

"Soon," he promised.

"Every night," she decided. "We must make love every single night."

God, how she pleased him. He leaned down and kissed her again. "Life with you is going to be an adventure."

IF YOU HAVE ENJOYED READING
THIS LARGE PRINT BOOK AND
YOU WOULD LIKE MORE
INFORMATION ON HOW TO
ORDER A WHEELER LARGE PRINT
BOOK, PLEASE WRITE TO:

WHEELER PUBLISHING, INC.
P.O. BOX 531
ACCORD, MA 02018-0531